Praise for C. Hope Clark...

Author of multiple award winning series receiving the Epic Award, Silver Falchion Award, the Daphne du Maurier Award, and most recently the Imaginarium Award for Best Mystery Novel of the Year.

"The story is addictive . . .Clark makes us question what's really happening."
—Brad Cox, Netgalley reviewer on *Reunion on Edisto*

"I will be looking for the others in the series. Well written, believable characters, and well plotted mystery combined to immerse the reader."
—Tammy Howard, The Protagonists Pub on *Reunion on Edisto*

"A great read and a thrilling ride. Couldn't put it down!!"
—Lisa Mclaughlin, Netgalley reviewer on *Reunion on Edisto*

Burned in Craven

Book 2 of
The Craven County Mysteries

by

C. Hope Clark

Bell Bridge Books

Bell Bridge Books
PO BOX 300921
Memphis, TN 38130
Print ISBN: 978-1-61026-171-5

Bell Bridge Books is an Imprint of BelleBooks, Inc.

We at BelleBooks enjoy hearing from readers.
Visit our websites
BelleBooks.com
BellBridgeBooks.com
ImaJinnBooks.com

10 9 8 7 6 5 4 3 2 1

Cover design: Debra Dixon
Interior design: Hank Smith
Photo/Art credits: C. Hope Clark

:Lcbh:01:

Dedication

This book is dedicated to Eleanor Hare, teacher and mother extraordinaire. Through her incredible devotion, morality, and intellect, she taught her daughter, Catherine Ging Huddle, to be just as extraordinary in her role as a school board leader, serving the greater good.

Chapter 1

LIKE DISTANT BOWLING balls taking the lane, thunder rolled across the South Carolina Lowcountry, warning of rain to come. To top it off, June measured unseasonably warm, and at seven thirty, the evening held a stickiness usually reserved for July.

As Quinn sat in her pickup, mashing her loose red curls under an Edisto Quail Club hunting cap and debating bringing an umbrella, she couldn't help but think . . . *It was a dark and stormy night.* A cliché and the only line she remembered from high school Lit class. God knows who the author was, but the quote was the best she could muster seated outside Craven High School auditorium. The last time she'd been here was to have a second transcript sent to the FBI, when they offered her a co-op internship in college.

By the time she stepped off the running board, small drops began to hit the asphalt. She might regret her sneakers in lieu of boots decision with this weather.

Quinn had hoped to slink inside unnoticed. Unfortunately, staff and, surprisingly, two county deputies, directed attendees through double doors via a metal detector. One of the uniforms winked.

"Hey, Quinn. You aren't armed, are you?" said Deputy Harrison, tongue-in-cheek.

Not her favorite uniform in the Sheriff's office, primarily because of a certain one-night stand on the eve of his wedding—a wedding she'd known nothing about.

She started to say, *Why, you expecting me to shoot kids?* But she quickly deemed that unwise. "Not today, Harrison." He let her through unchecked. She could get him in trouble for that, but she gave him a pass.

She'd never been to a school board meeting, envisioning them dry as dirt and boring as a phone book. She peeked in the door, and from the heads she roughly estimated a hundred people facing the stage. They were so serious one would think they were holding senatorial hearings for the Supreme Court. Usually it took the fourth of July or Christmas to draw this level of attendance for anything in Craven County, so maybe this meeting would be of more interest than she thought.

Quinn came to observe first-hand the nastiness her client professed took place at these meetings. The woman nearest the door smiled in recognition. Yeah, Quinn might as well go in now. The door squealed metal on metal, making half the room turn to see her enter. Completely recognized now—not that a five-foot-ten, red-headed female could go undetected—people spoke to her in whispered greetings as she hunted an empty place. Others barely snatched a glance before returning intense attention to whatever this was. Some texted hard on their phones. Nobody smiled.

Thick disgruntlement owned this crowd for sure.

Her client said this meeting would be controversial, and had told her to join the Craven Living Facebook group to learn more. Quinn had joined, but after five minutes of scrolling had tired of the bitterness, condescension, and small-minded tit-for-tat. More emotion than fact, typical of social media.

Maybe she should have read minutes of previous meetings instead. In what Quinn deemed overkill, the district website preserved videos of past meetings, providing the world proof of their incredible accomplishments. Who watched those things?

The folding seats in the auditorium were distanced, not unlike keeping kids arms-length from each other to avoid hands-on teasing, and taken. *Wait*. Thank God. She found a place in the rear butted against folded bleachers.

As niece to the sheriff and the last heir of the oldest family in the oldest county in South Carolina, Quinn Sterling rarely set foot anywhere local without somebody noticing and following up with the question of when she would settle down, marry her childhood friend, Jonah, and pop out babies. She expected a well-oiled rumor mill to crank up by tomorrow with her setting foot in a school.

Hopefully not. She studied the front of the room.

Her client, board member Iona Bakeman, age forty, sat prim and proper behind her name plate. She wore a crisp navy blue suit, seated second from the right. She had made brief eye contact when Quinn entered but not now.

She was in the process of making a motion in a forceful voice which sounded completely unnatural. "I move we accept last month's minutes."

Two others hands raised to second the motion, but Ella Mae Dewberry flapped hers with zeal.

The gentleman in the middle, chairman per his name plate, obliged

Ella Mae in a tired, droll manner, as though accustomed to her enthu-siasm. "Ms. Dewberry."

"I second that motion, Mr. Chairman." Ella Mae spoke as if to kin-dergarteners, the full time mom and school volunteer way too excited for an evening so glum. Not a bad Marilyn Monroe impersonation, though.

The chairman orally accepted, then a vote carried the day.

Iona had well described each board member with little chance of Quinn mistaking one for another. They couldn't have been cast any better in a sit-com. Four women and three men, plus the superintendent.

Curtis Fuller, retired Air Force, a past acquaintance of Quinn's father, sat rather unimpressed and disgusted from that scowl but silent about whatever plagued his mind. Next to him Harmon Valentine, a slim, middle-aged insurance agent un-extraordinaire, preoccupied with his phone. Then there was Guy.

Don't cry, call Guy.

Chairman Guy Cook was an ambulance chaser who advertised along the coast with offices in Charleston, Beaufort, and Savannah. The television jingle ear-wormed itself into minds. How could it not? The auditorium curtain resembled the commercial where dancing girls high-kicked, singing about accident claims. He lived in rural Craven County to avoid Charleston people knocking on his door and to pay lower property taxes.

The eight sat behind six-foot tables draped with black tablecloths, giving the appearance of judges. Guess the Supreme Court joke wasn't so far off, but per Quinn's client, this team of personalities represented serious threat. Quinn was here to vet Iona's interpretation of *threat*.

The naive had so many misguided definitions of the word.

Blatantly this board avoided eye contact with the audience. Quinn hoped they did more than silent passive aggression or this would be a wasted trip. Now half the attendees were on their phone.

As if someone heard her thoughts, a remark popped up from the far right, using the word *incompetent*. The crowd grumbled. Twisting around, Quinn couldn't see who spoke, but people were showing each other their phones instead of hunting for that voice.

To Quinn's right, a young woman scrolled, engrossed. So Quinn pulled out hers and popped into the Facebook group.

Good gracious. The group was roaring with comments so fast she found it difficult to read fast enough. That's where the activity was. These people were live reporting with gusto, but still, rumblings began traveling the auditorium once the man who'd spoken opened that door. Verbal expression in group mode could empower at an incredible rate.

"Vote them out," someone yelled.

"They're not used to being accountable," said another.

"We need the new school!"

"No, we don't!"

The chairman pounded his gavel. "Order in this room, please. If individuals cannot contain such outbursts, they will be removed by a deputy." Guy pointed his gavel to the back corner of the auditorium. Quinn leaned to see who he pointed to.

Son of a biscuit. Sheriff Larry Sterling himself perched in his seat and nodded with a cooperative smile to the chair. And was that . . . *holy sugar,* Deputy Tyson Jackson sat to his right. The two most senior uniforms with the Sheriff's Office.

More disgruntlement rippled the room meriting another rap with the gavel.

Her uncle never did after-hour events. She knew Ty well enough, however, to read his annoyance at being there. He was probably ordered.

That made three deputies and the high-sheriff present. What the heck merited this level of strong-arm theater?

This was a new type of case for her. As owner of Sterling Banks Plantation, a three-thousand-acre pecan enterprise of a family that dated three centuries, she selectively chose who and what she explored as a private investigator. Her FBI training had whet her appetite enough to deter her from the mundane. Her father's murder, her uncle's incompetence dealing with it, and the needs of Sterling Banks unfortunately switched her from FBI to PI.

Standard domestics didn't blip her radar much, and child support or disability fraud ranked little higher. It wasn't about the money. She'd inherited enough of that to take her to her grave and made enough more selling pecans. Her choices weighed on the side of importance and intrigue, sometimes simple loyalty to the people of her county.

A different board member's voice captured her attention. "I'd like to vote we accept the two new employees as discussed in executive session." Piper Pierce was a well-known, blue-haired native in her sixties who owned two large daycare centers, a dry cleaners, and a UPS Store in Jacksonboro, the county seat. Her brother was the county administrator. Frankly, as small as Craven County was, it was difficult to make a name for yourself and not be related to someone else already in authority somewhere.

Some seconding of minor motions gave Quinn's mind an excuse to stray again, though with one eye on Facebook. These board members seemed nothing special . . . just stereotypical big fish in a small pond so common in these parts.

In a nutshell, her client Iona Bakeman needed divorce fodder and her soon-to-be-general-contractor-ex-husband was pressuring Iona at home and in public about abusing her title. At first her husband leaned on her to approve certain two-bit jobs for him and his friends. That pressure morphed into Iona being coerced to vote for school district projects paying hundreds of thousands of dollars. And not just jobs for him.

Iona served as a freelance bookkeeper in Jacksonboro, handling payroll and tax accounting for a dozen small businesses. She understood accounting, and she recognized when to recuse herself. The husband retaliated when she tried to put a stop to votes for him, accusing her of not taking care of her constituents or the district. Why be on the board if you weren't voting to get important things done for the poor students and teachers?

Quinn smelled kickbacks making their way into Fripp Bakeman's pockets.

Iona was not only tired of harassment but sick of the husband and whatever he was up to. Problem was when Iona was first elected, she messed up by voting for several small contracts as her hubby wished, when their marriage still held promise. She'd told herself the deals were too small to matter. As the couple's marriage dissolved, the coercion increased not only from Fripp but from others in attendance who no longer liked her voting record. She'd begun receiving threatening phone calls of late. Texts came in from unknown numbers.

She reported the activity to the board, in particular Guy Cook, who told her that threats were part of the position. If she couldn't control her own husband that was her problem, not the board's.

Iona went to the sheriff's office, but they refused what they perceived as a nonthreatening domestic issue. No physical harm. Nothing they could do. Go tell the board, they said.

Then on the subject of a brand new elementary school, someone killed her cat and left him on the hood of her car. Someone else slipped a note in her daughter's bookbag at school. *Do your job, Ms. Bakeman.*

Sheriff Sterling labeled the cat an accident, with the driver nice enough to leave the pet in a spot to avoid further damage. The note was probably from a constituent who forgot to sign their name.

Her uncle's flippant disregard only enticed Quinn to take interest.

She snapped out of her thoughts when more protests mumbled.

"Order, order," demanded Guy Cook, the heavily-jowled man pounding that gavel with utter enthusiasm.

"That company got the contract last time," yelled someone against the east wall.

"And the time before," came another.

She leaned way out to put faces with the voices and caught the stare of her uncle.

"All procedures were followed. He's the successful bidder," said the chairman. "If you wish details, file a Freedom of Information Act request with the district office."

Another round of discontent. More gavel. Nope, no love lost between the board and this audience. Threats of handcuffs and ultimatums didn't help.

How had some of these members remained on the board for four and five terms when this was the reception given to voters? Most politicians, even at this level, ran on altruistic promise of a better future, which voters craved. But power ultimately drove these types, and power was most often wielded for the personal, not the greater good.

"We seem to have reached the Public Participation part of the agenda," Guy said, adeptly shifting gears. "Speakers should have signed up at the door. No late-comers. You know the drill." He rattled off the three-minute limit, a warning about misbehavior, and a few other vague rules from God-knows where.

Three board members immediately returned attention to their phones, as though they had no need to listen. How rude could these people be? Iona did not touch her phone, thank goodness. From the timing of the smirks on two of the members' faces, they texted each other.

"Let's see," Guy said, raising his head to read a piece of paper through his bifocals. "First speaker is Jonah Proveaux."

Quinn perked up. What was her Jonah doing at a school board meeting?

Well, not hers really. He would walk her down the aisle in a heartbeat, but the concept wasn't anchored in Quinn's mind just yet. She turned down his dates of late for fear he'd pop the question after only two months of officially seeing each other. *Seeing.* Funny. She saw him daily on the farm. As the foreman of Sterling Banks, he technically worked for her. As did his mother.

And they'd known each other since before she could walk.

Jonah rose and took the mic. She warmed at his appearance, admiring the slacks and open collared dress shirt, all six foot three of him topped with sweeps of auburn hair.

"Ladies and gentlemen, I am Jonah Proveaux. I've lived in Craven County my entire life, and most of you know where I live and work. But today I'm not here about me."

Like Quinn often did, he'd excised Sterling Banks from the equation. Many almost genuflected at the name Sterling Banks since it was ground zero of Craven's origin, and it could distract from purpose sometimes.

"I'm here to represent my neighbor, Miss Amy Abbott." He glanced down at his paper, closed it, then focused on those up front. "This district has attempted to purchase more of her land to build a new elementary school. She is unwilling to sell, yet you badger her with demands. You've even subjected her to threats. She's eighty-two years young, people. Let her live out her life in the only home she knows. She wants to avoid legal proceedings, so here I stand to inform you that she has given me power of attorney to handle her affairs regarding this matter."

Surprise swept the room like a current.

Whoa. He hadn't told Quinn any of this.

"I formally request you cease contact with her," he continued, "and you are hereby banned from setting foot on her property, which for clarity, is still not for sale. Thank you."

Before his butt hit the chair, the audience exploded in a blend of applause and opposition. Guy Cook's gavel failed to take charge. The crowd only clapped more enthusiastically, like a stadium of fans shouting too loud for the quarterback to be heard on the field.

Guy Cook stood and pointed his shaking gavel at the sheriff.

Sheriff Larry Sterling strode forward, motioning for Ty to head to the other side of the room. The other two deputies in the hallway entered, met Ty and took opposite corners, then the four began taking folks by the arm, strategically starting with the loudest men, to escort them to exits.

The rest of the room erupted in protest.

Several attendees turned to Quinn. "Do something," one lady said.

Quinn touched her collarbone. "Why me?" Then she got it.

Everyone understood Quinn's relationship with her uncle. And everyone understood her friendship with not only Jonah but also with Ty. Plus, she was a Sterling. In other words, she had the power nobody else in the room held to overcome this drama. Or so they assumed.

A man shoved Deputy Harrison, who used his skills to quickly extract him into the hall, arms behind his back.

The board stood and retreated through the curtain to an exit, leaving the poor district staff cowering to the side.

Unbelievable.

Rushing around the chairs, parting the proverbial sea, Quinn strode to the front of the room, snatched a microphone, and shouted in her best FBI voice, "Everyone stop where you are!"

Even the uniforms froze.

"This meeting is over. Everyone leave in an orderly fashion. Those who attempt to fight the authorities will be arrested."

All quieted, contemplating what just happened. Then one by one, wives nudged husbands, and friends prodded friends until most had filed out.

Ty had sense enough to retreat and let the crowd thin on its own, and when another deputy ordered directions, trying to force traffic, Ty hushed him.

Quinn remained at the mic, thanking people by name as they cooperated. "Thanks, Ms. Watson, Mr. Simms. Appreciate this." Control perceived was control achieved.

Her uncle, however, glared from the side. She smiled at him then pretended he'd vanished.

Jonah helped a few get by him and remained behind until most of the room cleared, then he slipped outside to leave. Quinn trotted to follow.

"Thanks, Q," Ty said as she scooted past.

"Sure thing," she said, escaping to hunt for where Jonah might have parked his truck.

Took mere seconds to find him surrounded by well-wishers, and she waited until his fans left to approach. "What the hell are we up to tonight, Jonah?"

Someone shouted, "Thanks, Jonah!" from four cars over. "Hey, Quinn!"

Both waved as if leaving church on Sunday, then Jonah turned back. "What's this *we*, Quinn? You've made it pretty clear of late there isn't a *we*. This is my project. What are you doing here?"

She leaned on his truck, trying to appear unfluffed. "I'm working."

He scoffed. "You took another case."

"Yes, I took another case. Is that so terrible?"

He shook his head and reached for his truck door.

"Wait a minute," Quinn said, not wanting to part on that note.

The parking lot thinned fast. Only three county patrol cars in addition to Iona's SUV, Quinn's pickup, and the district's white SUV being quickly loaded by the poor staffers left behind.

The other board members had disappeared fast.

Now parked like an island, Iona had remained to speak to Quinn, unless she was too rattled to drive yet. Either way, Quinn needed to check on her.

Jonah's truck door slammed.

Quinn spun. "Jonah, come on, don't leave like this."

Jonah pointed to the sheriff, message being her uncle came first, and he left.

That's when she spotted the sheriff, hands on his belt, glowering from the curb. With a nod and quick curl of his finger, he beckoned.

Screw her uncle. Quinn made for Iona's vehicle.

"Quinn?" Larry shouted. "Get over here."

"Not now," she shouted, and knocked on Iona's window to let her in the car.

"You okay?" Quinn asked as she slipped into the passenger seat and closed the door.

A nod, though shaky, said her client was safe, her wits not too far frayed to be communicative. Quinn marched on. "Y'all don't seem to play well with others."

"I told you the meetings were bad," she said. "Didn't you read the Facebook group?"

"That online stuff is mostly emotional gossip, but you grossly understated the contention in there. Didn't even get to see your husband show out." Made Quinn wonder if he really misbehaved in public as Iona described. "Guess I'll look at those meeting videos after all, but this isn't just about him, is it?" She pointed toward the auditorium. "None of that was about Fripp. Is that land situation part of your problem, too?"

Iona inhaled, then let it out long. "I didn't want to bring you into that one. I have no sway there."

"One vote out of seven for a multi-million dollar school is indeed sway, my friend." Quinn hated tight-lipped clients. "I don't work like this. If you can't be upfront with me, I'm done."

Iona's head snapped around. "No, please don't drop me, Quinn. I'll tell you everything. I didn't lie." She swallowed hard. "It's just . . . there's so much to tell."

An object flew past Quinn, grazing her shoulder. Only then did she register that it had shattered her side window to do so.

Chapter 2

QUINN DOVE ACROSS Iona's front seat. Head down, she waited, expecting another projectile.

Only heard were Iona's heavy breathing and yells from the deputies in the distance. As Quinn rose slowly, glass pebbles tinkled, dropping off her lap and back, and she avoided rubbing against anything. Safety glass didn't cut deep, but it could nick.

She finished sitting up, brushing herself only to feel the sting in her hands as a chip or two left their mark. "Iona?"

Buckled into her seat, Iona hadn't been able to move out of harm's way. "Quinn?" she whimpered, scared to remove hands over her eyes. "Am I bleeding?"

"It's okay." Quinn inched over and scanned the woman's exposed skin best she could. Iona continued squinching her lids. Not much glass had reached the driver's side.

Night was almost upon them, most light coming from the metal-halide streetlights in the parking lot. Her biggest prayer of thanks went to nobody getting bashed by the brick. From the looks of things, it came in the side window, across the front of her, bounced off the gearshift to knock it askew, then landed in the floor on her foot.

She knew she should have worn boots.

"Let's get out of the car," Quinn said, turning to follow her own advice, incredibly thankful nothing hit her head.

"Q?" Ty had reached them. "Y'all okay?"

She refused his hand, wanting to show she was fine, but as she stood she felt the bruise atop her left foot that would certainly shine purple in the morning.

Ty couldn't help but take her arm. He was her buddy, her swim-in-the-Edisto-River best friend from elementary school. Her take-naps-on-the-back-porch-in-the-summertime friend. His daddy had worked for hers for years, and since the ages of five, they'd been inseparable until Quinn went off to college. She, Ty, and Jonah had been tight for a lot of years.

She couldn't blame him for anything the Sheriff's Office screwed up and considered him their finest asset.

Instead she blamed Uncle Larry, and with her adrenaline still pumping, she threw her frustration in his direction. "How does the Sheriff's Office guard a school board meeting but miss the assault right under their noses?" Her uncle helped Iona from her seat. "How is she?"

Hesitantly he tried to brush off the school board lady, awkwardly deciding to let her do it herself. "I believe she's good."

Instinctively, Quinn studied the scene, seriously doubting they'd retrieve fingerprints off a brick. "You might dust this side of the vehicle," she said, hoping the person had balanced a hand against the car . . . and hadn't worn gloves.

Uncle Larry and Iona came around to see the damage, and the sheriff ordered one of the deputies to get his print kit.

Iona went to touch the door and the sheriff stopped her. "This is getting out of control," she said.

He acted the gentleman and could sound like he was doing his job, but Quinn knew that her uncle wouldn't break a sweat doing it well. Those prints were the brunt of what he'd do, and he'd give Iona a police report for her insurance company, but then the case was closed. Quinn would bet a hundred acres of the farm on that.

She hated being adversarial to blood kin, but what choice did she have? She didn't want her uncle being what the community thought of as a Sterling. The balancing act proved trying so often and in so many ways.

"Did you see anyone, Quinn?" he said.

Did *she* see anyone? Why didn't *he*? "I was in the passenger side of the front seat, facing her, and the brick came from my right side. No, uncle. The bigger question is did any of you protect-and-serve people see anyone."

That came out worse than she planned, but the brick had been a shock. Uncle Larry frowned with a harsh meeting of his brows. "Who says they didn't come after you, Quinn? You broke up the meeting. Hell, someone could've just followed you unrelated to the school. What is it you do again?"

She should have known better than to challenge him in front of people. Not to mention it was rude. Her daddy would've chastised her royally, even if this was the black sheep uncle.

While she and her uncle sparred as usual, Ty put the other deputy to scouring the grounds. However, with the dark and the shadows, and the fact the uniforms had been standing such they could only see Iona's side,

Quinn expected little fruit from the search.

Like her uncle said, she honestly couldn't say whether the person had been after Iona or herself. Quinn Sterling had drawn fire before. She scanned the parking lot. Almost empty.

"Could've been Fripp," Iona said.

"Could've been anybody," Quinn replied.

"Ain't that the truth," Sheriff Sterling said in his gravelly grumble. Cops weren't fond of private investigators, but Craven uniforms knew she wasn't some wannabe who'd never worn a badge, and sometimes she could actually be of help.

Quinn had worked for her uncle right out of high school, but to appease her father, had left the Sheriff's Office and gone to college, choosing criminal justice in addition to the business degree her father preferred. Graham, the wisest of the Sterlings, bowed to her obstinance and decided whatever his daughter did, she'd do and get it out of her system before he retired and she took over the pecan enterprise.

He just hadn't counted on dying.

The last walking, talking, living Sterlings, even after three hundred years of procreating and building Sterling Banks Plantation, had boiled down to his two younger brothers, Larry and Archie . . . and Quinn. Archie, an architect in San Francisco, sold his rights to Graham. Larry lost his claim through a sloppy divorce. The burden and the glory of owning Sterling Banks fell on Quinn.

She directed a judgmental stare at her uncle, a major part of the reason she chose PI work. If he'd done his damn job when her father was murdered . . . if he'd not tried to cut a real estate deal with a magnate in Charleston that led to that murder . . . Graham would be alive and she'd still be FBI.

And she also wouldn't have this incessant niggling in her that said magnate would attempt another coup. While brick throwing wasn't quite worthy of Ronald Renault, this incident, like the bigger ones of days past, only went to prove Uncle Larry wasn't much protection . . . of her or anyone else.

Her uncle equally met her stare.

Yeah, they were used to reading each other's minds. Everyone around them could read their minds. The love lost was no secret to anyone.

Enough of the family. Quinn needed to talk to Iona, and more times than not, a PI had to dig for the truth even with supposedly cooperative clients. Even paying them to listen, folks lied to both their doctors and their PIs.

She turned to Ty, her back to Uncle Larry. "I believe we might drop by Jackson Hole." He gave a discreet tip of his chin.

Then to Larry and the deputy pulling prints, "Iona and I are taking a drive while you finish with her car."

"Maybe we would like to hear your conversation," the sheriff said. "In case you two come up with candidates who might have done this."

A brief flash of panic crossed Iona's face, but the sheriff missed it focused on Quinn.

"No," she said. "This is woman talk and just calming down. We have no idea who did this. Odds are it's someone who wasn't happy during the meeting. Take your pick who that might be." Then in a second thought, "Heck, jump on the Facebook group. Bet you'll find suspects all over the damn place there."

From his look, the sheriff wouldn't bother.

"Since you guys attend these meetings, you're on top of things anyway," she said, then twirled a finger in the air. "*Round up the usual suspects.*"

She wasn't sure he'd catch the line from *Casablanca*. She was pretty sure, however, he missed the insult. Quinn ushered Iona into her pickup and left.

Captain Renault spoke that movie line, and Quinn had always loved using it. Although slick, shrewd, and quite likeable, Renault was easily manipulated if he could glean personal achievement in the compromise.

Then the name connection hit her like never before.

Renault. The Charleston real estate magnate her uncle had connived with back in the day. The man whose daughter Quinn had killed just two months ago, in addition to her henchman sent to Sterling Banks to kill her . . . the same man who they suspect killed Graham.

Disgusted, her heart pumped faster at the memories and what seemed a Freudian slip. She glanced over at Iona to see if she noticed Quinn's introspection, but her client apparently fought her own demons while silently studying the passing scenery.

They rode with high beams, the low steel-gray clouds making it feel like midnight. Still, Quinn couldn't shed the name Renault.

Think other stuff. Let's see, Humphrey Bogart was the good guy in the movie. Bogie. *There you go, Quinn. Think about Bogie.*

Which drew a smile. Bogie. Jonah brought her the pup after the Renault case. A black mouthed cur, which she hadn't believed was a breed until Jonah showed her the papers, the baby was going on thirty pounds, sweet but rolling-around playful. He was fast developing the normal color of blondish red with black muzzle. A mutt-looking stray to some, but perfectly adorable to her.

Her beams bounced off a dozen cars as she nosed her pickup into the parking lot of Jackson Hole, a diner by day and bar by night, operated by Ty's mother, Lenore Jackson. Both the eatery and the lady were well known throughout these parts. Being almost nine on a Monday, Quinn bet they wouldn't be busy.

She and Iona entered to the mixed scents of cayenne, tomato sauce, fries, and beer, the air conditioning turned up to beat the early season humidity. Quinn stomped her sneakers by habit, like she usually did her boots since she often came in off the farm. Lights dimmed, an aid to keep drinkers controlled, though few showed their butts out of respect for Lenore and the fact that her deputy son often dropped in.

"Hey, baby," Lenore said, standing straight from a table she'd just served. She gave a slight nod to her left. "Your booth is open."

Before Iona could ask how Lenore knew to hold a table, Quinn replied. "She means that corner booth next to the swinging doors leading to the kitchen. I eat there a lot." But what she didn't say was that the booth was more or less where she met clients.

They slid in either side, and Lenore arrived before Iona could open the menu. "Special's chili tonight."

"We could tell stepping through the door. Fine with me," Quinn said. Iona nodded for the same.

"Extra jalapenos on mine and tea for both of us, please," Quinn tacked on, also knowing there would be cornbread.

Quinn had scanned the room for familiar people from the board meeting but saw none. Tucked in convenient shadows, the booth gave them privacy from the better part of the room.

Tea arrived quickly, but before Iona could take a sip, Quinn launched into her. "There's so much more to this than you told me, Iona. You hired me because of your husband's coercion about contracts. You feel threatened by him and others, whoever they are. You want dirt on him to aid you in filing for divorce." That about summed the things Iona said she hired a PI for. "So why is it now I have a feeling that your domestic issue only scratches the surface?"

Iona twisted the tea glass in a slow circle between her hands. She peered around once for familiars, but Quinn had taken the side facing the room to keep atop of that. Always better for anyone to see Quinn than a client . . . equally important for Quinn to see who came and went.

"I won't be a victim," Iona whispered. "I feel like one, and I'm damn sick of it."

"That's the kind of stuff I need to hear," Quinn said. "Go on."

Iona leaned forward. "There's a conspiracy. I don't understand it, and I'm not sure who's in on it. I'm definitely on the outside looking in."

"How do you even know then?"

"Some of the board meet before I arrive at meetings, and they talk like they've held get-togethers I wasn't aware of."

Basically, Iona was the unpopular kid in school, pardon the pun. Not cool, but not breaking the law either. "Assuming you're right, conspiracy to do what?"

"Channel the district's money to certain people. Coordinate the district's actions to aid certain non-board individuals who can greatly benefit from what it does. A backdoor sort of fraternity, I think."

Iona clearly dodged naming who comprised this conspiracy, so Quinn waited for the rest of the story. The whos would no doubt become clearer as they delved deeper, but she preferred to hear them now.

"Are you making me ask who?"

"Unofficially, we call them the Board Corps. The board majority that pushes agendas through. And whoever their friends are."

"Corps?" Quinn asked.

Iona shrugged. "It sounded good."

Power players showed themselves in these parts. Some people just gravitated toward corruption, and every county had them.

But they'd get to that later. "Let's start with your husband and his contracts," Quinn said. "Start with the ones you approved."

Blowing out sadly, Iona collected herself. "It began as repairs to bleachers. I didn't care, so when Fripp said give it to him, I agreed. It was small money. Next came general repairs in six of the schools. He told me to go with his friend."

Quinn waited, hoping the obvious didn't need to be asked.

"Troy Cheverall," she replied.

Quinn knew of him. An average contractor common to the area. "Was he low bid?"

Iona shrugged, making Quinn frown. "You don't know?"

"Listen. Nobody tells you the ropes when you run for office." Iona wasn't whispering now, but her voice cracked trying not to be loud, her frustration evident. "When you're elected, you hit the ground running, and if nobody takes you under their wing, you trip over details, you know? Harmon Valentine, the member who sat at the opposite end from me tonight, sort of led my election campaign, and Laney Underwood sat me next to her at meetings, teaching me." She dipped her head at Quinn. "Nobody gets elected understanding the legalities of procurement, real estate, and hiring, much less how a board works. Nobody's ever qualified for this job."

Sure, Quinn thought. School board elections are *so* nerve wracking. So many babies to kiss. So many appearances to make. So much ground to cover . . . *in Craven County.* This woman had gotten in way over her head, but damn, the water was rather shallow. At least she was smart enough to holler for help.

"How many contracts did you sign off on and on how many did you refuse to cast a vote?"

"A dozen," she said. "I approved a dozen, but keep in mind I wasn't the only one voting. I probably would not have agreed with them if I understood procurement."

That didn't sound good. "And how many did you object to?"

"About the same," she said. "Once they exceeded a hundred thousand, I didn't feel comfortable rubber stamping my name. The Corps voted them through anyway, though. They don't need me since they had a chokehold on the majority. I started recusing myself formally, on the record, so nobody bullied me. Then Fripp started calling me out in meetings, and people started saying I wasn't willing to do my job. The Facebook group started leaning on me, and I suspect Fripp and some of the Board Corps rallied them. People can get malicious."

Quinn had envisioned boards as PTA moms, retired teachers, and grandmothers tired of their empty nests. "Let's address the Board Corps." Quinn didn't see any bad asses behind those black linen tables. "Which members supposedly wield so much power?"

"They're practically a militia," Iona whispered.

Glory be. Who'd of thought? Quinn saved the grin.

Iona glanced for anyone close and held up fingers. "First, Guy Cook who thinks he's God's gift to anything and anyone. Second," she said, holding up another finger. "Ella Mae Dewberry. She's on Guy's leash. Piper Pierce, because she thinks she owns everything, and finally Laney Underwood."

"But you said Harmon Valentine helped you get elected. Why isn't he in on things?"

"He is. He's the biggest insurance agent in the county, so sometimes he feels beholden to customers and avoid appearing one-sided. He's not, though."

Maybe Iona just lacked a strong set of people skills. The better answer might be she had no business being in politics.

There were few in the county Quinn hadn't at least heard of, much less met. Guy and Piper were arrogant sorts who measured life in terms of dollars. Ella Mae reminded her of the girl in school who'd do anything to be liked. But Laney Underwood? She was a mystery at the moment.

They leaned back as Lenore put down the steaming bowls of chili, cheddar melting on top, and an extra dozen slices of jalapeno on Quinn's. "There you go. What else can I get you?" She rubbed hands on her red apron like she always did. Before Quinn could say anything, a waitress slid hot cornbread on the table.

Iona smiled. "This is great, ma'am."

Lenore hurried off instantly tending to someone at the bar. Quinn kept watching Lenore . . . thinking.

"Laney *Jackson* Underwood?" Quinn said, repeating the name with emphasis on the name with bigger impact. Quinn knew the reputation well, had met the woman numerous times at affairs, but they traveled different professional and social circles. But she'd heard enough about her through Ty's family to sense that labeling her one of the district architects of corruption didn't fit.

Iona jerked at the hot spoonful, blew, then ate. "Yes," she said after the swallow. "I recognize I'm throwing a Jackson in the mix, but that group owns the district, and, therefore, much of the money that comes and goes in this county."

Quinn blended her jalapenos down into her chili. "You give them a rather embellished resume." They were five of seven. Wasn't that how a voting body worked? Majority wins?

Jacksons were the second oldest family in Craven County short of the Sterlings, and Laney was Lenore's sister-in-law and Ty's aunt. The family was respected and admired by whites and blacks alike even though the Jacksons planted their roots by working for the Sterlings going way back when. Quinn stood up for a Jackson as adamantly as a Sterling, and depending on which Jackson and which Sterling, she fought for a Jackson more.

Quinn had wanted to marry Ty in tenth grade. And later, his ex-wife refused to live in Craven County because of the long-spoken rumors of a relationship between the red-haired heiress and the black deputy. The Sterlings and Jacksons went way back in lots of ways.

But right now, Quinn couldn't stop noting Lenore.

"Yeah, I love Lenore, too," Iona said. "But Laney ain't no Lenore. Laney gets her way."

Lenore could, too. Quinn wasn't sure she wasn't listening to gossip rather than clues. "What are you wanting from me, Iona? I cannot tackle the entire school board."

Iona laid down her spoon. "And pray tell why not? You're Quinn Sterling."

Another customer came in, and Lenore waved them toward an empty table. The time was late, but diner owners never turned away a hungry stomach.

"No thanks, Ms. Lenore." Iona stiffened at the familiar voice. "Came hoping to find my wife."

Quinn watched Fripp scan the room, his gaze resting on their booth. He strode over, Lenore watching him with her stink eye.

He leaned stiff-armed on the table. "And here I was waiting for my wife only to hear that she had buddied up with the high and mighty Ms. Sterling."

"Someone vandalized her car," Quinn said, in no way inviting him to sit. "I happened to be at the board meeting, and while the deputies looked over her vehicle, I offered her dinner."

Iona said nothing. Fripp's stare dared her to do or say anything, wanting something to fan this spark he'd carried in. Long seconds passed.

"You didn't ask if she's okay," Quinn said.

"She seems fine," he said. "I'm here to take her home."

With a wave across her plate, Iona stated, "But we just got our meal."

"They've got take out boxes."

But Quinn wasn't letting him win. "How rude for me to invite her to dinner, pay, and her leave before we barely taste it."

"Then I'll sit here—"

"I'll see her home," Quinn said. "Her and her car. I'm sure I could talk my uncle into bringing the car to your house."

A couple of nearby tables took note of the face-off. Lenore scooted to Quinn's end of the bar, her fingers tapping her phone.

Fripp hovered over the plates. "Do what I say, Iona. Quinn, back off."

Quinn slipped out, stretching her five-foot-ten self to full height, which happened to beat the husband by at least an inch. She itched for him to twitch wrong.

Phones snapped pictures. Lenore hung up from her call. Fripp suddenly realized the whole diner had eyes on him.

Fripp turned to the onlookers. "Sheriff Sterling's on my side, people, so don't interfere."

Quinn scoffed. "Iona, sit here," she said. "Fripp. Let's you and me take this outside."

He grinned. "Sounds good."

She grinned wider. "I'm trained, Fripp. I just hope you feel froggy enough to jump."

Chapter 3

"QUINN," LENORE said with a firm, warning momma force, making her way around the bar at Jackson Hole toward the two adversaries.

Quinn held up a hand, keeping her gaze locked on the smirking Fripp Bakeman. "We're good. We'll be right back." Then after a pause, she motioned toward the door. "Fripp, after you."

Iona's husband hesitated, his jovialness dimmed.

"Come on. Let's do this," Quinn said. She went ahead of him in case gender was the issue. The room watched in silence.

Outside in the night, one streetlight and an assortment of neon beer signs in the windows lit up the parking lot ... plus Lenore's lit-up marquee. To avoid gawkers, Quinn continued toward the rear. Her opponent wasn't following very quickly.

She wheeled near the coach lamp at the employee entrance, away from the public's eye. "You want to test your Sheriff Sterling connection to mine?"

His chin up in defiance, he braced his shoulders like they were about to tackle fists. "Larry's on our side."

She stealthily shifted weight to the balls of her feet. "And whose side is that?"

"Those wanting the best for this county."

"Which means what?"

"Whatever we deem it means."

"Names?" she asked.

He laughed. "I'm not divulging names."

"Sounds shady," she said. "Besides, wouldn't take me long to figure them out. You're the first hint at who some of them are."

Blinking, Fripp seemed to replay their conversation, seeking where he'd erred. "What are you doing with my wife?" He deferred to more solid ground.

"Sharing girl talk over Lenore's scrumptious chili," she replied.

His scowl deepened. "Well, I don't like it."

"Not sure that's an issue." She raised her brows. "Where are we taking this, Fripp? People inside are waiting to see who wins, waiting to see what to tell their friends over coffee in the morning." Then she remembered. "Or on that Facebook group tonight. Just tell me how you want to play this."

"How about everyone shake and walk away?" said a much deeper voice from around the corner. Still in uniform, Ty appeared. "I'd hate to lock you two up."

Fripp took a step farther away from Quinn.

Quinn stood fast.

"Fripp?" Ty moved closer to Quinn.

"I could get both of y'all . . ."

The hollow threat didn't bother Quinn a bit. Ty, however, felt the need to finish the thought. "Fired? In trouble? What exactly are you trying to say, Fripp?"

The husband took another step back.

In deputy mode, Ty stared the man down. "I didn't think so. Give it up and move on."

"But my wife—"

"Came here to dine with me," Quinn said. "I'll get her to where she needs to be."

Fripp's frustration wasn't nearly as concentrated as before, but it hadn't disappeared. However, he couldn't win a fight behind a diner with a deputy present. He turned, and his feet crunched gravel until he reached his vehicle, cranked up, and left.

Ty waited until he was certain he'd gone. "Did I interrupt an ass-whooping or were you putting on airs?"

"I was leaving it up to him." She shrugged one shoulder. "Admittedly I poked the bear, but I did it more to get him off Iona."

Ty nodded like these things happened every day. He was a solid wall when it came to protecting his buddy, and her him.

"She's telling me stuff, Ty. Stuff to make me want to talk to you. You and your momma."

He gave a sideways look. "Trying to make me curious?"

"Maybe," she said, nudging him in ribs deeply protected behind a Kevlar vest. "Now you'll be clued in when I get around to asking."

"Good. We parked her car near the front," Ty said, as if nothing had happened. "The gear shift is bent, but it drives. She needs to get that fixed, just in case there's damage we can't see."

"Thanks. I best be returning before she gets worried."

"I'll cover Momma. She texted me, you know."

"I figured," she said, and they walked into the diner together, entering like normal with Quinn not minding in the least that Ty probably got credit for busting up a fight.

"Ain't a mark on you," someone hollered. "Must of kicked his ass, Quinn."

After the laughter died, Quinn returned to the booth, a half-grin still on her face. Part appreciating the camaraderie . . . part to show Iona all was good.

"Nothing happened," she said to Iona's nervousness. After another bite of chili, another one of cornbread, she returned to business. "Can you get me copies of those contracts?"

"They're supposed to be on the district's website. There's more than a few of them missing."

Big surprise. "There wasn't a thing mentioned about contracts tonight."

"Jonah interrupted the agenda," Iona said.

Which was a whole other issue Quinn would pursue once she got home. "So why the cops? Handpicked ones, too, from what I know of the department."

"The chairman is concerned about order."

"Sounds more like an intimidation factor."

School yard antics. Or jail yard tactics. Not too much difference. The uniforms were a façade to make folks draw up short or steer away. In this case, they made the public believe the sheriff's office was in the board's pocket, and those who dared cross the line would be dealt with one way or another.

That explained Ty's sour expression at the meeting.

Each took a few more bites, Quinn letting Iona set the pace.

"They live-stream the meetings, too," Iona said, ripping off a piece of cornbread. "Then recordings are posted two days later and are supposed to enable folks unable to attend to see what happened."

"But I take it not everything winds up onscreen?" Quinn asked.

Iona thought about that. "Not sure. I've not been made aware of them cutting things out, if that's what you mean."

But Quinn shook her head. "I mean they probably don't take everything before the public *because* of the videos."

The eating stopped. "What are you saying?"

Quinn had spotted enough naïveté in this woman to bet high dollars on the fact she wasn't aware of the board's full actions. Quinn doubted the game-changers of the board educated this latest, most gullible member on much more than the obvious.

"Never mind," Quinn said. "Tell me more about the stuff that isn't about Fripp."

Looking around, Iona leaned over. "Aren't they ready to close?"

Ten thirty. The jukebox was no longer on and the room almost empty. Aromas waned from the kitchen. Yes, it was late, and Quinn already expected the jalapenos to sit a tad heavy because of the hour.

She needed sleep and fresh footing. She smelled a whole different case than the one she took on.

Bless him, Ty hung around, now wearing an apron to protect his uniform as he cleaned the bar for his mother.

"What else?" Quinn said to her client.

Iona pushed the plate and bowl away. "There are regular locals at every meeting."

"Like who?"

"I could tell you a dozen names, Quinn. One complains about traffic around the schools. Another one or two fuss about school taxes. There's fussing about wanting a better football stadium, then another who claims our AP classes aren't good enough to give our students an edge in college. The list is as long as my arm. But then Jonah started coming in."

Stunned, Quinn hadn't pieced Jonah into any of this. "Wait. I thought tonight was Jonah's first appearance."

Iona shook her head. "Oh no, honey. He's quite informed, and he has come about five times, I believe. You'll see the videos. He asks hard questions of the Corps, and it wasn't until he started coming that they asked for more cops. He's also written the board. Emails and texts."

Quinn's gut plummeted, and she wasn't quite sure why.

Five meetings and written contacts over the last four to five months. That predated the time she and Jonah started dating, and he hadn't mentioned it once.

"What else do I need to know?" Quinn asked.

"I haven't talked to Fripp about hiring you."

"That cat might be out of the bag after tonight. Go on."

Even with diners mostly gone, Iona lowered her voice. "Five meetings ago, I noticed two strangers in the audience. I'd have pegged them as *suits* if they'd been wearing them, because they looked that much out of place. They wore khakis, polos, and windbreakers, like they'd escaped from a country club. After the meeting, they left with Guy and Laney in a large SUV that had to cost as much as the two bedroom my brother owns."

Outsiders . . . with money. Quinn didn't bother asking Iona if she got the tag.

"The next meeting," Iona continued, "I asked Laney who her friends were. She feigned ignorance, but she knew I knew. I could tell."

"What else?" Quinn asked.

"That's it. I'm in the dark about a lot and, frankly, haven't tried to turn on the light. Besides, I'm not running for office again. Just let me finish my term, and I'm done. Once the dead cat appeared on my hood and the note in my daughter's book bag, I told Guy that the experience was way too combative, and I'd developed a better appreciation for term limits. My clock is ticking down seventeen months to the finish line. Less if I resign first."

Chairs were going up on tables. Staff was leaving.

"Iona, I'm not sure what this is we're doing. You said you needed dirt on Fripp. This is a no-fault state for divorce unless he's got a woman on the side, stays drunk, beats you, or just disappears on you. Sounds like he crossed the line into your elected position, and that pisses you off more than anything. Is this about him or about the board? I need direction or I'm worthless to you, you're wasting your money, and I'm wasting my time."

Iona flared up. "Are you doubting me?"

"I'm doubting your focus. What is it you want me to do?"

Like she'd been thrown a foreign concept, Iona could not speak for a moment.

Lenore peered out. Quinn winked, begging for a few more minutes.

"I'm tired of him," Iona finally said. "He's into board business, and I don't like what the board is doing. I can't call the police on any of this."

Iona was rationalizing, to herself, mainly. She wasn't sure what she was doing. She needed help, expertise she didn't have, and the police weren't the right parties to call at this point in time. Quinn was her lifeline to sort it out for her.

In a gathering of Iona's stupid, scattered logic, Quinn got it. "Give me a chance to research, and I'll be in touch. You're sure it's divorce time?"

"Absolutely," she said, gathering her purse.

Then no holds barred on dealing with or inquiring about Fripp. Iona was trying to stay out of anything wrong, and with her husband having a foot in whatever it was, she was giving him the boot. Okay, Quinn thought she had a loose handle on this.

Frankly, if Quinn hadn't learned about Jonah's involvement, this meeting would've been to sever ties with Iona, but for now Quinn would dig. "Let me see what I can find out for you. Give me a few days. I'll get in touch, definitely in some place the community can't see us together again." More so due to the school board business than the husband. She called out. "Ty? Got those keys?"

He came over and laid Iona's lady bug keychain on the table. "Thanks for your cooperation," he said, and Quinn let it stand for both the sheriff's department and herself. "Need someone to go with you? With Fripp like he is?" he asked.

"No, I got this."

They saw her to her vehicle.

"How'd it go?" he asked inside, throwing Quinn a rag to help wipe tables.

She had to scrub extra hard on one booth. Surely people didn't eat this sloppy at home. "I'm definitely more intrigued, but not ready to talk to you yet." Especially about Jonah. Most especially about Ty's aunt.

He released that deep chuckle of his, and as she walked by he popped her on the backside with his towel. "You work it like you want, but talk to me before you talk to Momma, you hear? We just reopened." He lifted the last chairs. "She paid enough for your last case, Q."

Quinn remembered too vividly the fire from two months ago. A culprit had faked an inspection and sabotaged the fryer's fire extinguishing system, on behalf of a person Quinn pursued. Thankfully nobody got hurt but Ty, whose hand was tender but almost healed. It scarred, though.

"You both indeed paid a price," she said. "But sure. Can I go now?"

"Get out of here," Lenore said, walking in. Quinn gave her a hug, then in afterthought gave one to Ty, and then left. She was tired. She was disappointed about the state of her relationship with Jonah, but it was too late to go home and get into anything with him.

She really wished to God he'd brought his project to her. Being left out hurt more than the subject matter. Maybe she could have helped.

But hadn't she done him this way not that long ago dealing with the Renault situation? Left him in the dark as to her plans? She'd forecasted his dislike for her daring-do and kept quiet. He'd read it as deception. Worried him . . . scared him . . . thinking she knew best what was best for him to know.

How did that feel with the shoe on the other foot?

Wasn't long before she pulled up to the farm, the title Sterling Banks noted in lighted iron-crafted script across the brick and wrought-iron entrance.

She wasn't accustomed to so much going on in Craven County without her knowledge. Or was that pompous of her? Between Jonah calling her Princess and Uncle Larry perpetually trying to knock her off her pedestal, lately she tried to read herself before someone else could.

She didn't want to model Scarlett O'Hara behavior, but she was way too spent to decide what to do about it until tomorrow.

Plus she still had to walk Bogie.

She sat in her truck a moment reading her phone. She had an old Facebook account dating to her college days, and she'd updated her password of late. Iona told her that Craven Living had become the beating heart of the community, and what used to be filled with public service mentions about civic club meetings and downtown holiday events, had turned into a noisy chin-wag of rumor mongering.

School board information had taken it over.

She did a double-take at her Facebook icon shouting thirty-four posts since this afternoon, and when she hit the icon, the entire lot was affiliated with the infamous Craven Living group.

At a glance, she saw how Fripp learned she and Iona were at Jackson Hole. Someone saw and posted—others shared and copied—that fact with a pic. And further down, she found discussion about the thrown brick, explained in way more detail than Quinn could recall and she'd been there.

Even further down was what sounded like tittering co-eds.

Oh, and wasn't Jonah absolute perfection up there talking to that naughty, pompous board? Gorgeous, intelligent, so gallant, who couldn't love the way he took care of Miss Abbott going up against all that power?

Wait . . . what was this?

Jonah *himself* thanked one person after another, stating he was only trying to do the right thing, which infused energy into folks per the hashtags appearing everywhere like *#supportJonah* and *#saveamyabbott*. One faction spoke of finding different candidates for next year's election, maybe even Jonah, in an attempt to clean out the old members. On the other hand, some spoke of how devoted certain board members were to the children and the poor teachers who relied so heavily on their sixteen years of expertise.

But Quinn's scroll stopped on another post that caught her off balance. Some person piped up with this:

The sheriff's office says they have no clue who threw the brick.

Okay, who the hell was talking in the sheriff's office? But that didn't bother her nearly as much as the next post they made:

Iona has been seen with Quinn Sterling. What's up with that?

Talk bounced amongst others about the need for the new school versus the board being corrupt, maybe putting money in their collective pockets, then that frequent poster, Lincoln20, reappeared and took another swing at trouble:

Learning why Quinn Sterling is involved shouldn't be too difficult to discover. I'm on it.

Quinn had not a clue who Lincoln20 was.
And she wasn't taking that bait.
Or should she?

Chapter 4

QUINN AWOKE TO a slobber tongue in her ear. Hands over her face, she struggled to roll out of reach, but the cold nose burrowed under her grandmother's quilt to find her.

"Bogie, come on, dude." Talking only gifted her with a sloppy kiss in the mouth.

"I already took him out. Already fed him, too," came a familiar male voice from the corner.

She didn't even open her eyes. "You broke into my house."

"It's eight thirty. The crew has its work orders, and Jule is wrapped up with the goats. Besides, I'm the one who set up your security system."

"Jonah . . ."

He rose from the Victorian chair, having thrown her clothes on the end of her bed to make room to sit. "Guess you don't want to hear about the school board and their insane real estate ideas."

"Ideas?" she asked, as in plural. She sat up, which energized Bogie to pounce on her, then dance and bounce and downward dog himself to snare her attention. "He needs to go out again."

Jonah stood. "He needs to be walked. Throw on some clothes, and we'll give him a decent run." He left, his footfalls going downstairs toward the kitchen, the pup following the one more likely to offer snacks.

Both Jonah and his mother Jule lived right down the dirt road from the manor, on the property, and Graham Sterling had allowed employees to enter the main house freely between eight and six . . . at least until his death. Quinn ceased that practice, but she saw Jonah and Jule as family. They had keys and came and went at their discretion. She'd give Ty the same access except he declined. Larry Sterling? He had a key, and he occasionally let himself in, but not often since each time resulted in a fuss.

She got out of bed considering Jonah's remark. The farm went on for acres and acres, and he'd said Bogie needed *a decent run*. Guess Jonah had a lot to say.

Her wild curls would take a while to tame if it mattered, so Quinn decided it didn't. A rubber band worked and the turquoise scarf she wore to town two days ago. Jeans, socks, her most comfortable farm boots, and a three-quarter sleeve tee from a 2008 ZZ Top concert at the Charleston Coliseum. She gave a little umph at the bruised foot, but once on, the support of the boot seemed to work.

He had her coffee waiting in a travel mug when she arrived, flavored like she liked it . . . like his mother taught them both to like it . . . almost half full of goat milk from the herd. "I took you to that concert," he said, eying her chest.

"Oh." She looked down at the slanted double Z logo and the silhouette of Billy Gibbons' beard. "Yeah, you did." She was still in college then but had come home for her birthday. She, Jonah, and Ty partied in Charleston before, during, and after that concert, with Jonah the designated driver. Ever the caretaker.

"That thing ought to be vintage by now," he said, walking over to grab a leash from the mudroom wall hook.

She didn't tell him that she rationed wearing the tee, so that it and the memories that came with it lasted longer. Or that she purposely pulled it out to transition their conversation. She eyed him over the top of her mug. She cared deeply for this boy . . . this man. She forever slipped into thoughts of their trio as childhood friends, because adulthood was so damn complicated.

Maybe that was her problem. Her past couldn't connect seamlessly with her future.

Jonah snapped Bogie onto the leash and swung a hand toward the sliding glass doors for Quinn to proceed. The two strode through the massive living room of a house whose foundation dated over two centuries, a hundred years ago burned down and rebuilt by Sterling ancestors. Its rich paneling came from the trees out back, orchard after orchard of wide-canopies that greeted them in greens, gray-browns, dappled sun, and whispers for as far as they could see. They stepped off the patio into a private world that half of the county coveted, the trio's world from the time they were toddlers.

Walking alongside Jonah, she knew they appeared to be a matched set. Her red hair against his dark waves with auburn highlights. Her tall and lean . . . him taller and fit. Their Timberlane boots walked in sync through a nature they both understood like their own heartbeats.

As soon as the two entered the trees, the morning breeze brought a faint fragrance of those leaves. Quinn stripped a stem of leaflets and crushed them between her fingers, releasing the mixture of orange, black pepper, burnt sugar, atop a milder bitterness of turpentine. Some found the aroma of pecan leaves pungent. Quinn found it palliative.

These were Elliott trees. Other sectors held Sumner, Kanza, Cape Fear, and Stuart. Pecan trees were a juggling act, and the generations before her struggled like every other pecan grower since the nut first evolved from a hickory tree to find the best producing, nut quality, disease resistant, bug resistant, early maturing cultivar. Lowcountry humidity made selection tricky.

Jonah had a firm grasp and a keen eye on the crop, capitalizing on his Sterling Banks upbringing to write his master's thesis on pecans.

"I was surprised to see you at the board meeting," he said, Bogie strolling at his side. For Bogie's walks, one or the other of them worked the young dog each day, then once he had obeyed for enough time, they'd cut him loose to chase squirrels and smell the assorted wildlife that gave him running dreams at night. She'd been walking him alone for the last week or so.

"Ditto right back at you," she said. She could match his stride, catch his eye, and sensed without looking when he was not happy.

Even still, Jonah was more the empath. When Quinn's daddy hired Jonah's mother to be caregiver to his wife after the birth of Quinn and her twin brother, Jule inserted herself and her toddler son cleanly into the hearts of the Sterling family. The death of one-year-old Quincy only served to bond Jonah tighter to Quinn. Ty entered the scene around age five, the same age as Q, as he called her, and the two became three.

She'd kissed the one boy in tenth grade and lost her virginity to the other on high school graduation night. After that she decided she preferred things less complicated... more than platonic, far from amorous, just something strong and reliable in between. If only time could stand still that way.

This spring, she and Jonah had become a couple during the throes of a dangerous case that threatened her and everything that was Sterling Banks, to include Jule. The intense energy that threw the friends together as potential lovers ultimately scared her. She'd tried to walk things back to how they had been, but that door had closed. Now it was just . . . weird.

Not that she didn't love him. That kind of love, however, was hard to explain. Those on the outside looking in saw a defined couple. Quinn, however, hadn't quite articulated what they were. Wasn't sure she wanted it labeled.

She let her hand rub across the trunk body of almost every tree they passed. They were the lifeblood of this farm, and nobody understood that more than she . . . and the man beside her.

"I hear you've had an interest in the school district's business for quite some time," she said, the unspoken being that he hadn't told her, even when they'd been *that couple*. None of their pillow talk mentioned old ladies needing saving, which Quinn would've thought a lovely quest to tackle together.

Bogie saw a house wren land on a root knee then take off quickly, and Jonah reined him in with a reserved tug.

"Miss Abbott wasn't wanting a scene," he tried to explain after a few seconds of silence.

"Meaning I was too over-the-top for her?" She wasn't hurt by the message, just at the messenger who hadn't trusted her enough to tell her. "All you had to say was that she preferred a strapping young man to a wild-haired monster like me."

His half grin warmed her.

"So, what's the deal?" she asked.

"She asked me not to spread her business," he said. "That's why I stayed quiet." They took a few more steps. "Not unlike you and your clients. Were you planning on telling me about your client, who you have not mentioned? At least you know mine."

Surely he'd seen the insinuation on Facebook about Iona meeting Quinn. She, however, hadn't missed the slight-of-hand jab at her for the PI work he never quite understood. "You're a PI now?" she asked.

Only Jonah could sneak up on her so adeptly. Ty simply laid things out straight and clean.

"I'm simply helping a neighbor," he said.

While she was what . . . *not* helping neighbors? Was he drawing some sort of parallel?

"Show me yours and I'll show you mine? Is that what we're doing?" she said, not unkind, but not completely in jest, either. "Trouble is, my friend," and she prodded him in the shoulder, "you stood before a hundred people and proclaimed what you were doing. My client prefers to remain in the dark, and with the license the state gave me, I'm beholden to honor her wish."

"*Her*, huh?"

"I gave you that on purpose, dufus."

"Sure you did."

"You knew it anyway."

From last night to this morning, while tired, while getting dressed, while Jonah made her coffee, Quinn had not shut off thinking about her case. Not because of Iona but because of Jonah. Her client might stand on the wrong side of things in the eyes of Jonah and Miss Abbott as a board member attempting to take an old woman's home.

And technically, they might not be wrong.

Quinn wasn't sure which side of that situation Iona fell on, but regardless, there were things Quinn could say and things she couldn't based on confidentiality even if Facebook was abuzz with guesses.

Jonah wasn't bound by the same rules, though she respected his moral code.

But was this a walk about the case? Both cases? Or a walk about a couple? Some clarity would be nice.

"I'll forgive you for not telling me," she chose to say. "Miss Abbott has been friends with the Sterlings as long as she's been alive, and I'm glad she came to you. Only makes sense since her land adjoins Sterling Banks." In many eyes, Jonah was regarded as much a part of Sterling Banks as Quinn. Nobody remembered one without the other. "How much land has the district optioned from her, and how much of it touches our land?"

"Quinn." He gave a small chuckle. "She owns seventy acres, and they optioned thirty. Twenty-nine and two-thirds, to be more exact, and none of that touches Sterling Banks."

"Well, that's a relief," she said, though having an elementary school abutting the farm wasn't an apocalypse. Thirty acres versus three thousand wasn't an issue. Somebody had to be a neighbor, and it sure beat a subdivision. "So what's the controversy? She didn't have to sign, and I'm sure she's getting a decent price for it."

She took the leash from Jonah, unhooked Bogie, and let him go. They were far enough in the trees for the dog to run free. Then she slid her arm into the crook of Jonah's, feeling the too familiar coating of hairs atop muscle he earned in his work. He still held a miffed sense of neglect at her slowing down their courtship, and she hoped he'd put that aside.

"Miss Abbott had already signed a contract with the district when she came to me," he said. "She couldn't afford to hire hands anymore and decided that farming would be no more than a vegetable garden." He smiled. "And she asked me to till that come spring."

"And pull up the dead plants in the fall," Quinn added, squeezing his arm. "Then what?"

"She came to terms with being next door to hundreds of kids and school busses coming and going. But then the district approached her again. Her house was fairly close to the purchased property line, and they'd underestimated something to do with ingress and egress. To avoid paying an architect to redesign plans, they wanted more land, which included her house."

Quinn stopped in her tracks, letting loose of him. "They what?"

Jonah had lost sight of Bogie and shouted for him. Both waited until a panting, tail-wagging pup showed to continue.

"Yeah, the gall of them, huh?" he said. "Miss Abbott said no, of course. What eighty-two-year-old, who's spent her entire life on the same dirt, wants to sell in exchange for what . . . a nursing home? She has no kids. Her niece lives in Texas." He was calm but not settled. "The money didn't matter to her, and the board tried to keep it in the dark."

"Their lack of planning shouldn't be her problem," Quinn said, her dander rising. "Again, I'm glad she came to you." Damn, she wished she'd known. "I take it there's more to the story to make you stand up big and bad at the meeting last night."

"Someone tampered with her tractor, set fire to old hay in the barn, and someone she can't identify was none too kind on her doorstep telling her she'd sell one way or another. I wanted them to know they could no longer bully her. Instead they were dealing with me."

Jonah didn't take up causes lightly, and she trusted his judgment. "You feel sure the district vandalized her?"

"Who can be sure?" he said.

"Did you call Ty?"

"He's the one who said we couldn't prove anything. Kids, transients. Who's going to blame Guy Cook or Laney Underwood in lieu of them?" he said. "But the timing was awful suspicious. I put her hay fire out along with a couple of our guys. She was lucky I happened to be here. That's when she asked if I would get involved and I accepted. She was crazy relieved about that, let me tell you. Made me wish we had checked on her sooner."

Now Quinn felt guilty. How could she not know? She'd heard of the fire. A small thing. And she realized Jonah went over there. Hearing him made her feel heartless that she hadn't gone, too.

From Iona's side, however, this mess meant the district forked out a six-figure deal for a flawed plan. No wonder they wanted this quiet. "How did word get out?"

"I went to the next board meeting and told them to let her alone. Right after that was when that stranger came to her door. At the next meeting, I addressed the bullying. She *still* got phone calls. At the next meeting I almost lost my cool."

Quinn understood better now. "Explains the uniforms. Can't believe

Uncle Larry made such a fuss and took the other side. Four men? Seriously?"

Jonah sighed and twisted his mouth a bit. "It didn't become four until last night, because of the previous meeting when I accused them of trying to shock Miss Abbott to her deathbed to get the land cheap."

Oh goodness. Quinn wasn't sure what to say to that.

"Yeah," he said, clearly reading her. "I called each and every board member to apologize about the remark. Instead of accepting my apology, Guy Cook stated they had been to the district's attorney. He stated I had no standing to get involved, and then he told me to piss off."

"He said that?" she asked. "The chairman?"

Jonah nodded. "He did. So, to get them off her back without getting her or me in trouble, she and I agreed it best she grant me power of attorney. She told me she slept better that night than she had in months."

This abuse set Quinn on fire, but losing her temper would only validate why Jonah handled Miss Abbott without her. Instead, she took his arm again and returned to walking. "I'm proud of you, Jonah. Now I get why you didn't involve me. Sounds like a lot of this happened when my world was upside down with the Renault case." She squeezed again. "I had a lot on my plate."

He knowingly peered down at her. "I see what you're doing."

"Walking and talking with my friend. Listening to how he's kicking ass for a little old lady."

His melancholy smile cut into her. "*Friend*," he repeated, staring ahead as he resumed their stroll. "A friend who you obviously said you weren't ready to call boyfriend, much less fiancé."

She almost halted at the about-face of the conversation. "I never used the word fiancé."

"It's what you meant, or rather, what you're hoping to avoid."

To think she'd decelerated this relationship amidst this other stuff. "Listen, the entire county would hitch us between hymns next Sunday if they had their way, and your mother would drop everything to make a dress, but I never talked in those terms, Jonah. We officially *dated*," and she did crooked fingers on her free hand, "for two months."

"What do you call thirty plus years?"

She started to say *friendship*, but the word almost felt insulting. "Awfully good times," she said instead.

His fluid movements tensed under her touch. "You speak like we're in the past."

Cinching her hold, she attempted damage control. "We're never in the past."

"Yeah," he said. "But I'm not hearing much talk about the future either."

She drew him closer. "Let's talk business and tuck the personal aside for later."

"Will there be a later?"

"Of course." She was afraid to say much else about that. They'd strolled almost two miles, Bogie in and out and around the trees.

Work roads crossed and crisscrossed the farm for the trucks and machinery providing the necessities of irrigating, pruning, and harvesting pecans. She heard the three-quarter ton Ram before it appeared, turned, and came their way. The vehicle slowed.

Jonah trotted to the driver, querying him on how something was going in a different quadrant. He gave task direction, talking with his hands as he pointed south and nodded. So did the driver before he moved on, bowing his head toward Quinn in passing.

Some would take issue that the hired hand catered to the foreman before the owner, and some women would claim gender bias, but little made Quinn more proud than to see Jonah so naturally run Sterling Banks. Her blood was in the heritage of the land, and she could do most of whatever Jonah did to keep it alive and well, but he chose to be there and he chose to love the place.

He wouldn't leave because leaving would mean abandoning his mother, or taking her away with him, or disrespecting the profession he'd embraced in the honor of his mother and Quinn's father. He'd invested heavily in Sterling Banks . . . emotionally, professionally, even financially since he'd left a farm management gig in the upstate to return when Graham died.

She'd had the lifestyle handed to her. The *Princess*, as Jonah often said.

Scared her shitless to blur their lines. Her the heir, him maybe married to the heir, no longer the foreman, instead the . . . what? He wouldn't be just marrying her. He'd be taking on the yoke of hundreds of years of legacy. Not many understood what that meant, or how heavy a responsibility that was.

And how would that burden affect a marriage?

Marriage . . . a word that worried her to bits, and hearing assorted members of the community use it upon seeing the two of them dating made her put on the brakes. She interpreted things as slowed. Listening to Jonah now, he felt dumped.

She was so bad at this relationship stuff.

Bogie came running up, gnawing a stick. He dropped to the dirt, kicking his hind legs out behind him, then he quickly teased the old dry branch into shreds with his front teeth. The pup had fallen into a natural stride with Quinn's lifestyle from the moment Jonah presented him to her in this very orchard.

Bogie kept her company in that massive manor way too large for one soul, crowding out some of the echoes of days and family gone by. But Bogie was also a reminder of Jonah. His love, his laughter, the cuddling and his off-the-cuff jokes . . . wonderful until he talked of their future.

They weren't old by any means, but they weren't kids either. Mid-thirties. Truth was she was the last Sterling, and every native in the county understood the need for heirs, with Jonah right there for the taking. And more than willing.

She didn't want to marry for heirs. In today's world, she could have a child without marriage and avoid her concern that binding their relationship would change each of them too much. Or would that arrangement make matters worse?

Did she even want children? How vulnerable would she feel then with that level of responsibility? The PI work would be tricky. No, the PI work would have to go to avoid the threats like they'd had not long ago.

Again, the Sterling legacy robbing her of the thrill of law enforcement.

Damn, how spoiled was she?

But lastly, and this one touched her heart, how was she to behave around Ty?

She shivered, that last reason smacking more of truth than all of the others combined.

They walked silent for several hundred more yards. Saying anything else about their feelings, Miss Abbott, or Quinn's case . . . felt precarious.

"I need to get back and check on some things," she said.

"And I need to get back to work," he added. They turned for the manor.

Funny how they'd accomplished little on this walk except clarify why he was defending Ms. Abbott . . . and prove how awkward they still were. Even after thirty years.

Chapter 5

DID SHE EVEN want Iona's case if it came with the potential to clash with Jonah?

Quinn sat mindlessly at her corner desk in the huge paneled den. Was she right avoiding anything permanent with Jonah? He was a wonderful person, and he'd be her partner, so why couldn't she envision the future being incredible with him?

Because she couldn't stop thinking what it might do to Ty.

Her grandmother's mantle clock chimed once on ten thirty, kicking her out of her trance.

Before Bogie arrived, these times could feel the loneliest. Everyone else was at work, and while she technically was as well—just at a desk mired in plantation business, the thought of being so alone in so much house gave her a doleful sense of isolation. The pup made things better, even snoring from his bed near the fireplace, his half-chewed rawhide bone under his chin.

Yeah, Jonah had known what he was doing gifting her the dog. He usually knew what he was doing.

Work, Quinn.

Her plan was to dig up data on Fripp Bakeman, starting with her favorite of the database programs she and hundreds of other PIs subscribed to for baseline intel on clients, targets, and everybody in between. What information she couldn't get from them, she often acquired through Ty or her own nosing around.

But this niggling concern had attached itself to Quinn like a barnacle since learning about Jonah's latest project. Miss Abbott's problem had the potential to clash with Iona's in Quinn's world. Surely there was a way to tactfully sidestep a collision with Jonah.

She really didn't relish an additional quarrel atop the thin-ice they walked on now.

Investigation was fact-finding, though, which shouldn't impact Jonah. Really it shouldn't. Iona felt railroaded by a husband, the original bone of contention and the basis of the case. A domestic issue. Quinn considered Fripp a bully and feared to some minor degree for her client's personal safety. He was the primary threat, not the board. Keeping this arms-length from the board would avoid conflicting with Jonah. About their respective clients anyway.

Okay, good. She'd rationalized how to do this.

An hour later, she had a decent grasp of Fripp's life. Married to the same wife for fifteen years, a general contractor for longer, a father of a daughter in middle-school, and a lifelong resident of Jacksonboro. He and his family had lived in the same house in the center of town. He wasn't a sex-offender, had no record other than two traffic tickets, and had never been arrested. He graduated from the same high school where the board just met and had an associate degree in business. He kept his general contractor's license up to date.

Fripp was very grounded in the community with roots buried deeper than most. One would usually consider his type too leery of losing what he had built to be very daring in his business dealings. Then there were always those who felt so entrenched and important in the community as to be untouchable. The smaller the community, the more they felt they could get away with.

Maybe like the board members?

Fripp also did real estate deals here and there, flipping houses after buying run-down ones on the cheap. Sometimes he partnered the deals. Sometimes the other name was Iona's. That revelation then led Quinn into finding their company's charter, and the fact that it qualified for woman-owned status. Apparently Iona owned fifty-five percent of the business.

Why hadn't she told Quinn?

Companies often used a wife or female family member to better compete for government contracts, but in the IRS's eyes, ignorance was no excuse for tax fraud and malfeasance.

Iona would have access to both personal and company tax returns. Quinn picked up the phone.

"I've been researching, and I have a couple of questions," she said.

"Sure," Iona replied, eager to assist.

"First, do you do y'all's company books?"

"No, I don't," she said. "Fripp wanted a high school friend of his in town to do them to maintain some distance and honesty. Besides, Todd Avert's a CPA. I just have the degree."

Total BS. Iona could easily have managed those records, but Quinn didn't need to argue the frivolous right now. "Can you put hands on a copy of both yours and the business's tax returns?"

"The personal ones, sure. Not the business. Fripp keeps those."

The naivete she uncovered in this woman multiplied by the second, and, disappointed, Quinn only hoped that she didn't find so much gullibility that her client had unwittingly crossed the line into anything off-book, under the table, or simply false by doing whatever Fripp asked her to do. Yet another issue to make Quinn second guess continuing this case. Any more concerns about Iona, and she might just pull the plug. "Can you get off? Like, right now?"

"I work for myself, so sure."

"Good, I'll pick you up in thirty."

A pause. "I have to be someplace in a couple hours, so I need to drive."

"Fine. Then meet me at this address."

The office where they were to meet was six blocks from Iona's, which in Jacksonboro meant the other side of town. The narrow office stood squished in a strip of other narrow offices. Also a deli and a dress shop, with Harmon Valentine Insurance on the end.

The sign above the door they wanted wasn't lit, just two-sided plastic saying Todd Avert, CPA in red and blue. Quinn parked right outside. For some reason, Iona had parked down the street.

"We haven't called," Iona said, trotting up and realizing where they were going.

"Of course we haven't." Quinn waited at the entrance. "Come on. We don't want him leaving for lunch. Why didn't you park behind my truck?"

Iona leaned in, clandestine acting. "Don't like people knowing where I do any of my business. Fripp tells me to do it."

Hmm, odder by the day. Sort of opened a door to his behavior.

As they entered the tiny office, a bell tinkled their arrival. The air hinted of lilac freshener, plank floors, and old wallpaper.

"Just a minute," said a hidden voice from the rear of the office.

"That's Todd," Iona whispered.

Quinn was familiar with most of the folks who hung shingles in Jacksonboro, but she had never had the need for his services for many reasons. Small town gossip and the size of Sterling Banks' operation were two of those reasons. The Sterlings had always used a firm in Charleston.

The receptionist's desk looked too neat, almost abandoned, probably not used except during tax season or certain days of the week. Magazines showed year-old dates, and framed photos on the wall flaunted Todd posing with various ball teams, parade floats, and civic groups. The maple furniture with tweedy upholstery looked older than Quinn if not her uncle, and the thought of how many bottoms had sat on them gave her the excuse to remain standing.

Early forties in khakis a size too big around the middle and three inches too long from the fabric buckled across his resoled loafers, Todd Avert entered drying his hands on a paper towel. "How can I help you . . . well, hey, Iona." Then he peered at Quinn, a tiny squint saying he wasn't quite sure of what this visit meant.

Iona looked to Quinn to take over.

"Hey, Todd." Quinn didn't reach out to shake, because she couldn't get the visual of him just leaving the bathroom out of her mind. "I'm working with Iona on some personal issues. She can't put a hand on the business tax returns, and while you're looking those up, go ahead and shoot her the personal ones as well. Say, the last three years?"

He seemed to disconnect the way his expression froze, chin up, a fixed stare down a thin beaked nose.

Quinn dipped her head, staring at the statue man. "Todd?"

"I might need to call Fripp on that," he said, more like a question than a statement.

Iona accepted the remark, saying nothing.

Quinn didn't accept that. "That's why Iona's here, Todd. To save you that trouble. Since she has a fifty-five percent interest in the company, which I'm sure was done to designate Bakeman Construction a woman-owned business for contracts . . . which you know, of course . . . then you can honor her request. We'll sit right here."

His mouth formed this little round opening and held it, and Quinn almost made a joke about flies. "That's a lot of copies," he said, "and I don't have a receptionist here at the moment to run the copier . . ."

"Todd? Come on." Quinn pulled out her business card with her email on it. "There isn't an accountant alive that doesn't keep files on a hard drive. Three personal returns and three business returns. Click, click, click." She started to hand him the card, then hesitated. "Iona, is it okay he send those to my email as well as yours?"

"Sure, sure," Iona said, happy for someone else running the show. "Do you have my email?"

Was she serious? "Of course you have her email, don't you, Todd? How else have you done her taxes and not communicated, but for expediency, I'll write it on my card, too."

Todd gingerly took the card. "But I was working on—"

"As I said, Todd, we'll wait." She took a breath. "Unless you are refusing."

Like a light came on, Iona brushed Quinn's elbow and moved in. "You do realize I can do my own taxes, Todd. Refusing a client would hurt your license around here. In thinking about it, I doubt I've signed a single one of these returns, have I?" She did *signed* in air quotes.

Quinn did a double take at the short woman. Slow on the draw but finally some gall.

Without response, Todd left the room. Wasn't long before Quinn saw the email come through on her phone. Two of them, one for the personal returns and one for the business. They waited a few moments, but Todd didn't come out.

Quinn figured out why. "Let's go," she said.

"Don't we need to wait—"

"No, we don't, Iona. He's calling Fripp. Call me when you get in your car."

They scooted out, walking none too slow.

Iona hadn't reached her car before she phoned Quinn. "Fripp's calling."

"Send it to voicemail," Quinn said, getting in her truck. "Do you have a copier at home to print these out?"

"Yes, but what if Fripp's there?"

Good point. On her last case, to avoid being seen with a person of interest, Quinn had taken him to Sterling Banks. Evil had followed her there, so she wasn't making that mistake again. She wished they weren't in separate cars.

Quinn drove up beside Iona. "Sit here while I make copies so we can go somewhere and go over these. We'll raise eyebrows if we go together. I'll call when I'm done."

Quinn wanted to do this quickly, while Fripp was working elsewhere. Piper Pierce owned the UPS Store a block over. With a quick detour, Quinn ran in, copied the emails, and fifteen minutes later hurried out with a stack of almost 200 pages. The irony of using another board member's business to work on the case was more satisfying than she thought.

She called Iona. With neither of their residences suitable, and the library too public, Quinn came up with an alternative. They soon pulled into the Craven County Law Enforcement Center, an oversized spit-and-polished, blond-brick affair with a silver metal hip roof.

Iona eased in beside her, pale and concerned. The fencing with razor wire, bars on the windows, and patrol cars had her gripping the steering wheel. She left her motor running. "What are we doing?"

"Going someplace where we won't be interrupted," she said. "Fripp won't look here."

Parked in the general parking lot amidst ten other vehicles, they got out but walked away from the center, toward the eighty-year old, flat, tar-roofed concrete block building across the street. The gold on black, hand-painted sign over the door stated Sheriff's Annex. Rusted razor wire remained atop its old fence since the ancient jail had once been prone to escapes.

This old locale was where the sheriff held less-than-public meetings. Even if Fripp came by, and even if he spotted the truck or car in the parking lot, he wouldn't dare go in the Sheriff's Office and inquire. And he wouldn't dream of looking in some ancient, locked-up historic landmark.

Quinn unlocked the side door to the timeworn jail and let them into the musty structure and its stifled air. She turned a knob switch. The light overhead hummed before finally clicking on.

Dated light fixtures worked via cotton-covered electrical cords that disappeared into a plastered ceiling with water marks. Scuffed, wooden, swivel chairs parked helter-skelter at a long wooden table for eight.

But that odor . . . not so much negative but mind jarring. Quinn reverted to childhood when she used to visit her uncle. Then forward when she'd escorted a drunk or two during her short term after high school as one of her uncle's deputies.

One of those cells, around the corner and down the hall, was particularly ominous and heavily oppressive. Uncle Larry had carted in her and Ty at age twelve and locked them up for an hour for misbehaving. She had to go to the bathroom from the moment they slammed the metal door, and unwilling to pee in the open toilet like that, she held it until her bladder stabbed pains through her belly. When Larry let them loose, she ran outside and squatted behind a bush, begging Ty to distract anyone from watching.

Iona sat on the other side of the table from Quinn. "As the bookkeeper, you read the business returns." Quinn sorted through the papers, creating two stacks. "I'll go through the personal."

But instead of the papers, Iona studied the environment she'd been cast into. "Are we supposed to be in here?"

Quinn gave her a dubious look. "Did you not see me pull out a key?"

Which didn't answer the question, but Iona settled for it. "What are we looking for?"

Quinn had already spread out the oldest personal return, run down the first page, and turned to the next. "Anything that doesn't fit. Anything questionable. Any activities or income or acquaintances you find odd."

Wasn't five minutes before Iona gave an *oh my*.

Quinn waited for the woman to finish reading whatever it was that drew the response.

"Troy Cheverall's name is everywhere," she finally said. "So is Sy Bowers."

Two contractors familiar in these parts. "Not hearing a problem, Iona."

"The only names getting district construction contracts are those," she said. "They are mostly renovations and repairs. They don't build schools or add on wings. You have to be almost specialized in schools to land those."

Okay, some potential here. Again, Craven was a small county.

Iona went on. "Last year Troy got the middle school gym rehab. Sy got the playgrounds. Fripp won the job for refurbishing the overhangs where car riders wait to be picked up." She peered over. "But I'm seeing way more district money running through our construction company than just what Fripp won." Her eyes blinked, then blinked hard again. "I believe he's showing income from all three jobs, plus more." Paling, she sank in her seat. "Could my husband be a mastermind behind the district construction contracts?"

Mastermind seemed a bold moniker for the likes of Fripp Bakeman, but this was small county business and the district a big paying enterprise. So indeed, could he be somewhat of an organizer? Quinn gave Iona time to digest the fact these returns were in her name, too . . . as fifty-five percent owner.

Iona dropped the papers like they caught fire. "Oh my gosh, this looks like I directed work to my husband and managed the contracts through the district. I could go to jail for this!"

With Iona's tone escalating, Quinn kept hers level. There was always a moment like this when a client lost their head and Quinn had to catch it and return it to its cradle. "This explains why he hasn't asked for a divorce, I believe."

"Oh, God." Iona's hand went over her mouth.

"You are only one of seven board members, Iona." And if contracts were unanimous, or won regardless how Iona voted, then less problem. But if Iona could be deemed the deciding vote, say in a four to three vote, or if any of the others claimed they felt pressured by her, that was another story. Quinn still wasn't overly concerned. Not yet. Iona wasn't coercive, and she didn't appear to have strong allies on the board. They were far from worrying about handcuffs going on.

But there was still a concern as to whether this could escalate when Iona got home. Certainly by now Todd had warned the man. "Is it safe to go home? Has Fripp ever threatened you?"

"I sleep in the guest room," she mumbled.

"Not an answer. Wait, *you* are the one who moved to the guest room?"

She shrugged. "Less trouble that way."

Empowering for him, too.

"He yells but has never gotten physical," her client said.

But there was a minor involved. An innocent girl. "What does your daughter think?"

Iona dropped her head ashamed, and in this setting she looked like someone who'd just been read their rights. Quinn sensed the forthcoming tears and decided not to mention the daughter again.

A lot of clients reached this point, too. PI work came with a lot of hand-holding. Some cases could result in nothing but the client giving up and accepting the ways things were. All it took was learning the facts, or facing facts after a PI's sleuthing made suspicions real . . . and more palatable to any alternative.

Quinn sensed that crossroad. If Iona filed for divorce, she opened herself up for legal ramifications if Fripp got mouthy. The aroma of collaboration could take them both down.

And Fripp might be difficult about the divorce, might feel he needed Iona for other contracts.

"So, you were aware of these contracts awarded to other contractors, but not aware that he got a share of each one."

Iona nodded. "What do we do now? I'm implicated in a lot of deals."

"We call him," she said. "Give me his number."

The phone quickly went to voice mail, meaning he refused the call. Quinn dialed again. "Fripp, this is Quinn Sterling. Call me, please. As you've figured out by now, I'm helping your wife. She just perused y'all's tax returns for the last three years, and the numbers look, shall I say, unusual. She's about to come home. You've never shown signs of violence before, so please keep it that way. Continue being civil." She had mere seconds left to make her point. "Give her serious crap, and you go to jail. Consider yourself warned."

"Quinn!" Iona gasped, thank goodness not in time to make the recording. "How do I go home now!"

"You just do," she said. "If he tries anything, we have proof he was warned not to. If he threatens you, drive to my place with your daughter. I have security. And we shoot trespassers on our place."

Two died a little over two months ago, one in the manor and one amongst the trees, but Quinn wouldn't tell her that.

She didn't expect Fripp to call, though. Not after the showdown at Jackson Hole.

She started to ask Iona if she had a firearm at home, or a concealed weapon permit, but in thinking twice, she bet not on both counts.

"Finish the paperwork review," Quinn said, thinking that a book-keeper might settle with the number crunching so inherently comfortable for her.

There was only so much Quinn could do for Iona at this point without peeling away layers and doing more damage. Sooner or later, Iona would ask the critical question, *What do we do now?*

"Quinn? What do we do about this now?"

Okay, sooner rather than later.

And herein lay yet another crossroad. They'd uncovered that Fripp might be wheeling and dealing with school district contracts, but to oust him would cast aspersions on her client. This case might turn into nothing but damage control . . . or explode into a county-wide scandal. Quinn preferred the former, while thinking of a plan to contain the latter.

Chapter 6

QUINN HAD SEEN Iona's self-esteem and confidence diminish in steps ever since she was hired. How Iona had landed on the school board was beyond Quinn's comprehension, and the woman's timidity and questionable talents as a leader made Quinn try to recall her own choices during the elections.

She voted. She always voted, and she selected someone for every post on the ballot, but she couldn't recall a single name of who ran for the school board other than Laney Underwood who posted signs around Lenore's Jackson Hole diner. Seeing those signs so often and knowing she was related to Ty earned her Quinn's vote. She seemed to recall voting for more than just one, but no telling what other boxes she checked. How many people researched school board candidates anyway?

Having worked for the Feds, plus being the daughter of Graham Sterling who thrived on being a positive force for his county, Quinn learned to pay attention to federal, state, and county politics, but for the life of her, she couldn't recall discussion around the election of the school district board candidates.

She might've voted for Bakeman for no other reason than she was at the top of the list alphabetically, which in hindsight probably proved an asset for candidates. But the board had a Valentine and an Underwood, too, so some people apparently voted by other than alphabet.

Quinn had postponed Iona's question about what happened next with a directive to study the tax returns. Three years' research, however, showed the same contractors, and Fripp's income for contracts he didn't have but his friends did. Iona remembered voting for several of those contracts.

These guys might be *thick as thieves*, pardon the pun, in such a small county without a slew of contractors to spread jobs around. They had an arrangement to sub for each other, so that whoever got the job took care of his friends, and Quinn wasn't sure there was anything illegal about that.

What could look illegal was Iona voting for her husband's benefit while silently being the company's majority stakeholder. What the hell was she thinking?

The harder Quinn looked, the more this sucked for her client. If Quinn were on that jury, she'd think Iona should have known better.

They completed reviewing the returns. "Well?" Iona asked.

Well, indeed. Quinn wasn't exactly sure of their next step. She stacked the papers and kept them for herself for later reference, uncertain how to answer, but they needed to leave soon. Uncle Larry didn't even know his niece had a key to the Annex, and she wanted to keep it that way.

"Iona, go home. But . . ." and Quinn had to think about these words. "You need to help me here. What is it you want me to do? Whatever we throw at Fripp can easily stick to you. You funded your own company."

"But I do accounting. I don't do construction. That's his world. I just gave him my name to increase his chances when he bids. Not just for the board, for any government contract."

This just kept getting worse.

Yet Iona wasn't seeing it. "Look for anything he's done I can use against him. I won't be a victim," she said. "He might be in the board conspiracy."

The only conspiracy proven thus far had been Iona's. "I'm not seeing a board conspiracy," Quinn said.

"Yes you have." Iona rose and paced her side of the small room. "You saw them get the cops involved. Not sure that you've paid any attention to the county, but they'd rezoned some areas to entice development."

"We're dragging in county council, too?" Iona's conspiracy theory was spreading like a bad stain. "And you're saying this is connected to Fripp? And the board?" Iona needed to learn what was worth pursuing and what wasn't.

"We're a poor county, Quinn. We qualify for more federal grants. We'll get a fat check for any sort of new school, which can go to infrastructure which aids subdivisions and raises land values."

There was logic in her explanation, but how did it apply to Quinn's case for her? "And you want me to look into everything. County council, land purchases, permits, and construction contracts? We're straying from the original purpose of you wanting intel on your husband for a divorce. For one thing, you couldn't afford for me to go into that depth for the length of time it would take. And those are a lot of hornets nests you're asking me to stir."

Her client was desperate. She had access to a lot of knowledge but didn't understand how to use it. The truth was, due to her unintentional and possibly criminal voting record, her husband and the board might have more leverage on her than she had on them.

Quinn sighed. First they needed to stop the bleeding. Her proposed interim solution wouldn't exactly clear things up, or solve the marital issue, but it might stop Iona from sinking deeper into the quagmire. "I believe you need to resign."

Iona gripped the chair before her. "What?"

Quinn didn't need to repeat herself. She was definitely heard.

"But I hired you to fix things for me," Iona said, her tone raised.

"You hired me to get Fripp off your back in hopes you two could divorce and be done with each other . . . unless I misread you," Quinn replied, attempting to remain nonconfrontational. "And I cannot correct all the ills of a school board and county council. Remember what you said before about term limits, not running for office anymore, and having had enough of the board? Call this liberation."

Quinn released a purposeful sigh when her client seemed lost for words. "Go home, Iona. Take a long bath and think about this. You are in deeper than Fripp, my friend. Maybe the contracts weren't totally corrupt. Maybe the work got done and nobody bought yachts or took European vacations. You should've abstained from those votes from the outset. We're addressing damage control now."

"But they are doing wrong."

"And you did wrong. How much damage are you willing to accept in your personal life to point fingers at others?"

Iona paled. "I could lose my bookkeeping clients."

"Yes." Quinn stood and came around the table. "And you and Fripp could go to jail and your daughter wind up in foster care."

Quinn eased Iona into her chair before she staggered and missed it.

"That's so unfair," Iona whined, tearing.

"That's reality. I'm not trying to scare you, just attempting to put the pieces together and determine a solution. First, I'm not an attorney, and at some point in the not-so-distant future, I may have to direct you to one. Not one in Jacksonboro, though, because this could fall under state law enforcement. I doubt the FBI would want it unless serious money is missing. We haven't seen that."

Yet. It would take a forensic accountant to determine if money was misappropriated. Quinn prayed the school building work was performed properly. If they could drop this into a *no-harm, no foul* category, this issue might be mute.

"You're not going to barf, are you?" she asked when Iona didn't want to budge.

"No," came out weakly.

"Can you drive all right?"

A nod, then a shallow, "Yes."

"Good." Quinn helped her up. "Not only go home and relax, the bubble bath and such, but order out dinner. Have it ready when Fripp comes in, so he has nothing to gripe about. Then tell him you have a migraine, go to your room, and watch some mindless old movie until you go to sleep."

Another nod.

"And stay off Facebook," she added in afterthought.

This woman wasn't malicious or conniving and most likely had been outsmarted. However, none of that required Quinn put herself in the middle of a problem littered with political and criminal land mines. She needed a day or two to ponder options, and at least leave Iona with direction if Quinn bowed out gracefully.

She escorted Iona to her car, saw her in, and patted her arm for assurance. "Let me think. I'll be in touch. Call if Fripp shows his butt, but chill until you hear from me."

She watched the small sedan disappear out of the parking lot and up the street, turning left at the light toward home. But instead of climbing into her truck, Quinn struck out for the Law Enforcement Complex. She had a few questions for Sheriff Sterling before she made any quick decisions, and she had to be selective in how she asked them.

CARLA SAT AT reception, her dyed blonde eighties' ponytail high on her fifty-ish head and heavy loops on middle-aged ears. The hair-do wasn't a complimentary style, but she owned it. Carla was a woman stuck in the fashion statement of her teenage years, and because she controlled access to the sheriff, one simply admired the view.

"Where you been, Quinn? Saw your truck sitting out there."

"Met up with someone. Just needed a place to park. He in?" Quinn did a quick point toward the hall.

Carla gave a head tip of acknowledgement. "Yep. Nobody with him. If someone waltzed in there, don't hold it against me. Love the turquoise scarf, by the way. Damn, I sure wish I had your coloring. You make that red hair come alive, girl."

"It's a beast, Carla. Trust me. Try to be good." Quinn walked herself through the entrance.

"Gave that up years ago, honey. Besides, they won't arrest me anyway!" Carla cackled as Quinn made her way down the hall that still held the scent of paint, even a year after the complex's ribbon cutting.

She walked in on her buddy sitting in the straight-backed leather chair before Larry Sterling's wide wooden desk. "Oh, hey, Ty."

Ty looked over, and Quinn got the strongest sense she'd interrupted a conversation about her. "What did I do?"

"Who says we were talking about you?" her uncle said.

She did a fist bump into Ty's shoulder. "His look." She sat in the neighboring chair.

Ty started to rise.

"No, no, stay seated," she said, a hand on him. "I had a couple things to run by the sheriff. You're bound to hear them anyway." Ty's presence also might aid in keeping the air more civil with Uncle Larry.

Ty looked to his sheriff who nodded his okay.

She began. "First, I have this domestic case."

"Thought you didn't do those," Larry said.

"It's not so simple," she replied, and he shut up. She never told him about her cases, and he understood not to push too hard or he might not hear about this one.

"It's getting squirrelly," she said.

Both waited for more.

"Have y'all had any issues, domestic or otherwise, with Iona Bakeman or her husband Fripp?"

Both sets of brows went up. "Which one is your client?" asked her uncle.

"That shouldn't affect your answer."

He scowled.

"He can be an ass as you know from meeting him behind Mom's place," Ty said. "Seen him flare up at the board meetings, but he's not crossed any lines I'm aware of. No neighbor complaints, no abuse. More windbag than anything."

She turned to the sheriff, who added nothing. "I can't even say that much about him," he said. "What the hell is he talking about you meeting this guy behind the bar?"

"Don't worry about that. But y'all automatically spoke about Fripp," she said. "What about Iona?"

"Zero," Ty said. "Besides, her life is under a microscope being on the board. The world would hear if she wasn't flying straight."

Apparently not. "Speaking of the school board, why the hell are y'all pulling out the stops to thump your chests at their meetings?"

Ty didn't move a muscle. To relieve Ty's awkwardness, Quinn dumped it on her uncle. "A request for security comes through you. Sending one guy would be a courtesy. Sending two plus the county's detective and the almighty sheriff is over the top. You're kissing ass or playing politics, because I haven't heard a thing about any sort of threat warranting that much force."

She hadn't asked a question, so neither replied.

"Who asked you to be there?" she asked, just to confirm her own intel.

"Guy Cook," her uncle said.

She almost asked if he'd gotten a freebie deal on estate planning in return, but cops didn't take kindly to being accused of taking bribes. Besides, Larry Sterling had little sense of humor.

"What made him come to you?" she asked instead.

"Controversial topics of late have been drawing more public participation, like firing the basketball coach and building a school, and with the public feeling its oats, the board got nervous about someone getting physical. You saw how they reacted last night."

She scoffed and gave him her best dubious look. "When's the last time they had a brawl? Or made a substantive threat?"

"Never," he said, "but a show of force keeps it that way."

"These are small town parents, for God's sake."

"They are showing out, Quinn. When we're asked to be security, we do it."

She shook her head. "When's the last time you moon-lighted as security, Uncle Larry?"

"We're paid with taxes," he replied. "We serve as needed."

She peered over at Ty, silently mouthing, *Are you believing this?* for her uncle to see. Ty's lips flattened, and he studied his fingernails in an attempt at silent neutrality. She turned to the sheriff. "You're intimidation. I can think of no reason for you to be there personally without giving the appearance that you are a tool for the board."

Color showed in his cheeks. "I'm nobody's tool. *We're* nobody's tool."

Her own vexation kicked in to match his. "When Guy Cook stands with that almighty gavel in his hand and points to his buddy standing guard in the corner to do his bidding, you become a tool."

"Stop, Quinn."

She hushed at the surprise of Ty speaking up, noting his glance at her uncle before continuing. "Jonah is the problem," he said.

She clipped a laugh. "Jonah." Staring over at the sheriff, she waited for a different take, but he seemed to be siding with Ty. Had that been the discussion when she barged in?

"Him helping a frail, little old lady keep her home is grounds for SWAT? The district harassed her. He even got power of attorney so that she didn't have to deal with this and have a heart attack."

Both men held back, and while her uncle often did so out of spite, Ty didn't want to tell her something.

Uncle Larry tried to explain. "He comes to every meeting, niece. And each time he gets more emboldened, shall we say. The boy's a good guy, but—"

"He's a man."

Larry inhaled and gave her her say. "And I get that he's special to you. But he's given some rather questionable ultimatums to a few board members, both in the meeting and privately. It doesn't hurt for a few uniforms to sit and endure those prudish, stiff-shirts for a few hours, does it? If it keeps the public from losing its mind or keeps Jonah in check, it's no big deal."

"It empowers the board to play God and dominate," she spouted. "I've been hearing things from an entirely different perspective of late about those people."

"You watching that Facebook group, are you?"

Since when did her uncle do social media, and worse, when did he do it ahead of her? "Just started reading it," she said.

"Read to the first of the year," Ty said, making Quinn study him, taking in the anomaly of Ty and the sheriff oddly on the same team.

"Do so then we'll talk," Ty said. "And when you have a minute, we can discuss the emails he sent the board members."

Well, crap. She was letting them get the best of her because she wasn't as informed. Her fault. "I'd like to see them," she said, then changed the subject. "I had another issue, and you already opened that door. It's about Miss Abbott. Are you investigating her fire? The vandalism coincidentally happened around this land fiasco."

His utility belt squeaked as Ty shifted to see her better. "We looked into it, Q. Nobody saw anyone and there're no forensics to be had. I suggested she get more lighting out there, a fire extinguisher or two, and maybe even a cam." He did a wrist flip thing for the next point. "Even told Jonah to rig up a camera or two, like he did at your place. He's good at that."

"But?" she asked.

"He got pissed."

"This is Jonah we're talking about, Ty. How pissed could he get?"

"He went from plainspoken to red-faced in seconds. He said he expected me to cooperate with him on taking care of an old woman, not dodge my job."

Oh goodness. She couldn't stomach her two best friends at odds. Usually when they sparred, the topic was meager and the quarrel never long. "He cares, and you know how he gets about something he cares about, Ty. And this woman probably reminds him of Jule."

"Oh, no. He chewed me out and accused me of—" He cut a glance at his boss.

She enjoyed a laugh. "Let me guess. He blamed you for being like the sheriff. No heart. No drive."

It sounded cruel the moment she said it, but she couldn't unsay it now. The three of them understood the shallowness of Larry Sterling's loyalty to work, but saying it openly in front of him was another matter.

Her uncle let the insult go, sounding more like the parent in the room. "See if you can settle him down, Quinn, and I'll quit coming to the meetings."

Mark one up for Uncle Larry.

But none of this sounded right. Jonah had committed to a serious cause, but he was a peacemaker, choosing to attack only to protect his own. So why wasn't Jonah listening to Ty, or joining forces with someone to fix this situation instead of slinging accusations?

Clearly she'd stumbled in here unprepared, and before she screwed up more, she'd go home and orient herself with the facts.

"Your boy is causing trouble. Straighten him up."

Sheriff Sterling should've stopped while he was ahead.

"That *boy*," she said, rising, "is as noble a man as I've known since Daddy. If he has concerns, it would behoove you more to understand them before standing against him. Don't make me take a side, uncle."

He scoffed. "Girl, you've always taken the side opposite mine."

"And if you think you've seen me go up against you before, you haven't seen anything until you go after Jonah." She pushed the chair aside to leave but had one last thought. "And be glad it's only Jonah standing before that board. I could choose to stand with him."

As her words finished echoing, Quinn almost wished Jonah could see she hadn't really dumped him at all.

Chapter 7

ALMOST SUPPER TIME, and Quinn made her way toward home . . . alone. In twenty-four hours she'd distanced herself from both Jonah and Ty, and she couldn't remember a time when she hadn't been on the same page with at least one.

Guess she was eating alone tonight. One left turn ahead and she wouldn't have to. She wondered what Lenore's special was this evening. She texted Jule and asked if she or Jonah could walk Bogie once she was parked up front at Jackson Hole. Of course, Jule replied yes. Quinn texted, *Love you, goat lady.*

Wasn't long before Quinn occupied her booth, a glass of tea and appetizer of fried okra before her, the bowl arriving almost before her seat got warm.

When she needed mothering, she went to Lenore or Jule, one generation up from her two best friends. Neither had daughters, and somehow she felt she filled a special part of their hearts. It was too last minute to drop in on Jule for dinner, but as a restauranteur, Lenore always had eats ready to go on the table.

Tonight was meatloaf and mashed potatoes. Comfort food. Quinn could use some comforting. Wasn't long before she had plate before her, fresh tea, and some banana pudding in a small bowl to the side. Then napkin in lap, she positioned her phone to the left, held her fork to the right, and took her time reading and eating. She'd only glanced at that Facebook page before. Time to see what the hell Craven Living was so worked up about . . . and who the ringleaders were.

Somebody put a slow George Strait on the jukebox. She listened to the words a moment, familiar with just about every song on that old machine, then returned to her phone, letting the country song take on a white noise background effect.

Didn't take three bites into her meatloaf before she found herself chewing faster, caught up in the middle of an argumentative thread.

We need this school, and we do not need some arrogant rich bastard butting into where he doesn't belong. He doesn't even have kids.

Holy bejeesus at the toxicity. And Jonah wasn't rich. About the time Quinn read something civil, an adversary tacked on an insult and destroyed the effort.

He's saving a woman's house so she isn't put in the street. Show some humanity, you idiot.

Then like a see-saw, in came the other side.

Then let him move her into his house. I hear he has plenty of room over there on that plantation. They're loaded!

Some additional folks echoed the talk about being rich. Others took up for the Sterlings as hard workers and contributors to the community, *bless them.*

Which board members do you think he'll buy to stop this school?
Nobody, you moron. There's no money to go into anyone's pocket if you don't build it.

Yeah, right. And in the meantime, while this lady rocks away on her front porch, with her money in the bank from the first sale of land, our children miss out on a decent education because we can't build the school.
Then vote out the board that made the bogus deal. Ain't her fault they screwed up. More power to her.
Gotta give the old lady credit for scamming them like she did.
All this foolishness is going to kill her, people.
We can only hope it happens before my eight-year-old graduates high school.

Quinn's pulse quickened at people bashing Jonah. Quickened more reading his follow-up posts. He didn't hide behind some fictitious title or humorous nickname. There he was in full glory . . . Jonah Proveaux. He didn't type often and avoided the one-liner spit-ball contests. Instead, he presented in complete sentences and an intense attempt at explanation.

Admittedly, he escalated things a bit by pleading for Craven County to show more humanity.

He got particularly fired up about the vandalism, even more so at the bullying tactic of the person who appeared on Miss Abbott's doorstep ordering her to sign the second contract or else. Quinn could sense his attempt to point fingers without instigating a fight. In some places, his efforts fell short.

Sheriff Sterling would be all over that crap, rich boy. No one set a fire on purpose around here. Can't be true. Sure you're not saving that place for yourself and that lady friend over at Sterling Banks?

And Jonah replied. *Back off. I put the fire out in Ms. Abbott's barn. And we don't need the Abbott land.*

Back and forth, to and fro. True to his word, he'd kept Quinn out of it. He'd avoided any mention of her or the farm except for the slipped use of the word *we*. Such a powerful word between them of late.

He knew Quinn didn't do much social media. She hadn't known there even was a Craven group until she'd taken Iona's case.

Quinn clicked into the group's origin. In the About This Group part, someone stated, This page was created to share news and the positive things happening in and around Craven County, South Carolina.

News? Sort of. Positive? Not so much. Surely there was someone in charge . . . at least someone who founded the group. She scrolled to Administrator and found the leader by her first name, Birdie.

Birdie was a deeply Southern given name several generations old, but there was only one that Quinn could name from her time on this earth. She clicked on Birdie's icon. *Bingo.*

Birdie Palmeter.

She'd taught tenth grade English to Quinn, Ty, and, three years earlier, Jonah. A quirky woman that no student ever forgot, possessing an intense fire to drill the classics into students' heads. You loved Shakespeare like she expected you to love Shakespeare or you got docked an entire letter grade. They learned to fake it, which made them learn it.

Her trademark hurdle to pass her class was to memorize a two-minute soliloquy from any of the Bard's plays and present it in costume in a Friday class. The sooner you signed up, the better the selection. No duplication of characters. Romeo and Juliet went fast. So did MacBeth.

In hindsight, Quinn realized she might've been too narrow in her judgement of the teacher. The woman made students teach themselves each Friday. Birdie slipped in *Quicksand* by Nella Larsen, about a mixed race girl trying to find acceptance. Then they covered Twain's *Huck Finn* before swinging into *Catcher in the Rye*. She made students think. And she made parents nervous.

Not long after Quinn returned from the FBI, the year that Graham died, the school board fired Miss Birdie, by then identified by the closed-minded and culturally fearful as the mouthy spinster with the outdated Afro who agitated trouble and defied the administration. For over a year she was front or second page subject matter in each and every issue of the weekly *Craven Chronicle* as she fought a suit against the board.

They fired her for insubordination. As one of only four black teachers at the time, they wanted her to teach Black History instead of half her English classes. She declined. They stated English was closer to History than the subjects of Calculus, Auto Mechanics, and French taught by the other black teachers. She still declined, arguing that was not her training, and that she was not going to be pigeon-holed into a stereotype. Then a now ex-board member told her in a letter copied to the entire board and the superintendent that she ought to know Black History by heart anyway. Who needed a degree in it?

She won, not in court but via a settlement amounting to a two-hundred thousand dollar payout and an early retirement with health benefits. She didn't want to go back to the high school, and the high school didn't want her back, giving everyone a sigh of relief.

They'd become a bit more knowledgeable about diversity since then.

Quinn took another bite of meatloaf and flipped into Birdie's personal page. Sometime in Quinn's reading, Lenore refilled her tea.

Everyone had heard of Miss Birdie, still single, still living on her family land on the outskirts of Jacksonboro. She went from being the weekly topic in the paper to a weekly column contributor. She'd become such a staple for the paper's distribution that the editor wisely recognized she'd be sorely missed after the suit. A perfect fit for the English teacher and parties concerned. Apparently she segued into online reporting, too.

Investigative reporter, social media maven, and professional pot stirrer.

Quinn could relate. Except for the social media part.

Quinn wasn't sure how long she held that fork in the air, but her fingers had stiffened. Her plate was almost empty, and she'd just eaten mashed potatoes dipped in ketchup instead of gravy.

Blinking hard, she set the phone aside and rubbed her eyes. Then she reached for the banana pudding almost wishing she had a cup of goat milk coffee to go with it.

Dressed in civvies, Ty slipped into the other side of the booth. "Hey, you." His deep voice was a clash to the silence she'd encapsulated herself in. "Momma told me you needed checking on."

Quinn did a quick scan for Lenore, but she wasn't to be found. Probably in the kitchen making herself conveniently scarce. "I'm just having dinner and catching up on emails and stuff," she said. "You sure got here quick."

She wasn't a small girl, but he made her look tiny stuffed in the booth like he was. They usually sat out at the bar, just for that reason.

"You've been here almost an hour," he said. "When I called to ask if I should tend bar tonight, Momma said you looked troubled. She hates it when you eat alone. And I hated how things ended today."

Quinn gave a mild shrug. "I'm a single girl, Ty, and Lenore is genius in the kitchen. Why should I have to cook?" She gave the topic a second to shift. "And I'm okay about today. I could never blame you for my uncle's indiscretions."

"Thing is, he's not terribly off base," he said about the time Lenore arrived with his food, with double the meatloaf. She kissed his head as she always did and scurried away.

Quinn loved Lenore's concern. Jonah's mother, Jule, would also be calling Quinn to come to dinner before the week was through. Few orphans had such good surrogate mothers, much less two of them.

"You and Uncle Larry were talking about me before I walked in this afternoon," she started. "I should've hung outside the door and listened to get a better gist of things instead of the slanted version he gives me."

"Surprised you didn't, and I wish you had."

Halfway through the banana pudding she waved at the counter. A young girl came over. "Want me to get Ms. Lenore for you?"

Quinn smiled. "No, ma'am. Just asking for two cups of coffee." The dessert needed caffeine to cut the sweet.

She let Ty eat most of his supper in peace before she opened a discussion. "Remember Miss Birdie?"

"Who could forget," he said, speaking around his food. "You helped me find a robe to avoid wearing tights when I gave my speech."

"Soliloquy, dude. Not speech. Didn't she teach you anything?"

He peered off in the distance, pretending to remember, smiled and returned to his food. "Too traumatized by the soliloquy-ing, I guess."

He could be so funny. "How caught up in the school board is she?" she asked.

"How should I know?" He used a piece of meat to round up the remnants of his potatoes.

"Because you're black and she's black. Don't you know each other?"

He laughed aloud at her attempt at humor, a joke at the shallow mentality that had given Miss Birdie her win in court against the district.

"I imagine she's been laying low during this school building controversy," he said. "Not sure she has a dog in that fight."

Quinn nudged her phone. "But she sure is letting the crazies go at each other on that Facebook group of hers. Or the newspaper's. Not sure who owns it. Is she pro or con the elementary school? Is she familiar with Miss Abbott?"

He snapped his fingers. "From zero to sixty, just like that. From knowing nothing to spreading yourself all over it."

"I'm not far from running Miss Birdie down," she continued. "What's your take on her?"

He shook his head with a nonchalant air. "That her social media group is giving all sides an outlet, maybe? Or she loves being the conduit for people to piss off the school district. If she's on a side, she's not saying." He pointed at the phone. "But by now you know more than I do."

Yeah, that was the feeling Quinn got, that Birdie just offered a platform for debate, but that didn't mean the woman wasn't aware of the leaders, the liars, and the intricacies of the battle. Note to self, visit Miss Birdie.

"Okay," she said. "Let's flip to Jonah."

"No, let's stick to the investigation right now. Who's your client?"

She'd have thought Jonah made for more comfortable conversation. Fine, they'd discuss the case. She always ran cases by Ty anyway as the lone detective with the SO, and he never violated her confidence.

Garth Brooks came on. *If Tomorrow Never Comes.* Wow, at least the fourth sad love song tonight. Someone was in a melancholy mood. "Iona Bakeman's the client," she said.

His face clouded over. "You're representing a board member. Damn, Q. Seriously bad timing . . . in a lot of ways."

"Listen, I had no knowledge about the land controversy, honest. I took her on as a domestic. Fripp Bakeman is somewhat of a pistol, and they're on the path to divorce, I'd say, but their personal is crossing into the professional, and now the political. To better understand their marriage, I need to better understand the politics of the board."

"That made no sense."

"I'm still working on filling in the holes," she said.

"Is the domestic physical?"

"No, more like mental abuse, but legal issues have popped up," she replied, and she explained about Iona having been sucked into the school district contracts, having basically voted to give herself jobs. "Don't you tell anyone."

"I won't. She needs to come forward and accept the consequences, though."

Yeah, Quinn leaned that direction, too. "I told her to resign, but she's worried how Fripp will react."

"Sounds like work for an attorney, not a PI."

Iona truly needed legal advice, but the investigator in Quinn couldn't shake loose. If Fripp and his two buddies had a deal, were there others? With others? Worse, was this a board practice?

Originally, she had no interest in the land deal for the school, but on second thought, a multi-million dollar contract involved appraisers, builders, engineers, and God knows who else. How many back-room deals might be in that kind of mess? Iona alone couldn't push through contracts. Not with the Corps who held the power to pass anything and everything. Not that she condoned Iona's cluelessly complicit behavior, but Quinn wanted to look at the voting breakdown and see how much in lock-step these people were who spent the district's millions.

Quinn couldn't believe that the other board members were so stupid as to *not* question Fripp getting contracts and Iona voting on his behalf. What she could believe was them letting Iona have a pass on Fripp's bids to gain leverage for when they needed her vote on something bigger and better . . . or needed her silence.

In that moment, Quinn kept Iona's case. "Can we talk about your aunt?"

"I have four, but I assume you mean Aunt Laney, the one on the board. I smell your brain churning."

"The one and only," she said. "Heard of the Corps?"

He shook his head.

She elaborated on the key players, Guy Cook, Ella Mae Dewberry, Piper Pierce, and Ty's aunt, with Harmon Valentine in and out of the clique in their control of the district. Per Iona.

"You saying my aunt is crooked?"

"No, no, not what I said." And not what she meant . . . well, maybe she did, but . . . damn, she hadn't approached this right. She wasn't sure if anyone was crooked, frankly.

"I'm not aware of her business," Ty said. "Don't care. Not sure why you should, either."

Of course he'd be defensive. Laney was his dead daddy's baby sister, and Ty had worshipped his father. Better Quinn just gain access to Ty's aunt instead of discussing the finer points of her desire to corner the woman into spilling private board business. "Think you could get her to talk to me? She might give me another version of that board."

He seemed okay with that. "Sure, I'll call her tomorrow."

"You're a big teddy bear, dude, and I love you to pieces. Thanks."

An old Tanya Tucker ballad shut down and a mournful Alan Jackson took its place. Quinn was grateful she had business on her mind and Ty across the table to keep these downhearted tunes from taking root in her head. She returned to the topic Ty had pushed aside.

"Let's talk Jonah, okay?"

Ty didn't respond.

"What's the matter?" she said. He'd dodged discussing Jonah twice. "His activities seem to be common knowledge to everyone but me."

His lips mashed as he visibly battled something.

Quinn hated conversations that danced, and seeing Ty's reservations had her worried. "Talk to me, dude. You and my uncle said just moments ago that Jonah was caught up in the boxing match between those wanting the school and those not. Y'all made it clear he was the reason you attended those meetings. You said he throws fire on things." She reached over and playfully took a spoonful of his dessert to lighten his mood. "You're supposed to be here to give me the honest run down."

The waitress refilled their cups, and Quinn dumped tons of cream in hers. Two packets of sugar in his. She knew the guy. "I feel like the only person in the dark about this, Ty."

He pushed away his plate. "I know you do, Q. That's part of why I came."

She relaxed. Bless him. He could read her better than Jonah most of the time. She'd wondered a time or two, or three, how it would be spending a night with this man, and she'd bet the entire farm he pondered how that would go, too. Their friendship meant too much to ruin, she told herself, but the older they got, the more she felt pulled to choose. She favored Jonah, but wasn't about to hurt Ty.

The coffee cup looked tiny in his hand.

"So . . . " Quinn began again.

Ty looked down, and when he didn't immediately reply, she did. "He's aiding Miss Abbott. He started helping her five months ago. Seems a good thing unless you tell me differently."

Ty glanced back up. "He kept you in the dark and it stung, didn't it?"

Surprisingly she no longer wanted to ask about the board, or the threats on Miss Abbott, or this school business. Those questions sat front and center, waiting to fall off her tongue, but was another stood out more. "Yes, it did sting, Ty. Why didn't he tell me?"

A knot formed in her chest, and until now, she hadn't realized how much Jonah keeping a secret from her had hurt.

"Q." Ty set his cup down and reached across the table. "He wanted you involved, but when it got adversarial, he figured with you being the face of Sterling Banks that maybe you ought not choose a side. But nothing was secret, girl. Not a thing." He pointed at her phone. "You could see social media any time you liked. The meetings were wide out in the open. If you wanted to be involved, you could've gotten involved. That's what I'm guessing he thought. Anyway, he did tell me about protecting the Sterling name."

"Oh."

"Yeah."

"Okay." She had to think about that.

Ty took another sip, eying her. When he set the cup down, he seemed to have more to say, and his gaze settled on her. "Boy's got it bad for you, Q."

Suddenly she was the awkward one. "I . . . I'm not sure what to do about that, Ty."

His smile came across so sweet but not without a sadness in it. "Has to be him or me. We've always known that choice was coming even if you didn't."

Oh Lord, that hurt.

She'd known. She just didn't want to face it. She tried to smile and be as matter-of-fact as he was. "Why not find somebody else altogether? Who knows? I might do better." The joke came out wanly.

"I think maybe it's not your choice anymore. I'm stepping out of the way," he said. "Just know that I'm no longer in y'all's way."

She teared up.

"It's okay, Q."

"No, it's not," she said, no longer able to look in those sweet eyes.

Chapter 8

HOW COULD TY not see her heart beating so painfully fast? Thank God for the dim lighting. Suddenly she regretted never having kissed him, only not in their tenth grade manner, but adult-like . . . just to see what it would be like.

But she'd let that ship sail and she had to live with the consequences as well as the changes the future would make to their relationship.

Jesus, what best friend tells you to go be with the other guy?

She couldn't stop craving stability . . . for the three of them. It slipped through her fingers even as she and Ty sat facing each other, and the panic of the loss almost choked her. Atop it all, Ty had been the most mature in bringing that reality to light.

She had to live with the fear that they'd never again be quite the trio they were.

Childhood officially gone.

God, she wished they were still young. She wiped her eyes with a napkin, and they sat in silence. She couldn't decide what else to say until she noted they were the only ones left in the diner. "Let me help you clean up."

Having helped close Jackson Hole since she was a teen, she went to wiping tables. He went to sweeping floors. Ordinarily they raised the lights to better see the dropped crumbs and straws on the floor, but Lenore left them low. The country music continued, too . . . the slow stuff that mellowed folks.

And Quinn kept trying not to cry.

A big hand rested on her shoulder, then traveled down her arm to take her hand. Silently the big deputy took her rag away and dropped it on the table, and pulled her into a dance.

"What are we doing?" she whispered.

"Being friends," he said.

"But this . . ." and she couldn't complete the thought.

Dancing tight amongst the four tables they'd just cleaned, his hand behind her back, the other holding one of hers tucked between them, they drifted to the song. Quinn had long ago memorized the lyrics to *The Dance*.

Tears welled at the meaning of the words, and she let loose of their hands, wrapped her arms around the burly guy, and lay her head on his shoulder. She didn't want him to see her cry.

But the pat on her back said he was aware.

"Wish we were still kids," she said, muffled into her shirt.

"Me, too."

They let the song end but still swayed a while. No other came on. Then when it seemed right to stop, they parted, not quite sure what to say.

"I need to make sure the bar is stocked," he said.

"Yeah, and I need to go. Tell your mom good night for me," she replied.

He nodded. She nodded and left, so relieved the parking lot was empty.

BOGIE WOKE HER again, his front paws mashing his thirty pounds up and down her torso. It took one pounce on her bladder to make her jump up for the bathroom. This time Jonah hadn't been around and Bogie hadn't been out, bless his heart, which prompted her to hurry on her loose jeans, a Charleston Bridge Run tee shirt from a race she hadn't run, and what she called her slip-on *girlie* sneakers.

With the sun bright and the temps not too ridiculous, she gave the pup a solid hour of walking while she took the time to think of the case as well as inspect trees. The crew was ever aware of the owner and her impromptu walks, and the fact she understood the trees as well as or better than they did, and as a result, the pecans looked fine. Particularly within walking distance of the manor.

Bogie behaved well on his leash, so she cut him loose once she turned toward the house. Spring's tasseling had been remarkably good, and bug damage appeared less than the norm. With enough rain, Lord willing, and if hurricane season missed the lower tip of South Carolina, they might see impressive yields this year. The holidays would be hectic.

She brushed a hand across another couple of trees before collecting the pup and returning inside. Glancing a quarter mile up the long straight dirt drive, she barely made out the corner of Jule's place. Funny how Jonah lived there, too, but everyone considered it his momma's.

Noting no movement, no trucks, no hands between here and there, nobody consulting with Jonah, Quinn deemed herself not needed and returned inside. She fed Bogie and mulled over shower or no shower. Contracts, board minutes, and God knows how many two- and three-hour school board videos awaited her, and she sided on weathering the day as she was. After frying herself an egg sandwich and pouring a goat milk coffee, she settled at her desk with sights set on a long day of research.

She tried hard not to think of either of the boys.

The air conditioner kicked on, the only noise short of a snoring dog and a clock that chimed on the half hour. Tucked in the corner of the massive living room, to her left the incredible view of the orchard through a wall of glass doors, she faced the computer, embraced her aloneness, and dug in.

Some investigators preferred the paper and web searches. Others favored extracting clues through people skills. Bottomline was that any investigator worth their salt only cared about the results gained from whatever means and method necessary to get the job done. Still, a twelve-hour day of screen time would be mind-numbing. She chose to start the workday with reading contracts, when her brain was sharpest. She'd save the video watching to last, hopefully starting no later than right after lunch, depending on how many there were.

The goal was to find any pattern of impropriety, to attempt to catch the devil in the minutia of details.

Took her an exasperating twenty minutes to figure out how to dig down into the district's website and find the contracts. Either the school's IT staff could use some education or these contracts weren't meant to be found. But find them she did, or at least those posted, and it took her another while to make copies. There was reading online . . . then there was digesting, highlighting, and spreading-out-on-a-table study of the details on paper. And keeping copies in case the online ones suddenly disappeared.

Crap, no sign of who voted for which contract. Guess she'd find that in meeting minutes.

She could just file a Freedom of Information request for them over the time period Iona was in office. Two and a half years. But in more wasted time studying the process of making FOIA requests, she found they had ten business days to comply for some things, and thirty business days for other requests, and if the information was over 24 months old you had to add another so many weeks to the process . . . hell's bells. More road blocks.

One couldn't help but see that the district felt itself removed from scrutiny by the average public. Quinn's investigative diligence, however, wasn't average.

A serious crook with half a brain and an iota of perseverance would get away with a helluva lot between the website and the multiple layers of processes that hid the decisions, actions, and money spent by this district. No wonder people wanted to be on a school board. The hidden perks had endless potential.

Access to the board members' pictures and brief bios, however, was only a click away from the main page. Those items had been made available front and center, egos on display. Quinn noted how long each of the seven had held a seat. Guy, Laney, and Piper had maintained their seats for sixteen, twelve, and twenty years, respectively. The other three for eight years. Iona was the newbie. Quinn just wasn't seeing altruism as the driving factor of the first three running so often for so long. Not for Guy or Piper, anyway. Money drove them, and they made no bones about it in their universes. Ty's aunt, however, came from a family of different substance. Quinn wasn't quite ready to pass judgment on her. Note to self: push Ty to get her in to see Laney like he'd promised. He'd do a better job getting Quinn through that door, plus she sort of wanted to show him how much she still needed him.

Maybe not today, though. Last night remained too vivid.

She dropped her head in her hand. Jesus, why'd she have to think of last night?

And down that rabbit hole she went.

Jonah was as equally hurt as Ty. Maybe more so. She'd led him on. Not really led him on, but she'd welcomed his amorous overtures weeks ago. They'd crossed the line into courtship, with him doing absolutely everything right. Then she couldn't stop thinking about how their friendship wasn't the same as a couple plus one, and that Ty might be left in the cold.

She leaped up to get another cup of coffee and return to her real work. She didn't have time for anything but the case today. After today she either aided Iona or severed their contract, and it took homework to make that call.

She carried her refilled cup outside and threw a stick for Bogie for ten minutes, then came in. About the time she settled, she found the meeting minutes. Good, no FOIA business. She went to when Iona was elected and commenced to reading the stilted, dry-as-dust record when her phone rang, caller ID Iona.

"Hey, Iona. Sorry, but I'm still researching."

"But Quinn!"

The shout made Quinn yank the phone away from her ear. "What's wrong?"

"Fripp lost his shit when I told him I might resign!"

Apparently Iona hadn't come close to following the instructions Quinn gave her when she left the Sheriff's Annex yesterday afternoon. "Why did you tell him that?"

"I don't know. I just do not know!"

Fripp wasn't the only one who'd lost his shit.

"Are you safe?" Quinn asked.

Iona breathed heavily. "Yes."

"Then why are you out of breath? Where is he?"

"Sorry, sorry," and Iona sucked in hard a couple times as if collecting her wits. "He just left the house. I did exactly as you said last night. Had a wonderful night of rest, by the way. But this morning, oh my God, he was waiting for me when I got out of the shower. He said he needed answers, especially since I've been spending time with you. Did you know he had me tailed, Quinn? We were seen at the Sheriff's Office! That's exactly why I don't park anywhere I'm doing business. He likes to follow me."

Gracious, this woman and her logic. Damn, she wished Iona had told her Fripp was the tailing type. Quinn hadn't expected that. She should've been more aware of her surroundings. "What else did he say?"

"He said his career was at stake, and that *more* than *his* career was at stake," she whined.

God help her. "You didn't expect him to roll over and ignore your remark about resigning, did you? That's his livelihood." But those were strong remarks from Fripp, sounding as if he'd bet his money on one horse in some manner or another. "Did you ask him what he meant? What's *more than his career* mean?"

"All he said was he expected big money, and if I resign, he gets none of it. He even promised to call SLED if I resign, and he'd turn me in himself." The state's law enforcement agency carried pretty strong clout.

An empty threat from a desperate man, which Quinn found quite intriguing. "No, he won't, Iona. That board would turn on him so fast. What's he going to say to SLED without incriminating himself anyway? The man's scared."

"He's scared of me?" She spoke as if Quinn had told her the man was from Jupiter, the concept of her husband being on the defensive so foreign to her.

"He's scared of something. As I said, stick to business as usual while I study the facts, Iona. No board talk to anyone, okay?"

In a world that thrived on headlines and soundbites, Iona had believed that she delivered sufficient details anyone needed to take action. But that simply wasn't the case. "I need facts to corroborate your side. Just chill until I call you. Call me if something else detonates. But Fripp is not the best person for you to confide in, my friend."

They hung up after a few social platitudes.

Quinn pulled out her file on Iona and added the conversation and abbreviated coding of what was said, then returned to searching through the board minutes. The voting record of these people had to be on that website somewhere amongst those files.

Eventually she found them, each one in its own separate file by date, mixed in with the minutes of every meeting. Digging was the proper word for it, too, and for each meeting, she had to canvas pages, hunting to see if a contract was even voted on because there was no evidence anywhere else.

Lots of reading, lots of digging, lots of saving voting records and matching them with the contracts so she could tell what the voting was even for. By quarter to one, Quinn began to make sense of it.

Her phone rang. Iona again.

"Listen, Quinn. I've been thinking."

Rarely a good comment from a client. Often a red flag of justifying their own theory. Or a way of parting ways.

"I'm having second thoughts about having a private investigator."

There it was.

"I work for you, Iona. I'll tell you what I find, and I won't report what I find to authorities. Unless you murder someone."

Iona gave a weak, wobbly laugh, and Quinn waited.

"All this has me too nervous. There's no point paying you if I need an attorney, right? I'm not made of money like . . ."

Like the Sterlings. Quinn wasn't insulted at what was almost a cliché remark in these parts. "Let me get to an educated position, and we'll talk then about whether you keep me or show me the road. Suit you?"

Two deep breaths came across the call. "That's fair."

Crisis averted, they hung up. If Iona called again like this, Quinn would concede and give her wishy washy client what she wanted. If she didn't, someone like Fripp, or Iona herself, could accuse her of being overbearing, or worse, oppressive. The sheriff already gave the Sterlings that sort of image, and Iona was a personality who could easily feel strong-armed.

A half hour later, Quinn had a spreadsheet of the contracts approved.

She'd skipped contracts like the ice-cream machine replaced in the high school cafeteria, or the repair agreement for the copiers, and retained only those that Fripp Bakeman might bid on.

Out of fifteen such contracts, Iona abstained from voting on two, was absent for one, and voted against the Corps on just one, the first contract after she was elected. Otherwise, she voted in sync on eleven contracts.

Iona could almost be considered a member of the Corps.

Quid pro quo was the unwritten rule of politics at every level.

Any law enforcement investigation would recognize the glaring pattern and practice. They'd address Iona first and get her to roll on the others. With or without Quinn, that could eventually happen.

With this contract evidence so . . . evident, why had Iona even come to Quinn in the first place? Was she that adolescent?

Maybe the thoughts of divorce clouded her thinking. Maybe she was pressured, or more, feeling overwhelmed with the politics. Iona didn't appear too bright. After all, she'd said, "My vote was never the deciding vote."

Quinn would find no record of executive sessions, which were considered privileged in discussing contracts, hiring, and highly sensitive personnel matters. With no record, Quinn bet talk ran more freely, comments and opinions less opaque. Demands more clear.

She needed to talk to more of these people face to face, but she hadn't touched the videos yet. Maybe she could read something into their behaviors there first.

She opened the first video involving Iona, and after thirty minutes of boring talk of attendance and truancy policies, she went to another. So much of this was yawn material. Nothing animated. Nothing oppositional. Hardly anyone was even in attendance except for the board, the support staff, and whatever teacher or staff received some sort of recognition.

She flipped several months.

The minutes mentioned the proposed school. *There we go.*

First thing Quinn noticed was more folks in attendance. She wished the videographer had had enough innovation to do other than pop a camera on a tripod and snooze, but he hadn't. The picture was nothing but a wide-angle view of the seven and the superintendent. The voices echoed. A fifth grader with a smart phone could've done better. Plainly the recordings were minimally done to check some regulatory box.

Public participation made the camera guy rotate to the speaker at a

microphone off to the side, where he locked the camera again. No pan-
ning or close ups. Someone spoke about wanting the school built faster.
Another was more concerned about rising taxes if the county couldn't get
enough federal grants. The third speaker, however, took her time shuf-
fling forward, and the video showed just the empty mic for a couple of
minutes. Three members of the board were already reading their phones,
so the delay hadn't even caught their attention.

Finally, Miss Amy Abbott arrived. Frail bodied, her skin was pale, like
old lace in a hope chest. She started speaking before someone stopped her
and readjusted the microphone. They asked her to start over, promising
she'd be permitted her entire three minutes. *What was with them and their
almighty three minutes?* Her voice came across elderly, but nowhere near
feeble. No sign of dementia, and her sweetness shined through.

Quinn smiled at the old woman who'd dressed in slacks, a turtleneck,
and a long dangling locket necklace. Her cardigan hung almost to her
knees. Her white hair was coifed beautifully in sweeps with a tortoiseshell
clip to hold it in place. Slowly she explained who she was and how long
she'd lived on her land. About how she'd never been blessed with children, and this was the Lord's way of filling that void. As if in an old-
fashioned town hall meeting of half a century ago, she expressed her love
for the community and willingness to sell her twenty-nine and three-
quarter acres to the district, for the greater good. She looked forward to
watching the children playing on the playground and seeing the future of
Craven County grow.

"Miss Abbott, we are honored to have you here and thank you
immensely for agreeing to sell your land for this much-needed school. I'm
afraid we limit speeches to three minutes in order to keep the meetings
from extending so late, and we must cut you short right there."

Oh, he didn't . . . oh, the arrogance. Guy Cook could've graciously
just given her those minutes he just ate up talking. Or been willing to give
that wonderful lady as long as she needed. What little stock Quinn held
for that man plummeted into the toilet.

Miss Abbott was a jewel and acquiesced to the rules. She thanked
Guy and shuffled to her seat.

"Excuse me," spoke a man from the room. The video guy must have
had orders to not move the camera, because he didn't follow the voice.

"Mr. Proveaux," Guy said, announcing as if to five hundred people.
"Anyone wishing to speak must sign up before the meeting. If you wish to
address this board—"

"This lady just sold you her land. This lady took time from her evening to come in and thank the community, and this is her treatment?"

The gavel banged. "Mr. Proveaux, if you continue in this manner, we'll have a guard escort you from the room."

"Just as long as you put the camera on me. Feel free, because it just might bite you later."

A white-haired security guard headed toward Jonah, as if he were a match for the thirty-seven year old.

"Gracious . . ." Quinn's jaw dropped, mouth open, but instead of concern, her chest pumped up full of admiration for her Jonah taking on the bullies.

That's my guy.

Chapter 9

QUINN STOPPED THE video, leaving Jonah paused in his affront on the school board contesting how Miss Amy Abbott was being treated by the district.

Uncle Larry called this troublemaking. She called it honorable.

She unpaused the video. Attendees in the high school auditorium grumbled after Jonah's eloquent exclamation, completely broken from their usual tether to Robert's Rules of Order.

Only when the noise escalated did the cameraman turn the camera onto Jonah.

The fussiness halted the security guard in his tracks, puzzled at how to handle the hoopla alone, and the delay was long enough for Jonah to see he'd made things worse. He held up his palms to the guard and returned without another word to his seat.

Quinn waited for more bru-ha-ha from the audience, but instead, they slowly subsided with Jonah having silenced himself. Public participation ended and the camera returned to the board. Quinn weathered the audio to its lackluster ending then quickly clicked, clicked, clicked the stupid number of times she had to in order to back out and go back in to find the next meeting.

There it was. February. And, God love him, Jonah appeared again in the public participation part of the agenda. Once again he railed on them for their treatment of Miss Abbott and stated he hoped they named the school after her or at least the auditorium because she'd been in Craven County since her birth, longer than anyone in the room. Other than a few harrumph comments of support behind him, nobody addressed him one way or the other.

Then March. No mention of the school on the agenda, but Jonah spoke, saying he'd heard rumblings about the school plan being screwed up, and he and the district's constituents would appreciate a detailed update. He also found it astounding that the appraisal and engineering studies had been done before Miss Abbott agreed to the sale. For that reason, he was helping her from this point forward. Again, the board gave him no feedback, almost as if he wasn't even there.

April's meeting was an entirely different story. Quinn had been in the middle of her own case with Renault at that time, and she'd even used Jonah to amp up security on the farm due to the break in and the assault on Jule's goats . . . ultimately a threat on her own life. In hindsight, he'd been pulled in two directions, three counting his own mother's despondency at the loss of a goat, which explained some of his vacillating behavior at the time. His then frustrations at Quinn made more sense.

The video showed an auditorium much fuller than prior meetings. She wouldn't put it past Jonah to have phoned people to attend. Quinn's heart flipped a little at being omitted from all of this. She'd have supported him. Two deputies stood to the side in lieu of security guards this time, one being Harrison who never missed a chance to make an extra dime picking up sideline gigs.

Jonah came to the mic and demanded more details about the school: where the money was coming from and what was the status. Nobody answered him, and when he asked why nobody did, they directed him to file for details via Freedom of Information rules. However, a few others spoke up making similar inquiries. How much will taxes go up? How much grant money had been found to avoid raising said taxes? Again, they were redirected to making a Freedom of Information request.

Then came May. An even fuller room. Three deputies this time, the youngest guys, which wasn't saying much since the Craven's Sheriff's Department force fell on the younger side. A lot of deputies began careers under Larry Sterling's oversight then soon left for better pay and working conditions, except those with families entrenched in the county.

The board let everyone else speak at first this time. Comments centered around the school, the festering topic. More personalities. Guy Cook anchored the three-minute limit in stone, without exception, with an administrator from the district in charge of holding up placards indicating how much time was left. Guy Cook's gavel kept the momentum going.

Until Jonah's turn.

Quinn had been scribbling on a pad, noting each meeting's topics and who voted for what, who argued, and who couldn't care less. When Jonah appeared, her pen poised. She bet this would be about that fire in Miss Abbott's barn. Quinn had been recovering mentally and physically from her case, and Jonah had mentioned the fire merely in passing as a minor incident. Something told her now it wasn't.

"You know who I am and why I am here," Jonah started, a hardness in his tone, a laser stare focused on the powers-that-be. "And I want all of you to put your phones down and listen for a change."

Three phones disappeared, each acting like Jonah surely couldn't be speaking to them.

Someone said, "Damn straight," from the rear, but when nothing else happened, the deputies let it go ignored.

"Miss Abbott's barn was set afire two weeks ago." Jonah projected, enunciating, giving time for people to hear and not miss a word. "Her equipment was vandalized. If not for me and my workers, her entire place might've gone up in flames."

"Mr. Proveaux." Guy Cook interrupted. "Are you stating that this board had anything to do with that incident?"

"Mr. Cook, I didn't say that, and you just tried to steal part of my speaking time. Put it back on the clock, please."

The room erupted in applause. The gavel pounded. Jonah, however, stood calmly waiting for Guy to do his job as chair and pull things together while enjoying watching the scrambling to do so.

Jonah let it go on for a full minute then turned to the crowd and softly pushed his hands down. The room slowly silenced.

Guy's red face couldn't hide his contempt. Iona stared stunned. Piper Pierce looked about to bust wanting to say something.

"Time back on the clock, please?" Jonah asked, but without waiting for a response, he continued. "You people have screwed up this new school. Your plans fall short of approval on the acreage you bought from Miss Abbott. Now you want more of her land to fix your mess. Land that includes the home her own father built."

The crowd gasped. The board looked ready to crawl under the black drapes covering their tables.

"How dare anyone do this to her!" he continued, not hiding the tremor of emotion in the least. He wanted this to be dramatized. He wanted this to be remembered. He wanted this to be front page in whatever paper, television station, or blog would cover it. "She is scared to death, and rightfully so."

"Mr. Proveaux, I'm warning you," Guy Cook shouted. "You can't come in here and blame this illustrious group—"

"Did you hear me blame any of you? That's the second time you've taken my words as some indictment of this board's guilt. Do you have a guilty conscience, Mr. Guy?"

Guy's mouth hung half open. Board members cut eyes at each other, afraid to do much else.

Jonah continued. "Whoever is doing this, and I only bring this here to this meeting because it's no doubt connected to the building of the new school, best lay off. That is the message I want you to hear." Then he turned to the camera, "That includes anyone who watches this livefeed or video."

He gave a notable pause, and Guy appeared unsure whether Jonah was through, thinking twice about interrupting again. The audience waited for direction from either. One could sense them on the edges of those folding chairs.

Simply seeing the recording had Quinn hanging on his words. She would have killed to have been there.

Jonah took a breath. "Do not bother Miss Abbott. And I mean anyone. Thank you very much."

The room exploded, and with fifty people patting Jonah on the back and only three deputies in place, Guy made the wise move of moving the agenda to adjournment. Amidst the jeering and noise of the audience, the board couldn't even be heard making the motion and seconding the meeting's end. Then they promptly vanished behind the curtain.

Jonah had created a movement. No wonder the board had asked a stronger show of force from Larry Sterling's office.

Then Quinn remembered her purpose. The meetings had little discussion about contracts. They were voted and pushed through in a blink, with the public more hungry for talk of the school. Done and done. And whether they were quid pro quo or irregularly handled, nobody could tell, because nobody cared.

In reviewing the hours of footage, even fast forwarding, Quinn had paid more attention to Jonah than the board, except for Guy, maybe. Who could ignore that presence? She needed to go in again and read the faces of Laney, of Iona, of each of them. How were they reacting about the contracts? How were they—

Her phone rang. She assumed Iona, and was about to agree to part ways when she noted caller ID. Jonah?

"Miss Abbott," he said, huffing, maybe running. "Her house is on fire. Grab your boots. Meet me in the drive. I'm leaving Jule's now."

QUINN RAN THROUGH the mudroom, grabbed work boots from under the bench, dirty work socks from the hamper, and a windbreaker off its hook. It might be June and it might be hot, but layers beat skin touching fire.

Jonah barely slowed but Quinn hopped in the pickup with little trouble, leaving off the seatbelt to change into boots. "Did she call you? Is she okay?" She felt like she'd just been with both of them after spending so many hours on the screen.

He drove crazy fast, gravel kicking up as he took the road to the highway, and she twice rocked into the door as his intensity took his foot almost to the floor. They had to reach the highway then drive down a mile to Miss Abbott's drive to get to her house. If they traveled as the crow flew, they'd have cut two-thirds the distance.

"I rigged a security system at her place last month," he said, "and made myself the contact. If an alarm goes off, I get notified. Fire, glass break, I get the notice. They all went off."

Quinn laced up the second boot. "She didn't call?"

"No. That's what bothers me."

"9-1-1?"

"Automatic, plus I called. But you know where they have to drive from. It might take—"

"Drive faster," she said, snatching her seatbelt in place.

Once they reached the highway, off to the left, gray smoke climbed upward, the plumes way more than Quinn preferred. "That fire is cooking fast, Jonah." She prayed Miss Abbott hadn't tried to save anything. She prayed Miss Abbott hadn't been in the house to begin with. She prayed hardest that she'd find Miss Abbott standing in the yard waiting for help to arrive.

The truck's rear-end slid around, in and out of the edge of the highway ditch as Jonah turned off the road. Quinn scanned the property for the little lady only to find nobody. "Jesus, Jonah, she might be in the house. Come on!" And like she got in the truck, she got out with it still in motion, her windbreaker on one arm as she fought to put it on.

"Quinn, wait!" he called, but she beat feet to the front of the old two-story clapboard house with the wraparound porch, halting ten feet from the steps.

Flames seemed worst in the living room, but before long there'd be no worst part of it. It'd be a hundred percent engulfed.

"Miss Abbott!" she shouted moving left, then right, trying to peer in windows. "Jonah, you go—"

"To the back. Do not go inside, Quinn!" Jonah disappeared to the right.

She ran left to the north side of the porch, hoping it was less invaded. Heat gushed out the window at her, the hot breeze taking her breath, rifling her hair. She turned away to find cooler air, inhaled, and turned around to push closer.

The heat enveloped her, toasting her arms through her clothes, but she moved as close as she could stand, calling. Through the opening, flames lapped furniture, striving toward the open window, leaping from curtain to cushion to rug having swept through the living room and hallway already. She couldn't even see through the room for the wall of orange and gold . . . in places bright cherry red.

"Miss Abbott?" she screamed. God, what if she was upstairs, sleeping, already knocked out from the smoke? Or worse, what if she were in the middle of . . . that!

Fear ripped through her at the image of Miss Abbott on the floor someplace. Then it tore through her again at the thought of Jonah barging in looking for her.

He'd sent her to the safest part of the house, away from any doors.

"Jonah!" She ran toward the back, where she hoped to God he hadn't attempted to enter. He'd gone the other direction around the house but hadn't met up with her to coordinate what else to do.

The kitchen exited out the rear door, like so many hundred-year-old homes, toward the old outhouse. Toward the well.

Good God Almighty, Jonah wasn't outside, which only meant he'd gone in.

A roar raised up into the sky, the heat making waves in the air, making way for the flames which sounded like a living, breathing animal. A pop jerked her attention toward the right side, where she'd been. Then another. Then a sickening vise gripped her as a crash exploded inside.

Without thinking, she ran in.

The crisscross ventilation of these old homes only served to channel flames. Quinn could barely see through the kitchen for the smoke. Wetting a dish towel, she wrapped it across her mouth and nose and ventured up the hall. While she prayed the fire hadn't reached the stairs, she'd visited Miss Abbott enough times to realize if the living room was the fire point, and the dining room engulfed, the blaze had crossed the hall and therefore the stairway entrance to get there.

"Jonah!" she screamed, only having the ability to call for one of them, so she chose the one she'd hear best. Choking on the name, she realized in an almost panic that she couldn't grab more air to call again. She could barely breathe.

One siren sounded outside, maybe two.

The crash had been a beam falling in the living room. Now the upstairs was unsafe with other floor structure soon to follow.

Where were they? Out of pure terror and dire need to find them alive, she inhaled to call, only to swallow smoke.

Suddenly she couldn't breathe but the barest of amount. In or out. She wouldn't breathe without the rag, which was fast losing its moisture. Tears dried on her face as fast as she cried them.

This wasn't working. She reversed, looking up through the stair railings one last time, praying to catch sight of one of them. To not see them created so many horrific pictures in her head. To leave them, left them to die.

But in her retreat she misjudged. A closet door handle snagged her windbreaker, and in a blast of fear she assumed her escape blocked and screamed the last air in her lungs . . . losing her ability to breathe.

She couldn't inhale. She couldn't cough. And in her effort, she lost orientation of which way was out. The smoke had turned dark, and she couldn't see a foot in front of her. Little spits of light flashed in the periphery of her sight, and she understood she had precious seconds to get herself out.

Turning, attempting to orient, she bounced off a wall.

What was wrong with her? *Drop, you idiot.*

She went to her knees, the floor hot but not melting hot, thank God. She crouched lower, putting her face inches above the hardwood. Her eyes stung terribly, but they had to stay open, despite the instinct to shut them. Blinking, squinting, she sought daylight. She turned almost one eighty before she thought she saw lighter smoke. She had to dare to believe that was daylight, prayed that was the direction to the back door.

She didn't think she had time to make a mistake and try again.

She exploded a cough and rued it, unable to take in any oxygen to replace it.

Suddenly hands gripped her under each shoulder and dragged her stumbling into the sun.

She hadn't been eight feet from the porch.

"Come on, Quinn. Move your hands." Water poured over her face, in her eyes. "Now let us put this over your face. Come on now, let us help."

She hadn't realized she'd been fighting them, and once she stopped, the cool sweetness of clean oxygen slowly returned her ability to breathe as they cinched the mask in place.

They'd propped her up against the old outhouse, away from things. A medic was taking her pulse. "You're a stubborn piece of work, aren't you?"

Sandy. He went to school with Jonah. Played football. Way fatter than he used to be.

"I—" she started, filled with questions, but the effort threw her into a coughing fit.

"Quit trying to talk, dammit. Just sit still. I'm already trying to decide whether to cart your butt to the hospital."

"Hospital?" she mumbled into the mask, a cough cutting her short again.

A siren whipped to life. She sat straight, searching. Who was in it? She tried to yank the mask off and scoot her legs up to stand.

The heavy hand on her shoulder told her otherwise. "Leave that on or you're going next," Sandy scolded. "Try to stand, and I'll tie you down."

But she couldn't see.

"Sandy," she said, then coughed.

"Shut up, Quinn."

He avoided telling her who was in the ambulance. She felt it, and she saw it in his lack of eye contact. Heart pumping, she'd wait until Sandy got distracted to make her break, but instead she got distracted as lights rebounded off the partially burned barn to the south as the vehicle left.

The siren seemed to grow louder as the ambulance pulled onto the highway. Lights flashing, the siren reached its rhythm, and Quinn caught a quick sight of it as it turned left, to Walterboro.

"Jonah?" She fell into coughing again, but continued rolling to her side to roust herself up.

Sandy was on her in a second. "You're not—"

She punched him. His heavy shoulder only absorbed the force, but it distracted him enough to let her roll to her knees. Hands on the dry, warped outhouse wood, she crawled up to stand and leaned her back against it. "Get out . . . of my . . . way." She sucked in, coughed, sucked in, coughed.

"Son of a bitch, Quinn. Promise me you'll stay here and let me find out what's going on for you, okay?"

Jonah and Amy Abbott she tried to say, but Sandy didn't hear because she couldn't finish saying it. But he'd left. That's when her heart leaped into her raspy, smoky throat at the realization they could've fit two people in the same ambulance.

She told herself to hold on. What else could she do but hold on?

Backed against the old boards, she slid to the ground and held the mask tighter, forcing herself to breathe more, breathe better, so she could get up and go.

"Quinn!"

She jerked her gaze up to see Jonah run past Sandy toward her.

He was covered in black, both forearms wrapped in gauze, his eyebrows not quite gone but heavily singed under the black smudges coating his face.

He dropped to the ground before her, started to take her hands, but hesitated, scanning her for burns.

Sandy stooped as well. "She's going to be fine."

"I'm fine," Quinn said at the same time, croaky, not coughing this time.

"I *told* you not to go in," he said, a crusty edge on his voice as well.

"Was that her in the ambulance?" Quinn asked.

His expression fell. "Yes."

"You found . . . her." The hacking resumed.

"Stop. Yes, I found her. She was upstairs. I barely got her down before the floor caved. They're rushing her in. She's unconscious but alive, Quinn. We did it."

Good gracious, the floor beam Quinn saw. God, that had to be mere seconds of opportunity. Leave it to Jonah to make it happen, because she did nothing but get in trouble.

But she was glad she was here. Tiny bits of timing could've taken things in another, more deadly direction. If Jonah had come alone . . . and something had happened . . .

She removed her mask. Jonah helped her up, but he wouldn't let loose of her. His arm around her shoulder and hers around his waist, they returned to the front, giving a wide berth to the firefighters.

Jonah moved his truck further away, and they sat inside the cab watching, drinking bottles of water someone handed them. From the looks of things, the station had sent everyone. Men covered over the place, the pumper truck giving its best.

The ancient farmhouse wasn't big, and the fire had consumed it with vengeance. Bit by bit, board by board, they watched the place surrender.

"What is she going to do now?" Jonah said, as though to himself, unable to take his stare off the disaster.

"Fight harder," Quinn said. "And if she can't do it, we can."

He turned. "We?"

"Yes, we," she said. "I'm not letting you fight these people alone, Jonah."

No telling how this community would anger now. Without even knowing if Iona voted to take this farm, Quinn struggled not to be mad as hell at her. Hadn't she been voting alongside the Corps?

No hurry, though. She'd find out soon enough. For now, she and Jonah had things to talk about. And someone had to check in on Miss Abbott. She'd need lots of tending after this.

Chapter 10

STILL STUNNED AND distanced in Jonah's truck, they watched the firefighters slowly overcome the fire as evening arrived. The gagging smell reached them even two hundred yards away, atop the stench in their damp clothes, and Quinn bet the smell to some degree reached all the way to the manor. She could taste soot and imagined it lining her lungs.

But this house . . . Seeing the charred remains only made the setting more hopeless with an ache-in-your-chest sorrow as to the permanence of the damage.

What a woeful reality that Miss Abbott had no more residence, and God knows how many century-old antiques, doilies, books, and memories had been consumed to ash. How did someone eighty-two years old and living alone pick up and start over without family?

Quinn hoped this didn't kill the poor woman.

"She was gathering photos," Jonah said, adding a huge, heavy sigh. "And what appeared to be the family Bible. A big clunky thing . . ." His voice trailed, Quinn suspecting his description had understated the importance of the item. His gaze moved from men at the pumper truck to the house, like he should oversee the woman's affairs. As if he could see through the black timbers and locate where important remnants lay.

He'd called the Walterboro hospital twice in the last two hours. Nobody could tell him Miss Abbott's status.

Quinn looked over, silent, not wanting to interrupt his thoughts. His dejection had filled the truck and left little room for Quinn, but she understood. He'd committed to Miss Abbott, adopted her, and Quinn was sure he felt he'd failed.

"She'd passed out," he said. "I left the things right there on the floor, scattered in every direction around her. They're ashes now."

Quinn had already heard how he'd found her, and what Miss Abbott had probably been doing, but she listened again. She reached over to take his hand again, too, missing the bench seats old trucks used to have that would've let her slide beside him. Her daddy kept such a truck until he died. She'd sold it. So many times she wished she hadn't, but that loss was nothing compared to the losses Jonah believed Miss Abbott sustained. Losses he'd insured by ignoring the importance of those items. The man would torture himself over this.

"You had to get her out safe, Jonah. You did that. I heard that floor cave. I saw the damage. You couldn't afford the time."

He nodded and agreed, but nothing would wipe away the loss. The cherished remnants of an old life were no more, as well as that of many lives before her. Regardless the heroics, loss couldn't be talked away. Quinn understood that far too well.

Jonah mumbled something else.

"What?" she asked.

"I said, let's just hope I saved her."

He'd said that already, too. Quinn wasn't sure how to address that the second time either.

The ambulance had left before the deputies got there. They'd spoken to the both of them, then the firefighters. One remained behind to see the event to its completion and had told Quinn and Jonah they could leave.

It seemed sacrilegious to do so.

Her phone rang. Ty calling.

Neither Ty nor her uncle had come. Maybe they figured there was nothing they could really do. It was rural. No traffic to handle.

"How are you two?" he asked with no hello.

Jonah looked over, brow raised, part of what was remaining anyway.

"Ty," she mouthed silently to him.

He gave a tip up of his chin. Expected. Understood. Jealousy didn't enter in their relationship.

"We're hacking up smoke," she said, and promptly demonstrated without meaning to, "and our clothes are ruined. Jonah's hair is singed. We're smutty, stinking, and whatever else you can imagine."

"But not hurt?" Ty asked.

"Jonah has some gauze on his arms but okay," she replied.

"We sent two guys . . ." he said, not finishing the thought.

"Yeah," she said, disappointed one of them hadn't been him and that he hadn't called earlier since he'd known enough to send out officers.

"Well, I'll relay to your uncle. He asked about you, by the way."

"Good." She wasn't sure what else she was supposed to say to that. Why hadn't he called himself? Another disappointment.

Today was full of that.

She hung up. "It's getting on to supper time."

Jonah said nothing.

"They already said we could leave," she added, ending on a sputtering of small hacks.

He stared off a couple more minutes then started the truck. In their long wait, Quinn had texted Jule. She'd had to tell the mother not to come, that she had her son's back. In reply, Jule had ordered Quinn to let her know when they were on the way. Dinner would be waiting. No matter how late.

With little discussion, Jonah dropped off Quinn at the manor while he went home to shower. She hadn't dragged herself upstairs yet before Jule texted and said dinner would be ready in forty minutes or so.

And there was her second surrogate momma, taking charge. How could anyone be so blessed?

Bogie assuming his place on the bathroom rug, Quinn ran the water lukewarm and was glad she skipped the morning shower, more glad she put on old clothes because these would go in the trash. But the soap hardly made a dent in the odor the first and second scrubbings, and it took a double dose of her best scented shampoo to touch the stink in her hair. She took the opportunity of having no one in earshot to cough her brains out, craving to cut the smut loose, but she stopped when her throat turned raw. Bogie whined, nose against the shower door.

Guess this would take time, like Sandy told her. *And if it doesn't get better in a couple days, you find a doctor, okay?*

The coughing tired her. A lot of tired, actually. If Jonah felt the same, dinner might be short-lived. Jule would see to that.

As she rinsed, she imagined Jonah doing the same, his hands resting against the wall of the old, soft blue tiles, letting the water run and run. She'd used that bathroom to clean up before, and she kind of wished she were there to help him now.

No, she *really* wished she were there. Or better yet, him here. Something about shared danger served as an attraction. She felt a little ashamed at having such thoughts.

She got out and checked the clock. She was pushing the time a bit, unable to dry her thick hair, so once braided, she finished off with a leather tie and threw on her better jeans, a simple navy tee, and sneakers. A soap and water face would do.

She walked the quarter mile to Jule's under the cover of early night, at the last minute letting Bogie come along to comfort Jonah. As the dog sniffed the path ahead, she listened to crickets and cicadas, and the whooshing sound that only breezes through pecan leaflets can make. Every now and then a tree frog sang. The humidity seemed higher than usual, but the temp wasn't high enough nor the walk far enough to raise a sweat.

About the time she reached for the screen door, she caught a whiff of the menu. Jule's homemade chicken pot pie, and unless Quinn was wrong, buttermilk pie. The goat lady had gone for her own version of comfort food and couldn't have hit the target better.

Quinn let herself in, taking note of the unlocked door. Unless left open for her sake, she'd chide Jule for going lax on security. After a trespasser killed one of the goats a few months ago, and after Jonah set up fresh security on both houses, Quinn would like to assume this exception merely an instance of manners.

She entered with Bogie going nose up at the aromas, and she locked the door behind her. "Jule?" But all that met her inside was a stronger smell of dinner.

Gold placemats and cutlery set in place on the table, but the pot pie remained on the stove with a dish towel over it. Nobody answered her calls.

After going through the rooms, she exited to the next logical place. The goat barn. After that would be the business barn where they processed pecan gift basket orders and cooked up different flavors of coated nuts. The pecan barn belonged to the farm . . . the goats to Jule. Jule was in charge of both.

Quinn found the elder woman in her customary dress of overalls, seated on the fence to an empty corral, the goats put up in the barn for the night. Bogie reared up for a pat on the head. "Hey, what's going on?" Quinn asked when Jule only glanced over, then returned her stare into the night.

"How bad was it over there today?" she asked, business-like. Jule was rarely anything but business. Jonah was the more passionate soul.

"Why?" Quinn tried staring into the darkness to see what kept Jule looking. "Where's Jonah?"

Jule turned to her. "I asked you a question."

"It was bad, horribly bad, but I didn't see Miss Abbott," Quinn said, trying not to croak. The frogs in the orchard had clearer tone than she did. She remained standing to keep her height level to Jule's. "They took her away in the ambulance about the time they were hauling me out."

"Hauling you out?"

"Wasn't as awful as it sounds." Though it kinda was . . . or could've been.

Jule stared at her, the coach light on the barn giving her a younger appearance. "Hunh, I know better. Listen to your voice, girl. And don't think I didn't hear him coughing and spitting in the bathroom." She gave another *hunh*. "Like I wouldn't notice his eyebrows missing."

Jule had a strong constitution. She loved as hard as she worked, and she didn't spill emotions as readily as most moms. Though she wasn't teary-eyed and wringing her hands, that didn't mean her head wasn't filled with concern for her two children. And she expected each to take care of the other. Always had.

"You can tell me the details another time," she said and nodded toward the dark. "Woulda thought the woman died the way Jonah came in here all maudlin, though. Then after his shower he talked to you on the phone and blew past me out the door. By the time I got the pot pie out of the oven, he'd gone off out there," she said. "Y'all have another falling out?"

Puzzled, Quinn looked into the night again. "He didn't call me, Jule."

"Well, he talked to somebody," she said. "And he wasn't willing to spill to me." Jule turned to Quinn and waited, the stare meaning one thing.

"I'll go hunt for him," she said.

"I'll have dinner warming when you return." Jule hopped down, a good foot shorter than Quinn now. "And I don't want no arguing this time, you hear? I'm sensing he isn't up to it, Quinn. Tuck that red head personality away and be what he needs. That clear?"

"Yes, ma'am."

Jule left for the house, her long gray braid swinging down her back. She whistled and Bogie followed her inside, while Quinn struck out through the trees. Her gut sent her toward Windsor. The treehouse fronted the Edisto River, hidden in five acres of live oaks older than the pecans, a tract saved from becoming an orchard by a long-ago Sterling ancestor who appreciated what nature had chosen to put there. Graham built the treehouse for his daughter as a haven when her mother died. Quinn named it Windsor when Princess Diana died.

Ever supportive of their best buddy, the two boys adopted it soon after. Jule's unspoken directive was for Quinn to start at Windsor, not that Quinn needed the push.

Only three people set foot in that ten-by-ten hideaway: Jonah, Quinn, and Ty, aka JQT, aka JACKET. Jule designed them matching windbreakers with the name when they were nine or ten years old.

But adulthood came quickly and the trio drifted away from JACKET meetings after graduation. Quinn, however, often returned solo, especially after Graham's death, and everyone left her alone to do so, including the guys. The place had reverted to being only hers, their matching jackets outgrown and stored behind winter coats in closets. Quinn went off to college. Ty joined the sheriff's office and got married for a short while. Jonah was already in college and took a job in the upstate at a major commercial farm.

When Quinn returned from the FBI for Graham's funeral years later, Windsor returned to its original purpose, her own personal retreat as she struggled with loss. She used the treehouse to return in time and remember how things were.

The last JACKET meeting had revived the childhood group. What had started as a kids' clubhouse affair in Windsor, morphed to gatherings of serious substance.

Two months ago, when Sterling Banks and its occupants were assaulted by actions Quinn ultimately affiliated with Ronald Renault . . . and to her Uncle Larry, to some degree, with law enforcement involved and crime happening on sacred Sterling Banks grounds, Quinn brought the JACKET meeting back to life. The boys responded as if over a decade had not flashed by.

Funny how the three of them so easily returned to the security of their youth.

Quinn fast walked through the front tree quadrant. A full moon wasn't due for two weeks, and in spite of a cloudless sky, she couldn't see as well as she'd like, negating the desire to run. She relied on hearing, listening for his steps cracking brittle branches. She fell back on familiarity walking in the dark, her keen memory coming from a childhood of relentless hide-and-seek, and an adulthood of maintaining the grove.

Trickling sounds of the river reached her long before she saw the oaks.

A stranger wouldn't see the treehouse. Live oaks didn't lose their leaves, and Windsor's entrance faced the water, away from the access to the five-acre grove.

Quinn came around the massive, six-foot wide trunk and climbed the steps to the house. The organic scents of the unique flora that died and colored the water black, saturated the air. The river location raised humidity higher than at the houses.

The room was pitch, the lone light off. She sensed Jonah's presence before she reached overhead and pulled the cord, the twenty-five watt bulb giving shape to the darkness.

Instinctively she glanced toward the childhood trunk covered with an old tablecloth, ensuring the area remained undisturbed, her .22 safe and sound. She used to keep it there for snakes. After the Renault deal, she kept it for whatever proved a danger.

She sat in the old rocker, deemed hers eons ago. The bean bag was his. The straight-backed chair would've been Ty's if he were there.

"Jule's worried," she said, setting a rhythm. Her feet weren't six inches from his.

"Yeah, I know." Long and folded up, he was despondent-looking wedged in the middle of that bag, the low light giving him age while the position reminded her of him at twelve. She made a note to move a sofa up there.

She let the chair creak, knowing he wasn't fond of the noise, hoping he'd open up, talking to take its place. She paused one time, to see if it mattered, and the silence of the room allowed her to hear him sniffle. "What did the hospital say?" she said, assuming that had been the call Jule spoke of.

He sighed so heavy.

"Today was rough," she said. "Rough on us, so most likely a horrible experience for her. She's older, Jonah. I'd say go see her after dinner, but it's late, and she needs her sleep. Poor thing has to be out of it." She stopped rocking and leaned over. "She'll take a while recuperating. I've been thinking. With her homeless, you know good and well we can put her up here. Hire a nurse. With the three of us we ought to . . ."

He started shaking his head, like he wanted her to hush. She did. But when he didn't talk, she continued. "She can stay in the downstairs bedroom. Bet she'd like some of Jule's—"

"She's dead, Quinn."

She tried to tell herself she heard wrong while a frigid jolt coursed through her, telling her otherwise. "But . . ." However, there was no but. The shock and smoke had been too much for the feeble woman.

Quinn slid down to the floor, taking Jonah's face in her hands and felt the moisture on his cheeks. "Oh, honey, I'm so, so sorry." Then she was crying with him.

She crunched herself in that bean bag next to him best she could, with only the subtle river noises around them. Up against him she could feel the beating of his heart, the tension and rage in his muscles. Jonah's sadness was half anger, and Quinn didn't blame him a bit.

She was pissed as hell, too.

At first she wanted to cast Iona Bakeman to the wolves for being part of the board that could've had a hand in that fire. People would cry coincidence, but with a fire in the barn then the fire in the house, only the guilty would call it that.

Jonah reached around and hugged her to him. "Thanks for being here, Quinn."

"Where else would I be?" and she kissed him. "Don't hate me, Jonah. I can't take that anymore. I'm here for you. Please know that I'm here for you."

He'd tried so hard to lift the burden from Miss Abbott when the board had miscalculated the design and assumed they could capitalize again on a woman too frail to fight . They hadn't counted on Jonah.

"What happens to the land now?" she asked.

He sniffed a final sniff and patted her in his embrace. "She didn't just make me power of attorney, Quinn. She updated her will and made me executor."

Oh wow. Miss A had fallen in love with Jonah. Many trusted him, and he was worth every smidgeon of that trust. People saw it all the time, often telling Quinn how lucky she was to have him running Sterling Banks. How lucky she'd be to have him as more than that.

"Her niece gets it?" Quinn asked, sadly assuming that the distant Texas relative would sell that place quicker than a broke drug dealer, and the eager district would be as hungry a buyer as any. Not that Quinn minded having a school next door. She just hated thinking how it got there.

He nodded. "Her niece gets a lot but not the land. It's a decent amount though."

"Especially since Miss A sold the thirty acres to the district. How much did she get for that?"

"That thirty acres sold for two hundred fifty thousand," he said. "But she doesn't get that. Miss Abbott wasn't crazy about the niece but felt the need to leave her something. I suspect she'll get close to a hundred K."

"Nothing to sneeze at," Quinn said. "And the sale of that first tract sort of dictates the value of the remaining forty acres. Who'd she donate it to? And the money from the sale of the first?"

"Me," he said, a heavy, heavy sigh behind it.

"Oh, Jonah," she said, feeling the burden in his reply, reading the heaviness of responsibility that came with his inheritance.

"Yeah."

Footsteps sounded outside. "Quinn? Jonah?"

Ty laid a hand on the screen door. "Y'all in here?"

Quinn scrambled out of Jonah's arms. Even in the dim light, Jonah's disappointment in her shone clear, and she felt like a dog.

"Hey," Ty said, coming in. "Came to see how you guys are doing. One of the firemen said you two were inches from going to the hospital yourselves."

Just the thought made Quinn clear her throat, and before she caught herself, she stepped aside, forming a neutral distance between the two men. "We're good. A sore throat maybe. I'm still smelling smoke. Jonah has bandages."

Jonah pushed himself up and out of the bean bag. "Hell of a day."

Ty looked from one to the other. "Listen," and he seemed hesitant. "I also came to talk to you guys about Miss Abbott."

"We heard," Quinn said, just as Jonah said, "We know." They glanced away from each other.

"Um, okay." Ty studied the two, the awkwardness thick as pudding. "Well, I'm sorry. I knew her, but not like you guys, and from what I've seen, not nearly as well as Jonah."

"Yeah, well, it's not over yet." Jonah pushed around Ty and left the treehouse.

Ty turned to Quinn. "Did I interrupt something?"

"I don't know, Ty," she said. "I just don't know." She touched his arm and left, calling for Jonah to wait up.

Chapter 11

JULE INVITED TY to eat with them.

The pot pie served up flaky, and the buttermilk pie presented as perfect as ever, but Quinn found no taste in the bites, using tea to wash them down a scratchy throat. She spotted Jonah attempting to do the same. Ty ate fine, but his conversation seemed reserved to Jule, at least until the meal was done.

"It's late," Jonah said, though the time was nine thirty.

"I told y'all not to fight again," Jule said, reaching across to collect and put each one's dessert dish in a stack.

"We didn't fight," he replied, irritated.

When nobody wanted to talk to her, she squinted at Quinn, cut eyes at Jonah, and then carried plates to the kitchen. Water started in the sink, the unspoken message being for the three to get whatever it was out of their system.

"She doesn't know about Miss Abbott, does she?" Ty said.

Quinn and Jonah shook their heads with Jonah adding, "Let me tell her later."

"She can hear us, you know." Quinn was acquainted with this house as well as her own. The walls weren't that thick. "She's damn observant, and if you don't think she read you, Jonah, you underestimate your momma."

Ty studied each of them then tried to find someplace else to rest his attention.

"Y'all discuss Amy Abbott if you can't talk about anything else," Jule said, slipping in, and they jumped. She'd left the water running to distract. "You're no longer children, so stop acting like it. You're adults, with adult feelings. Surprised this day hasn't come before now, but in my opinion, now ain't the time. You're still friends and that woman needs you." She wiped the placemats in front of each, them holding up their hands to let her. "She didn't deserve any of this, if you ask me. If you need me to get involved, I'd be happy to go to that damn school board, and—"

All three yelled, "No."

She straightened, the rag in a hand on her hip. "All right then. What are you gonna do? Or is there anything that can be done?" She made one final swipe at a crumb. "Just call me if you need me." And she left again for the kitchen.

"I just wish Miss A hadn't sold the first thirty acres," Jonah said. "She regretted it, you know. After they leaned on her, she wished she hadn't gone through with it. She made it damn clear to me they weren't getting another acre." Then under his breath, "The thieving bastards."

He meant all eight including the superintendent. To most taxpayers, the board was the board. The county council was the county council. Even the town politicians functioned as one. Candidates lost their individuality once the final determining vote was cast, and the reputation of the chosen body became the reputation of the one.

Which made people even more afraid to go up against them, which was part of why Miss Abbott had so readily sought an ally in Jonah, Quinn thought. With Jonah being the noble guy he was, he accepted the quest. She reached over and laid a hand on his arm, hoping he recognized the peace offering, praying he accepted her silent apology she made in front of Ty.

"You didn't expect this, Jonah. But I'm in it with you." How could she not be?

"What can I do?" Ty asked.

"I say do nothing." Jule leaned against the doorway frame. Quinn hadn't heard the water go off. "They have no contract on the remaining land and the poor woman's dead, isn't she? That asinine board may tuck their tails and disappear, especially once they hear the place belongs to you. Son, . . ." She strode over to him, laying a hand on his shoulder. "I'll go with you tomorrow afternoon to pick through the debris and see what of value is left, but first thing in the morning, you call the company that had insurance on the house, then we head to Presleys and make the funeral arrangements." She lightly rubbed his cheek. "And give that attorney who prepared that will a call first thing."

Nobody was surprised she figured on her own that Miss Abbott died.

Jule slipped into her chair. "Though Amy was old enough to be my mother, I was closer to her age than any of you. She and I visited periodically. I have a much better feel for what she'd desire in a service than you kids."

They'd turn fifty years old and Jule would still relate to them as her kids, but there was a wisdom in her words, and no doubt Jule would have a better sense of these things. She and Uncle Larry had handled Graham's funeral, and Quinn barely remembered her mother's.

"I'll go with you to both," Quinn said.

Ty seemed relieved. "So, we're hoping this just goes away."

Jule answered with a pat on her son. "That's right."

Smiling warmly at the mother and son, Quinn was relieved that Jonah didn't have to break any news and was touched at the support system gathered around that table. However, she didn't see the future as neat and tidy as Jule wanted to believe, and in a glance to Ty, saw him feeling that, too. Jonah leaned briefly into his mom, letting her be his consolation, but Quinn saw damn good and well he didn't see this as a closed book, either.

The school board had spent six figures on a piece of land they could not use, spending taxpayer dollars that the taxpayers didn't know had been erroneously managed. To the west of the thirty acres they owned was Miss Abbott's remaining forty. To the east of it was a creek that rose wide and strong during hard rains feeding the Edisto, meaning that land was a floodplain and unbuildable. To the south was Sterling Banks, and while Quinn would love for them to dare try to buy some of her land, the logistics of it didn't help their cause. They needed road frontage.

They'd bet on that thirty acres and screwed up. They'd be back. How they'd make their appearance was the question.

THE NEXT MORNING, with funeral home director Peyton Presley at her elbow, Jule wandered from casket to casket, weighing the intricacies of wood color, satin interiors, and details of trim and handles. Miss Abbott died from smoke inhalation, so an open viewing set Jule busy with the details. They didn't have small, medium, and large. Quinn imagined Miss Abbott needing an extra small if they did. The one-size-fits-all seemed such a waste.

Crazy the twists a mind took when faced with uncomfortable situations.

Once the three of them finished at the funeral home, they would change clothes and head to the burnt house. Jule explained if there wasn't anything worthwhile salvaged for Miss Abbott to be buried in, she might head to Charleston tomorrow.

Quinn was immensely grateful that the woman had a grasp on the steps to take. Jonah would be lost.

The place smelled like a florist with a double dose of the chemical they sprayed on greenery. The odor only mingled with the char aroma Quinn hadn't been able to shake, and she'd gladly taken the peppermint Jule offered when they walked in the door.

Quinn and Jonah stood closer to the entrance of the casket room, under the guise that they weren't comfortable to walk amongst coffins. Maybe not so much a guise as a preference. Jule didn't question why.

"I'm so glad she's here," Quinn said.

Jonah gave a sad scoff. "You and me both, but I'm feeling guilty."

She reached around and tenderly took his bandaged arm. "Don't. I think Miss Abbott would like seeing your momma doing this. I'm really sorry, Jonah."

His halfhearted grin showed appreciation.

She was sorry for the loss of Miss Abbott for sure. Sorry for him having to deal with this. Even sorry for leaping up when Ty walked into Windsor. If Jonah needed an explanation, they'd iron it out later. For now, she was there for him, and he just needed to know it.

However, she still felt bad for Ty. Though last night she'd danced over it with the mildest of a scolding, Jule had also read that the three friends struggled with an emerging couple. Without question, she would prefer Quinn be with Jonah, but she'd accept whichever two partnered up with avid support. The three couldn't remain three forever.

The service was set for four days hence on Monday. Tomorrow was Friday, and churches were taken on weekends. Poor Miss Abbott had left no instructions, having told the attorney she preferred to think on that for a time.

Jule refused to consider cremation. Someone of Miss Abbott's generation didn't meet eternity in such a manner, she said, and after the funeral home, Jule had an appointment with the church's administrator to see what plots were available at the Pon Pon Presbyterian Church. In the same efficient manner she ran the pecan basket operation, and the goats, and Jonah and Quinn. Jule arranged a funeral in about three hours.

At home they changed into clothes they were willing to throw away afterwards, and the three headed to the farmhouse.

Jonah drove with Jule in the front seat. From the backseat, Quinn watched the two. This was how they often went to church on Sundays. Jule had silently kept a strategic, watchful eye on her boy the whole day. Jonah had moved past the depression and into something more mission oriented. Quinn sensed worry in Jule about that. He'd given no mention of his intentions to either of them, and neither believed there were none.

But Jonah wasn't ever verbose or demonstrative with his intentions, to include those about his feelings for Quinn. They were thirty-four and thirty-seven. His surge of interest in her for the prior two months had swept her up in an urgency, only with his was entwined an earnest commitment to make their future permanent. That scared the crap out of her, and upon seeing her reaction, he retreated. He wasn't fond of releasing his feelings, and if they weren't welcomed, he tended to mentally disappear.

Right now, both women had reason to wonder what bounced around Jonah's skull.

Quinn wasn't looking forward to wandering through Miss Abbott's destroyed belongings, but the dread dissipated when they arrived at the scene to find three people wandering like they owned the place. Or wished they did.

The fire marshal would've been in an official vehicle. These people arrived in three sedans: a BMW, a Lexus, and a Buick. "Son of a bitch," Jonah said as he pulled behind the Buick.

Throwing the gear into park, he left the truck, then in an afterthought, spoke to the women. "You two wait here." He left and approached the nearest party, who happened to be Guy Cook.

Jule peered over the seat at Quinn.

"Don't worry," Quinn said, opening her door. "I'm not about to let him go tackle them by himself."

Jule started to get out.

Quinn leaned in and rested a hand on her. "Not sure you ought to get involved."

She patted Quinn's hand but continued to exit the truck. "Not about to. I said I would search the house for anything to save, so that's what I'll be doing. Y'all call me when you're done with your business."

She shut her door, some plastic kitchen trash bags at the ready, and walked around Piper Pierce to get to work, speaking to the woman in passing, wishing her a happy day.

Compared to the three visitors who looked leftover from Sunday service, Quinn, Jonah, and Jule presented rag-tag, almost homeless in their disposable attire. The two groups represented entirely different missions, yet similar, with the goal being to study the dank, charbroiled disaster for nuggets of the salvageable.

As Jule moved off to survey for remnants, Piper Pierce moved toward Guy even as Quinn approached Jonah. Laney hadn't left further than two steps from her Lexus, but she was close enough to hear and chose to stay where she was.

"I got this," Jonah whispered to Quinn, but she gave her back to the *guests* and uttered to him, "Trust me, hard head, you need a witness."

She righted herself alongside Jonah, discreetly hitting record on a wonderful app she kept on her phone for moments just as this. Then she wondered where the others were, but as soon as she thought the question, she answered it. Ella Mae Dewberry sided with the strong personalities in whatever capacity they told her to, so no point muddying the waters with her presence. And while Iona voted with them most of the time, she hadn't earned her stripes. Add to that she'd been seen with Quinn.

No point having any more witnesses than necessary. These were the heavy hitters of the board.

Jonah straightened and stood fast as Guy closed in. "Jonah," the man said in greeting.

But Jonah had no patience for a preamble. "Your two obstacles to acquiring this land are gone, Mr. Cook. The house burned . . . the owner murdered. I bet you think life's looking up for you and your posse."

Piper took in a breath at the harshness of a man widely noted for his easy demeanor. Maybe she was stunned a bit by the thinly veiled accusation. Very thinly veiled.

Quinn stood to his side, primed to run interference for a temper Jonah rarely used. It didn't appear often, and it didn't last long, but it flashed white hot when a nerve was struck, enough for him to invariably regret it later.

Inside the debris, Jule pretended to hunt for valuables, pretending not to listen.

Guy wasn't deterred. "Who decided it was murder? I hope you're not accusing us—"

Jonah poked his chest out. "She's not even in her grave yet, Cook."

"We're still buying it," Guy said. "We'll pay market value, but it will be ours. Count on it."

Jonah glowered, so rare on him. "You three show up like buzzards feeding off carnage, you know that? Cold, man. Really cold."

This was a side of Jonah not readily seen, but Quinn had to give Guy credit. He hadn't flinched. Instead, he nodded southwest. "We own that acreage right over there, young man. In light of what happened last night, we made an impromptu decision to visit it and consider our options."

"Apparently you aren't familiar with the property lines yet."

Guy lightly shrugged. "Call it the human nature of curiosity, I guess, but we wanted to see how bad the damage was. It's a tragedy, for sure."

Jonah spit words out over the top of Guy's. "You're a lawyer, right?"

The board chairman nodded.

"A shyster, right?" Jonah added.

Guy almost nodded in agreement before hearing the slur.

Nobody moved a muscle.

Jonah squinted. "Attorneys know better than to trespass on posted land. Decent ones anyway."

"We weren't aware—"

"You almost ran over the damn sign." Jonah pointed toward the road ditch, and there it was. One of those generic squares on thin metal legs found at a Home Depot. The night the barn burned, Jonah had placed it there as a show of his promise to Miss Abbott to better secure her place. And when he and Quinn left last night, he'd gotten out of the truck and paid particular attention to righting it into place from where someone in the fire hubbub had knocked it askew.

Tentatively, Piper approached. "We are terribly, terribly sorry about what happened to Amy Abbott. Not a soul wanted this, Jonah." She peered at Quinn, a silent pleading for her to assist. The rather angular woman was trying to soften the situation, empathy not exactly inherent to her nature. "But it's best for the county that we use this land for the betterment of the children, don't you think?"

Quinn wasn't about to aid her cause. Jonah wouldn't get physical, but once he crossed a line, he delivered decent tongue lashings, and since last night, his pent up pain needed a release. Better he deliver it to these greedy bastards than those he loved.

Cue the muscles in Jonah's neck. "I can tell you're all broken up, Piper." He shifted full attention on her. "But since you want to talk, and since Guy won't answer me, explain why you're trespassing. I've read your school board rules. You can't represent the board without the others, so what exactly do you call what you're doing?" Jonah hungered for a fight.

Maybe Quinn could make them see this summit wouldn't end without someone driving away. "Let them leave, Jonah. They've seen the damage and have no need to stay, do you, Ms. Pierce? Mr. Cook?" Quinn ran her hand lightly down Jonah's back as a signal to lighten up.

Laney Underwood pushed off her Lexus and strolled over, and Piper took a step aside to give her the metaphorical podium. Funny. Quinn would've put Piper over Laney in the hierarchy.

"Accept it. We'll get this land," Laney said. "We cannot help that the poor woman died, but now the opportunity presents itself for this school to become a reality, which ought to please you as well as us. Our community is long overdue in meeting the needs . . ." She stopped.

Jonah had pulled out his phone, clicked off pictures of each of them with the burned house in the background. Then he placed a call, putting the phone to his ear.

"This is Jonah Proveaux. Is Sheriff Sterling in?"

Guy's tension released with a laugh. "You're embarrassing yourself, son. Quit wasting your time." His politeness had acquired an edge.

From the tumble of his expression, Jonah wasn't immediately put through. He watched the ground and waited, though, fully conscious they were there.

The smugness shared between Laney and Piper shot a hot current through Quinn. Even Jule headed over, sensing a conversation taking too long.

Guy entered his own smug grin in the mix, and Quinn couldn't take it any longer. She held out her hand, and when Jonah didn't quickly respond, she raised her brows at him, her mouth forming a silent *please.*

He turned the phone over, and when he almost turned away, she held his sleeve. "Hold on."

Carla, the sheriff's receptionist, was explaining how the sheriff wasn't available.

"Hey, Carla? It's me, Quinn."

"Hey, girl. I was just talking to your man. He wanted to speak to your uncle, but the sheriff didn't want to be disturbed. You know how he is." She gave a teeny bopper sort of sigh to segue into something else. "Tell me. How are you wearing your hair today?"

"One braid tied with a lanyard."

"Damn, I wish I could do that."

"Be grateful for what you've got, girl. Your fashion sense isn't anything to sneeze at."

Jonah stared at the one-eighty direction of the conversation, but Laney and Piper watched wary. Only a woman would understand what was going down on that phone.

"You're needing to talk to the sheriff, aren't you?" Carla said.

"You read me like a book, girl. Yeah, need to in a really big way."

Carla put her on hold, and Quinn turned to the two ladies and smiled, a feigned apology for the unexpected delay.

Her uncle came on the line. "What's up, Quinn?"

"I hate to bother you, Uncle, but Jonah and I are at Miss Abbott's place in hope of finding some items for her funeral—"

"Should've called you myself yesterday. I'm really sorry about what happened. Heard you and Jonah tried real hard to save her. Stupid you two going in the house like that, but I understand you bought her a few hours. Just too old a woman to weather that, I imagine."

"Yes, sir. Jonah is especially torn up about it. He'd rather adopted her of late."

"Yeah. So, back to your call. You two are out there and . . . what?"

She hesitated on how to label the three before her. "I guess there's no other way to describe them other than trespassing," she said. "They won't leave."

"Who won't leave?" he asked, becoming cautious. He fully understood the wiles of his niece. "What are you sucking me into?"

"Guy Cook, Piper Pierce, and Laney Underwood," she said.

"Jesus, Quinn. Jonah's sparring with them again, isn't he? In reality, with Miss Abbott dead, none of you has a right—"

"Actually, Uncle Larry, that's not so. Mind if I put Jonah on?"

"Do I have a choice?"

She passed the cell to Jonah.

"Sheriff Sterling," he started. "Thanks for taking the call. I've asked them to leave. I know this sounds like playground stuff, but—"

"Son, this falls under probate court now. Just leave these people be, okay?"

"Actually, Sir, probate makes me executor of Miss Abbott's estate." He laid a stare on Guy. "And the will gives this acreage to me."

Like statues, the board members stood locked in the knees.

Piper was the first to break loose and walk away. Guy, however, glanced at Laney while speaking to Jonah. "Probate doesn't work that fast, son."

"The paperwork is clear," Jonah said.

"We'll fight you," Guy replied. "We mean business."

Jonah's eyes widened. "You mean, you'll do more of this?" His phone-free arm swept across the landscape.

"Not saying we did this, and you know it. But we don't need this situation to get dirtier, Jonah. It's dirty enough."

"Get off this property," Jonah ordered.

"Mark my words," Guy said, turned and left.

"Wait, Mr. Cook and Ms. Pierce have decided to leave," Jonah said into his phone. "I think you can cancel sending anyone out here, Sheriff."

"Y'all need to break that up and settle down, Jonah. Glad to hear they're leaving. Okay, now that you've used me," the sheriff said, "just let them save face and go. I've got work to do."

Jonah tucked away his phone. Quinn slid her hands in her butt pockets, not seeing the need to utter another word. The less voices on the recording the better anyway.

Jule approached and stood beside Jonah. "Since you're in charge, son, would you mind if I dug up some of those daylilies she had in that front bed? The leaves are burned, but I believe I could salvage the bulbs."

Bless the woman for trying to dispel the mood, yet make a statement to Laney at the same time.

But Laney remained. "I'm leaving, but we need to meet over this," she said. "The other tract is worthless without this one. The whole county is watching, and this board owes them to build a school. We are this county, Jonah. Regardless who owns it, we need this land."

Jule looked up from her dirty hands holding a smudged and filthy grocery bag full of what-nots. "The funeral's Monday, Laney."

Laney gave Jule little more than a glance. "Jonah, surely you don't intend to keep this land for yourself."

Jule half-stepped into Laney's line of sight. "I said the funeral's Monday, Laney. Would look awful bad for you not to make an appearance." Then she turned to Jonah. "We really need to get on with our task, son."

They left Laney standing alone, and it didn't take long for her to leave.

Quinn retrieved her phone from her jeans pocket and clicked off the recording, wishing they'd used Jule to start with.

Chapter 12

"YOU DON'T HAVE to be a damn PI to tell Miss Abbott was targeted," Jonah said, cramming shrimp casserole in his mouth then pointing with his fork. "And those three people are part of it."

Jule was the queen of throwing meals together, and her freezer was a testament to that fact. She, Jonah, and Quinn sat around her dinner table yet again, freshly showered after returning to the farm covered in soot and grime. They hadn't eaten until after the goats had been fed, a standard rule. Quinn had brought Bogie over to be loved on, after being alone for so long that day. A bird clock in the kitchen chirped like a chickadee, meaning seven o'clock. They weren't eating as late as last night, which was good since everyone seemed a bit spent after the day's stress.

Quinn slipped the pup a shrimp, thinking nobody saw.

"Won't eat it," Jule said, and Bogie proved her right by licking the casserole sauce off and leaving the pink meat behind on the rug.

Quinn picked up the piece with a napkin and took it to the kitchen trash. "Ty said it's arson, by the way." She'd checked in with him twice that day. "Gasoline in the living room." That paralleled what she'd seen arriving at the fire, the living room already hot and blazing destroying that corner of the home first. "They want the security video, if there is any," she added.

"They have what I have," Jonah said. Apparently he'd been talking to people without her knowledge, too. "With the weather nice, she had the windows open. Someone only had to toss in the Molotov cocktail and run."

Something had to be wrong about the scenario for Jonah not to be somewhat glad at the crime being recorded by the very security he installed. Instead, he seemed to carry twenty pounds on his shoulders, growing heavier by the hour. Quinn wasn't sure what else she could do to help. This Good Samaritan plan of his had swelled into something horribly ugly, and it was taking his personality with it.

Jonah was a sweetheart and a person who cared about others, but he could also be a worrier, taking things deeply internal. This whole ordeal had turned on him, and he wasn't sure what to do with the tiger he had by the tail.

Quinn thought she could pinpoint his issue of the moment. "The arsonist wasn't identifiable, was he?" Then before he answered, she filled in the rest. "Your cams didn't catch a car or the culprit, because he'd cased the place, parked down the road, slinked in and hauled ass leaving. A mask or hoodie covered his head, and Miss Abbott didn't see a thing. Probably at her age didn't smell anything until the fire was out of hand, which is why you never got a call directly from her."

Jonah put his elbows on the table, his face in his hands, and rubbed his eyes.

A mile was considered a hop and a skip in the country, and with Miss Abbott being a mile from Sterling Banks, she might have felt safe, especially with Jonah's security additions. But one of the negatives of living rural was the ease in which crime could be carried out unnoticed. No witnesses. No traffic. No interchanges or crosswalks with CCTV cameras mounted on corner posts.

They abandoned the talk of fire. Wasn't until they moved on to the pie leftover from last night did the conversation boil down to what everyone hadn't said aloud. Jule asked first. "What do you really want to do about the land now, son?"

He looked to the side, away from them, his left hand scratching through his long, collar-length hair, making Quinn wish she could reach over and do that for him to console. "I don't know," he said. "I still think of it as hers."

He had two hundred and fifty thousand dollars and forty acres valued as much or more. If anyone would make good use of such a gift, it was Jonah.

Jule studied her pie, mashing crumbs with the tines of her fork. "What would Amy Abbott *want* you to do with it? Maybe that can help you."

"She's not even buried yet, Mom."

The word Mom sounded odd. Everyone, to include Jonah, called her Jule. This change showed how in need he was of a mother.

"Jonah," his mother started, "you made a lasting impression on an old woman who had nobody. She might've seen friends at church on Sunday, even had the occasional lunch with a lady in town. I was right here, her closest neighbor and the closest to her age, yet I was too busy to visit more than every couple of weeks. When people get to her age, they get forgotten, even more so as their friends die before them."

Jonah removed his hands from his face and laid forearms on the table, watching her, apparently open to listening.

Jule slipped another sliver of pie onto his plate and motioned with the knife for him to eat. "You listened to her. You visited her. You took care of her. Though only for a few months, she royally appreciated you taking time from running Sterling Banks to tend to her. Trust me, she was grateful. Then when you committed to her, she committed to you. I'm proud of you."

Quinn almost choked up and thanked the Lord for the privilege of being present at this mother-son talk. Suddenly she missed Graham more than she had in months. Only when Jule handed her a paper napkin did Quinn realize she was crying.

"Yeah, Jonah," and Quinn sniffled, glad she'd gone bare-faced to dinner. "Something in that woman told her you would do right by her. Not that she expected to die so soon, but she pictured you making the right call. What do you think that is?"

"I think it was no more than a desperate woman saying thank you." He reached down to pet on Bogie.

"Go with that then. Let's say the land and money are a thank-you. Now what?"

He peered, brow meeting in the middle. "What do you mean *now what?* I'll clean everything from the fire first." He thought a second, now realizing he hadn't had a chance to go down that road yet. "I wouldn't build a place and live there. Too close to the road for my taste."

Thank God for that. For some reason Quinn saw Jonah forever living with Jule . . . or herself at the manor. . . maybe.

His eyes lit up, and in turn that gave Jule a hopeful glow about her. "What?" she asked.

"We can use it for a store," he said. "A lot of traffic takes this route between Charleston and Savannah. Not as much as the main highway, but we're a farm, right?"

Quinn wasn't sure his meaning. "Right."

"Yet we only sell online novelty and wholesale bulk. Who says we can't have a store? Right now, nobody in Craven can buy straight from us. It doesn't have to be big. The land is paid for and the money is sitting in the bank for the construction. We can advertise in Walterboro, Charleston, Beaufort."

Jule rolled the idea around. Quinn wondered who would be in charge of running it.

"Sterling Banks can't take advantage of you that way," Quinn said.

"So rent the building from me," he said. "We'll share the profits."

Look at this man. He hadn't had a chance to gnaw on the concept that much, but it undoubtedly enthused him. He didn't own an inch of Sterling Banks yet here he was willing to invest his windfall into it.

A trickle of guilt seeped into her heart at how much more devoted to Sterling Banks he was than she most days. To be honest, he'd run it better than she.

And Quinn wondered if Miss Abbott had had an alternate motive. She'd all but given Jonah a dowery to make him a better catch.

"On another note." The daydreaming was a pleasant change, but Quinn couldn't shed what likely lay ahead. "What are you going to do when the school board returns for it?"

With color back in his cheeks, mention of Miss A's adversaries brought Jonah even more to life. "Already thought of that. First, if they have the gall to approach me, I'll counter to buy their thirty acres back since the money's still in the bank."

Jule busted out laughing. "They won't even think of that."

"Good place to start," Quinn said.

Jonah needed to ponder the options, the obvious and the not. Laney had warned she'd be back, but what would the board do when Jonah declined their offer? What would he do when they declined his?

Someone pushed Miss Abbott to her end. If they'd go to such extreme measures, how high would they step up their game to convince someone as stubborn as Jonah?

This recent landowner was family to Quinn. His land adjoined hers. If anyone set foot on Sterling Banks, they'd learn that Quinn fought dirtier than Jonah. He always thought right and wrong came with clean lines. She knew better.

They cleaned up dishes and Quinn struck out for home, weary from the day. She added to her notes, recording the events of the day, of which there were many. Then she went to bed a little after ten leaving a text for Uncle Larry that they needed to talk without others around.

He wouldn't dare call this late, and before he called in the morning, she'd be at his office.

Jonah carried too heavy a burden to do everything himself.

SHE ARRIVED AT the sheriff's office at seven a.m., normally too early to be out and about, much less dressed. Unthinkable for her. The lobby and hallway carried heavy whiffs of strong coffee, and she grabbed her one with an inch of milk, using someone's cup from Disney World. Then

Carla led her down the hall into the boss's office.

At a quarter to eight Uncle Larry strolled in, balancing newspaper and coffee mug. He almost dropped the latter finding Quinn settled across from his desk.

"Told you we needed to talk," she said. "Need a towel?"

"No," he growled as he brushed the front of his shirt. "A drop or two won't kill me." He sat in his chair, the familiar creak answering to the weight. "What's got you so spry this morning?"

"Miss Abbott's murder."

He found a napkin and a tie in his drawer. He dabbed the final moisture off his shirt then put on the tie to cover it. He'd done this before.

She got up and shut the door quietly.

"It's too early for you to lose your temper, niece."

"Have no intention of doing so," she said. "On the contrary, I'd rather not make a lot of noise. I'm here to ensure you've opened an investigation on Miss Abbott's murder and the arson at her house."

"Ty's in charge. And since it's an open investigation, I can't discuss it with you."

She chuckled at the irony of him keeping information from her when it usually went the other way around. Then she went solemn. "I'm here to emphasize that this case be treated properly."

It was too early to quibble and take jabs, so she laid the phone on his blotter and hit play.

"Not this again—"

"Listen and don't talk." She reached across and started it over.

Not the best quality, but the board member voices were defined well enough. He obliged her in listening, blowing on his coffee, finally deeming it cool enough to sip as he took in yesterday's conversation in front of Miss Abbott's shell of a house, raising his brows when he heard his own voice tinny and distant in the background from Jonah's phone.

Quinn clicked it off. She left the device sitting there as a reminder. She'd play it again if she had to.

"Appreciate you recording me," he said.

Not what Quinn had planned, but a positive for sure. The sheriff had witnessed the semi-threats of the board.

"You heard. Laney Underwood warned Jonah he best listen, after Guy Cook emphasized Jonah best be wary." She pointed at the phone. "You were in essence there. They are persons of interest. They may have engineered the threats against Miss Abbott, the last of which led to her death. They went too far, Uncle Larry, and they aren't done."

"Seven upstanding members of the community collaborated to take down an eighty-year-old woman, huh?"

"Don't patronize me," she said, deadpan. "And don't downplay the loss of this woman. This is arson and murder. The fire marshal confirmed the arson. The coroner confirmed death by smoke inhalation. Jonah's security system gave you footage showing someone throw an incendiary device in the living room window. You can use that footage to compare height, weight, age, maybe sex . . . right hand versus left hand . . . then catch who this is and turn them against who hired them, very likely this damn board who need interviewing ASAP."

He scratched his neck. "Quinn, you're sticking your nose in where it doesn't belong. We'll handle this."

"Did you not hear what I said?"

"Yes. You want me to interview every board member."

"All seven."

He looked down on her, a look she'd come to hate, the one that prejudged her. "How many voted for this land?"

"Six for, one against. There are seven members. The one who voted against buying the farm could easily have knowledge they wish to get off their chest, and I believe Iona might be wishing she hadn't gone along with the rest. Make them talk about each other."

Quinn didn't want his normal lick-and-a-promise effort. She pushed. "There's an election for Sheriff in a little over a year, and if you can't investigate an innocent old woman's death, then how's the average voter to feel safe?"

His eyes went hard. "That a threat, little girl?"

"No, just the promise of a public ground swell of disgruntlement about ignoring the deaths of seniors."

His expression darkened. "Don't pit yourself against me, girl."

Anyone poking their head in the door wouldn't first see the depth of animosity. Quinn and her uncle could present like they conversed about the next family cookout, but up close within earshot, others would hear a back and forth of a stronger caliber.

There were no hugs and affection amongst the three Sterlings. One remained distant in California and the other two regularly squared-off on opposite sides of almost everything.

"I'm not trying to fight you. I'm seeking your help," she replied, letting the message gel between them. "The sabotage at Miss Abbott's place failed. Someone overplayed their hand, underestimated the old woman, then screwed up with the fire. They thought removing her would pave their way." She lifted her phone, waving it once before putting it away. "You heard Guy Cook. You heard Laney Underwood. What does this sound like to you?"

He eased more in his chair, blowing hard through his nose. She felt the division between them lessen.

Nobody understood better than Sheriff Sterling how politics could get dirty.

"So Ty's in charge?" she asked, bringing the conversation around.

He dipped a nod.

"Now, about Jonah. How do we safeguard him?"

"He been threatened?"

"Not any more than what you heard on that call," she said. "But he is to soon become the owner of the land they want. He's also a symbol of Sterling Banks. He's family, uncle. I'm not letting anything happen to him or Jule." She gave a few seconds for him to forecast where she was going with this. "You've seen what I'm capable of when my world is threatened."

"Indeed," he said, not seeing the need to mention the two bodies he'd had to handle in April.

"Now, about you using Ty," she started.

He didn't hide his surprise. "You're questioning Ty now? Thought he walked on water for you."

He did, but . . . "He'd be investigating his own aunt. Is that fair to him?"

"You trust him?" Larry asked.

"I do," she said.

"Then that's it. Besides, he's all we've got. My others are barely more than road deputies. Can you see Harrison investigating anything? He's my second most seasoned."

Harrison couldn't find his own wife under his own roof. Assuming he'd want to. She wasn't his favorite lady if the rumor mill could be believed.

She tread on familiar ground again. "What about asking SLED to assist? And I still know people with the Bureau. Arson can be considered a federal offense, and this has the smell of public corruption. They investigated Beaufort's school board three years ago. Remember?"

"Nope."

"It's no reflection on you," she said, though he would see it differently.

"It stays in-house," he said.

"Then deputize me to assist. I had nothing to do with Miss Abbott."

He snorted a laugh. "You represent a school board member."

Well, that was true, but Quinn wasn't sure that relationship would last much longer. She might fire Iona herself. "Let me make some calls."

"Nope."

Damn, this man could be stubborn. "Then it's on you. You know I'll be on top of this. I prefer not to see you embarrassed."

"Don't you worry about me."

But she had one more concern, and there was no way to ask but pointedly. "You're not involved are you?"

He glowered. "Get the hell out of here, Quinn."

She sat forward, a palm up. "No, listen to me. Regardless what you think, you being at the last board meeting was not a good image. You *send* the protection. You don't trot yourself out like a dog whistled to heel." Quinn thought through the videos, the overwhelming show of the sheriff's department that came off rather inflated.

"He needed a show of force to maintain civility," he said.

"Guy Cook, you mean. Was Jonah a threat? Really? Or any of those parents? I'm not seeing it, Uncle Larry. You may think you were the epitome of intimidation that night, but I think otherwise."

"I'm listening." He hated saying the words, but she'd obviously dropped a notion he hadn't considered, one with the potential to demean his position.

"Did Guy Cook mention any contractors or visitors or strangers he had to appease or maybe attract to do business in our county? Was Guy Cook trying to impress someone?"

He shook his head. "Not that I'm aware."

She envisioned the suits on the video, the suits that bothered Iona, the suits catered to by Guy and Laney after a meeting one evening. Quinn hadn't seen them the night she was there, hadn't known they existed. Maybe it was time she looked at that video.

Their coffees were gone, their conversation waning, and two people had already knocked and tried to see the sheriff. He leaned over his desk. "Guy Cook looks like a buffoon on his attorney ads on television, but there's a reason he's been on that board for two decades. Piper Pierce owns half of Jacksonboro, and Laney has a Craven County bloodline as long as ours with a hundred times the progeny. Keep that in mind when you step on toes. There's a ton of self-preservation involved here, Quinn. They lead with it. No differently than you or I. You use it if you have to." He leaned back in his chair, ending the chat. "I've delayed my day enough, niece."

Quinn left. No hug, no embrace, no *have a good day*. In spite of their Southern genteel upbringing, she and her uncle didn't practice any of that between them. After a word exchange about earrings with Carla, Quinn headed to the parking lot, but it wasn't until she sat in her truck that she seriously sifted through Larry's parting words. *You use it if you have to.*

Was he honestly giving permission for her to dive into this mess? Was this trust for her sleuthing or admittance of his lack of resources? Or was this the sheriff's way of distancing himself from a much needed school board investigation?

Chapter 13

PICKUP STILL IN the sheriff's office parking lot, windows down, Quinn replayed the conversation with Larry Sterling, eating mints she kept in her cup holder. A quarter past nine. That talk with her uncle felt way longer than that, and she came away with a different layer of meaning than expected.

As expected, he didn't want outsiders like SLED or FBI coming on his turf, but Quinn caught a smidgen of embarrassment in him today. Like he'd been caught on his back foot, or someone had used him and he hadn't seen it coming.

And in a move so unlike him, he'd just about given her permission to hunt. He wouldn't tell her that outright, but he'd never respected her enough to drop that hint before.

Such an odd, uncertain feel to the dialogue.

He'd delegated the entire case to Ty, omitting himself . . . or so it seemed to her. She needed Ty's interpretation, both inside the SO and about the case. She had really hoped to talk to him before she left this morning, hoping to hear how he'd been given his assignment and the level of emphasis he'd been told to give it. Just what were the informal ground rules of running this case? Who should they pursue? Who was deemed off limits?

She called Ty's private number, left a message, and resumed her thinking. He'd call the minute he could. Probably already on task. Since she and Jonah witnessed the fire, he'd want to talk to them anyway.

To her left, a couple of officers exited a cruiser, laughing, in no hurry. One looked up and did a double take at her. "Hey, Quinn. What're you up to?"

"Keeping your boss straight," she said.

"Ain't touching that," he said, signing off with two fingers. "Be good."

Most of these guys made her smile and miss her eighteen-year-old days on the force. The others made her glad she'd moved on.

She lowered the truck's visor. The day was bright, the temperature in the eighties, and people enjoyed going about their lives in this beautiful, temperate climate, but Miss Abbott was no longer a part of it. Remembering what Jule said yesterday about old people's lives shrinking and people in their busy-ness forgetting to visit, Quinn carried her own share of that guilt for not tending to her neighbor any more than she had.

Thanks to Miss Abbott, which also meant Jonah, the more Quinn learned about this board, the less she wanted to do with Iona. The woman spoke of cutting Quinn loose, and her wishy-washy tendencies had grown into a nuisance. Maybe quitting was the answer since there was a certain ick, untrusting feel about her now. But sticking with Iona could grant her insight into what happened, too. Not an easy ethical decision. Strategically, however, the choice was clear.

She put the truck in gear. She drove the few blocks over, parked at the curb, and made the call.

"Hello? Quinn?" She answered on the second ring.

"Hey, Iona. Are you home right now?"

"I certainly am. Just doing some books. Why? Did you find something?"

Her car must be in the garage. "Fripp isn't there, is he?"

"No, he's gone for the day. Got a job in Charleston."

Quinn opened the driver's door. "I'm right outside. Let me in. We need to talk."

She didn't wait to be invited when Iona opened the door. "Close it," Quinn said, stepping over the threshold. "We don't need to be seen."

Iona's eyes widened like they so often did. "Care for some coffee?"

Already revved on two cups of the sheriff's high-octane, Quinn declined. Scanning the living area, she noted where Iona had been working, sprawled out at the dining room table, and wondered why a bookkeeper didn't at least have a bedroom office or a desk in the living room corner. Quinn headed to the paperwork and assumed a seat at a place less covered by spreadsheets and receipts. Two two-drawer filing cabinets sat in a corner. How many of Iona's business clientele knew this was the office? Maybe they were the types of small businesses who didn't care.

As Iona stiffly sat, Quinn moved papers aside a few inches to make room to rest her arms. "Miss Amy Abbott died day before yesterday."

"I heard." The reply came out breathless but not quite sincere enough to suit Quinn. At least not today.

"What are the rumors you're hearing, Iona?"

Hand to her chest, she took on the damsel look, something Quinn held little patience for from anyone at any time, but much less from this woman now. She wished she'd had the time to revisit those videos to be better armed for this moment, but chances were if Iona would spill to Fripp, she could easily be pressured to spill to her.

"I'm not sure what you mean." Still saucer-eyed, Iona seemed thrown so far off her game that she had no idea where the playing field was.

"Miss Abbott died from the fire someone set in her house. I just left the sheriff's office. They have opened an investigation. Be prepared to answer questions. Lots of them. Difficult questions. Questions that will back you in a corner if you aren't sure where you stand."

"I'm not sure . . ."

"Don't tell me you aren't sure what I mean," Quinn said. "That only makes you look worse."

Iona's hand on her chest now gripped the blouse. Apparently, the train wreck in her brain blocked her from forming a thought, and her effort to pick through the rubble for the right, proper, and least condemning reply made her comical at best.

Quinn kept the pressure on. "Now, since you look guilty as hell . . ."

Iona covered her mouth.

"Let me help you by giving you a taste of the questions you'll have to answer," Quinn said. "Did you vote to buy the first tract of land from Miss Abbott? The thirty acres?" Not that Quinn didn't already know.

The woman was too afraid to answer.

"It's a yes or no answer, Iona."

"Yes, I voted for it."

Quinn gave a satisfactory nod. "Did you vote to proceed with an offer to buy the second tract?"

She started to reply in the positive, probably since the first yes response hadn't hurt that badly, then stopped. "We didn't take a vote on that."

That was unexpected. "But you pursued Miss Abbott. You asked her to sell. You harangued her enough for Jonah Proveaux to get involved."

"Oh, no." Iona got animated in her denial, hands flitting. "I voted for none of that. I agreed to absolutely none of that. That was executive meeting conversation."

"But you were there."

"But I didn't get involved!" she shouted. "And much of that was between them outside of the room. I told you they did stuff like that."

Which was where Quinn had wanted her to go. "What you might not understand, Iona, is that you are the board. Each of you is the board.

When one of you speaks, you speak as a whole. Why do you think they record the meetings?"

"But they do not record executive meetings," she said.

"Meaning you have no proof you didn't go along." Now Quinn would see which Iona feared most . . . the board or the law.

Iona looked around for something to drink, grabbing the coffee cup to her right only to find it empty. She just stared into the bottom of the mug.

"Need some water?" Quinn asked. Iona nodded, forgetting this was her house and she was the hostess.

"It's just—" Quinn stopped, slowing down the conversation's momentum as she filled two glasses found on a dish rack in the kitchen. "It's just they have to query the board members about the murder and arson. Are y'all still going after the second tract of land?"

"Last I heard we were." She welcomed the water glass like she'd been stranded for days without it.

"Last I heard you were, too. Laney Underwood said that just yesterday. Told Jonah that he best consider their upcoming offer."

"That's just Laney mouthing off," Iona said.

"I was witness," Quinn said. "And she said it on Miss Abbott's land where she was trespassing."

Iona sort of froze again.

Quinn coughed once. Then again before taking a sip to smooth over the residual rawness. "One member speaks for all, Iona." A smaller cough, and another sip. "Sorry. Left over from the fire."

Iona stared. "You were in the fire?"

"Yea. Scary." Quinn sat, taking her time with her own glass of water. Time for Iona to decide what to say. Time for Quinn to wait and take measure.

"I don't know what to do," came out first, and when Quinn didn't reply, "They told me to go along or stay out of the way, but if I interfered or opened my mouth, I was going down. I'm really not sure what that even means."

"Well, it doesn't sound good," Quinn said.

She shifted and came forward, crossing arms on the table. Iona did the same. "We need to insulate you," Quinn said, "but first, do you even want me anymore? You said on Wednesday—"

"Of course I want you," she exclaimed. "I'm sorry about what I said. I'm sorry—"

"Okay, okay, I hear you." This woman was ridiculously malleable, a trait of Iona's that Quinn bet the Corps had learned quite some time ago. "This has gotten real. I believe one or more on that board is responsible for one or both crimes. With you having benefited from contracts with the district, you are vulnerable, but believe me when I say this . . . murder, conspiracy, and fraud are far worse. *This* is your focus."

Iona gave little child-like nods.

"Keep your eyes and ears open, you hear? Glean conversations for intention. Do not let on you are speaking to me, and frankly, if they ask, say you fired me. I don't care if you say you can't stand me, hate my uncle, or accuse me of lying, just distance yourself from me if it comes up." Quinn motioned toward the door, and Iona flinched. "My truck parked out front? If anyone asks why it's here, say you asked me over to give me my final payment and cut me loose."

Lots of little nods this time. Quinn imagined her frantically thinking, *I can do that, I can do that.*

"This time, don't tell Fripp a damn thing! He will throw you under the bus, tell the others, God knows what else. If he threatened to turn you in to SLED, how easy would it be to accuse you of conspiring about Miss Abbott?"

"So true," she whispered. "He would."

"The moment I hear you've betrayed our confidence, I'm done. I will not be able to help you. I cannot make it any clearer than that."

"Very clear," Iona said.

Every response was a hammer blow now. Quinn gave direction and Iona hammered it home. Amen and amen.

This is how Quinn wanted her. Compliant and loyal. Even if Ty got hold of her, she'd be loyal to Quinn. Or so she hoped. She now had an undercover operative in the Craven County District School System, and if Iona broke the rules, the only harm would be self-inflicted.

"What do I do?" Iona asked. She ripped off the top paper of a notepad she used for her bookkeeping. She poised to write, but Quinn shook her head.

"Memory only," she whispered. "No evidence."

Her client laid down the pad, dropped the pen, clasped her hands and laid them in her lap as if to keep them from straying on their own to write.

"Okay, listen to what I need you to do. One, find out what started this land acquisition business. Why that tract of land? Why even that road? Is it the owner or the location driving them? Did they go after Miss Abbott because she was easy or because her land was in the right spot? See what I mean?"

"I think so."

"No active sleuthing. Just ask the occasional stupid question. Blame it on being the novice on the board."

"I can do that."

Iona had quit panicking and with the water glasses empty had gone into the kitchen to make them each a cup of tea. Now they sat at the table, legs crossed, sipping like lady friends who felt the need to meet and discuss how the church social was ever going to come together properly.

"This is better," Iona said. "I was worried you would get me in trouble the way you were ramrodding things."

"All the reason I came over," Quinn replied, not a fan of lukewarm tea. She forced down the last swallow and rose. "By the way, before I go, see if you can find out who the suits are?"

"The suits?"

Bless her, Iona had forgotten she'd nicknamed the mysterious guys *suits*. "Those strangers who Laney and Guy took out after that board meeting, what, three months ago?"

"Yeah, yeah. I'll see. They've been to more than one meeting, you know."

No, Quinn didn't know. "How observant. That's what I'm talking about." She made a mental note to review those videos again, from a different perspective than just Jonah.

Beaming, Iona rose like a proper hostess to walk her guest to the door. Quinn almost asked the woman about Fripp's involvement with the board irrespective of his involvement with the other contractors. Did he have any interest in the school, in other words, had he been promised any contracts. She'd love to know how tight he was with the board members, but asking Iona to investigate her husband could be lethal. He'd see right through her.

Hand on the door, Iona stopped Quinn. "I'm still not sure I shouldn't fire you."

"So fire me."

Her hand fell off the door knob. "Pardon?"

"Doesn't change a thing. Doesn't change your mission. Right now you're painted with the same brush as the rest of the board. What you're doing is helping me extract you from that band of thieves. You voted for that land, Iona. Remember? You are whatever the board does."

"But what if I resign?"

This poor woman. "Leave before you know the truth? Outside the board you learn nothing. Resign and you appear guilty for sure. You'll be accused of developing a case of conscience about Miss Abbott, see? Your future is on the line here. Maybe your life."

But to that, Iona scoffed once, grinning. "My life? Now you're exaggerating."

Quinn gave her a sober look and a blunt assessment so she couldn't miss the point. "What if they don't want a witness? What if they need a scapegoat? What if you appear to commit suicide over the guilt?"

A current of reality must've run through Iona the way her color slid away.

"One murder already happened. You're safer inside the clique than outside."

Iona wasn't as eager to nod this time. Like anyone caught up in a scary situation, her instinct was to escape. From the surrender in her shoulders, however, she wasn't seeing an easy way out.

Quinn stood six inches taller, her arms and legs much longer, and she often used the advantage to take possession of a moment. Resting hands on Iona, she rubbed her upper arms a little bit. "Why did you run for school board?"

"To make a difference. To make sure our tax dollars were invested in the classroom. To raise our school scores in the state."

"For the children."

"Yes."

"Where'd you get the idea to run?" Quinn expected a warm story about talking to a classroom during career day or a situation with her own daughter. Her client needed to rally. With zero motivation, she was worthless to the case.

"Fripp asked me to run, believe it or not. Then Laney took me to lunch, telling me how I would be a good level head in the group. Guy and Pierce helped run my campaign."

The light-hearted question had unexpectedly led to something darker, meriting discussion. Quinn almost walked her to the table again to drill down the details. "Fripp is friends with them?"

She shook her head. "Gosh, no. He doesn't travel in their circles. They told him to talk me into it. They didn't want the other candidates to win. I'm not so stupid not to see I was the lesser of evils, so to speak. The pool of candidates in this county isn't that deep."

"Who were the other candidates?"

"Well, Laney and Guy were running, of course . . . there were three seats open, but after old Mr. Lynch passed away, they needed somebody. Most of the time nobody runs against them, you know."

Making it easy to hide misdeeds, for sure.

"Nice of them to let me run alongside them," she continued. "Especially since I was up against Miss Birdie."

Quinn's brows went up. She really liked Miss Birdie. She assumed she voted for Miss Birdie. She itched to give this further discussion, but she'd pummeled Iona enough. Too much more and the dynamics might shift. "Well, you won, and that's saying something. I voted for you, you know." Might've actually been true, too. Bakeman would've topped the alphabetical list on the ballot. Her third vote went to Laney with her being Ty's aunt. She really hadn't put much thought into anyone's platform or campaign promises, especially not having kids.

Iona lit up. "Aww, thanks, Quinn."

She smiled at the bookkeeper. "You've got this, girl."

"I've got this."

Quinn let Iona have her warm moment. "The sheriff will dig to the bottom of this mess. Just answer their questions to the best of your knowledge and you'll be fine. Remember, I'll be in the background dealing with things."

More of Iona's little nods. "What will you be doing?"

"Best you not know," she said, and opened the door.

"Thanks, Quinn." The whisper was endearing, shaming Quinn a smidge.

The door closed promptly. Quinn made for her truck with a thought smacking her. Damn, she hadn't asked how Fripp had stalked Iona's movements. Had he simply followed in his truck or had he used technology? She doubted the latter. He didn't seem the type.

Fobbing open her own pickup, the beep triggered a notion.

Aware neighbors might be watching, she did a cursory inspection around her Ford. Wheel wells were clean. She ran an arm's length search of the undercarriage. But when she reached the spare tire under the bed, her fingertips hit treasure. An electronic tracking device.

Some would ask if the tracker was legal, but that didn't matter. Bad guys weren't known for following the law.

Chapter 14

RETRIEVING A GLOVE from the truck, she pulled the tracking device off her vehicle and saved it in a plastic bag, both gloves and bags a staple in her console.

What now? It was just after noon, and Quinn couldn't remain parked in front of Iona's house with this GPS tracker in her hand and somebody on the other end knowing. She cranked up and left for home, but at one particular turn decided Jackson Hole was closer. She didn't want to drive to Sterling Banks only to divert to Charleston to query a particular source of hers.

She pulled into the diner's parking lot, tucking in amidst the heavy lunch crowd, and instantly called Knox Kendrick. The FBI agent had befriended her in the latter part of her brief three years with the Bureau, and they still kept each other's cells in their contact lists. He worked at the smaller Charleston office now. She'd asked him a favor on the Renault case not long ago, not that he'd been able to come through, but from the text she'd gotten afterwards, he'd noted how the case had blown up around her. He'd even kidded her that the bureau would've done better.

Surprisingly, he picked up before it went to voice mail. "Quinn. I don't hear from you in, what, six years, then I hear from you twice in a couple months. I feel stalked. Buy me a movie and dinner so I feel better."

She laughed easy with him. He'd been one of her better enjoyments with the bureau, just not for long, because they dumped her when she couldn't return promptly after her daddy's murder. "Wait, thought you had a girl? That blonde?"

"What girl?" he replied. "Oh, yeah, her. That was three girls ago."

"You're getting old. Better find one and stick with her or you'll wind up in a one-bedroom apartment spending your retirement drinking beer and watching Netflix."

"I could say the same to you."

"But you're forty. I have more time." She was enjoying this. "Tell you what. If neither of us is married in, say, five years, I'll meet you at a chapel and we'll take care of business."

He belly laughed. "I like it. Putting that in my calendar . . . as we speak." He paused, and she wondered if he was really doing it. Finally he said, "Now, I assume there's a favor in this call?"

She smoother out the bag with the tracking device. "Someone tagged my truck. Any way to route this to the owner?"

"Not any more, Quinn. Go online. You find Wiki instructions on how to install one, how to find one on your vehicle, how to avoid getting caught, you name it. Amazon will ship you one by tomorrow if you can't get to Walmart to get one this afternoon. In this state, they can't tag your truck without your permission, but, assuming they even got caught, it's only a misdemeanor. A year and/or five hundred dollars max."

"So, nobody cares."

"And nobody can prove it without fingerprints which I doubt are on it. So, right."

Quinn was glad she didn't bother with a trip to the Holy City for that advice, though dinner with Knox would've been nice. Just dinner. On second thought, he'd expect more.

"You're obviously mixing up trouble," he said. "Don't get hurt like last time."

"Good thing I have bureau training."

"She says sarcastically. Thought your uncle was the sheriff?"

She could hear Uncle Larry now, asking for her to turn over the tracker to him. *I'll handle it, Quinn.*

"What about your boyfriend deputy? That guy you came with last time?"

"Ty Jackson," she said. "He's not my boyfriend." But she'd get him to dust this thing for prints.

Knox scoffed. "We may not all be profilers, Quinn, but that man had a protective streak a mile wide for you."

"He's working on the case," she said, deflecting. "Listen." She'd had enough of her uncle for the day and didn't care to explain more about Ty. "When's the last time you had a school district in your cross-hairs?" The FBI had done public corruption cases before.

He blew out a mocking snort. "That two-bit, local political stuff is not worth the sweat and is best handled by the state. Not a soul likes those things, you know. Unless you hand SLED or the Bureau an iron-clad, readymade case, they'll give you a string of excuses and obstacles why they can't get involved. You understand return-on-investment, Quinn. They measure the manpower it takes to retrieve a dollar, and if there aren't enough dollars . . ."

She cut through the chase. "It's not about justice anymore."

"Or even the law."

"It's politics, and the bigger politics doesn't like the little politics." Maybe she was glad to be out of the Bureau. "Well, a little old lady died this time, Knox. Arson. They were trying to force her to sell. They want a school there." Then she tacked on, "She was my neighbor."

"So it's personal. I seem to recall the last case being personal, too. What are you, the Craven Avenger?" He chuckled, then ceased when she didn't in kind. "You think your school board committed murder. Okay, and you can prove this how?"

Admittedly, she didn't have it trussed up, and the paths to clues still held potholes, but Laney made her point distinct enough standing on Miss Abbott's place. Who else would set fire to that house unless they were wanting to scare the old woman, or kill her, thinking intimidation or probate would open it up for a good price. Miss Abbott's distant relationship with her niece made it more than an even bet the "expected" heir would want to sell.

"I'm still working on a theory," she said. "But if I prove it, I'm not handing it to you with a bow. You guys love having locals do your work for you, then taking the credit."

"We're extremely smart that way."

No point wasting her connection with Knox on this yet. She needed more than she had to go over Uncle Larry's head or risk making Ty look bad.

She hung up, enjoying one final laugh over an old inappropriate joke repeated about her long legs, and she opened her truck door. While at the diner, she'd visit Lenore for lunch and eat her go-to bowl of fried okra. Then once she got to Sterling Banks, she'd just pop that tracking device on one of her pecan trucks that never left the grove.

SHE WAS DOWN to half a bowl of okra and a half glass of tea, seated back against her normal booth, feet against the opposite side, staring at the spinning Budweiser display hanging on the other side of the room. She'd let Lenore force some chicken salad on her, and some might won-der how okra went with that, but to her, fried okra went with everything. Her brain food, as Lenore called it. She slowly nibbled on one piece at a time when she had things to mull over. The more worrisome the concern, the slower the nibbling. Sometimes it took two bowls.

She was stalling, too, knowing Lenore would inform Ty that poor Quinn ate alone again, and took her time doing it. But by the bottom of the bowl, Ty hadn't shown.

She needed to check on Jonah by day's end, but as to the case, she played with speaking to Laney Underwood, especially with Iona saying Laney had taken her under her wing. Sounded rather opportunistic . . . or a way to preserve the way things had always been.

Her opponent Miss Birdie wouldn't have been so easily managed. Miss Birdie had already proven she was a force to be reckoned with, plus nobody in that district administration wanted that former teacher as one of their seven bosses, with the power to do to them what they did to her.

She flipped into the Facebook page to read up on the reaction to Miss Abbott. Didn't take her long to see how factions had formed and allegiances made. One side thought the burnt acreage should automatically go to the district. Nobody could name an heir, which to the ignorant made the land appear up for grabs, with dibs to a government body. Some admitted there had to be an heir someplace, but hey, they'd get a tax write-off if they donated it, as they should. As thanks, the school should name the building after Amy Abbott. Some inserted crosses and angels in their posts, sanctifying their suggestions.

The other side exploded in contention, emojis, and graphics demanding the heir sue the board. Nobody outright said the board killed Miss Abbott, but the insinuation left little to the imagination. The harshest of the critics said the district did not deserve the land and should be brought to task for screwing up in their poor planning. Someone might even need to go to jail. Didn't anyone know someone with SLED or the FBI? While that gave her a jolly, Quinn tended to side with them. Unmeted justice was hard to take.

Nobody, however, seemed to know that Jonah would soon own the land.

And Jonah was staying quiet.

The members of the Craven Living group had noticeably increased from one thousand to two, with the newbies appreciably more vocal. Quinn couldn't decide if that was good or bad.

Lincoln20 stood on the side of meting justice. There wasn't a post made without his comment. Sometimes he left simple emojis while at other times he spewed diatribes about the government wielding too much power, which in this neck of the state carried a lot of *amen* and *damn right* remarks.

A little man with a big social media mouth? Or a legitimate concern? She took a moment to dig into Lincoln20 but kept hitting walls.

She'd been accepted as a member of the group a few days ago to have full access to discussions, using her real name Quinn Sterling, but not being a big social media fan, her profile was sparse at best. Something about privacy and private investigations didn't marry well with spilling your guts to strangers.

Maybe this once . . . feigning innocence.

She typed the post three times before hitting send. Fresh to the group. Sad about what happened to Miss Abbott. She didn't deserve that. Would love to speak with Lincoln20 about it. Send PM, please.

She waited, but he, she, they didn't reply. Maybe later. Sometimes people like that were armchair blowhards, empowered by a keyboard. Some turned genuinely mad, however, using a forum like this to drum up followers for a plan down the road. There was no doubt that Lincoln20 read her post, though. They seemed to be living online.

A few Lincoln20 fans told him to ignore Quinn. Others said to reply and feel her out. Some praised Quinn for having helped with the fire, bless them. One said Quinn was an Iona Bakeman fan, and if that was the case, she wasn't to be trusted. The board was just scum.

Quinn couldn't imagine the blowback if she posted a real opinion, but in pondering that, she recognized something. The pro-school side, the side that would want the district to build the school, take the land, do what it took to improve education, didn't seem to have a leader. It was almost like they feared uniting too tightly for concern of being shot at.

Searching through the members list, she hunted for names she recognized, studying who was on what side. The board members were easy enough to find, using their full names because they'd had to when running for office. They might've been loud during the election, but no way in hell they'd speak up in this environment. This was a damned-if-you-do/don't scenario if there ever was one. Four, five, six board members had joined, though remained silent, but one remained absent, namely Curtis Fuller.

Curtis Fuller had known her father, of the same generation. Maybe not the best of buds, but they crossed paths in charitable causes, which indicated like minds. Late sixties, she guessed, and with him being retired Air Force for quite some time, she couldn't see him being too Facebook friendly. He'd been pretty quiet during the last board meeting, and in her afternoon perusal of the videos, he'd left no indelible mark in her memory. Just seemed to love to vote like he wanted to vote, regardless the direction of the board.

Harmon Valentine, the insurance agent, made not much more of an impression. Thin, middle-aged, benign yet nice, he seemed a gentleman who tried to stay positive but with minimal sound. He was on the

Facebook group but had said absolutely nothing since its existence. She did recall Harmon usually voting with the Corps.

She wondered what the mouthier members thought of their board representatives. She also wondered how said representatives behaved behind the closed doors of executive sessions.

Ah, there was the superintendent, but he never commented either. Smart. Fripp Bakeman was on there, mostly silent. He echoed a friend or two, on the side of the school, getting the land as quickly as possible, but not loudly. Seemed most of the noise originated from about twenty-five or thirty who spent a major part of their day glued to their screens. The rest watched from afar, sensing the pulse, popping up after work or dinner.

Those who spoke, however, did so with gall and gusto. If that anti-school group discovered who really killed Miss Abbott, or who might be suspected as the killer, these self-anointed justice seekers would lose their minds.

Most would demand the land from Jonah.

Social media was more bad than good, in her opinion, yet here she was, scrolling, scrolling, reading people yelling at each other and making accusations they could not support. Her pulse rate revved just taking in the silent screaming. She didn't realize until she bit into a hot piece that Lenore had replaced her empty okra bowl with a fresh batch right out of the fryer.

She peered over at Lenore giggling behind the bar.

She smiled back, returning to her phone but deciding she'd read enough. Yeah, she needed to chat with Jonah. Maybe she'd suggest he get legal advice before he asked the district to sell back the first tract of land. Last thing they needed was a mob with torches marching through Sterling Banks' wrought-iron gate to coerce him into giving in.

She didn't like her little county behaving like this. She and most of those who lived in it enjoyed the lack of development and minimal traffic. Rush hour barely existed unless leaving Sterling Banks during picking season, church on Sunday, or the wrong road when a school let out. Even then nobody slowed more than five miles below the speed limit.

She bet the editor of the *Craven Chronicle* lamented the day he let Miss Birdie take the paper into social media. Right now with the noise in the group, there was no way one could announce a summer sale, a class at the community center, or a fundraiser at the Presbyterian Church. Who'd want to amidst all of this? Too much nasty being slung around.

Which begged the question why did Miss Birdie, the founder and administrator, let the group go wild and loose? She could halt things, or at least temporarily put a stop-gap measure into place until everyone cooled their heels, with the click of a key. While understandably she might not want to shut down such a powerful media tool, why hide and say nothing? Especially after running for school board. Even more so after beating the district in her lawsuit.

Miss Birdie hadn't typed a thing in a couple of weeks. She still posted weekly editorials in the print paper, however, so she remained alive and kicking.

With Iona reminding Quinn that Miss Birdie ran for school board, Miss Birdie just got added to her list of people to interview, too. Question was whether Quinn wanted to speak to Laney, Guy, or Fripp first.

Thinking about interviewing made her wonder why Ty had not gotten back to her about his aunt. Laney Underwood was a big exclamation mark in this, especially after her brazen admonition to Jonah yesterday. For the first time, Quinn wondered if Ty was choosing his work over his friendship in pushing off his promise to schedule Laney. Especially with events of late being awkward.

For the first time in a long while, she left Jackson Hole without a word to Lenore, who was too busy for more than a wave, and without Ty having come by.

She sat in the parking lot trying to decide her next course of action, though it didn't take Dick Tracy to tell she stalled. She needed legs on a plan. This flying by the seat of her pants would spin her in circles.

She'd see Jonah tonight for his update on probate.

Fripp was in Charleston, per Iona.

She preferred to give Ty the chance to connect her to his aunt rather than going around him, so she put Laney Underwood on the back burner, though she couldn't afford to for long.

That left Guy Cook. She looked up his number on the district's website and placed the call. Voicemail. With no explanation, she left her name and number and asked to meet. Then she called his commercial number from his ads, resulting in nothing other than the same message given to a secretary.

She'd also love to ask Ty how much he'd done on his case, but the onus was on him to contact her. She'd prefer to be better armed with facts beforehand. They were running parallel in their efforts, which wasn't necessarily bad. It was just something they'd never really done before, because they'd promised each other at thirteen years old, swinging in a hammock on the manor's sprawling porch, never to keep secrets.

She felt pretty certain they'd honored that promise, so far. Guess that left her with seeing Miss Birdie.

Chapter 15

EVERYONE KNEW where Miss Birdie Palmeter lived on the outskirts of Jacksonboro. The two-story clapboard house dated back eighty years and looked amazingly similar in style to Miss Abbott's and a few others, the ones that hadn't been torn down and replaced with brick and mortar, central air and built-in microwaves. Still single, the retired teacher owned a hundred acres, also coincidentally similar to Miss Abbott, except hers was a stone's throw from town limits.

Quinn soon turned onto the entry road to the property, and took the quarter mile drive to the homestead. She wondered who would get Miss Birdie's place when she was gone since she, like Miss Abbott, had become a spinster with no known hope of marriage.

She bet the district wouldn't dream of going after this place for a school, and surely they had better sense than to hope for it to burn to the ground. If that wasn't another lawsuit made in heaven, nothing was.

Quinn smiled at the vehicle in the dirt drive, a cream-colored 1989 F-150 that had belonged to Mr. Malachi Palmeter, the teacher's father. He'd babied that vehicle, and today, everyone recognized Birdie coming long before they could see her behind the wheel.

Miss Birdie was home. The first break Quinn had had that day.

With this visit being impromptu, Quinn hadn't planned a formal list of questions, but she had more organic knowledge of the woman than the others. She and the boys had been in her literature class, giving Quinn a foot in the door, especially if she recalled Quinn's ill-attempt at reciting Shakespeare.

Quinn rapped on the latched screen door, the entrance to the wraparound porch one had to cross to reach the front door. The house was maybe thirty-five hundred square feet top and bottom combined, a lot of house for a lone lady, and while painted white, could stand to use a fresh coat from the signs of natural wood showing through places. Eight weather-worn rockers rested in a line, four in both directions, once painted white. None looked particularly favored by the owner, leading Quinn to believe she didn't sit out there. A favored rocker had its tells.

Another older lady living alone. Like Quinn would be if she didn't make some decisions in her life, a life that the world was already dictating. Though she considered herself a take-charge person, Quinn eyed those rockers on a deeper level, not sure why here . . . not sure why now.

But she could be inhabiting one of those on her own back porch in thirty years while she watched others gather the pecans, take off for Christmas to head home to enjoy their children and grandchildren. Jule would be gone. Maybe even Lenore. The boys would have tired of Quinn's refusal to step into adulthood and moved on, leaving their childhood clubhouse behind them.

Footsteps echoed through the high-ceiling hall and drew Quinn to the present, embarrassed at her distraction.

Miss Birdie quizzically peered out, her afro tamed with a scarf across the front of her head and knotted at the nape. Very mod and seventies in style, and very apropos because these days the style had come back around. Miss Birdie, however, had never deviated from her look.

"Quinn Sterling?" She wore a caftan, nothing flashy in its browns and federal blues, which flowed when she hurried across the porch to let her guest in. "Gracious, girl, I haven't seen you in forever. Not since—" but there she stopped. It's where a lot of people stopped, because it meant they'd attended Graham's funeral. There hadn't been a larger funeral since.

"Come in, come in," she said, letting Quinn through then latching it behind them. She led them inside.

"How are you doing? In case you're wondering, I'm taking you to the back. Porch isn't very big, but I like it better." En route, she liberated two bottled Cokes out of the refrigerator. Quinn considered herself honored to share in what was probably a treasured stash with everyone drinking out of cans and liter bottles to save a dollar.

This side faced south toward a distant pond, woods encroaching most sides of it. No sunsets, no sunrises, and no winter winds reached this porch, with the woods stopping the brunt of summer sun. Someone thought twice before setting this house on its foundation. The hostess pointed to two chairs.

"Beatrice at the masquerade ball from *Much Ado About Nothing*," she said, sitting in a wicker rocker that creaked heavily, continuing another type of squeak when she began her motion.

Quinn stopped mid-sip from her Coke, swallowing the bubbly bite of the drink which made it hard to get a word out. "Oh my God, you remembered."

"*You may light on a husband that hath no beard,*" Miss Birdie recited, playing Leonato.

The words came to Quinn in a rush. "*What should I do with him? Dress him in my apparel and make him my waiting gentlewoman? He that hath a beard is more than a youth, and he that hath no beard is less than a man; and he that is more than a youth is not for me, and he that is less than a man, I am not for him. Therefore, I will even take sixpence in earnest of the bearherd, and lead his apes into hell.*"

Miss Birdie fell into the role, bobbling her brows. "*Well then, go you into hell?*"

"*No,*" Quinn said, adopting the humorous role like it was yesterday. "*But to the gate, and there will the devil meet me like an old cuckold with horns on his head, and say, 'Get you to heaven, Beatrice, get you to heaven; here's no place for you maids.' So deliver I up my apes and away to Saint Peter. For the heavens, he sows me where the bachelors sit, and there live we as merry as the day is long.*"

They stopped there, Miss Birdie's eyes twinkling, their smiles shared bright. "You made Tyson Jackson stand in as Leonato," she said, "which he agreed to do because he had to wear nothing but a cape and a big mask to hide his face." She warmly grinned. "Those Fridays were such fun for me. Always my favorite part of teaching."

"I still have our masks." Quinn coughed a little, the soliloquy having irritated her throat. "Never could throw them out."

Miss Birdie rolled her eyes. "I hope you kept that gorgeous cape. Someone went to a lot of trouble making that."

The soft chuckle carried Quinn to those days of practicing with Ty on her patio. The threat to put him in tights was real, and when he drew the line on leotards, she got Jule to sew the cape, taking it all the way to the floor. "Yes, I do have it," she said, picturing it in the back of her closet, velvet, braid, and all, protected in a dry cleaners bag. She'd kept the costume, fearful Ty might not see it as full of memories as she did.

No wonder Miss Birdie refused to give up her literature classes. Quinn remembered the Bard like that class was yesterday, and she bet dozens of other kids did as well.

"That character suited you," Miss Birdie said. "Beatrice was single and independent, the idea of giving herself to another felt like defeat."

Quinn laughed uneasy, recalling one of the next lines. *I had rather hear my dog bark at a crow than a man swear he loves me.*

Damn if her sixteen-year-old self hadn't predicted her adult self to a tee. And incredibly coincidental was Ty playing Leonato, a patient, protective, kind man with a strong sense of justice. Likeable and trustworthy.

"Karma must've brought you here," the teacher added.

"Ma'am?" Surely they weren't getting into matchmaking. That subject was taboo to every breathing soul in her life to include the guys everyone would have her hitched to.

"Guess there's no wrong with telling you about the special edition paper coming out tomorrow." Birdie gave a shrewd smile, proud. "Half the size of the regular paper, but I talked Wallace into doing it to notify everyone about Amy Abbott's funeral . . . and assorted other things that will feel old news by our normal Wednesday distribution."

Shakespeare flew out of Quinn's mind. She swallowed a cough. How much would be in that paper? "You want to connect the gazillion dots out there, I'm guessing. Might as well cover the district's business while you're at it since the paper will surely report how Miss Abbott died and the suspicious circumstances."

Feigning innocence, Birdie used her mouth as a shrug. "It's news. It's connected. Hard to pick and choose what to print now and what to save until Wednesday."

"Plus, it's what your Facebook group is ravenous about," Quinn added, clearing her throat. "Just how much are you saying?"

Birdie studied her. "Hold on." She went inside and soon came out with some cough drops, placing them on a rickety little table between them. "Still feeling that smoke, huh?"

"Yes, ma'am." Quinn gratefully accepted the help, unwrapping one before realizing Miss Birdie'd heardabout Quinn's brush with the fire.

"Now, on to what's in the paper." The teacher held up her fingers, starting with her thumb. "A long human interest piece on Amy Abbott, culminating with her death and funeral arrangements. That funeral home will be packed, let me tell you." She gave a soft wink. "Then there's the human interest piece on Jonah."

"Jonah?"

She tapped Quinn's knee with her fingertips. "Honey, he's so loved in the county, such an upright, principled man. He runs Sterling Banks, the Camelot of Craven County, and he's the jilted lover of the rich owner."

Halting the chair, Quinn almost choked on her own spit. "Jilted? What?"

Birdie snickered. "Messing with you on that last part . . . Beatrice."

God help her, Quinn remembered a sense of humor, but not this much spunk. Well, she *had* bucked the school district.

And she wasn't done. "Then there's the crime and corruption piece." Her voice deepened as if talking into a mic. "Sources close to the school district believe that without Miss Abbott's tract of land, there can be no new school. That quarter of a million dollar loss for the district leaves the public disturbed as to the identity of the person or persons responsible for destroying the farm house . . . with Miss Amy Abbott trapped inside."

"Damn," Quinn whispered. "You're going for the gold, aren't you?"

Birdie held up a different finger, indicating more to come. "And while we're on the topic of board members—"

"You just took a crazy leap there. Are you seriously blaming them in print?"

". . . while on the topic of school board, district records show that Iona Bakeman, the most recently elected of the board, has voted to give contracts to a business for which she is the primary owner."

Quinn melted in her chair. "Son of a bitch, Birdie." She stopped short of saying Iona was her client, though after today's conversation at Iona's place, Quinn could legitimately claim she wasn't any longer.

Iona was a naive woman in many respects, and Quinn suspected she had been taken under the Corps' wing for manipulation, but she'd hoped to research the matter quietly, more discreetly, mitigating some of Iona's screw up.

Fact was fact, though. Iona figured no harm done since her vote was not the deciding one. She saw the contract as Fripp's, claiming he coerced her vote, but people would see clear through that.

Miss Birdie was as good a reporter as she was a teacher.

"You want another Coke?" Birdie asked, standing.

Quinn nodded, regrouping about what to do here . . . her throat welcoming another drink. When Birdie returned, Quinn took a sip and sighed. The first nip of a fresh Coke just had that special snap.

"You follow every board meeting," Quinn said, not revealing she'd been playing catch-up trying to watch the same videos, too.

"I attend most of the meetings, and I scrutinize the recordings," she said. "The board never voted on that second tract of land. No record of pursuing it anywhere except for Jonah standing up each meeting to speak his mind. He put that botched up school business in the public's eye. Him and him alone." As if reaching into her memory, she paused, then recited, *"How far that little candle throws his means! So shines a good deed in a weary world."*

Quinn had no idea what she recited.

"Merchant of Venice," Birdie added, reading the blank look.

That did sound like Jonah. She had to remember to tell him.

Quinn stared past the woman's shoulder at a macrame plant hanger. Miss Birdie lived in the past in a lot of ways, while daring to embrace the present just enough. Quinn worried the woman hadn't thoroughly analyzed the repercussions that could occur mentioning these names, and wished she had waited a few days, a week or two. "I hope this doesn't hurt him, Birdie," she said. "He's awful close to me."

But Miss Birdie remained unfluffed. "That's something that doesn't need a newspaper headline, honey."

She was glad Miss Birdie hadn't chosen to write about *her.*

Birdie stared harder at her former student, no more humor in her eyes. "I also attend the county council meetings."

"Meaning?"

"Meaning the council has to approve where a school goes in this county," Birdie said.

Quinn didn't know that. Hadn't seen the need to know that. She didn't follow county council that often, except for here and there when something held potential to affect Sterling Banks. "Are you saying county council followed the school district's lead in approving a school on a piece of land that fell short of being able to get sufficient infrastructure and frontage?"

"Yes, ma'am, but more than that. There are other projects being discussed for that same highway. Tracts are being optioned for subdivision development not a mile south of there. Old folks die and their progeny don't want to stay or live here. Not everybody has a Sterling Banks legacy to maintain. But I sense a developer behind that school movement."

"How?"

Birdie did a mouth shrug. "Putting two and two together, girl. The county's getting development requests at the same time there's a fight over the school down the road."

"A school would make a subdivision investment more certain." Quinn thought she got it. "Are you seeing interest from outside the county?"

"Yes."

Pieces were coming together. "Someone might be pulling the strings of the school board, hoping that their grant, loan, and tax monies will help fund the infrastructure for subdivisions and commercial ventures down the road. Plus, the county would love to have those property taxes."

"There you go, girl."

Quinn couldn't help but see how close to home this could get. Growth happened everywhere, and transparent organized growth could be a plus, but it pissed her off that outsiders pushed the movement. Slip in, throw up houses without any thought to controlled development, then slip out to some other unsuspecting county, leaving harem scarem sprawl.

"Do we even need the school?" Quinn asked. "You know better than I about numbers, rankings, growth."

Birdie leaned forearms on her knees, hands clasped. "Nobody turns down money for education, but stop and think. You can justify a school just about anytime and anyplace you throw up houses."

Miss Birdie should've taught more than literature, but why weren't more people aware? Certainly other people attended council meetings. "Where are you getting your information?"

"The Palmeters are cousins to the Jacksons, Miss Sterling. You may have the longest lineage in Craven County, but we have the numbers. There's hardly an office in the county that doesn't have someone I'm kin to."

But that also applied to Laney Jackson Underwood, whose loyalties were highly questionable at the moment. Maybe catering to the *suits*. Manipulating Iona. Practically threatening Jonah.

"This why you came?" Birdie asked. "Cause of Jonah?"

Guess she did read minds like everyone thought she had in high school.

There wasn't just one reason, though. This situation had layers and levels. Quinn felt a battle coming, led by money. "I came because you are an expert on this school district, you run the Facebook group, and you're wired into everything. The sheriff would kill for such a resource."

"Honey, you have no idea," Birdie said under her breath. "I also submit Freedom of Information requests to both county and board. Come. Follow me." Birdie hopped up quicker than expected of her age, and Quinn followed her into what would be a formal dining room on the main floor. Papers lay in neat stacks, and those stacks in neat, compartmentalized subjects. A laptop sat at the head of the dining room table, and instead of china, a wide, seven-foot cabinet on the far wall held file boxes across the buffet and odds and end supplies and notebooks inside the glassed shelving atop it.

"Got so used to gathering and categorizing intelligence for my lawsuit, I continued doing so on the school district and the county council. I can tell you who's developing what in this county. What stores have requested licenses and which contractors asked for permits." Hands on hips, Birdie admired her accumulation of knowledge wealth. "The lawsuit is in file cabinets upstairs."

Birdie looked over, reached with a finger, and lifted Quinn's chin to shut her mouth.

"Jesus, Miss Birdie."

"It's what I do," she said, beaming. "My people feed me so much stuff I don't know what to do with it."

But Quinn saw danger, vulnerability, and the potential for Miss Birdie to wind up like Miss Abbott, even wondering why Birdie hadn't been threatened before.

"Yes, I have," Birdie said.

Quinn did a rerun of their conversation, trying to find the question to that answer.

The teacher continued the thought. "Been threatened."

Again with the mind-reading.

Birdie smiled as though acknowledging the ability. "But they don't dare come after me."

"Oh no, don't believe that—"

But Birdie shook her head in gentle disbelief, still smiling. "They don't want to fight me again. They give me a wide berth, little girl. Retaliation for EEO activity is a real thing. They can lose a lot more money if they come after me."

But it might not be the board. Birdie was too sure of herself for Quinn to argue, so she walked around the table, stopped and glanced up for permission to read the stacks. Birdie nodded her go-ahead.

Surveys, building plans, sewer designs, but what she wanted more was a name, or names, of the Charleston people. She struggled keeping them straight, the developers versus the contractors versus the subs, the latter whom Quinn was convinced would eventually include Fripp Bakeman. Lifting a page here and there, she recognized a half dozen pieces of property being optioned for development, three pieces within two miles of Sterling Banks, one of them within just one.

She saw contractors, big ones, but what wasn't here was the money behind them. This scheme felt orchestrated. Who funded this scheme? Those people, the money people, were the culprits, if one was so inclined to call them such. She bet none of these thousands of pages of data, justifications, and project forecasts would name the big dogs who sat in paneled studies the size of a small farmhouse, wielding their Scotches, designing projects they never had to drive by. The kind of people who didn't take no for an answer.

"I'm worried about you," was all Quinn could find to say.

The teacher grinned to herself, walked past Quinn with a squeeze to the arm, and left the dining room, a crooked finger telling her to follow. "Don't get worked up, Quinn. It's getting on toward supper time. Got some leftover pulled pork in the refrigerator unless you care for a breakfast supper."

"Breakfast supper sounds wonderful," Quinn answered, not wanting to leave until the stun wore off and she had a chance to ask any questions hung up in the overwhelming, understated realization of this woman's impact on the county. She could be considered serious opposition.

The kitchen was quaint and worn, the appliances at least two decades old, the curtains double that. Birdie apparently ate at a small table for two in the same room she cooked her meals. She pointed for Quinn to sit. Eggs and grits were a one-person creation and cooked pretty fast.

Two paperbacks were wedged in a napkin holder, one fiction and one, not surprisingly, Shakespeare. Coincidentally, *The Merchant of Venice*.

A skillet went on the stove and water in a pot, and Quinn soon waited with hot coffee in a mug with a peace sign on it. "Guy Cook seems to be the local alpha on the board," she said as the water started boiling for the grits.

"Guy Cook's name does float to the top, but while he's arrogant, he has no spine." Birdie seemed to think about the question harder. "Not really sure who the real top dog is." She held up a mixing spoon. *"The first thing we do, let's kill all the lawyers."*

Quinn laughed at Guy Cook's name triggering another quote. *"The Merchant of Venice?"*

A humorous scowl crossed Birdie's face. *"Henry VI."*

Quinn gave a sour expression. "Never could keep those king plays straight. Henry, Richard, George, William."

"No George, no William."

"Something else. Why aren't you reining in that Facebook group, Miss Birdie?" she said. "It's scary to read those folks becoming almost mob-like."

Bacon sizzled, and the grit water boiled, so Birdie spoke over her shoulder as supper commanded her attention. "Why control it? These people are waking up to what's happening under their noses."

Admirable in concept, but Birdie assumed too much. In her world, Quinn had dealt with the wealthy who wanted their way. Ronald Renault, the high-powered Charleston entrepreneur, continued to run free with Quinn holding no doubt he'd helped snuff out more than a couple lives, the family greed even costing him his own daughter . . . at Quinn's hand. That vendetta wouldn't fade until one of them left this world.

She lifted *The Merchant of Venice* and leafed through, not wanting to distract Miss Birdie from her meal prep. She'd told Birdie to watch herself and warned her of how rotten some people were. There wasn't anything left to do but stay here with her or invite her to Sterling Banks. "Aren't you concerned?" she asked one last time.

"Not a bit, girl." The plates went on the table.

Quinn sank two pats of butter into the steaming grits, worried as hell about what would happen after tomorrow's paper came out at dawn. Her next interview needed to be Laney Underwood, with or without Ty's permission, because no one else would. Nobody else would question Laney's ability to broker deals with her husband's real estate affiliations in the Holy City up the highway.

Chapter 16

AT ALMOST DUSK, Miss Birdie walked Quinn to her truck. "Watch yourself."

Quinn laughed once. "You're telling *me* that?" On second thought, she stopped stepping into the cab and turned to her old teacher. "You willing to say who Lincoln20 is?"

Miss Birdie stood, hand on the open door. "I have no idea. I don't think it's a housewife or some high school kid, and like you, people think I know everybody on that group. When I couldn't ID him, and since he wasn't doing anything worth banning him over, I quit trying to find out. These days I mostly watch."

"You haven't posted in ages," Quinn said.

The smirk went all the way to twinkle Birdie's eyes. "Well, haven't had to since Lincoln20. Not sure he's even local."

The poster's comment on the group, *I'm checking on it,* when mention was made of Quinn and Iona, however, gave him a more local feel.

"Remember what I told you in there?" Birdie nodded at the house, the porch light a gentle gold aura against the aged siding.

Quinn squinted. "You sure it isn't you?"

Birdie winked. "I'd pick a much better name."

He did sound rather male, but a middle school kid could adeptly hide identity on social media.

Miss Birdie reached out and hugged Quinn, who squeezed in return, meaning it. "Miss Amy was a good, good woman," Birdie said, stepping aside to let Quinn get behind the wheel. "You tread lightly, girl. I sure don't want to be writing in the *Craven Chronicle* about you getting hurt, or worse."

Quinn left, watching Miss Birdie in her rearview mirror wave goodbye, the layers of her caftan swirling around her legs in an afternoon breeze. At the road, out of sight of her old teacher, Quinn took a moment to send a group text to Ty and Jonah.

JACKET meeting in two hours. RSVP please.

She turned for home, but she hadn't gone a mile before she heard from Jonah. A half mile further, Ty answered. Nobody turned down one of those.

SHE ARRIVED AT the manor with enough time to quickly let Bogie out, feed him, then go to her desk. With a little fast forwarding, she replayed the latest school board video when Jonah spoke his mind and announced to the world he was in charge of the Abbott farm.

Damn that videographer. She wished he'd panned the room a few times to note the troublemakers and the guests, but alert he wasn't, or lazy he was, since he'd set his camera on a tripod, lens locked on the board and superintendent, and probably read his phone. One could barely make out the expressions on board members' faces, much less hear them distinctly. Then at the proper moment, he turned the camera and locked on the public participation microphone. There was one broad pan of the audience at the beginning, and another when the cameraman changed from the board to the public speakers. That was it. If she could slow that down . . .

But when she did, she only noted parents. The *suits* weren't there. Quinn caught no sign of Miss Birdie or Miss Abbott.

She looked at the mantle clock, just under a half hour left before she had to be at Windsor. Quickly, she flipped a month to the previous meeting and froze it. The board trustees sat like statues, like kids afraid to sit anywhere but the seat they'd sat in last time, and the time before that. The seating was most likely strategic to share discreet messages.

Heavens, the foolishness in these people, yet they probably thought nobody saw these things. They might not care. Once on the board they couldn't be ousted. There were no rules on taking someone down short of an election . . . or the governor removing someone for incredibly egregious behavior. In her searches Quinn had found no evidence of such action in the state for a dozen years. These people wielded incredible power for four years. Iona hadn't figured out how to use hers. Instead, she'd been used and still didn't understand the depth of that exploitation.

A fist banged on one set of the sliding glass doors, scaring her out of her skin. She rolled the chair back to see Jonah, cooler in hand, the white of his arm bandages almost shining in the dark. She held up a finger, ran to get her own cooler from the frig, as well as her keys, phone, and one last item she'd set on the kitchen counter, and she hustled to find him inside the open door.

"You left it unlocked," he said.

Good Lord, she had. Probably from walking Bogie. "Old habit," she said. She struggled adapting to Jonah's latest security demands.

She didn't bother with Bogie's leash this time, and when she spit a clipped whistle, the pup bounded over, thrilled to be invited.

Jonah locked up behind her. "Saw the light. Surprised you're not already at Windsor."

Nobody called it the tree, or the treehouse, or the clubhouse. The structure had more three-dimensional character than that.

Bogie took off, glancing to see which way his masters walked, coming around once he realized they headed toward the river. Jonah and Quinn's thirty-year-old friendship fell into place like the old days, to which she thanked the heavens. She related to it like she showered, with routine muscle-memory. Probably also why she resisted any other type of relationship with Jonah. With Ty, even. Change, maybe growth, if one could call it that, went against her grain.

Jonah took her hand, like they'd done regularly as children. Was she forever going to weigh who they were as adults by the way they behaved in their youth?

Sometimes she wondered how the mix would go if she found a guy who'd never heard of Sterling Banks, Windsor, or the trio's childhood. Would he be forever twisting in the wind, anxious to be let in, to share a piece of Quinn the two boys were so in tune with?

No, she couldn't see another guy having half a chance, and honestly, she preferred one of her guys. She preferred both, not for the love, which was undeniable, but for the loyalty. To choose one would be to deny the other. How was that to work without ruining whole bloody lot of them?

A bat swooped overhead, chasing mosquitoes. "You get payroll taken care of okay?" she asked. Jonah was still the foreman, and with it being Friday, his afternoon would've been busy. "Nobody got canned today, did they?" He usually ran that sort of thing by her, but she hadn't exactly been available.

"All paid, nobody fired," he said. He gave her hand a little squeeze when Windsor came into view in the beam of his flashlight, though they could find the way blind. When she didn't squeeze back, he gave it another go. She returned the gesture, not wanting him out of sorts, but tonight was not about dates, marriage talk, and scared expectations of the future as a couple.

That was much too hard to think about in light of everything else.

Bogie ran up to the wide tree trunk, sniffing, jerking once as some small creature brushed his nose. He squatted and peed once, then twice, too young to cock his leg yet but with enough instinct to mark his territory.

At a couple minutes short of nine Ty hadn't arrived, but he had the furthest to come. He probably brought something from Lenore's which meant a quick stop en route.

Jonah contributed to the cause through Jule. Quinn usually brought a bottle or a six-pack. Nobody partook of anything or entered Windsor until the three had arrived. Funny the little customs they'd accumulated.

One couldn't see into the pecans from Windsor, day or night, the five-acre tract of trees a natural hideaway bordered on the southeast side by the black-water Edisto River. The old oaks offered a vacuum from the outside, the acoustics changed by the thick, moss-laden, low hanging limbs. Jonah shut off the flashlight, saving the battery, and for a little while they listened to the sounds of bugs and the occasional reptile, and the water as it lazily slid around limbs and rocks, but he didn't let loose of her hand.

"Is this about Miss Abbott?" he finally asked.

"A lot of it, yeah," she said. "But let's wait for Ty."

"Ty," he repeated, and she wasn't sure how he meant that the way he said it. "Without question I love the guy," he tacked on.

"I know," though the impending *but* she didn't want to hear seemed imminent. "I'm going to interrupt you right there," she said. "It's not that I do not love you. It's that in committing to you, he's cut out."

"Inevitable, Quinn. Bigamy is illegal, last I heard."

No, no, not what she wanted, not what she meant. She had to make him realize how scared, hurt, mixed-up . . . damn, she couldn't find the right word, that she felt. Guess if she couldn't define it, how was Jonah supposed to?

"What if I'd chosen him?" she asked, jumping into this thing from a different angle before Ty arrived, because she damn sure couldn't once he did. "You'd be on the outside looking in. How would that make you feel?"

"Are you saying you care for him equal to me?"

"No, just answer the question."

He sucked in through his nose deep and long, then blew it out hard from his mouth. "It would be difficult." He said it shaking their conjoined hands for emphasis.

"Would you hang around?"

"None of us is going anywhere, Quinn, but he doesn't live on Sterling Banks."

Odd comment to make. "That doesn't give you points," she said.

"Didn't say it did."

They saw the headlights about the same time, and it seemed a good place to hush. This time Jonah released her hand. In respect for Ty? Flustered over the discussion? She couldn't tell, but welcomed the fact he did it instead of her.

Ty parked at the edge of the acreage and walked to them, his own flashlight leading his way. Bogie ran up, haltingly, then recognized a friend. "What's up?" Ty said, rubbing the dog's head. "We're getting started a bit late, aren't we?"

"It's Friday," Quinn said, heading toward the stairs. "We can sleep in tomorrow." Regardless what each brought to the meeting, they rarely left with empties.

He lifted his cloth bag. "Frankly, this is long overdue, if you ask me."

They were attempting to be normal, but the frivolity that usually accompanied them to these meetings seemed missing. Regardless, time to delve into the problems at hand and leave their personal issues at the roots of the tree.

THEY PULLED OUT the tablecloth-covered trunk, sliding it closer to their three seats to serve as a table. Quinn checked quickly to insure her old .22 remained inside before setting out the spread, pimento cheese sandwiches from Lenore and homemade granola bars, humus, and crackers from Jule. The two mothers usually took their contribution to these meetings as seriously as the group, but this last minute call meant they packed whatever was at hand. The trio topped things off with Jonah's wine, Ty's bourbon, and Quinn's beer.

Sitting in their respective chairs, the lone lightbulb lit and hanging over their heads, they poured their drinks of choice. Bogie draped himself across Jonah in the beanbag, the most comfortable lap. Since Quinn called the meeting, the guys waited for her to kick it off.

"I just came from Miss Birdie's place," she said, taking the two men by surprise.

"Whoa, that's a lot of history," Jonah said.

"I still have nightmares about tights," Ty said, busting them out in laughter.

Good, Quinn thought, because a lot of this conversation wasn't funny. "Why haven't you called me, Ty?"

"About . . .?" He waited for her to finish the statement.

"What the sheriff's office has uncovered about Miss Abbott."

"I cannot always tell you things, Q. Your uncle—"

Bullshit. "Ty, come on. My uncle expects you to tell me what you're doing, and you know it. He learned a long time ago he couldn't stop us from talking. If he had issues, he'd have made a point of it." She finished the last swallow of her first beer like the punctuation on a sentence.

A JACKET meeting meant no holds barred in terms of information. If you couldn't divulge, you refused to come, but not a one of them had ever exercised that rule.

"The investigation is young, and informing you is pure courtesy," he replied. "Come down off your damn high horse, Q."

Ty had always attempted to censure her, but always in fun, or in correcting a wrong assumption. This was something different.

Quinn softened her approach. "Okay, then tell me this. What are your marching orders from the sheriff? Are you to take this investigation seriously or give it a light polish and move on?"

Ty finished his bourbon. "He doesn't talk like that. He just assigned me the case. Deal with it."

She popped her second beer by feel, holding his eye. "Fine. Next topic. Are you going to set me up with your aunt? We held that conversation twice already. You promised."

"I gave you no deadline," he said. "Besides, I wanted to meet with her first." His stare held with hers. "And that isn't changing."

He wasn't budging. He wasn't playing nice, either. "Please don't tell her I want to talk with her, too."

"Not part of my investigation," he replied. "Not my business."

Well damn. Since when did he recuse himself like this?

Quinn had a bossy side, and she could ride it hard. These guys understood that and tossed it back at her on many occasion. She wouldn't know how to behave if they didn't. She needed checks; she could be chided without leaving marks. But they needed to feel free to talk, to release feelings, to criticize.

"Then don't be surprised if I make my own appointment with her," she said.

"Why should I feel surprised at anything you do?"

That question had too many meanings to choose from, most of them hurtful. She opened her cooler and placed two more beers on the trunk. "Don't let these get hot."

The adversarial nature of the young man she'd chased fictional criminals with in and out of the trees, who'd worn a cape for her in Miss Birdie's class, who'd popped a kid upside the head for badmouthing Quinn as a rich bitch in sixth grade, was rare. He could actually be the most mature one of the three, and he would normally cut off his hand before aiming a slur at her.

Jonah remained cautiously quiet, and coupled with the dark shadows, she couldn't read him.

"Heard from the school board?" she asked Jonah, for a switch up. The meaning was had Laney gotten in touch as she'd promised would happen.

But he shook his head, stroking the dog.

Tonight wasn't going anywhere. They couldn't function like this. The guys weren't even talking to each other much less over her in poking fun.

Their relationship felt like it had already made a permanent turn.

She tried tossing the talking stick to Ty again, nonconfrontationally. "Do you have any questions about the Abbott fire?" she asked.

"No, and if I think of any, I'll be in touch. Why did you call this meeting, Q? Miss Birdie, right? Something apparently happened there to call us together like this."

He'd tossed her a total change of subject. She caught it and took him on, updating them on Miss Birdie's involvement on Facebook, her newspaper column, and how she'd researched Jonah. Ty agreed to add her to his interview list, and Quinn suggested he show up wearing that cape, which cut through his ice and allotted a smile. She couldn't help but reach over and pat him on the leg.

"But the reason for this meeting is this: there's a special edition *Craven Chronicle* coming out tomorrow," she said. "I'm worried that paper will cause trouble for the board members and for Miss Birdie." She nodded toward Jonah. "Maybe for you."

She went over the details of what to expect in the morning. "The world will probably know you are the heir to that land after you broadcasted the news to those three board members," she said. "Wills are recorded, you know."

"It is what it is," he said.

She continued. "I've seen you on the newspaper's Facebook page. Reading it much of late?"

"Yes," he said. "A few months ago, I got on simply to let people know what a good thing Miss Abbott did. Then later I spoke up more when the board leaned on her to sell the second piece. There's one guy on there who spins anything and everything and can't stand for voices to quiet down. Keeps people absolutely nuts."

"Who's the guy?" Ty asked.

"Lincoln20," the two replied over each other.

"Who the hell is Lincoln20?"

Jonah shook his head.

"No one knows," Quinn said. "I tried to find him. Failed."

Ty pointed his paper cup at her. "How can Miss Birdie not know?"

"If you know what you're doing, you can hide your identity."

He turned to Jonah. "Have you had it out with him on that site? With anyone on the site?"

"He didn't—" Then Quinn stopped herself. She'd read Jonah's online remarks, but he was seated right there. He needed to speak for himself and to keep it from looking like he and she functioned as one.

Jonah's Facebook remarks weren't as caustic as others and nowhere near as frequent, but he'd made himself known protecting Miss Abbott. Nothing posted since her death, though.

He started explaining himself, touching upon his feelings about what happened. "I can't stop thinking that my public displays at those meetings put her in harm's way. Anyone would realize how little pressure it would take to kill someone her age." He sighed. "Feels so wrong for her to give me that land."

"Wait," Ty said. "She left that place to you?"

Quinn nodded instead of Jonah.

Ty shook his head and took a drink. "This just keeps getting better and better."

Quinn reached over to Jonah's awkward repose in his beanbag chair and rubbed Bogie, brushing across to Jonah's knee where she briefly rubbed in consolation. "Well, expect some of those yahoos to make demands of you, Mr. Samaritan, and if they don't like what you do or say, be cautious of them coming after you."

That they understood. Sterling Banks needed to be on high alert. Strangers had trespassed on the farm before. "I'll tell the workers," he said, with extra protection for Jule assumed. He reached across and tapped Quinn's calf, about the only part he could from his position in that bean bag with the dog on him. "You need to lock your doors, Princess."

She shot a glance at Ty at the use of her nickname. No reaction.

Then she reached in her windbreaker pocket and extracted the bag holding the tracker. "Different topic. Found this on my truck today."

Ty snatched it from her hand and pulled out his flashlight. "Tell me you know who."

"Per Iona, I was followed by her husband or one of his minion the other day, because he told her where and when we'd met, so I could assume him? But I'm not that quick to stop there."

"No," Ty said, shaking his head. "That would just be too simple, wouldn't it?"

She couldn't tell if he was irritated or not, but she sided on the former. He wasn't particularly cordial tonight.

Chapter 17

JONAH REACHED out, asking to see the tracker, and Ty reluctantly handed it over. Quinn nursed her beer, watching. The mild tension between the two guys was a strange creature to her, and she didn't want to feed it.

But when Jonah tried to hand it to Ty, Quinn reached over them, simply because it was hers to control. Jonah halted, uncertain who to give it to. Ty leaned further and took it, with a side-glance at Quinn. "Believe I'll hold onto this."

"It was on my truck. It is mine. I have not asked you to do anything with it, and you cannot connect it to an investigation to claim it as evidence."

The minute she spoke she felt childish. She wanted it, but not like that. They acted weird. She still needed Ty to dust it and check it for prints.

Ty conceded. "What the hell do you intend to do with it?"

"I'll leave it on Sterling Banks. Maybe hook it to one of the farm trucks so nobody follows me."

Jonah scowled. "And lead them here?"

She should've thought of that. She started thinking of options. "I don't want them to change their game and think they've been discovered." She could change vehicles . . . and the plan. "I'll put it on a farm truck I drive to routine places like the grocery store, maybe the sheriff's office. Show them that I'm unaware of the tracker, and keep them hooked."

Ty hadn't yet discounted the decision, weighing options.

"You." She pointed to him. "Would dissect the thing and therefore let them know someone's onto them." She held out her hand again. "My business, Ty. Not the sheriff's." He returned it. "If I go see someone relative to this case," she said, "I'll take a different vehicle. It's not like we don't have enough on the farm."

"I've got a better idea," Jonah said, shifting under the weight of Bogie who'd made himself quite relaxed across a lap the pup had no inclination of giving up soon. "We've always got a truck going out each week with a bulk pecan shipment. Attach it to the bottom of a container. Next one's headed to Savannah."

Ty nodded. "Those things have a limited range anyway. It would basically fall off the radar with nobody the wiser. They'd think it got dislodged and run over somewhere. It happens when those things are not installed well."

Quinn laughed, more for the relief and satisfaction of them thinking together, but she wasn't keen on the pecan shipment. She wanted to turn the device against them downstream in case this was affiliated with the board. As she told the guys, Fripp Bakeman might be the obvious instigator, but he wasn't by any means the only suspect.

"I'd still rather keep it, y'all. Sooner or later this bird dog could bring them to me, which is what I want."

Jonah's humor vanished. "So right now it's here on the farm? Where we live? We, Quinn. Not just you. Just get rid of it. Quit playing like you're bait."

Ty echoed agreement. They were ganging up on her. Sorta, kinda a good thing.

But leaving the tracker on Sterling Banks would tell them Quinn had found the device. The guys couldn't see that this tracker, this scheme, empowered her more than the other way around. She was less likely to stimulate actual contact with her surveyors if she left the tracker live and managed her movements. Her managing them instead of the other way around.

She emptied the wine bottle into Jonah's cup. "What if I had a better idea?"

They listened. Bogie released a snore.

"What if I took the truck to the shop? Say the engine's skipping, whatever. Let them keep it for a few days."

"It's Friday," Jonah said. "Nobody's open on the weekend."

"Open or not, surely Peyton would do it," she countered.

That garage took care of their farm vehicles, and the owner fancied himself the manager of the Sterling Banks fleet. He was older than Quinn's father, but they'd been friends, and he took a shine to continuing the tradition with the Sterling daughter.

The guys had to agree.

"Well, regardless, I'm having the rest of the farm's vehicles checked every day," Jonah said, his way of agreeing to disagree.

Quinn finished the last bite of a pimento cheese sandwich square. Lenore'd removed the crust and shaped her renowned recipe into hors d'oeuvres, making the bite-sized morsels more appealing than they already were. There weren't but two squares left out of the dozen they'd started with. She picked at the one in her hand. "This way if they put a tail on me, I'll spot it."

She attempted to play down their apprehension. They used to be about the adventure of things. They never used to avoid trouble. Instead they'd been more about digging up the cause of events, the solving of mysteries, and the fun side of being in the middle of a challenge.

Listen to her. They used to, they never did, they always had . . .

Suddenly, getting older saddened her. In the recesses of her mind, like the steady clicks and chimes of her great-grandmother's clock on her living room mantle, time slid by with stealthy feet and clear reminders she wasn't a child. Jule would discount Quinn's interpretation of *getting older*, but from the exchange sitting here in their childhood hideaway, Quinn couldn't stop trying to affix them permanently in their childhood ways.

Jonah wanted to move on . . . and marry her.

Ty wanted to move on . . . and let her.

She had spurned both, holding their adult decisions against them.

She saw it now. She was spoiled. How was she supposed to raise children if she couldn't quit being one? Honestly, she wasn't seeing herself as mother material. Maybe that was her problem.

"Are you drunk already?" Ty asked, kicking her shoe. They rarely left these meetings without being at least tipsy. Windsor was their safe zone to tie one on and act foolish or drown feelings. This time nobody was letting down their hair.

"Not anywhere near drunk," she said, popping to the present. The tracker had been talked to death. She'd keep it in the evidence bag and carry it around. Dust for prints next time she saw Ty alone and avoid another drawn out conversation. Besides, time to discuss a meatier issue.

"Your turn, Ty," she said. "What can you tell us?" He'd been pissy when he first arrived, and she hoped by this point he'd be mellower, and more revealing about his recent activities.

"Coroner says smoke inhalation with a resulting heart attack." He nudged Jonah. "Sorry, man."

There was the old friend she remembered.

"And I looked at the paperwork on that first land deal. Pretty routine," he said. "They just didn't do enough due diligence with the state and pulled the trigger too soon in the purchase. There are issues with ingress and egress, and something to do with parking. Makes them look pretty stupid, if you ask me."

Quinn concurred, but you'd think with Laney being married to a hot shot real estate agent in Charleston, and Guy being an attorney, even the shady type he was, the board would've covered the bases before handing over money.

"Jonah?" she asked, a different hunch rearing its head. "Did they try to buy all Miss Abbott's land from the start? Or maybe more acreage than they got only to settle on the thirty acres? Maybe they miscalculated something."

Ty raised both brows, appearing to grasp where Quinn was going.

"They did ask for all of it at first," Jonah said. "But if you look at a plat, there's somewhat of a natural divide between what they bought and what she kept. She gave them a simple rectangular piece that didn't infringe on her homeplace. She was close enough to see the school, but it wasn't right on top of her."

The purchased land did have neat structured dimensions, and as a seller, the shape maintained the integrity of the remaining homestead.

"Jonah, do you think they took what they could get, in the hope that they could get more later?"

Jonah spoke first. "They recognized the shortfall from the get-go, and figured they'd coerce the extra land from her once they sank their teeth into the thirty acres? Is that what you're saying?"

Quinn didn't like it either. "While there's probably no proof of any of that, it makes sense. It sure didn't take long for them to harass her and make you step forward. They just never saw you coming." She hated watching him hurt again. "The sons-of-bitches stepped up their game."

Jonah released a huge sigh. "There's a nasty bunch of people on that board."

Too late he darted a glance at Ty, realizing that remark meant Ty's aunt, too.

"You're assuming the board was behind the fire," Ty said, without emotion. "Like you said, no proof. We don't know who else might've approached her for the land, or who made a statement against the school . . . or for it. That Facebook group has a few nuts on it, and who says the arsonist is even in the group or on the board?" His voice had risen. "Most likely some low-life hired by some other low-life," he added with a final shot.

Quinn recognized the attempt to move the spotlight off his aunt. Just like Quinn might've taken up for her misguided uncle a time or two, blood was blood, as distasteful as it may be.

"Anyway," Ty began again, "as for the investigation of the fire, it was clearly arson. Cocktail thrown in the living room window."

"Don't take this wrong, but has my uncle tied your hands in any way?" Quinn asked. He would understand what she meant.

"Just said don't leave Craven County," he replied.

Of course there was a condition. "What if your leads take you elsewhere? You follow the evidence."

Not denying or endorsing, Ty picked out a piece of something from his teeth, the granola bar, maybe. "It's like if I find something, that's fine. If I don't find something, that's fine, too. Admittedly, he's not pushing very hard. I'm not telling y'all anything you haven't seen before."

Uncle Larry never pushed hard. But Ty would turn over rocks unless the sheriff pulled him off the scent, and he usually went the extra mile regardless what the sheriff's orders were. Limiting him to the county might have meaning.

"What about your aunt?" she asked, hoping he'd discuss her now.

His tone lowered. "What about her?"

Quinn tried to pick her words. "How well do you really know her? I mean, she's from your daddy's side."

His gaze cooled. "And what does that mean?"

"I'm not foreign to your family, just like you're not foreign to mine, Ty. With your daddy gone, do y'all keep up with her?" She paused. "If you want to interview her before I do, I get it. If you want to warn her, I get that, too, but I need to move forward. Birdie is about to raise a ruckus, and I really wish I'd spoken to Laney beforehand. She'll go on the defensive big time tomorrow." The unsaid being accidents may start happening, and if Laney had been more forthcoming before, she'd be less of a suspect.

Unexpectedly, Jonah came out of the chute. "She may be your aunt, but I'd never met her before these board meetings. Sorry, dude, but I don't trust her. She's had a threatening way about her since the first time I laid eyes on her."

Ty stiffened more, but Jonah hadn't said anything that wasn't on school board video.

"She's a politician, man," Jonah continued. "Trusting one of them means putting your life in slippery hands. Never heard you talk of her before. I mean, she's in your family tree, but you've never really spoken admirably about her, so just saying maybe she's not who you think."

Ty really clouded over. "I've never spoken about her because there never was a need."

"I know, I know," Jonah said. "But she warned that I'd best consider the offer. Clearly, I might add. That's got threat written all over it. I'm not

afraid of these people, but I'm responsible for Jule and Sterling Banks."
He pointed at Quinn. "And yes, her. That's my world sitting there."

Air left Quinn's lungs. Up to this moment she'd entered Windsor as
moderator, aiming to keep everyone on an even keel. At this moment she
couldn't think of the right thing to say.

God, Jonah had never been so openly candid about her.

Her heart drummed her ribs, part for Jonah and his sudden open
honesty, and part for Ty finally hearing the depth of Jonah's feelings.

Bogie woke, maybe at the tension. Jonah took the opportunity to
slide him off to stand. As the tallest, his head almost brushed the cross
member, and he reached up to hang the single bulb over a cup hook
they'd screwed into the wood to get it out of the way when needed. The
change cast a distorted shadow over the trunk table. Bogie leaped into the
warm bean bag, warily eying the silhouettes.

"Laney was the first person I spoke to when this started," Ty said.

"Wait. You said you had to talk to her before I did." Quinn wasn't
happy with what seemed a half-truth. "You've already interviewed her?"

"Yes, and I still have more to ask her, but she's my connection inside
the board, Q. Like Iona's yours."

His aunt was his CI? Laney was Ty's CI within the board? Even
better. Quinn gladly made the leap from talking feelings to talking school
board. "Somebody's dead here, Ty. Did she tell you she was going out to
the burned house? How does she feel toward Jonah? How is she reading
the others?"

Ty gave a quick glance at his other friend who'd remained standing,
his hands resting on the cross member overhead. "We still don't know the
board had a thing to do with that fire."

"No, no, no," Quinn said, setting down her third beer. "Wait a
minute. Three members, including Laney, challenged Jonah at the burned
house, and you think they're not involved? I cry bullshit there. You have a
CI amidst that board for a reason, my friend."

From his expression, Ty started to oppose her, but she wasn't through.
"After the board got involved, a barn was burned, threats made to Miss
Abbott, her house destroyed, and ultimately the woman killed. Come on,
Ty. You're a much better cop than that. Don't hide this case from me . . .
from us."

Jonah was letting Quinn go with the conversation. She was growing
irritated enough for the both of them, because surely Ty wasn't putting
blood before murder.

Ty gave her a try-to-understand expression, one that always irritated the crap out of Quinn. "She admitted they shouldn't have gone to Miss Abbott's place," he said. "*Bad optics*, she said. They didn't expect to see you guys out there, and she said she hoped nothing said was misconstrued." He peered up at Jonah. "And while she had to play the part, she also said Jonah might've been a little emotional."

Even in the muddled distortions of the light, Jonah's flat-lined expression read clear.

Quinn pulled out her recorder. "Then listen to this."

Ty didn't seem surprised at a recorder in her hands. Ty listened to Laney repeat her message to Jonah, steeled by the end. Whether disturbed at Laney, or at Quinn for catching him off base with the recording, or maybe even at Jonah for standing adversarial at him, Ty's natural gentleness was replaced with a hardened glower.

"This is my investigation, not yours," he said. "I'll be thorough. Hopefully you realize that. Accept my findings, my methods, or not." Then specifically to her, "You don't get to challenge me, Quinn, and I am not accountable to you."

Temper crawled through her, and she felt the heat bloom into her cheeks. "That's not how we work here, Ty. Y'all danced around that tracker talking about danger and finding a way to get some party off my tail to remove any jeopardy from Sterling Banks, but suddenly you want to flash your badge, claim authority, and renounce accountability to us? We've always been accountable to each other, and you know it. Jonah might be in danger, Ty!"

"Quinn as well," Jonah added. "The tracker on her truck, for instance."

"I know!" Ty said, that deep voice of his reverberating in the tight space as he rose.

"We share," she said, standing to face him, reaching for him. "We're a team."

"Oh, it's still *we*, is it?" He shrugged off her attempt, his shoulders absorbing so much of the limited space.

Hearing the almost identical words Jonah had used at her a few days ago, hearing the cynical, skeptical use of the word *we*, stunned her into silence. The investigation and their camaraderie had hit head on, and like a driver stumbling from a crash, she wasn't sure how to address the wreckage.

When she didn't reply, Ty pushed Jonah aside and left Windsor, slamming the screen door behind him.

"Ty!" she called, following.

Jonah ran past her to the door and down the steps. "Hey, man, don't leave like this."

Alone, Quinn listened for Ty to retort, change his mind, stop running away, but his steps became the crank of his car's engine.

Jonah returned to find Quinn inside at the treehouse window. From that position she couldn't see, but she could catch headlight reflection off the neighboring oaks. She could hear the car turn around, and she could tell when the tires hit the rutted path that led to her house and beyond. She could sense when he left the plantation.

Only when Jonah wrapped arms around her from behind did she realize she'd been holding her breath listening so hard.

"I can't lose the both of you," she said. "I can't lose either of you. How am I supposed to deal with this?"

His cheek against her red mane, he softly whispered, "The three of us cannot put our lives on hold forever, Quinn. We can always be friends, but I will not give you up for fear of hurting Ty." He turned her around. "I love you, and I'm darn sure you love me. We've been tangled in this union since we were babies, and it's scary to change how we were . . . but we grew up. We can change or we lose everything."

His words were valid. But this core of hers remained heavily laden with guilt about Ty.

Standing in the treehouse, rocking, she let Jonah comfort her. Reaching up, she crossed her arms over his, caring little he smelled of wine. Took her a moment to realize he was gently humming an old Creole song Jule brought with her to Sterling Banks.

Pauv' Piti' Mom'zelle Zizi. A very old bayou lullaby sung in French. The song was simple, but it held a haunting, soothing melody sung to her by her mother, then by Jule, and yes, even by Jonah when Jule ordered him to watch over Quinn as a toddler. She didn't learn what it meant for many years. *Poor little Miss Zizi. . . . she's as sad as can be in her little heart.*

Tonight the tune helped, and tonight the tune hurt, but most of all it validated she was heartsick and sad. Tapping an old place in her soul, she hummed it with him, swaying, and they took a long time to break apart to go home.

To her home.

And on the manor's patio, Jonah gave Jule a quick text saying, *I'll be back in the morning.*

Chapter 18

QUINN AWOKE LYING diagonal on the mattress, her head on Jonah's shoulder, Bogie wedged between the two of them atop the quilt, pinning them from their legs down. The purple shadows across her vanity table told her the sky hadn't yet met the sun.

Gently she nudged Bogie aside, forcing him to relocate so she could take up residence full-length against her partner. Jonah gave a shut-eye, drowsy grin, pulled her to him, and fell back into a coma. Unaccustomed to having someone in the big old house, she observed him, pretending what-ifs until her own lids got heavy, then repositioned herself so she wasn't laying on his arm still bandaged from the fire.

THE COMBINATION of Saturday, alcohol, and Jonah's visit should have kept her sleeping until nine at least, but Quinn awoke just after seven . . . with Ty on her mind. Right on the heels of Ty, she recalled the newspaper would be out. At that point, her brain engaged.

She looked over at Jonah and stalled worrying about the day's events just a while longer. Funny, having him here seemed to blur the edges of her worries.

Slinking out of bed, she donned her satin robe, a luxury she stole from her mother's closet. A closet that had never been cleared of either parents' clothes in a master bedroom that remained just as it was when they died. She still vacuumed and dusted, preserving it, replacing a lavender air freshener every month. She had this image of being able to show her kids that room, and retell the stories of who their grandparents might have been.

She didn't care how weird anybody thought that was either.

She stole downstairs, hit the on button for the coffee pot, and opened the refrigerator, deciding on eggs and bacon. Wasn't twenty minutes, with the bacon almost done, before Jonah slid in the kitchen barefoot, in jeans, going straight for the coffee pot, the puffiness around his eyes and the scruffy hair making him more cute than unkempt. Bogie loped down with him as if feeling the same.

"I see where your loyalties are," she said to the dog, putting the last of the bacon on paper towels on a plate. She pointed to the eggs still lying on a dishtowel, eggs from his mother's flock. "Scrambled or fried?"

"Not fried," he said, wincing.

"Doesn't mesh with last night's wine, huh?" She quickly cracked five eggs into a bowl and whisked them together with some feta thrown in. Again, from Jule's farmstead. In afterthought, the way Jonah looked, she pulled out bread for toast.

Jonah let Bogie out for a few moments, then came in, setting the alarm behind him. "Get used to doing that," he told her, and she nodded. He fed the dog then opened the refrigerator to do the same half and half thing with goat's milk that Quinn did. "Heard from Ty?"

She shook her head, not wanting to go there and attentive to the skillet instead. While she was pretty sure Ty, a senior officer in the small department, didn't have weekend duty, she didn't want to disturb him. He'd be at Lenore's diner or mulling over the fight, or both. Since she and Jonah had made their relationship as clear as they ever had last night, she figured he needed space.

She noticed her inherent use of the word *relationship*.

Jonah refilled her cup on the counter, returned the pot, and came back to lean against the counter, pretending to watch her cook.

"Are eggs that interesting?" she asked.

"You're that interesting," he replied.

"Jesus, you sound like one of those mawkish Hallmark romances," she said, scooping the eggs on two plates.

"One of us needs to." Smoothly, he kissed her on the cheek and took his plate to the small table in the bay window of the kitchen.

He was loving this.

She joined him with her matching coffee, matching breakfast, neither one having brought their phones with them. Nobody put a napkin in their lap. So damn much like an old married couple.

They didn't speak for the first few bites. She caught herself watching him eat. He could do this couple thing with his eyes shut. Maybe Jonah was right. Hell, Jule had practically said the same thing to her the other evening. They'd grown up. Some time ago, actually. "You have trouble shutting off, Princess."

And . . . he could read her. He'd always been able to read her, but then, so could Ty. Just on a different level and about other things.

"In spite of how it started, I enjoyed last night," she said, in a left-handed apology. She wasn't good at apologies.

He patted her on a bare knee that had come out of her robe under the table. "Me, too."

But he left his hand there. It traveled along her thigh, slowly working its way north.

She put down her fork, shut her eyes and let him. "You are so bad, Jonah Proveaux."

"No," he said under his breath, teasing and tickling her skin in little circle motions. "I'm very good, Princess."

In a serpentine move, he silently slid his chair closer. She turned and drew his mouth to hers, his hand still out of sight.

The eggs grew cold.

An earsplitting klaxon noise of the alarm jerked them apart. His hand caught in her robe before pulling loose, then he bumped the edge of the table, tilting his chair as he tried to balance.

But she was up, robe offset and half tied, and against the wall peering around the door frame into the living room before Jonah could stand. She held a snub-nosed .38 in both hands, listening.

Jonah set his chair upright and scooted to stand with her.

"Quinn?" shouted Jule, attempting to be heard over the ruckus. "Jonah?"

Jonah ran out, reaching the nearest alarm box, punched in the code, and shut off the noise. "I'll take the security call when it comes in," he said.

"With what phone?" said his mother, with only a quick note of his bare feet and ungroomed appearance. "I've been trying to call y'all. So has Ty. He called me to find you."

Wordless, Jonah patted his pockets, coming up empty for the phone, and turned to run up the stairs.

"Here." Jule tossed him a tote bag. "Change your clothes."

Quinn let an embarrassed Jonah enjoy his escape from his mother's witness of the obvious.

Jule did a motion thing with her finger, and Quinn realized how much of herself was exposed. Red-faced, she set the weapon down on an end table, rewrapped the robe and cinched it tight. "Is it an emergency?" Quinn asked, eager to change the unsaid subject. She replaced the .38 in its place atop the high kitchen shelf, strategically where she'd imagined needing it if ever caught off guard while cooking or washing dishes. She had four other such places in the house.

"*The Craven Chronicle* put out a surprise special edition today," Jule said, not having known beforehand. "I haven't seen it. Always wait to pick one up when I go to town, but Ty said you needed to know. People are flustered. He said to find you two and tell you to be careful." Then like a mother, she sternly asked, "What does he mean, young lady?"

She had every right to know if trouble was coming, especially if it was coming to Sterling Banks. She'd been injured when Graham was murdered, everyone amazed she hadn't been killed. That's when Jonah gave up his upstate career and returned to Sterling Banks fulltime. That's when Quinn had done the same.

A few months ago, too, in the name of getting to Quinn, Jule had been targeted and a goat slaughtered to scare her. Jonah adored Jule to pieces, and both of them continued to have concerns about Quinn's PI "hobby."

"Um, you know how Jonah helped Miss Abbott?" Quinn started. "Well, the school is apparently still pushing for her land."

"What?" Then Jule thought. "Which means now they are pushing Jonah for her land."

"Yes, ma'am."

Jonah appeared down the stairs with shoes, socks and a better shirt on, his hair quickly combed and both phones in his hands. He raised his. "I've got five calls and texts, and you've got, I don't know, ten?" He passed it over to Quinn.

While they scrolled, Jule moseyed into the kitchen, poured herself the remnants of the coffee, and started washing dishes. Quinn scanned messages from Ty, Iona, and even Uncle Larry. In over a half dozen attempts, Ty wanted to insure they were okay, but after reading the article, also wanted to talk to Quinn about Birdie, Iona, and maybe even Fripp. Whoever she'd talked to, he wanted to as well, with the inside scoop from Quinn beforehand.

"You should've hung around last night instead of running off mad," she uttered, still perturbed that he'd stormed out before they could hammer out their business.

Jonah moved over to read her screen, having just finished reading and listening to his.

She listened to another panic-filled message from Iona. She was worried what the board would do to her, what Fripp would do, what Birdie thought, what Jonah thought. She would lose her business and her daughter would be harassed at school. The list went on and on.

However, Quinn put Uncle Larry's voicemail to her ear. No telling what he'd say or how he'd say it. "What has that fool Birdie woman done now?" he said. "Did you put her up to this?" He paused a second, a throaty growl still heard like an echo. "Pick up this damn phone, niece. If this is some lame-brained strategy of yours . . . Call me. And I mean now."

That was the last one. She slid the phone in her pocket. "I was afraid of this. They're losing their minds."

Jonah returned to his caretaker self. "It's Saturday. Who says we have to do anything? I'll slip out and get a paper and come right back."

While Quinn was itching to jump into the fray, the smart move might be to sit and see how the fracas played out and ultimately settled. The paper was out and the damage done. "Sure, good idea. Let the two factions raise the hell, chew the fat, whatever. Meanwhile we'll spend the day here. If there's something Jule needs us to do with the goats, or a quadrant of trees needs anything, we can do it and stay out of the way. I'll text everyone that matters that we're fine and home. Iona can wait."

Jonah's cocked up grin showed his approval, and he seemed rather enthused playing the quasi-hero venturing into the pandemic of idiocy to get a paper.

Honestly, they didn't have to be out and about. Though Quinn had a gnawing inclination to interview Laney Underwood on the heels of Miss Birdie's exposé, Laney likely fielded other calls right and left, if not circling the wagons of the board.

Ty would be jumping from person to person, no longer off duty. He'd be trying to see Laney, Birdie, and the rest of the board. At least Quinn would if she were in his shoes, and they thought incredibly alike when it came to cases.

"Jule, stay with Quinn while I'm gone, if you don't mind," Jonah said, pulling keys from his pocket, and he was gone.

Peering over at Jule leaning on the kitchen doorframe, Quinn grinned. "He's rather cute when he thinks he's in charge, isn't he?"

Jule winked. "One of his most endearing qualities, I think."

Both returned to the kitchen, Quinn wolfing down the remnants of her breakfast then assisting in the final cleanup. When she pondered what to wear, envisioning a day of kick-back laziness instead of the work load she'd told Jonah, she almost decided to leave on what she had, let Jule return home, and entice Jonah to return to the business they'd started before the alarm went off.

"I'm headed up to change clothes," she finally said.

"Take your time. Might want to shower," Jule replied.

"You're something else," Quinn said, heading up the stairs.

"Y'all think I'm old and blind."

Quinn paused on the landing. "No, ma'am. Not in the least."

Right there, in that moment, Quinn felt that if Jonah were here, and he got down on a knee, she'd possibly say yes. She loved him. She loved his mother as her own, because she in essence was. She loved this lifestyle, and the fact they felt this house already home. What was there not to feel right about?

Other than Ty.

She ran the shower hot, afterwards drying and braiding her hair wet and tight, the fastest way to deal with it not wanting to leave Jule alone for long. In her softest jeans, a hole in one knee, and a tee shirt from a Neil Diamond concert, she came down in her Keds sneakers, sans socks.

Jule had the sliding doors open, standing in the gentle air. The late morning temperature measured a comfortable eighty degrees per the thermometer on a post, a slight breeze snaking its way from the river. Jule handed Quinn a glass, and the two women took iced tea to the patio and assumed their places in two iron rockers.

"So what prompted the JACKET meeting?" Jule asked. She understood the importance of those events.

Quinn shrugged. "You know. The whole land thing with the board. I also spent a few hours with Miss Birdie yesterday once I learned this paper thing was happening. You remember her, right?"

Jule paused the glass at her lips before giving a laugh. "Craven County's claim to fame for a long while. Never met her though. I think I'd like her."

Turning in surprise, Quinn looked down at the tiny woman. "Jonah took her English class. Surely you had to help him with a costume like you did Ty."

Jule did a light wave with one hand. "I remember, and I tried with the costume, but he isn't nearly as flamboyant as you and Ty. Best I could do was—"

"A crown." Quinn laughed. "I remember now."

"And he was mortified at wearing that."

They laughed together again, then reverted to rocking.

A pair of squirrels raced up and down two pecans, a third nearby chattering a scolding. There had to be a nest up there somewhere. "This is nice," she said.

"It is. Now, how are things with you three?"

Jule had a cagy way about her tucked inside that short, overall-clad body.

"Well, Jonah and I seem to be better."

Jule smiled with a soft chuckle at the obvious. "And Ty?"

"Let's just say when he's good, I'm not, and vice versa. It's hard, Jule. It's damn hard. He's my mud-pie and freeze-tag buddy. He gets my PI work. He yanks me in line when I'm out of hand." Then she thought about that. "Guess both of them do that."

Jule *hmphed* in agreement.

"But I'd never do this with Ty," she said, nodding back at the house.

To that, Jule raised a brow as loud as any request for explanation.

"That didn't come out right, did it?"

Jule stared at her, no longer rocking either. "No, it sure didn't."

Quinn sighed, highly uncomfortable in this metaphorical corner. She hadn't meant to say that. Hadn't realized she'd thought it, but there it was.

"I don't want to start comparing the two, I guess is the best way to put it," she finally said. "Those two men are the best friends I could ever have, and I do not want to lose either one. Please tell me you understand that."

"Of course. Anyone who knows you sees that."

Quinn wasn't sure where to go from there, because what was next in her mind was proving quite difficult to say. "It's not like I can date Ty and eliminate my 'what ifs.' If I crossed the line with Ty . . . if I started seeing them both as not just pals . . . if, damn it. Damn it to hell, Jule! I don't want to compare them as men. Catch my drift?"

Her momma-figure returned to rocking, the two of them with their braids hanging down, one gray, the other red. The simple shift in repose told Quinn that Jule got it, or most of it. Quinn had slept with Jonah, but not Ty. She'd said it. Jule heard it. So why did she feel the need to explain further?

"I don't want Ty to feel he's not special, or he's less of a friend, or that he's not as appealing." She blew out hard. "Son of a bitch, you can't say this without it sounding wrong."

"Like I said the other night, baby, you three grew up together as close as anyone can be. This predicament was inevitable. Do you not remember that Ty got married when you went off to college? Did that upset you?"

Actually, it had kinda bothered her, but she was off to be a federal agent, and Jonah was off running that big commercial farm. Ty thought he'd found a soul mate. "We were scattered then," she said. "Striking out, seeking our futures."

"Please tell me that's not your way of saying you were out of sight so you were out of mind? You saying he settled for second place?"

Well, that sounded rather harsh. "No. We were each doing our thing." Then she could not help herself. "He did divorce her after I came home."

Jule stopped and slapped her on the knee . . . hard. "There's a small part of your problem. You're too damn full of yourself."

"Ouch." Quinn rubbed the spot, the pain more in her heart than her thigh.

"Do you love Jonah?" Jule asked.

Quinn stilled, surprised at how easily she could answer that question. "Yes, I do."

"There you go."

Wait. Where was the follow up question? The one where she was asked if she loved Ty?

"The fact you slept with one and avoid sleeping with the other says a lot, honey."

That felt like a summation, and it had taken what Quinn thought as complicated and had simplified the hell out it. They relaxed in their chairs, but Quinn hadn't thought of things that . . . defined. She couldn't say Jonah was easier to sleep with. In no way did that sound right, though from a certain angle it did.

Maybe she was overthinking this on purpose, for fear of hurting Ty and avoiding the inevitable pain.

She watched sideways at the older woman. Jule rocked, all wise-looking. Quinn could not imagine being half as good a mother. Jule thought of others first. Quinn wasn't sure she had enough of that ability in her to be a wife, to raise a family. While she could love Jonah, she wasn't sure about the rest of the responsibilities that came with wife . . . and mother.

They heard the truck come up the drive, then the chime as Jonah entered the house.

"Got it," he said, holding up the paper. "Got several so we could each have one." He slid one of the other chairs over and passed out the newspapers. For a solid ten minutes the only sound came from flipping pages.

Quinn was amazed at the depth of this *special edition*. Miss Birdie had some serious insight, some serious sources, and what some might interpret as a serious motive to get even with the school district.

Jule broke the silence. "I hope Birdie lays low for a while. I'm surprised the editor went along with this."

"That editor is drooling," Jonah said. "I'm getting a tea. Y'all want a refill?"

Quinn handed him her glass, but Jule shook her head. "Thanks, son, but I got work to do. Think I'll go on home." She stood and headed through the pecans, but a few steps out she turned around. "Let me know if you leave the farm so I don't worry. And I promise I won't bother you again." She went home.

Jonah remained standing, watching where his mom had been. "That wasn't the least bit awkward."

Quinn pretended a scowl at him. "And you left me here alone with her."

"Sorry, but you could handle that better than I could. Be right back." He headed to the kitchen.

Eager to take in the paper, Quinn's apprehension grew as she reread the various features. Miss Abbott, Jonah, the fire, the school fiasco, Iona voting for contracts for herself . . . the other board members letting her. But the worst part was the byline, over and over. Written by Birdie Palmeter. Quinn had thought the article would simply be a reporting piece. The paper rarely ran a byline on anything. But this . . . .

Everyone knew her. Everyone knew where she lived. A feeling in the pit of Quinn's stomach told her to give the woman a call to hunker down. No, come out to Sterling Banks. Nobody would expect to see her here. She regretted the last time she did that with a victim. She hoped she wouldn't again.

"Jonah?" she called, rising from the chair, dialing her old English teacher. "We've got a mission."

The call to Miss Birdie went to voicemail.

"What?" he said, meeting her in the living room.

Quinn tried again. This time she left a voicemail. "Miss Birdie? This is Quinn. Sit tight. I believe we need to come get you for your own safety. No argument, you hear?" She hung up.

Jonah had heard and headed for his keys.

Then she remembered the tracker. No time to drop by the mechanic's place. No need to leave it here with Jule being left alone on the farm, so she put it in her pocket. She'd plant it on a stop sign along the way. Maybe retrieve it on the way home.

Miss Birdie not answering was a concern. Hopefully she was coping with curious friends . . . not those affected by her eloquent words about fraud, waste, and abuse that of Craven County would be well aware of now.

As Jonah pulled away from the manor, Quinn opened into the Craven Living Facebook group. She gawked, scrolled, her mouth falling open. "Oh my God, Jonah, get to Miss Birdie's, fast. These people are insane."

Everyone hated the board now. Some challenged Birdie while some labeled her a savior. Many said she should've been elected to the board instead of Iona, because none of this would've happened.

But nobody realized what Quinn believed, like Miss Birdie had explained, that there might be a stronger power behind the curtain, and a shrewd culprit would take advantage of turmoil like this.

A financier with any semblance of self-assurance would want to take out any sort of heroine trying to, metaphorically, rise out of the ashes.

Chapter 19

JONAH IGNORED THE speed limit, and at the first four-way stop, Quinn jumped out and slipped the tracker into the recessed portion of the metal pole, snagging it in the screw holding on the sign. Inside, Quinn tried calling Birdie three more times between flipping in and out of the Facebook page.

"But is *she* on there?" Jonah asked once Quinn had read him several caustic posts.

"She was early this morning. She announced the paper and went silent. Her last post was four hours ago."

"Not sure if that's good or not." He turned toward Jacksonboro, rolling through a T stop.

"But gracious, there are so many responses from other people I can't keep up." Quinn's eyes glued to the words, her fingers working the tiny screen.

Some wanted the entire school board impeached and replaced. Some wanted them in jail for egregious sins from fraud to embezzlement to murder. Others wanted financial restitution from board members' own pockets for their spendthrift ways.

Suggestions were made to ban any businesses friendly with existing board members, or owned by the members. The nastier posters had already found company Facebook pages and openly blasted names, telling the public to ban those businesses.

Others, however, wanted this school built come hell or high water. With so much invested already, the only right choice in their mind was for Jonah to donate the Abbott property to the school district. Since he had plenty of money, and since the land was handed to him, nothing lost. One said he only assisted Miss Abbott to get into her good graces and steal the acreage. One idiot asked if he could've killed her with that fire once he realized the old lady put him in her will.

Lincoln20 played devil's advocate. And still, not a damn soul on the group questioned yet who he might be.

"I need you to be careful, Jonah," Quinn said, laying the phone down a moment. "You're mentioned too many times in here."

He glanced over with a gentle grin, but when he saw her expression, he lost it. "Any threats?"

"Not directly, but there's some strong innuendo. I'm texting Jule to stay home and keep the doors locked. The security system is hooked to your phone, right?"

He frowned, doing double-takes over at her. "That serious?"

"Could be."

She texted Jule the message and got a thumbs up. Jule wasn't one to argue, ever one to err on the side of caution. She'd seen her own share of nasty in her lifetime.

Quinn kept scrolling, afraid to miss anything. A couple of participants shouted in caps that this behavior was unwarranted, to which she could agree, but she wasn't typing a damn word to this mob. They wanted the Craven County Sheriff's Office to stand guard. Stand guard where? For fear of what? About the time she thought it, answers rolled in. At the board members' businesses, also their homes. The newspaper office, the school district office, but when Quinn read one suggestion, cold water flooded her veins.

This damn reporter needs to pay for misleading us. It isn't like this.

Then the retort. *This reporter needs a Pulitzer for bringing crimes into the light.*

The two went back and forth over the merits of Miss Birdie, an online cat fight between two women Quinn had hugged at church, one a teacher, two women who wouldn't dream of talking like this in public. Good Lord.

Miss Birdie's dawn comment had mentioned the special edition of the *Craven Chronicle* with no ledes or one-liners, just the fact they'd released a Saturday edition. She probably could've said nothing, because enough people had noticed it to start taking screen shots to post photos of the articles. The paper hadn't put anything online yet, probably with the intention of selling more papers. A bit low-tech, but the paper had little income.

But Wallace, the editor, expected a windfall with this opportunity and had sold an exorbitant amount of advertising to give the paper its normal bulk since there were no town hall announcements, marriages, sports, or obituaries, except for Miss Abbott's on the front page. Ironically, the ads included most of the current board members.

Guy Cook's mantra, *Don't cry, call Guy,* shouted big and bold on page two, the same page where they'd continued the story about how the plans for the school were screwed up. Piper Pierce had three ads, for each of her biggest Jacksonboro enterprises. Harmon Valentine's company offered deals on term life insurance on page four. Iona had even paid for a small boxed ad on the last page bragging about her bookkeeping prowess and her two openings for clients. Quinn thought Iona would've wanted to keep her head down. Fripp's construction company posted a double ad on the same page as Iona's.

Ella Mae was a stay-at-home mom and Curtis Fuller retired Air Force, with nothing to promote, but conspicuously absent in the advertising was anything from Laney Underwood's husband, the big shot real estate agent. He'd advertised locally many times, partly to attract business but mostly to show some sort of allegiance to the town and county they lived in.

Also noticeably absent was Sterling Farms.

"Did you get something from the paper about advertising us in here?" she asked her foreman.

"I did," he said. "It's off season. I saw no need."

She blew out. "So glad you didn't. Everybody else and his brother has advertised in this thing . . . now probably wishing they hadn't."

The absence of an advertisement from Laney's spouse stood out. Either she was concerned what this paper might contain, or she was smarter than the rest. For the umpteenth time, she was the party Quinn wanted a one-on-one with ASAP, and the longer events dragged out, the more she wanted that talk.

"Uh oh," Jonah said, peering in his rearview. They weren't a mile from Birdie's.

Quinn twisted around. A blue light came up on their tail, a siren keeping it company. She'd paid no attention to Jonah's driving. "You do something?"

"A little over the limit." Jonah spent as much time eyeing his mirror as the road ahead. "Unless they are in need of a quota—damn, he's coming on awful fast."

She studied the cruiser, trying to identify who was driving like a bat out of hell. Then he wandered into the other side of the road, passed, and sped on, LEDs on fire.

"That was Harrison," she said. "He didn't even wave."

She couldn't help but think of what she'd read on Facebook, and the potential of so many of those threats and challenges. While the odds were they were armchair threats, she read enough bullying for someone to possibly have acted on their warning.

Hold these people accountable, was the last remark Lincoln20 had said. What if he was one to stand by his remark?

Quinn wasn't one for coincidences. "Hurry, Jonah. I'm worried about her."

They reached the turn off the highway, and Quinn realized they'd delayed too long. "Quick, pull up, but don't get boxed in." She had a grip on the door handle, her seatbelt off. Jonah hadn't come to a complete park before she bailed and ran toward the lights, hunting for Ty. Smoke choked the air.

That old cream-colored, antique pickup truck stood burning, a path of scorched ground leading to Birdie's porch, the front door blackened. A gasoline trail.

Several SO cruisers and a fire engine filled Miss Birdie's front yard. The fire barely breathed anymore, the old truck sitting in the middle of a dead black circle, it's body crusted dark, paint gone except for the left fender of the bed. The heat had shattered truck windows and melted half the screen on the front porch, the nandina bushes on either side of the steps just black sticks.

"Miss Birdie?" Quinn called, darting around the damage and the first responders, hunting and finding no sign of her. Someone tried to grab her arm, and she jerked them off. Then someone must have reminded them who she was, because nobody did it again.

She tried to soothe herself with no sign of an ambulance, but that didn't mean it hadn't come and gone.

Déjà vu Miss Abbott.

Her heart leaped into her throat. "Miss Birdie?" she shouted, standing in front of the steps, peering through the damaged screen.

Jonah came up, Ty at his side. "Quinn."

"Where's Birdie?" she asked. She kicked and kicked herself for not forecasting this could occur. If the school confrontation had turned on Miss Abbott, why not as much or more for the English teacher?

"Jesus," she said under her breath, hand up over her mouth. "I had the tracker on me when I visited her yesterday."

Ty shook his head. "No, Q. This happened today, after the paper went out. If your tracker had instigated anything, don't you think they'd have done something in the middle of the night?"

"Not if they wanted to let the paper take the blame. Not if they wanted to distance themselves from connection to the tracker. Not if— Where is she?"

"She's at the hospital," Jonah said. "They don't think it's life threatening."

"But it's intentional," said Ty.

Quinn waited for the rest.

"They set fire to the truck, with gas poured for flames to follow to the porch. Miss Birdie called 911 and came out with pitchers of water to dowse her porch while she was still on the line. Dispatch heard her yell."

"Yell?"

"Yeah." He motioned to the steps. "Look there, on the side."

When she couldn't see, he turned her and made her look down his arm to where a trip wire had been attached to one of the nandinas and run across to the other side of the stairs.

"She wet down the porch first, then headed out to stop the trail leading from the truck. She fell over the wire," he said. ""Broke an arm. She was also scuffed up and injured from sprawling into the burning grass. At least she fell into some of the spilled water."

This crime appeared more targeted and open than Miss Abbott, but the duplicity in which these two women were attacked rocked Quinn to her core. This wasn't petty, small town, tit-for-tat crap. Hot letters to the editor were one thing. Attempted murder was quite another.

She was stunned. She should be numb to death and violence by now, but this was happening on home soil, amidst people she'd known as far back as she could remember. A theory awoke inside her, telling her that this wasn't anywhere near as straightforward as everyone imagined, but she'd be hard pressed convincing anyone of her gut feeling

Another deputy came over, showing Ty his phone. "Get a load of this."

Everyone followed the Facebook group now. Quinn hit the app icon, then hit the home part. "Holy bejesus," she said, glancing up at the guys. "Yesterday it had two thousand people, a huge number for these parts. Today it has five? Is every other person in the county on this damn group?"

Jonah pointed over and moved her screen to show her what had their attention. "Guy Cook is resigning from the school board."

"Wait, so is Piper Pierce," she said.

Jonah lowered his hand to his waist. "They're bailing."

"A day late, I'd say."

Lincoln20 and a dozen or so other vocal citizens had taken full grip of the group and had directed the flow, choosing who to denounce, and berating anyone who thought otherwise, and the resignations were proof of their power.

"I've got to think," Quinn said, moving from the fire hose, the cops, the half dozen first responders finding themselves gazing at Facebook when they had half a chance, listening to their partners explain the latest when they couldn't.

Ty and Jonah followed her, no longer out of sorts with each other.

"Someone's hiding behind this," she said, letting herself settle on the truck bumper. Iona had smelled something wrong, something she wasn't privy to. Her husband Fripp hinted of great financial reward to come, which he hadn't elaborated on in detail, not that he even knew, but which Iona interpreted as jobs associated with the school. Birdie had noted those numerous permits and options.

The mysterious two *suits* intrigued her a lot.

"Someone drives this mess from outside Craven." She motioned with her phone. "For the two most powerful members of the board to step aside says they are outgunned, outmaneuvered, scared, and over their heads." She peered up at Ty. "Where's Laney in all of this?" And to Jonah, "Any of the other board members stepping down?" She couldn't study everything.

Her buddies could share the tasks. This was and wasn't local, but the parts that were local were important, too. The three of them would have insight into these personalities and how this county worked, and they had enough connections to the powers-that-be. If they couldn't cipher through the smoke and mirrors, nobody could, and if they didn't, if Craven County didn't police its own problem, there was the risk of other authorities coming in and taking over.

Hate crimes, right-wing terrorism . . . the first mention of these causes, and SLED would be on site if not the FBI.

For a change, Quinn agreed with her uncle that Craven must try and solve its own problem first.

"Haven't talked to Laney in two days," Ty said.

"If she resigns, that's one message," Quinn said. "If she doesn't, that's something entirely different. We must talk to her. Now. Before someone else gets to her."

Ty's hard gaze on Quinn showed he understood.

"I mean in any way, shape, or form," she clarified, with getting to her financially being as much in the mix as anything else. "Can you call her? I mean this moment."

If he refused, she'd go without him. He moved off, searching for a number, and she returned to the online activity.

Comments entered the conversation like a hard rain. She found it even more difficult to keep up. "Jonah?"

"I see it," he said. "She isn't helping, is she?"

Miss Birdie felt better because she posted from her hospital room. Short phrases and abbreviations, probably much to her chagrin being an English teacher. She mentioned a guard at her door. She thanked the community for their support, explaining she only tried to report facts, and she wasn't taking a hard stand on one side or the other. Sure, she was a career educator, and she'd had problems with the district, she explained. But she was also a taxpayer, and she wanted whatever educational tools taxpayers paid for to be not just useful, not just needed, but also economically sound. Perfectly middle of the road.

In pure seconds, the thumbs up replies mounted. She'd been injured for shedding light on an issue without passing judgment. Most understood. Few didn't. Quinn worried about the silent ones . . . and the new arrivals. "Gracious," she whispered. "Six thousand followers. It's not even Twitter!"

Now Lincoln20 spoke as if he were Birdie's best friend, Miss Abbott's ally, and a comrade to all in the name of education.

Ty came back. "Aunt Laney will see you."

"When?" she asked.

"Whenever you can get there," he replied. "She's nervous. And Harmon Valentine just resigned from the board, she said. That's three down of the seven."

Quinn headed for the truck, Jonah on her heels, but when she opened the door and peered back, Ty remained behind, watching them leave. "You coming?" she called, assuming the trio was together again.

He shook his head. She told Jonah to get in, before running to Ty. "We need your expertise, buddy."

"I'm senior on this scene, Quinn. Gotta do my job."

She couldn't stand the gloom hanging on him. "It's Q," she corrected. "My name will always be Q to you, Ty. You and you only. Nobody fills your shoes. Absolutely nobody. We might change but we don't disconnect. You hear?" She kissed his cheek, waiting for his response. He motioned for her to go on.

She hopped in the passenger side, but twisted, watching the deputy as Jonah drove away. If she didn't have an interview to do and likely some sons of bitches to chase, she'd go home and down half a bottle of bourbon to chase away the sadness in those eyes.

Chapter 20

ALL THE WAY TO the Underwood residence Quinn watched her side mirror for a tail.

She'd never been in the Underwood home, but she'd heard Laney and Sealy lived high versus the grand majority of Craven County, thanks to his lucrative real estate activity. Laney was the younger sister of Ty's daddy who'd died when Ty wasn't quite driver's license age. Laney was a Jackson, a family as old as the Sterlings, and like Miss Birdie stated, a prolific genealogy. The Palmeters and the Frasers perched far and wide on the cousin branches of the Jackson tree, extending the reach into probably a tenth of the county's people.

Laney had always considered herself somewhat of a queen bee, with one foot in the common population having taught eighth grade for thirty years, the other in a more affluent side of society to match her lifestyle. Unlike her fruitful clan, however, she had no children of her own, so after a couple of years of retirement, she politically returned to education. As Iona explained, Laney enjoyed the attention, the power, and the control, and when Miss Birdie ran for the board, Laney had assisted Guy and Piper in recruiting Iona to seize control of the campaign's dialogue. Quinn bet Iona still hadn't figured out what hit her. Nor had she realized Laney wasn't necessarily an Iona fan . . . just anti-Birdie.

Per the advertising in Charleston and across the Lowcountry counties, Sealy Underwood had carved a huge name for himself. What started as a novice plan of selling quantity versus quality via boxy government subsidized housing to rural lower income, had smartly grown into elite luxury homes planted on country acreage. Still with an emphasis on rural, he now specialized in million dollar estates . . . like the twenty-acre one Jonah pulled up to now.

The Underwoods held no desire to hide the heights to which they'd climbed, the white stucco, fifty-five hundred square foot two-story sprawler impressive at the end of the long drive beside a four-car garage. The land was cleared a hundred yards on either side up to heavily mixed hardwood and pine forests, in a parallel corridor affair. The landscaped asphalt drive seemed to aim at the wealth. No apology, no humility, just a statement that Sealy and Laney worked hard to reach their pinnacle.

A lot of the Underwoods and Jacksons cried foul at Laney and Sealy's fortune. Most of the homes sold during Sealy's beginnings were to them, and after he'd sold them the land, house, and insurance of every type to cover each and every possible need, he climbed up and over them to Charleston, Dorchester, Colleton, and even Georgetown Counties. He was good at what he did, and people on both sides of a ledger sheet recognized it, whether they liked it or not.

Jonah took the straightaway drive to the sprawled estate faster than manners usually permitted. Quinn sought signs of life—cars, gardener, garage door up. She hoped the trip wasn't for naught.

A housekeeper met Jonah and Quinn at the door. She wasn't much younger than Laney and had lived in the county her whole life. "Hey, Ms. Fraser."

"Hello, Ms. Sterling."

Too formal. Quinn almost corrected her to use her first name, but she wasn't quite sure whether doing so would be a compliment or a censure. With her employer likely nearby, Quinn let salutations go.

They stepped onto tan, marbled floors, beige walls going up forever, and thirty feet further, geometric rugs and three different colored elongated sofas of chocolate, gray, and beige awaited visitors. They looked little used, unless recently vacuumed to run the nap in one direction.

Columns took up space where supporting walls would be, giving the place a cavernous feel. A decorator had splashed drapes and pillows with turquoise to keep the design from looking too sepia, but the color fell short of dispelling the showroom feel.

"I'll take them from here, Hanna," Laney said to who surely had to be a cousin relation from the Fraser name.

The housekeeper disappeared as ordered, her footsteps eerily silent.

The lady of the manor lacked luster, which fit in with the atmosphere. She was minimally though tastefully dressed in black yoga tights and a flowing, floral top that hid the ills of middle-age. Leather flats. Tiny diamond studs, the understated kind.

But dress could not hide the worry sculpted in her forehead, deepening her crow's feet, and rutting the sides of her mouth. Whether due to lighting or reality, her hair seemed dreary in spite of the coifed waves and tint job meant to downplay her age. Stress had caught up to Laney Jackson Underwood, at least compared to her older board appearances.

She hadn't said a word to them yet, unlike her reputation of taking charge.

"Ty called you, right?" Quinn asked. She didn't care if their drop-in was inconvenient or not. The urgency mattered more.

Laney nodded and held out a welcoming hand to the congregation of sofas. She held up another, holding it in the air, and shortly after, low key music sounded through a speaker system so embedded in the décor Quinn couldn't find it. Ms. Fraser must be watching. The music was probably turned on to prevent their voices carrying to the help. One couldn't hear about the county's latest calamity and gossip from under *this* roof.

The *Craven Chronicle* lay on the mahogany coffee table, obviously worked from the way the pages no longer fit evenly. Quinn got to the point. "Anyone threaten you yet, Ms. Underwood?" The woman was her elder, so Quinn addressed the woman accordingly.

Her phone on the table, Laney did a hesitant point at it, as if it were infected. The device had vibrated on the table several times since Quinn and Jonah arrived, and had gone unanswered. "Just that Facebook business, but people are doing Internet stuff, too."

"Stuff?"

"Sealy understands more than I do, but folks are leaving comments on Google, Yelp, and I forget the other ones he mentioned." Laney was holding a staunch façade, her discomfort not nearly as noticeable in her dark complexion as it would flash in Quinn's freckled, ginger countenance. She seemed to be fighting hard to show control.

Nobody asked if they wanted anything to drink, but Ms. Fraser showed with a tray and left.

"Take the phone, Hanna," Laney said, and the housekeeper tucked it in her apron pocket. "Where is your husband?" Jonah asked, peering around, having waited for Hanna to get out of earshot.

"Working," she said. "He's always working, and with what's happening, he's beginning to feel the crunch thanks to this board thing."

Today's Facebook activity may have instigated brush fires for him, but that shouldn't mar his reputation, not as influential and far-spread as he was. Folks in counties outside of Craven shouldn't give a damn about their neighbor's school board misbehavior, much less connect it to Sealy Underwood. Facebook and online reviews, however, cared little about geography, and today's activity might be chinking his armor.

Quinn feigned ignorance. "I would think he's rather removed from that, Ms. Underwood."

Suddenly there was so much to say reflecting from that woman's face. "Call me Laney, please. But tell me . . . why are you here instead of Ty?"

"I was hired by someone close to the board to look into this." Quinn wasn't about to elaborate on the who or the original why of her involvement because it wasn't her place to do so. But even if Laney was aware, the situation had grown bigger than Iona. Quinn's PI involvement had stretched to a broader, more meaningful purpose since Miss Abbott's murder and the attempt on Miss Birdie. This was home garbage, and she called herself taking it to the curb, insuring it didn't pile up like this again, so it didn't fester and rot.

Quinn could walk away and do nothing, too, but someone today or tomorrow would call her callous and uncaring for not getting involved. Of course when she got involved they called her arrogant.

There was a certain responsibility that came with having been born into a family that helped establish a community, and while residents didn't want you in their business, they likewise expected you to make the village better by using the clout the good Lord gave you.

Like in the school auditorium, when Guy Cook called upon the police. When the crowd couldn't believe how they were being bullied . . . when those sitting near Quinn turned to her and asked her to step up and do something about the unraveling of things.

And she had taken the mic and cleared the room.

"The school is the first step of something bigger," Quinn said. "And you aren't the first person I've met with."

Jonah listened in tight observance while also with a wider study of the house. Quinn had caught him watching the doors, the windows, the wide, marble stairs to the other floor. His guard was up.

Quinn had explained to him about Miss Birdie's snooping into county council business, and her sense of someone bigger sliding into their area, but that was it. He'd listened intently and was just as worried about these details. He was personally invested, he said, thanks to Miss Abbott, but Quinn sensed his current purpose being of a bigger, more protective stance. Bless him for remaining quiet and alert.

Still, she wished Ty also had come. "You've been confiding in Ty for a few months, I hear," Quinn said. "He stands by you, Laney, but today, when I asked him to come along, he declined. That was his way of saying there's a lot you're not saying, I believe. Like he felt you'd talk better if not in front of him."

"Or say things he didn't want to hear," Jonah added.

"Ty's a sweet boy." Laney glanced briefly at Jonah who didn't shy from her focus. "We always wondered if Quinn and Ty would tie the knot one day as close as they are."

A distraction, possibly. A shot at Jonah, but Jonah didn't take the bait, with only the slightest twitch of a brow. Confident now that she didn't have to worry about Jonah, Quinn recognized Laney had side-stepped the question about her confiding in Ty.

Then out of what most people saw as a rude habit, Quinn pulled out her phone. Jonah frowned a little. "Jule says she's good on the farm," she lied, as she hit record and returned the phone, face down, to the sofa cushion beside her. Jonah glanced at his own phone, then tucked it away, unaware.

"I went to Ty when the first track was purchased from Amy Abbott," Laney said. "What started as a simple plan to build an elementary school, one of the easiest schools you can build, turned into something rather complex before even I saw it. I told Ty I would play along." She tilted her head toward Jonah. "My remark to you on Miss Abbott's place was for Guy and Piper's sake. I had to be careful."

Quinn started to interrupt, because there seemed a big gap in time between buying the first tract and threatening Jonah on the grounds of the second, but when someone being interviewed yearned to spill, you heard them through.

"Guy assured us that the engineers confirmed feasibility of the thirty acres," Laney said. "Since none of us understood the technicality of construction, surveys, and design, we took him for his word. He's the chair. It's what he does. We approve so many contracts without understanding the specifications, like all boards do. You pay the right experts to make the right decisions then just vote. Either the chair or the superintendent sign off."

Typical political thought process.

"What about the two men from Charleston who attended dressed in business casual, who you and Guy took out afterwards?" Quinn asked, before they got too far past that point in the timeline. The *suits* were there for the original land purchase vote.

"Developers," she said. "Or at least high level admin types for the developers. Their primary job focus is to keep their ears to the ground listening for school growth across the state. When rumblings start about the need for new schools, they make their appearance. They'd been speaking with Preston, the superintendent, and Guy for the last year. I didn't see anything wrong with the process after speaking with my husband. He explained the logistics of how communities thrive, with a lot of that progress having to do with schools. Most people have no idea how the concept of schools, subdivisions, shopping centers, and medical facilities come together."

No, they didn't. Quinn hadn't pondered the process much herself until lately, but in the same second she admitted that, she recognized the myriad of opportunity for criminal behavior.

"Names, so we don't have to call them *suits*?" she asked.

"Anthony Chase and Marvin Mauney," she said without blinking.

"You remember them like they made an impression."

"They knew Sealy," Laney said. "Or rather, they met him before me. When they attended the meeting, they asked Guy to dinner afterwards and told him to bring me. I refused, at first."

As Quinn thought, Laney wasn't accustomed to being told what to do.

"But Mr. Chase told me to confirm with Sealy."

Quinn could read the loathing in the retelling of the evening, and she guessed the suits' next move before Laney explained.

"Sealy called me before I could get to my car," Laney said. "He told me to go with them. Told me to listen to their proposition. Told me not to decline before coming home to speak to him." She paused. "We voted for the first tract at the next meeting."

In other words, Sealy Underwood had promised them his wife's vote. Laney just couldn't say it.

As for the other board members, Piper Pierce didn't go to the dinner with the *suits*, because she probably voted in lockstep with Guy. Laney confirmed Quinn's suspicion on that. Ella Mae Dewberry routinely did what Guy told her to do, loving the reputation of the winning side. Iona went along with whatever Laney said, obligated to her for the campaign win; plus, there wasn't enough substance in Iona to fight solo too terribly hard for very long about anything. Maybe part of why she'd hired Quinn . . . to help her break those shackles.

Iona hadn't had an original thought, or vote, since elected, and Quinn saw that now. She was chosen to be a tool.

"Was it your idea to elect Iona Bakeman or Guy's?" Quinn asked.

Laney had lost some of her starch, but she spoke plainly, retaining some dignity. Maybe that was why she hadn't resigned. If suits held a grip on Sealy, did Laney even have that option?

"Fripp's idea," she said.

"He doesn't seem powerful enough to sway Guy Cook, Laney."

"Because the idea wasn't Fripp's in origin."

Piece by piece, Quinn's suspicions meshed with Laney's accounting. Chase or Mauney, or their subordinate assignee, had convinced Fripp that in order to acquire serious contracts on the new school, Fripp had to convince his wife to run to assure no surprises in board voting. Those men had experience with boards and their frequent unexpected and illogical moves. Who better than your spouse to convince you that you're intelligent and charismatic enough to run for office and win? Then for Laney to offer to take Iona under her wing, well, how could Iona say no? The simple plan sure shined Laney in a poor light.

After patiently listening, Jonah asked, "What did they have on Guy?"

Laney gave a lady-like shrug. "Not my place to ask."

Jonah laughed with an edge. "It was especially your place to ask."

But Laney shook her head. "Might open the door to him asking what they had on me. We were afraid to discuss the causes, promises, threats, and projections. A lot of unsaid going unsaid. I didn't even try to question Piper. If you knew her—"

"We know her well enough," Quinn replied. Piper was the eldest board member, and Quinn remembered her father talking about how the lady only lived for turning another dollar. Growth would mean more opportunity for more business in her existing and future stores. She wasn't related to a county name, and her children had relocated to the four corners of the United States, which maybe said something about her family skills. Her reputation survived through her storefronts where a silhouetted sandpiper served as her logo, keeping in line with the Lowcountry flavor. One could easily guess that she might be bought for the right price.

But Piper had resigned the board just a couple hours ago.

And Guy had resigned just minutes before her.

Quinn turned to Jonah. "Can you check Facebook to see if Ella Mae Dewberry has resigned from the board yet?"

He started scrolling.

Quinn didn't need to ask if Iona had resigned. Iona would wait for instructions from Laney. Or Quinn herself.

"Yes. Ella Mae resigned about ten minutes ago," he said, for a minute unable to quit scrolling. "Jesus, these people are roaring." Then realizing now was not the moment, he put the phone away.

The pieces were coming together so ridiculously clean per what had to be Birdie's plan that Quinn almost heard them click.

"Those three lost their nerve," Laney said.

Scoffing, Quinn did a half grin. "Looks to me these are the three who found it. You, on the other hand, have no intention of leaving."

To which Laney didn't respond.

"You've probably already received your phone call this morning," Quinn said. "You've already been told to assume your place behind the reins, and you'll control things until the three empty seats can be filled."

"That will take a vote," she said.

Jonah let loose a sarcastic laugh. "Give me a break, Laney. Not only will you run the board, but you'll assist the three newcomers in their runs in the special election. Trick is, which way will the wind blow after you take charge."

Laney didn't deny, didn't act ashamed, didn't seem to be anything but middle-of-the-road resigned to do just what they accused her of.

"Well, how about this?" Jonah rose, in a short huff, and strode to the large glass picture windows facing the pool and manicured courtyard. Hands on his hips, he seemed caught up in the view, his question left hanging unanswered.

"Jonah?" Quinn prodded.

Without looking at her, he held up a finger. He needed a second.

She had no idea where he was headed in what appeared frustration, and Laney seemed perfectly willing to wait for him to sort it out. He'd inadvertently become the troublesome squeaky wheel of a scheme much bigger than anyone saw coming. A scheme that would've matured before anyone could do anything about it. A school thrown up, the infrastructure paid for with grant and tax dollars so that developers could use water, sewer, road upgrades, and the traffic to build subdivisions along the routes of school buses. Modern homes, upscale living. An influx of teachers. An influx of families wanting to leave the city. High school graduates possibly deciding to remain in Craven instead of fleeing to a more urban life. Then would come the gas stations, the grocery stores, and so on.

The results sounded so pretty on the surface until prices rose beyond the average family's budget, and the roads and sewer couldn't handle the growth. The original schemers, however, would've long collected their profits and moved on to another county.

Quinn had seen it happen before. Exploding growth controlled by opportunists from outside the area. Bluffton, West Columbia, Rock Hill, Mount Pleasant, even places once deemed as country as Jacksonboro. Places like Chapin and Newberry.

"Laney," Quinn finally said when Jonah seemed to need more time. "Who's behind all of this?"

"Above my pay grade," she said. "You'd have to ask Sealy, and even then, I'm not certain even he knows for sure. Way more money and clout than we have."

That was saying a lot, assuming it was true. "But Sealy can offer an informed guess."

Laney softly nodded.

Quinn could recite a few of those names. "Someone who travels mighty high in his real estate circles?"

Laney didn't react.

Jonah swung around to face them. "Tell you what."

"What?" Quinn replied, knowing Laney wouldn't play the game.

"What if I ran for school board?" he said. Then to Laney, added, "And what if I also ran for board chair?"

Laney tried to rein the shock in her eyes, reaching over to the refreshment tray, pouring coffee into a cup and drinking it cold.

Chapter 21

JONAH STOOD in front of the broad plate glass window at Laney Underwood's, in the stale silence of the estate, and made his announcement about running for school board without accolade, just a guy wanting to do the right thing by an old lady he befriended. Honoring a promise to take care of Miss Abbott's business for her, Jonah wasn't going to let her death be for naught.

Quinn could not be a damn bit prouder of this man.

But pride quickly slid into worry about whether he'd wind up in somebody's crosshairs like Miss Abbott, or Miss Birdie. Or pressured like Laney, Guy, Harmon, and Piper. They weren't exactly lightweights.

With this land adjoining Sterling Banks, Quinn understood Jonah well enough to see that on a secondary level he protected the farm's interest. She wasn't sure he realized the depth of what he might be taking on out of some sweet sense of loyalty.

Laney didn't have her phone on her, but somewhere in the house, a phone kept echoing, going to voicemail. After a while, it would ring once and stop, someone apparently clicking the *can't come to the phone right now* or answering on her behalf. The phone had been carried into the deeper recesses of the house, too, because Quinn could barely hear it now.

Just how long would Laney be able to ignore the public, the press, and the power players?

"Who does that leave on the board?" Quinn asked, trying to consider where to go from here. Was a school dead in the water thanks to board members bailing? Or would they regroup and find another piece of land? Or would someone start playing dirtier? "Who do you think *won't* resign before the day's over?" That answer would help Quinn better define the board's direction.

Laney tilted her head with a hint of a shrug. "Iona and Curtis Fuller."

"Iona will follow your lead," Quinn said.

Laney didn't argue.

"I know nothing about Curtis Fuller," Quinn continued. "I mean, I know who he is, but he hasn't said or done much."

"He votes against the majority," Jonah said. "Sometimes the only one. He was the the lone vote against buying the original tract."

Laney focused again on her cold coffee.

Quinn noticed. "What's your take on him, Laney?"

"Can't win but stands on principle."

Being anti-school from the start, was this direction to his liking?

If a man, retired military at that, wasn't happy with the status quo, how far would he go to turn the tide? How far would he go standing on principle?

"What about you?" Jonah asked.

"I'm not resigning," Laney said, in an upper crust pout.

"Why not?" Quinn asked.

Laney gave pause. Even Jonah seemed perplexed.

"While Facebook isn't my choice of entertainment," Quinn said. "Nor source of credible news, it can give you the pulse of a community at a point in time. Have you seen the numbers on that Craven Living page? Have you seen how many times your name is mentioned in vain alongside the others? As I tried explaining to my client, the board acts as a whole in the public's eye."

"I'm not giving social media the benefit of my attention," Laney replied.

"Be naïve if you want, but social media is a core part of any politician's existence," Quinn said. "Those people have the power to take you down. Go ahead and be blindsided. They've apparently taken out four of your board thus far. Jonah, what's that group's membership up to now?"

He flipped into his phone. "Damn. It's up to seven thousand."

Quinn pointed to Jonah's hand. "Laney, that's a lot of people caught up in the future of Craven County, and whether or not you believe it, your future, too."

"Not falling for it." She put the cup down too hard and rose. "There are bigger people who have no time for Facebook and way more power, thank you very much. *They* control my future more. I believe I'll take my chances with those with greater influence. Now, please leave."

Quinn hadn't expected hugs and friendship from this meeting, but had at least hoped for collaboration. Laney was an integral part of Craven with a voice that could make a difference. Acknowledging errors in how the board had performed, making amends for how things fell out, could go far in keeping her a viable player. And Quinn had hoped not to alienate the woman for the sake of Ty and Lenore.

It seemed that saving face, however, was first and foremost in Laney's vision.

Quinn kept trying. "You went to Ty asking for help. I am part of that help. I'm fully aware of Charleston influence. You recall what the grapevine said about me as a result of my own such run-in. You have to choose between Craven County or Charleston, Laney. I'd hate to be in your shoes, for sure, but which side can you live with?" Then she asked the more pointed question. "What do they have over you?"

"Besides pressure on Sealy," Jonah added, and Quinn expected that to be some mighty strong pressure

Laney paced to the massive windows, and Jonah gave her the space and returned to the sofa. Musical chairs. "I was sent a photo of my sister's children in front of the elementary school," she replied.

Yep, quite the game changer. The Underwoods didn't need money and probably had no skeletons in their closets, even as many and spacious as those closets were. And since they had no children, someone went to the next best family . . . nieces and nephews.

"I told Sealy this had a bad feel to it from the start," she continued, "but after the photo, we hushed and went along. Every county can use a school and residential upgrading. He explained that the average person wasn't wise enough to see how rural development worked anyway. The ignorant would hurt the plans." She turned to Jonah rather than Quinn, as if he'd already become a like-mind by running for the board. "You cannot tell the people everything we do, Jonah. Nothing would ever get approved." She pointed to the phone in his hand. "Especially with Facebook and such."

Jonah listened without condemnation, making sure she was done. "You may not give them a choice in who coaches the basketball team or builds the senior class parking lot, Laney, but you do not insult them by excluding them from the big plans and major choices that affect their lives and wallets."

Laney rolled her eyes. "But the Birdie Palmeters of this world would ruin everything."

"It wouldn't take much to approach her, offer the pros and cons, and solicit her support," he said. "The Birdie Palmeters have the power to support you as well as oppose."

Quinn looked sadly at the woman. "So do people like me." She waved at Jonah. "Like him. You've got to quit playing to the elite, Laney. Those thousands on Facebook are not wealthy people. They want their kids educated, their property protected, and their feelings appreciated.

They feel lied to right now. Their votes matter."

Crossing her arms, Laney gave them her back. Quinn and Jonah glanced at each other, uncertain how long to wait . . . whether or not to leave.

"Guy kept saying the plans were for the children," Laney finally said. "We have a lot riding on this *for the children*. I assumed he meant the county, the board, the taxpayer. Now I wonder about what *we* he meant."

"*We* possibly being the outsiders," Quinn said.

Laney nodded. "You'd have to ask Guy for certain, but good luck with that. After Miss Abbott, he started losing his nerve. Jonah," and she nodded toward him, "messed with Guy's head out there on the property. He wanted to see the fire damage, just not go by himself, which is why he dragged Piper and me. I'd told him off the record way before this that we needed to give up on the Abbott land, but he said no. We had too much invested. So I went to Ty, told him about the photo, Guy's strange behavior, and Sealy's concerns. He said to keep a low profile, listen, and report to him."

A low blues tune drifted from the hidden speakers.

"Might be time for an emergency board meeting," Jonah said.

Laney shook her head. "We just lost four of seven."

"Those resignations have to be accepted," Jonah said. "A Facebook resignation isn't legit."

Quinn had a different take. "Ella Mae will feel left out in the cold and might be looking for another mentor, Laney. Wait and see how the day plays out. A lot of this is knee-jerk behavior."

Ms. Fraser came in, a cell phone in her hand. "Ms. Underwood? Mr. Underwood asks to speak with you. He told me to interrupt immediately."

With a sigh, Laney reached out to take the phone but didn't put it to her ear until she was out of sight. Someone turned up the drowsy Mississippi blues in the background to ensure Quinn and Jonah couldn't hear the conversation.

Which meant the house staff couldn't hear theirs.

"Want to wager on how many other board members are getting such calls?" Quinn asked.

Jonah watched where Laney disappeared.

"Jonah, if you were the people wanting the contracts to build a school, put in infrastructure, develop subdivisions, and construct strip malls to make a few million, would you take a frustrated Facebook comment as absolute?" Quinn shook her head. "By nightfall, some if not all of these people will rescind those hasty resignations. Trust me."

"So I can't run for office," he said. "I'm not sure whether to be relieved or disappointed. Who are these people, Quinn? Laney is no wuss. To be honest, the ones resigning are the stronger members."

"Money and politics are behind any development," she said. "You and Ty have listened to me whine about the growth in Charleston and Beaufort. I've been smelling it coming ever since I came home for Daddy."

He couldn't deny that. The guys avoided the topic around her.

Laney's flats echoed on the kitchen marble a dozen steps before she appeared. "We've about talked this out, so if you don't mind—"

"Are you staying on the board?" Quinn asked.

"Yes, that hasn't changed," she replied, walking toward the door. Jonah and Quinn slowly headed that way.

Quinn stopped a few steps short of the exit. "None of this is personal, Laney. I hate you got caught up in it. Please help us."

Laney homed in on her guest. "Help you do what, precisely, Quinn. You're just a PI."

"Oh, Ms. Underwood, I believe you know I'm a lot more than that."

"I can call the police if you refuse to leave."

She could, and being the sheriff's niece didn't necessarily give Quinn favor, so she decided departure the better side of valor.

Laney held open the door. "Looking forward to seeing you run for office, Jonah." Then she shut the door before they reached the bottom of the steps.

"Where to?" Jonah asked once they'd settled in the truck. He cranked the engine while waiting for an answer.

Quinn pointed ahead. "She's probably watching. Head to the end of drive, first."

Speed slower than when they arrived, Jonah headed out, both of them holding thoughts to themselves. Crape myrtles, barren and painfully pruned too tight for her taste, passed by them as Quinn mulled options, not yet willing to cease pursuing answers to both what had happened and how to fix the future. Eyes still on the road, Jonah reached over and took her hand.

She quickly withdrew it at the sight ahead. "Who's that?" A gray sedan sat parked off the drive, barely off the highway, the driver dead on watching them. Everything about the car screamed nondescript, and once Jonah pulled alongside, the driver did, too. Almost.

Jonah stopped and rolled down his window. Bless him, because like Quinn, he was aware Laney was alone with only one staff that they were aware of, and in the current environment, unscheduled visitors weren't particularly welcomed . . . or safe.

"Hello," Jonah said. "Can I help you?"

The gentleman was fortyish in age, dressed with a tie this time. "Mr. Proveaux." He craned his neck a little. "Ms. Sterling."

"Mr. Chase or Mr. Mauney?" Quinn asked.

The man only grinned, accepting he'd been recognized . . . somewhat.

"Nobody's home," she said.

Again the grin. "Then I'll leave the delivery with the help."

"No help either."

"Guess it gets left on the stoop. Nice seeing you again, Ms. Sterling. Mr. Proveaux."

When Jonah didn't pull onto the highway, the man drove around them and toward the house.

"She didn't want us there when he arrived," he said, watching his mirror. "Should we go back?"

Quinn shook her head. "No. She doesn't want us to hear the conversation. I'm wondering if we were followed. The tracker's still on that stop sign, so that didn't give us away."

He started to turn around. "I sense a threat."

She laid a hand on his forearm and squeezed. "Don't. Just sit for a moment. Be a visual presence for both of them. He's already seen us, so he won't do much." While speaking, she sent a text to Laney relaying where they parked, hoping the woman hadn't returned her phone to Ms. Fraser for safekeeping again. Even so, at least Ms. Fraser would know.

Quinn was surprised that only ten minutes went by. Maybe he did only leave his calling card in the door. Or in Ms. Fraser's hand.

The sedan stopped alongside them. "Waiting for me?"

"Just making sure you made your delivery. If it's edible, the wildlife might get it."

"Not a problem," he said, his grin growing into a laugh. "We good now?"

She wasn't sure how to answer that. "Yeah. Honestly, we were taking a moment to plan the rest of our day," she replied. "Busy one for us, and our tasks keep shifting."

He laughed again. He was way too jovial for her. "I hear you." He waved and eased onto the highway without a goodbye.

"Got his tag," Jonah said.

"Good." Quinn wasn't sure the tag mattered. The man hadn't done anything they could prove, and she bet her entire retainer with Iona that he had several visits just like this one on his itinerary. Laney had probably been one of his last by this time of day.

Jonah kept staring after the car. "He's too sure of himself for my taste. Surprised he exposed himself like this."

"I don't think he's worried about exposure. Laney never would've said he came out, I imagine, and he only accidentally came across us. Nothing risky." Besides, one couldn't be bold without feeling rather invulnerable. It's how powers-that-be became powers-that-be. This guy was probably little more than a messenger, but even working for power was empowering.

"Where to now?" Jonah asked.

"Look at you." She smirked at the man who perpetually rebuked her for private investigations. "You're hungry for more."

He didn't blush as expected. "I'm hungry for justice."

She motioned in the opposite direction the man took, toward Jacksonboro. "That's how it starts, sweetheart. Meting justice can be a strong addiction."

"Did you just call me sweetheart?"

She let him enjoy the endearment, because what thrilled her more was his desire to see wrongs righted. If she could not be a federal agent, and God knows she didn't want to be a deputy for her uncle, she could do her best as a private investigator, and Jonah accepting that choice was a huge leap in the right direction. Not only in understanding her, but in them becoming more in tune with each other.

"Someone coming up fast behind us. Looks like a pickup."

"Where's a deputy when you need one," she joked.

Jonah's gaze darted forward then to the mirror. "A little too fast. I'm pulling over."

"He'll pass," she said, turning to see who it might be.

"Quinn!"

Her head jerked into the headrest then forward, the seatbelt gripping her fast to the seat. Breath whooshed out, emptying her lungs. The truck spun, but the metal against metal didn't register until she opened her eyes to see the bottom of a muddy ditch rushing to meet them.

Chapter 22

QUINN OPENED HER eyes. She faced downward. Her seatbelt restricted her breathing, holding her fast at a forty-five degree angle, the airbag filling her vision. She snapped around to see what hit them, on the outside chance of identifying the person, the truck, the tag, but all she saw out the back window was sky . . . then black spots across her vision. She clinched her eyes shut and moaned, afraid to move anymore. Something wasn't right. Something hurt like a bitch.

She heard Jonah before she saw him clamoring past the air bags. "Quinn? Quinn?"

Gently moving hands, arms, shoulder, she attempted to analyze her damage, only to clench her teeth and suck in hard at the first effort. "Damn."

Jonah rested his hand lightly on her left shoulder, and she winced again. "Quinn, are you okay?"

Pride made her want to say she was fine, but she wasn't. "Pretty sure I dislocated a shoulder."

Lightly he touched the area. Why did people do that? Quinn flinched, zapping pain from her neck into her arm. "Don't touch it, Jonah, please." She had to take a few breaths to get in front of the hurt this time. Jonah could only call 9-1-1.

The same damn arm she was shot in two months ago. The same arm on which she'd finished therapy last week.

She wanted out of the seatbelt but feared the pain, so she sat, afraid movement would make it worse. With the airbag deflated and pushed down by Jonah, she saw how the grill of Jonah's truck had mired in the mud.

He remained hitched in his own belt, awkwardly but it kept him stable in watching her. When he told dispatch he was not injured, Quinn let go of her worry about him.

"Son of a bitch," she whispered again.

When she was still at Quantico, a fellow agent trainee had dislocated his shoulder during a tactical exercise in Logan's Alley, a fake town at the

Training Academy. Another overly eager trainee went to yank the ball into the socket only to wind up disciplined, having done more damage. Just like the shoot outs on television never get it right, popping a shoulder back into place wasn't as they depicted in a drama series. There was nothing noble about tearing a ligament.

The memory had her afraid to move.

The dispatcher said to remain on the line, and Jonah agreed but put the phone in his pocket for convenience. "Anything else hurt?" he asked Quinn.

"No, don't think so. See the guy?"

"I think it was a white Dodge Ram. A lot of grill. I was too busy trying to keep us on the road."

"Was it on purpose?" she asked cutting her eyes down the road toward Laney's, not wanting dispatch to hear everything.

He caught on. "Could be. The truck came from the direction of that car we saw."

"Yeah," she said. "Too convenient, too random."

"Sir? Did you recognize the driver of the other truck?"

Yea, Bonnie was listening . . . doing her job. The best dispatcher in Craven County. She was the fallback when any of the others went sick. A true dispatch junkie.

"No, we didn't, Bonnie," Quinn said, making it more personal.

"Want me to request your uncle?" she asked.

But when Quinn took in more pain, Jonah replied instead. "No, he has enough on his plate, Bonnie, but send uniforms. Personally, we're good with an ambulance. Thanks. Can you tell Ty to call me?"

"Sure can."

This had just stolen the rest of their day unless Quinn could push her way through the ER and grab the right meds. Thank God, for a myriad of reasons, they were closer to Colleton Medical Center than Charleston's Roper St. Francis. Though Craven shared a long rural line with Charleston County, the two counties were miles apart in understanding of each other, and a lot of Cravenites much preferred the sister services of the county on the other side.

Ty quickly phoned, and Jonah answered his questions. Bonnie had already put out a BOLO for a Ram, maybe ten years old, with a damaged front.

The ambulance arrived, Quinn noting the different siren of another vehicle riding its tail. Soon she heard Ty talking.

They assisted Jonah from the vehicle, and in deliberate movements freed Quinn and soon had her strapped to a gurney ready to load while they checked him over. Bruises from the seatbelt was about the extent of his damage. They rebandaged the burns on his arms.

Ty and Jonah stood barely three feet from Quinn and the EMTs, Ty getting more details from Jonah, the former looking way more upset than the latter.

She could almost read Ty's mind, doing the what-ifs. What if he'd come along. What if he'd been driving. What if he'd been with Quinn for Laney's interview instead of refusing and remaining at Miss Birdie's?

"Someone can ride with her," said the EMT.

Jonah hopped in without question, then paused a moment to speak to Ty. "Two guns in the glovebox."

Ty gave him a finger salute as the medic locked the doors, but his gaze was on Quinn.

THE DISLOCATION didn't need surgery, and when they prepared to pop her arm back in, Quinn begged them for the minimum pain relief. She might not be able to physically run someone down, but she wasn't dulling her mind such that her day was completely shot.

They heard her yell all the way to the lobby.

Slinged up and lightly medicated, they assisted her to meet Jonah, who looked paler than she. "God, was that you?"

"I'm good, I'm good," she assured. "Let's go." Not that she left the ER perky and ready to trim pecan trees. No, she felt more like she'd lost a bout of extreme wrestling. She could use a week on the living room sofa which wasn't far from what the doctor instructed her to do.

She felt foolish being wheeled to the hospital exit as he rolled up in her Ford. He'd arranged for someone to take him home to retrieve it. His had been towed.

"After we fill your prescriptions, are you up to going to your uncle's office?" he said, gently strapping her in, a light brush across her cheek with a finger. Jonah was the best nurse on the planet, and regardless of how she felt, he'd read her and act accordingly anyway, regardless how she lied. "I told Ty to keep me updated on anything going down," he said. "I informed him of our visit to his aunt's place, so he decided to lean on her after he finished processing the accident. He just left Laney's."

"How is she?"

He did a weird thing with his mouth. "She mentioned we inquired as to any threats directed at her. She denied any outside pressure. She said nothing about seeing Chase or Mauney, and she wants to stay on the board, but she isn't sure what's going on."

"Hmm. Half truths." Why wasn't Laney coming completely clean with Ty, unless she was indeed threatened so strategically she didn't dare. Which probably meant their representative *suit* had reiterated that threat. Plus, Laney'd already told Quinn and Jonah. Ty would get the scoop and Laney wouldn't have to embarrass herself rehashing the same material.

"Your uncle called him in right after that. But then Ty said he needed us at the sheriff's complex, so I'm not sure what's going on. Question is, are you up to it?"

"My uncle's doing what?"

But Jonah had shut the truck door. Quinn waited for him to come around. With her being run off the road right after Laney's visit, after she and Jonah met Chase or Mauney in the driveway, after the board started dropping like flies, and thousands of Facebook creatures lost touch with reality, Quinn could see Ty wanting a face-to-face with them. She would. Much had changed in just a couple hours.

But her uncle . . . what was he up to? Or trying to stem in the name of squelching trouble.

Sheriff Sterling hadn't called her, and with a 9-1-1 call involved, he had been made aware of her incident. Maybe he had his hands full. Maybe he relied on the guys to keep him apprised. He forever found ways to fall short in her eyes, and as many times as he'd disappointed her, she still found herself depressed about him. She didn't go out of her way to think ill of him, but after a slew of life's experiences with him, she'd accepted his norm.

Jonah got in.

"Were you trying to say my uncle called Ty *off* the investigation?" She tried to suppress her red-head temper with a controlled whispered, "The man couldn't be legit law enforcement if he tried."

"Y'all couldn't agree on the day of the week, Princess, and no, I didn't say that."

She hosed him down with a gaze.

He pretended she hadn't. "We're headed to the sheriff's office. Okay?"

"Fine."

The ride wasn't thirty minutes, but she filled it with tasks. Her first move was to call Laney, to ask if she'd met with a *suit*. Mauney, Chase, didn't matter. Quinn got voicemail and left that message then inquired if she was familiar with a Ram pickup. Quinn hung up to then dial Iona.

She answered on one ring. "Quinn? Have you seen Facebook? I'm afraid to leave my house. Jesus, I'm feeling so bad about Miss Abbott, Miss Birdie . . . "

"And now me since I just left the hospital. I was run off the road."

After a squeak of a squeal, Iona's voice choked up. "Oh my gosh, are you okay?" Then before Quinn could answer, "I've caused all of this, haven't I? By pulling you in, I've upset the whole county."

"Not by a long shot," Quinn said.

Iona lowered to a whisper. "Did *they* get to you? Someone's coming after us, aren't they?"

Quinn's laugh wasn't real, but Iona needed to hear it. Quinn could see her sequestered at home, blinds drawn. With the other board members resigning, however, Fripp might be feeling his future disappearing, too. "Fripp isn't bothering you, is he?"

"He left in a huff hours ago. A huge huff. I'm done with him, Quinn. I've done nothing but help that man, and he cannot blame me for a damn bit of today. I studied those contracts and tax returns like you asked me to, and he comes out smelling like a rose. I'd say he owes me, yet he blames me instead. Blames me! The shithead sucks me in, I land him contracts, then he blames me for screwing things up. I told him I hadn't resigned, so what was his problem!"

Quinn was almost with Fripp on this one . . . Iona was a screw up.

Iona blew out hard, directly into the phone. "I'm so fucking done with him, Quinn." More huffs and puffs. "Are you watching the shit on Facebook?"

Quinn was surprised at the language, but happy at the first sign of backbone from her client. "Don't read too much into the Facebook stuff, Iona. However, if you don't want to be questioned at every turn, keep to yourself and don't partake in that social media craziness."

"Can I just read it?"

Iona wouldn't honor a request to abstain anyway. "Just don't respond," Quinn said. "Not a word. Do you hear? You don't want to shine any sort of attention on yourself. That piece about you approving contracts for yourself isn't wrong. You messed up. But you don't want people knocking on your door, do you? Neither you nor your daughter need that."

Iona choked on that gasp. "Good heavens, no! Thank God it's Saturday and I don't have to pick her up from school. Should I skip church tomorrow?"

"Yes. We'll know more in a few days."

Iona cleared her throat again, now a nervous habit. "But what about

Miss Abbott's funeral on Monday?"

Aw, damn.

Iona gasped again with another thought. "And what about the emergency board meeting on Monday night?" At that question, Quinn put the call on speaker. Iona rattled on. "Laney said to expect one. Told me to be prepared to vote on the school land and assorted resignations. She said she'd tell me how to vote. I told you she looks after me."

"Vote how on the land?" They could vote to make an offer to buy out Jonah on tract two or ask Jonah to buy back tract one. Or simply ditch the project and hunt elsewhere. Or worse, contest Miss Abbott's will.

"She didn't say. She has a lot on her agenda, she said."

Quinn almost wished Iona would resign, but her vote could be a positive. Plus, the constituency voted her in.

"Don't say anything about Monday, though," Iona said. "The meeting's not formalized yet, but they only have to give a day's notice to the public, and when they don't want a herd of attendees, they announce it on the website exactly twenty-four hours ahead of time, only doing the minimal. Expect the post on the district site no earlier than six o'clock tomorrow night. Facebook doesn't know either. The fewer that show up the better."

Not exactly the best line of march, in Quinn's opinion. The board needed transparency, not more secrecy.

Quinn had to think, but at the moment her brain was fuzzy around the edges. "Stay home until Monday." Then she remembered Laney's mention of anonymous photographs of her nieces in front of their school. "Keep your daughter home Monday, too."

"Oh, Quinn. Now I do want to resign." Her voice squeezed out thin and needy. "But look at how Facebook went after those who resigned. Like sharks! We can't do anything right."

That's the way the public worked. Targets were targets, and the board fed a frenzy right now. "I know you want to make it all disappear, honey, but let's hold off resigning. The less attention the better. I'll call you the second I think otherwise."

"Oh." Iona's inhale belied her tears, wet and shallow with a whimper on the end. "Some of these comments are merciless. I don't like Guy or Piper, but these people get brutal online, don't they?" She would probably read Facebook the rest of the day.

Brutal, ruthless, the internet culture of today was about criticism. Even if they were on your side, posters seemed to lose any of the good judgment God gave them. Morality and manners had long gone out the window, and tomorrow, over half of them would sit in their Sunday pew, sing those hymns, and shout amen like the Christians they professed to be. "We'll talk, Iona. Promise."

Quinn hung up and tapped into the Facebook group, not so simple with one arm trussed up. She had to hold the phone in her bum hand, up against her belly, with her good hand scrolling and tapping. She expected a crick in her neck before the day was over.

On top of everything else, aches were taking up residence, from her neck to her butt, most likely from the slinging she'd received. Tomorrow would be a bitch which only fueled her desire to learn more as quickly as she could today.

People lived in front of their screens, waiting with baited breath for the next caustic comment to shout at. They were energized, primed, waiting on the balls of their feet for a different spin on the district spectacle. The superintendent hadn't said a word, in spite of a few teachers attempting to take up for him. The board was in hiding.

Literally hundreds more comments had appeared since they left Laney's, if not a thousand. People burned bridges with each other as fast as they could, with Lincoln20 supporting the creation of a school, cleaning up the board, and demanding accountability. He'd get riled then attempt civility with a plea they pull together. Quinn had first labeled him a troublemaker, but in this melee, a theme took form, like he thrived on the pandemonium. Empowerment and change without total destruction. He could almost be a Miss Birdie protégé, only with more raucous, more noise, and more often. Still sounded like a man.

Miss Birdie had reemerged with a different strategy of darting in and out doing her best here and there to temper the inferno. Unsuccessfully.

With tempers flaring, the pro-school people demanded Lincoln20's true identity, either from himself or Birdie. He articulated the reasons why who he was would remain a mystery, for now.

With the propensity of this group to become incensed, I'd rather just state that I am a long-time Craven County resident with a sincere interest in the school district, he typed.

We're not hiding our identities, said several. Why should you?

Each of us has our own prerogative, he replied. And our own reasons. One has to think short term and long term.

That last part sounded odd to Quinn.

But you sound anti-school, argued one.

Not anti-school, he explained. I just want accountability in this district, financially and ethically. If we can do that together, fine. If not, find the right people who can.

Then there were the retaliatory, over-the-top posters in response to him. *If I knew where you lived I would show you some accountability. We need that school. We need it on the Abbott land and we need it now.*

Or . . . *The old woman was pro-school. She's dead. There ought to be a way to condemn the land and give it to the district.*

Sorry, everyone, but this is why I post as Lincoln20. I don't want who I am to dictate the narrative. I only want the facts and events to steer us. We are in the trenches together.

Impeach them all came from several more.

That mantra appeared repeatedly.

Let's avoid a nuclear option, he said.

Quinn found his identity explanation posted a half dozen times, cut and pasted, because not everyone was able to read the incredible volume of text. He wanted change. He wanted things done right. Without saying it, he considered himself a rescuer and protector of the county's tax dollars. A downright patriot using the rancor and fury of thousands to draw attention with flamboyance in order to educate.

She couldn't argue much with his message. Avoiding *a nuclear option* was repeated several times.

She kept trying to dissect his verbiage, match his wording to anyone she remembered, but drew a blank. "Who do you think this guy is?" she asked Jonah as he turned onto the block of the Sheriff's Office complex.

"A weirdo," he said.

"But he's a local weirdo," she mumbled, thinking how Lincoln20's loyalty felt genuine, which meant she ought to recognize him. Of course, that was assuming he spoke truth and wasn't someone like Chase or Mauney raising crap to the surface and keeping it afloat for some choreographed end game. She couldn't afford to underestimate the cunning of these guys.

But wouldn't they preach the new school?

Surely Miss Birdie wasn't wearing two hats, was she? Playing two identities on Facebook. Could you do that? Quinn wasn't sure.

Jonah parked the F-150 in the complex parking lot. "Sit there."

He slid out fast, came around and opened her door, undid her belt. "Turn slowly. Just slide out. I've got you."

If she were clicking on all cylinders, she'd balk at the coddling, but

she hurt, she was slightly dull-witted, and she wanted to get inside and see
what her uncle was up to. Also, she'd like to hear they found the truck that
hit them. Mostly, she wanted to get Ty aside and the three of them collect
their knowledge and see if they could link any of the day's activities to a
culprit of some kind. The day certainly had thrown enough clues at them.
Enough to make Quinn feel this more than the hand of one person, or
even one organized group. Sometimes people just went off the rails, and
the smart ones were intelligent enough to work their magic amidst the
mayhem.

They entered the sheriff's complex, Jonah hanging tight, opening
doors, ensuring nothing got in their way. Carla rose at her desk, hands
clasped as though afraid to let them loose or they'd hug Quinn. "Oh,
sweetheart, look at you."

"Yep, look at me." Quinn tried to sound put together, but couldn't
quite pull it off.

Deputy Harrison happened to come up the hall to head out and
stopped. "I'd hate to see the other guy. You okay?"

"Fine, Harrison." But there was no hiding the fact she wasn't
together. "Just get us to my uncle's office, Jonah," she whispered. "This is
embarrassing."

"It's okay, her uncle asked us to come in," Jonah said, knowing
nobody would question, especially the way Quinn looked. "We're late."

The ad lib made Quinn proud . . . and more aware she wasn't
thinking sharp.

They passed a few others, each staring in their own way, but when
they reached Sheriff Sterling's office, the door was closed.

"Knock?" Jonah asked.

Quinn just opened the door.

The sheriff sat behind his desk. Ty stood off to the side, against the
wall. Guy Cook, however, sat front and center before both of them, like
he'd been caught stealing candy from the dime store.

Chapter 23

THE SHERIFF'S FACE clouded at the state of his niece. Ty leaped to move a chair for her. Jonah eased her into the seat, and joined Ty against the wall.

Guy silently watched.

Ty's request to meet them at the sheriff's office was his way of inserting them into things. This could go well or badly.

Between Birdie and Laney, and most definitely Iona, Quinn had developed this evil ogre image of Guy Cook. "Sorry to barge in unexpectedly," she said. She'd twisted to see him, and at the discomfort, Jonah ran over and adjusted so she could talk to Guy head on. "But I'm not your problem, Mr. Cook, and I imagine nothing I say matters versus what the rest of Craven County would like to say to you . . . or do to you."

Shoulders lax, jowls slack, the attorney seemed drained. Wearing brand names from stores on Charleston's King Street, his clothes hung as if slept in. Maybe he *had* slept in them. Or maybe he'd wallowed in them unable to sit still with so much heat blistering his reputation. He acted seriously dethroned.

"Quinn, how are you, honey?"

The authenticity in Uncle Larry's asking drew her around. He hadn't called her honey since her father died. "I'll be fine, Uncle Larry. Just not feeling it quite yet. Thanks."

His heavy sigh told her that he still had the capacity to care, but he'd done his duty, and his posture resumed to one of authority. "Quinn, there's no need for you to be here if you don't want."

Were they welcome here or not? She'd err on the side of being needed. "To get the elephant out of the room, we got rear-ended leaving Laney Underwood's house," she said, speaking more to Guy. "Laney's scared, by the way. Her family's been threatened." Giving the update only raised her irritation with this man, and she drilled him with a stare. "But *she* hasn't resigned, Mr. Cook. She told us that there's a force outside Craven County coercing the board to build that school, but their desires are a bit more self-serving than doing everything *for the children*." She did one-handed air quotes for his well-known catch phrase. "They are attempting to buy up acreage and develop subdivisions and whatever commercial they can manage, using the funding of the school to lessen their cost for water, sewer, electrical, gas, and so on. And since we are one of the poorer counties in the state, we have access to ample federal funds. You know the drill."

Guy dug deep to clear his throat. "Miss Sterling, I assure you—"

"Guy, your assurances are about as worthless as a wooden frying pan. You got suckered into some sort of scheme and then bailed when the water got over your head. You think if we uncover anything illegal it won't stick to you because you resigned?"

Guy sought the sheriff for help from the onslaught. Sheriff Sterling watched, silent and apparently happy with the questions she asked, so, she kept going.

"Who burned Miss Abbott's place?" Quinn continued.

"I . . . I don't know."

"Who do you *think* set the fire?"

"I . . . I really don't know, Miss Sterling."

"Then tell me something you *do* know," she said, hammering.

Sheriff Sterling leaned arms on his blotter, his wide chair giving its familiar groan. "Quinn." He tilted his head at the chairman. "He came in here on his own. Back off and I'll let him tell you what he told us, please."

"He's why I called Jonah to bring you in," Ty said. "His story's something to hear."

She wished she could record, but she couldn't discreetly access her phone with her injured arm. She had no pad, no way to write, and the residual pain killer, no matter how light, was detrimental to her ability to remember verbatim whatever Guy had to say.

"Record it, then, please," she said, repeating his nicety.

"There are four of us," her uncle reminded.

"Who'll remember it four different ways."

Ty left to grab a recorder. Guy, however, showed fresh reluctance. "Not sure I want to do that without my attorney present."

"See?" Quinn said. "An upstanding private citizen wouldn't think twice about getting his statement on the record, but put your ass on the line, and you want to rethink what to say. I say don't bother." Her newfound lack of interest surprised the man. Quinn pointed to Jonah. "We have their bullying recorded from Miss Abbott's place. Let that represent him."

Guy peered at the ceiling, frustrated. He received no assurances from the room.

"Laney Underwood is scared, Sheriff," Quinn said, breaking the silence. "So's Iona Bakeman. Ella Mae Dewberry probably has no clue which way to turn since she's Mr. Cook's protégé." She gave him a stare. "Have you talked to her today?"

He didn't answer.

"Would we find she's been desperately trying to call you since the paper came out?"

The moisture beading on the man's temple answered for him.

Ty returned and plopped a device soundly on the sheriff's desk, and silence filled in around them as they waited for Guy Cook to decide what to do.

Quinn could blame him for Birdie, too. She could also ask if he had a hand in having someone run her and Jonah off the road, but the more he worried who would sue him, the less likely he'd talk. He needed comrades. He needed to feel a degree of safety, at least a way out of being crucified. She needed to settle her own ass down.

"Sorry," she said, realizing her pain was coloring her actions. "You came in on your own. I interrupted. For all I know, you're just as much a victim as Miss Abbott and Miss Birdie."

Her shoulder throbbed, and she tried to push aside as she paved the way for Guy to feel exonerated.

He blurted, "They paid me ten thousand dollars."

Sheriff Sterling flipped on the recorder, mumbled in the date and time, and positioned it toward the ambulance chaser. "How much did they pay you?" he asked, like he hadn't heard.

"They gave me ten thousand dollars," Guy repeated. "Payment for voting properly. Though I want to go on the record saying I voted how I would have without the money."

Nobody agreed or disagreed.

"Who gave you that money?" the sheriff asked.

Guy seemed more relieved being asked questions than presenting the scenario from scratch. "I was sent a letter to come to a hotel in Charleston. To a certain room number on a given date and time."

"Do you still have the letter? Email? Whatever?" he asked, just as Quinn was going to.

But Guy shook his head.

She bet he trashed it in a dumpster between his house and Charleston, disposing of the evidence. "Which hotel?" she asked.

He gave the name and address. She was familiar.

"Was it Chase or Mauney?" she asked. "You know, the suits from the board meeting videos."

Hand on his belt, Ty shifted for her benefit. He didn't recognize the names, and he was letting her know. He'd learn in due time.

"Neither," Guy said. "A stranger. He never told me who he was. He only said we had mutual friends who needed that school built. I didn't even know what was in the envelope, and as I looked in it, he snapped my picture."

"Got the picture?" Ty asked.

Guy reached in his inside coat pocket and laid it in front of the recorder. They circled the desk and the Polaroid shot. Looking like a kid caught sneaking a peek at a Playboy spread, the board chairman posed in bad lighting, dimmed by the reflective, flimsy paneling on the motel wall, his mouth open and a hand on the cash.

Bribed. How about that.

"I declined at first, but he got me on record. Spontaneously, I decided to play this out and see where it went."

Sure he did.

"Where's the money?" Quinn asked.

"In my safe at home. Every dollar of it. Wrappers still on the bills. Told you, I decided to play along. Part of me was afraid to turn it down, and part of me wanted to see if we could flush out the identity of these people. My vote wasn't being bought, by the way." The second time he'd made the point.

"Of course it wasn't," Jonah said, speaking up for the first time as he held his place against the wall.

Guy raised his voice at him. "I wasn't bought! I voted as I believed."

He was the smallest person in the room, and his short stockiness did little to enforce his exaggerated declaration of innocence, painting him in the light of a Southern Danny DeVito.

This was great, though. This, atop of Laney's quasi-confession, held some potential. "Who do you think supplied the money. The suits?"

Uncle Larry scowled, unsettled being in the dark. "Who are these suits you keep mentioning?"

"Sorry," she said to him. "The two men from Charleston who attended the meetings. The two men who Guy and Laney took to dinner after one of those meetings. Men whose jobs are to listen for school construction opportunity across the Carolinas in order to buy up the surrounding lands to capitalize on development. Building permits have jumped in the county, in case you don't know, and most of them on the Sterling Banks highway, down the road from that school. We're about to get flooded with development if that school goes through," she said.

Guy feigned ignorance with his brows, his mouth, his sudden lack of words.

"Got that from Laney, by the way," she said, as an aside to him. "The suits' names are Anthony Chase and Marvin Mauney, one of whom visited Laney this afternoon. Then right after spotting us, a Ram pickup forced us off the road." Which she hadn't been updated on yet. "Y'all find him?"

Ty shook his head. "BOLO's out. Sent to Craven, Charleston, and Colleton counties."

"Someone's trying to take us over," she said, bringing them around. "Someone with deep pockets sees our little county as cheap, easy development with nobody in the way."

Every person in the room suddenly understood that an imperceptible authority had inserted itself into their county like a virus. Everyone there had heard the dialogue before. Outsiders loved to waltz into a poor county like theirs and claim to be saviors willing to improve the quality of life for the poor residents since they'd never accomplish much on their own.

"They'll take over, uncle," she repeated. "You've heard about development in this state. I bet if we looked harder, we'd find school boards in the middle of many such ill-planned explosions."

Jonah had been antsy against the wall, shifting and crossing and recrossing his arms. "I'm the only non-cop-type in this room, but I still have a question. Apologies, Mr. Cook. And, Sheriff Sterling, you stop me if I cross a line or anything."

The sheriff nodded.

Quinn was eager to hear this. Jonah was the guy who normally stood in the back of the room, but he listened hard. Inserting himself into things of late had exposed a charm in him, and she wasn't the only person to notice. When Jonah spoke these days, people listened.

"What made you come forward today of all days, Mr. Cook?" Jonah said, very controlled.

"Miss Birdie," Guy said. "Seeing what someone did to her and reading her articles opened my eyes. I honestly didn't realize how we were coming across. We thought, I mean, the board members and I thought . . ."

"Are you sure you want to speak for the entire board?" Quinn asked.

Guy held up his hands, refusing to engage. "We thought we were doing right by the people who elected us. We were as incensed as anyone about Miss Abbott and Miss Birdie. When the paper came out this morning, we could see how everyone would view what was going on, like we were some kind of intrusive missionary group forcing its way into a culture. We meant nothing like that. We were just—"

"Doing what you thought best for the little people," Jonah finished. "Who else got bribed?"

The shrug wasn't believable.

Ty wasn't convinced. "You don't know? Are you serious?"

"I was afraid to tell anyone I was bribed for fear none of them were. What if it was just me because I'm the chair?"

Or the most reachable, the most influential, the one with the most sway.

Or the most crooked, the most easily convinced. The list went on and on in Quinn's mind.

"We don't want crooks infusing money into Craven County," the sheriff surmised.

Quinn, however, couldn't believe such an organization would rely on this one man, who, from the looks of how he handled pressure, wasn't strong enough to carry through. Each board member needed to be interviewed, and while Quinn would love to steer this ship, the sheriff needed to turn the direction of the boat. He'd shown influence by attending the meetings. Time for him to use it for everyone's protection.

Control over Laney seemed to have come in the form of a threat against her family. She didn't need money, and someone had sensed that in coercing her how to vote. Iona had mentioned nothing to Quinn about a bribe offer; she would have said something. She wasn't cunning enough to talk around the board's activities without making a slip about an anonymous wad of cash. There was that note in her daughter's bookbag, however. A dead cat. Pressure from Fripp. Maybe that was the angle on her.

Quinn wouldn't trust Piper as far as she could throw her. Money, promises of more storefronts, who knew? Harmon liked being in the spotlight but only so long. Ella Mae might've been part of Guy's deal, one of the conditions of his bribe being to keep that board member voting properly. If Quinn had been bribing any of these people, Curtis Fuller, the quietest, retired military, would've been her last choice. He would've spoken up the soonest about an attempted bribe, would be her guess. That and he had a voting record indicating he didn't often go along with the majority. She bet he was clean.

"This is how it starts," Jonah said.

"Old people dying and the heirs wanting to sell to the highest bidder who's usually from outside the area," Ty added.

The entire situation was a loud and scary warning. "I have an FBI buddy who lives on Lake Murray." Quinn addressed his Christmas card each year to Jake Meetze Road. She always had to double check the spelling. "He used to live in the country, no traffic, tons of wildlife. Says the development around that lake is ruining everything, and none of the developers are local. They come in, clear every tree and rock and ounce of topsoil, toss up side-by-side houses, screw up the infrastructure, then head off to another county. It took an hour to get an ambulance to his neighbor . . . who died, by the way."

Lots of head nodding. Edisto Island was their Lake Murray. It wasn't forty-five minutes away by road, a half-hour by boat from the farm. Edisto was a safe haven being strong-arm-pressured to develop, with people from high-taxed states wanting the more realistic cost of living. Thank God the island had preserved much of the acreage in conservation land trusts.

Like Quinn's grandfather had applied to much of Sterling Banks. He'd seen this coming.

"My buddy says they're having a rough time around that lake," she said. "The county has raised taxes ten percent two years in a row."

"Thank God we don't have a lake," Jonah said.

"But we have the coast," Quinn said. "That's even bigger. And we're in between Charleston and Hilton Head. We're cheap opportunity waiting to be gobbled up."

Everyone, including Guy, went silent.

"Guy," Quinn said. "You're going to walk back your resignation."

"No, I'm not."

Quinn glared at her uncle for support.

"Yes, you are," he said. "You accepted a bribe. That's public corruption. You're doing as we say to help us wade through this mess."

"Be glad Sheriff Sterling isn't more fond of the FBI or this could fall in their lap," Quinn said.

Ty gave a dry chuckle at what they recognized as obvious. Sheriff Sterling hadn't let SLED or the FBI cross his county line for his entire thirty-year career. Guy didn't know, but the point was well taken. These sins of his could be considered egregious enough.

Guy could cooperate or go down, but nobody could tell who was in bed with whom. And with everyone resigning, how could they cobble clues to find the puppeteer pulling the strings if board members were cutting their strings?

Quinn's head spun at some unsaid options, though. Was this muddle an even deeper mystery? One where the board members' resignations *were* the intent? Were others waiting in the wings, others more easily bought and directed? County residents couldn't help but match the tragedies of Miss Abbott and Miss Birdie to the current board members. Fresh faces would be construed as more honest, the innovative guys who came in to clean up the dirt, a situation ripe for change.

The naive always gave fresh faces the benefit of the doubt.

"We've got to think this through long and hard," the sheriff said, as though reading his niece's mind. "Guy? Are you still holding a board meeting Monday night?"

"Have to in order to accept resignations and decide how this board ought to proceed."

The sheriff gave him a slow, understanding nod. "Ty," he finally ordered. "Accompany Mr. Cook to an interview room and get him to write down what he just said here. Then take him to his home, collect the evidence, and lock it up here at the complex."

Ty reached to help Mr. Cook stand. The man seemed unsure how to behave. This had to been too easy. Guy wasn't much of an attorney not asking for immunity, and if Ty got that statement down, more power to him. Maybe Guy had some sort of self-preservation instinct. As a minimum, he had to be seasoned enough to understand how the first pig to the trough wins.

She wasn't sure where her uncle was headed after this. What was the plan? What about the others? What if he had six more cases of attempted bribery, and that didn't even include people like the superintendent and Fripp Bakeman.

"Quinn?" Sheriff Sterling said, primed to give another order.

Maybe she'd spoken too soon. "Sir?"

"Go home and rest. Jonah, make sure she does. I'll handle things from here on."

Wait, this was really it?

"Why didn't you come to us earlier, Mr. Cook?" she asked, because Sheriff Sterling certainly should have.

"Just afraid to," he said, which was bunk to Quinn. The guy wasn't a high school dropout. He was an attorney, regardless the clientele he entertained, and in maneuvering his own clients in pleas and settlements, he'd recognize the importance of cooperation earlier in the game. He was coming across awful ignorant. Too much so.

Sheriff Sterling waved toward the door. "Quinn, let him go on with Ty."

She had a half dozen more questions, but Guy was already in the hallway, Ty behind him.

"Uncle," she complained, a jump to her feet shooting pain to too many places to count.

"Our business, now," he said. "Go on home."

With Quinn being sanctioned in earshot of him, he glanced back with a look of pity.

Quinn, on the other hand, her uncle behind her, gave Guy a somber wink.

He caught it, too.

Chapter 24

JONAH HELPED HER into the truck. The sheriff's complex parking lot hadn't been full to start with being Saturday, butnow the lot was desolate.

Quinn noticed a bit of a limp in Jonah as he rounded the front of the pickup. She should've known he'd be sore after the wreck, but when he climbed in, he did his best to appear spry and unaffected.

He didn't immediately crank the engine. "What are we doing?" He peered over, and she caught a hint of tautness in his turn, his eyes moving so his body didn't have to.

"You're hurt," she said.

"I'm stiff. Slipped up on me while I stood still in there."

She appreciated the aches, and wished she'd considered him earlier. God knows he'd taken care of her. "You're holding it together for me, Jonah. I love you for it, but be honest. Are you functional or do we need to follow Uncle Larry's orders and go rest?"

Funny how at this moment they stood in each other's shoes. Him acting unhurt, like she often did in front of him. Her stepping into the role as caretaker because he wasn't taking care of himself. The eye-opener made her release a laugh.

He appeared puzzled. "What?"

"You. Me." She pointed back and forth. "This."

Her wit softened him, and he chuckled.

"I like us working together," she said. She couldn't help but feel this experience a test, him maybe attempting to go along with her PI daring-do. He was holding his own. She'd always held Ty on a higher rung of the ladder in investigations because of his career path. Jonah just used his brain and gut, but she'd underestimated how sharp he could really be.

Then his smile faded. "They tried to intimidate us."

"And we weathered it."

He made a motion to her arm.

"We are incapacitated." She hesitated to then add, "We aren't dead."

His wince touched her. "I feel like we're in the middle of . . . whatever this is."

"Chaos, shitstorm, brouhaha. I always liked that word," she said, trying to act more put-together than he. No joke, she could crash on her sofa right now. Take one of those pills tucked in the glovebox, still in the drugstore bag, and sleep through church, lunch, and evening supper tomorrow. She couldn't think about moving, much less move, without pain.

She one-handedly took out her phone and tried to make a list under Notes about Guy, then gave up. "Let's run down the board members, please."

They remained parked in the complex, and Jonah slid around to see her better.

"You've got whiplash, don't you?" she said.

"A bit. Back to the board members. Are we just talking about them? Calling them? Going to see them? Do we ignore the ones resigning or pay more attention to them?"

She held up her free hand. "Let's not jump too soon. Go down the list for me. Then we'll decide."

"Guy Cook. Don't believe a word he said in your uncle's office," he said. "Laney Underwood is made of tough stuff. Don't see her being bribed, but I do see her being affected. She'll ponder her vote, the pros and cons. She's pro-school, we know that. Not sure if she's convincing herself that her vote being what the powers-that-be want makes it right. Who next?" He motioned with a finger and answered himself. "Harmon Valentine. In my book, and that's from just knowing him around town and watching his exchanges at board meetings, he's malleable. Nothing noble about him, and he hasn't the spine to go out on a limb for anyone."

"Agreed." She liked seeing Jonah perform like this. "Who else? Ella Mae," she quickly added.

"I don't see her sticking around for the mudslinging if Guy doesn't."

"True that. Not sure she'll stick around even if he stays. Not if the heat gets too hot."

They continued through the other three. Curtis was Curtis, doing what he wanted. The only genuine person on the board. Iona was pretty much an open book but could be guided as needed. Piper was usually Guy's partner in all things school board, as were Laney and Ella Mae, and she'd made a big enough name for herself in the county to not want to muck it up. She wasn't one to forecast herself, and she loved her money. To her, resigning would be cutting her losses.

Quinn and Jonah sat in her truck, wondering what to do next.

"Your uncle doesn't really want us involved."

"He never wants me involved. He's just never had to cope with you before. He likes you, but with you aligned more with me than him, he's stuck with more of me."

Shadows grew longer across the parking lot. A text came across both their phones from Jule, inquiring if they were coming to supper. She'd made spaghetti sauce.

"You hungry?" he asked.

"Famished," she replied.

He cranked up and left the town, heading home in silence. Jonah bounced the day around in his head just like Quinn did in hers. She wasn't sure he relished more what he was doing or the fact he was doing it with her. She counted her blessings either way.

She wished she knew more about Chase and Mauney. She wished she could put a finger on the money behind the scenes. As much as she might want to curl up under her grandmother's quilt tonight, even if Jonah was there, she craved more to stay up and dig deeper.

Time was not on their side. Monday's board meeting could alter the composition of the board, which in turn could alter decisions on the school . . . on development in the county . . . and ultimately the future of Craven County as a whole. Sheriff Larry Sterling usually fell on the side of least resistance, and whoever took control of the financial side of Craven would find a place for a man who wouldn't make waves. Quinn, on the other hand, wasn't so quick to bow down to people who ate up communities to line their pockets.

"Technically, nobody has really resigned," she said, when the silence got too long. They were three miles from home. "They still have to tender those resignations and have them accepted at a meeting, right? Then the board announces the need for a special election?"

Jonah stayed quiet like he hadn't heard. He went internal when he thought.

Ty's call lit up Quinn's phone. "Hey," he said. "Where are you?"

Being it was her truck, the call immediately went Bluetooth to speaker. "Jonah and I are on our way home. Why?"

"Guy Cook got cold feet on giving a statement."

Surprise.

"What about the ten thousand?" Jonah asked.

Ty gave a dry laugh. "Oh, I followed him home and got that. We'd recorded him admitting to bribery, thanks to Quinn, so he had to. It's secure. But while I was in his house, he received a call that wide-open rattled him."

"About what?" Quinn asked.

"No idea. I asked if he wanted to share, and he flat out refused. Whoever it was has talons sunk into the man."

"Could've been his attorney laying out options," she said. Might be Chase or Mauney, or whoever they worked for, too. Developers could take on a dominant air.

"Thanks, Ty," she said aloud but did a spin thing with her hand, telling Jonah to turn the truck around. "We might get in touch with Guy."

Ty didn't respond.

"Don't tell uncle."

"Tell him what?"

"Precisely. Oh, and thanks for the update."

He gave her a humph. "Don't make me regret it."

She laughed the laugh she always gave him when he warned her to behave or be careful.

He didn't laugh in kind. "I mean it, Q. We haven't found that truck that hit you. They're still out there."

"You'll find them, Ty. You're like . . ." She paused. "Who's a famous black detective?"

"Just call me Denzel. He played a few."

"Ooh, I like that," she said, grateful he'd finally latched ahold of some humor.

Jonah spoke up louder, to be heard over the speaker. "And my eyes are all over the road, dude. You'll be the first person I call if I see him."

"You better, man. What are you going to do now?" Ty asked.

"Eat," she said, even as Jonah turned the truck.

"Be careful doing it," he ended, not believing a word she said.

The cool thing was she knew he knew. It was how they rolled.

Finally, their old rhythm was back.

QUINN DIDN'T SEE a cam on the Cook family's doorbell but she found the one overhead in the corner. More sophisticated than one of those boxed jobs one could pick up at Costco, but a five-thousand square foot mansion merited more. She rang the doorbell and smiled up at the cam which the resident probably saw on his phone, his television, and some oral announcement on top of recording the visit in crystal resolution. The attorney could afford pretty darn whatever he wanted.

Jonah hung to Quinn's left, guarding her hurt arm. When Guy didn't answer, Quinn motioned for Jonah to knock on the door, hard.

"We know you see us, Guy," she said loudly. "If you don't answer, I can canvas the neighbors about your well-being."

She held up a finger to Jonah, head tilted, listening. Before long, distant steps became more succinct, then Guy Cook himself opened the door.

"We need to talk," she said. "You can't cooperate then change midstream without damage."

"What damage?" he asked, more scared than an attorney ought to be.

"Can we just come in?" Jonah asked, hand on the door. "Better than airing things out here."

After a second of hesitation, Guy welcomed them through. He led them to the den of the mansion, and when he didn't immediately sit, Quinn did, indicating the men should as well. Guy sat like his legs gave out.

"Who's smothering you?" she asked. "You got a phone call a little while ago that frayed your nerves, and why'd you decide not to give Deputy Jackson a statement? That would've gone far in helping your case."

Guy didn't ask how they were aware. "Can't say who called. Can't say why. But they said they had control of another board member, whatever that meant, and if I wasn't careful, they'd get ahold of me and do some serious damage."

"News flash, Guy. They already think they have control over you," Jonah said. "Don't get lulled into their demands. Do the right thing." He did an aside to Quinn, phone in hand. "I'm texting Jule to tell her we'll be late," he said.

"You know who called?" the attorney said in almost a whisper. The man wasn't accustomed to serious courtroom confrontation because his potency under fire was weak as summer camp Kool-Aid. He apparently excelled at chasing ambulances, however, because from the furnishings and Italian marble, the drapes, the art, and his custom loafers, Guy loved a certain standard of living. Nervous, he gripped his tufted leather chair as if they were about to take it away.

"Chase and/or Mauney," Quinn guessed.

He didn't argue, but he didn't volunteer either. Instead he acted like he wanted them to leave but was afraid to ask.

"Spill it, Guy," she said, once Jonah put his phone away. "We assume you didn't tell them you've been to the sheriff. Surely you didn't tell them you gave the deputy your ten thousand."

There he was, stuck between a rock and a hard place. This was the damage she'd referenced. He'd gone only so far with the sheriff then reneged, and now he was facing his adversary alone, without support. He'd screw up sooner or later, with one or the other or both. As an FBI agent, she loved interviewing those this tangled in their own stupidity.

Guy ignored the talk about the sheriff. "The caller told me to call an emergency board meeting on Monday."

Hmm, Quinn already heard that from Iona, and Laney said that much, too. The question was whether the idea had been Laney's or that of the outside power.

"They said a particular board member would make a motion, and that I would recognize it, support it, and push it through. But I said I only had one vote. I cannot control the entire board."

Jonah laughed, loud and indignant. "You've controlled the direction of this board for over a decade. Don't even *try* to sell us on the fact you only vote your conscience and everyone else votes theirs. You've manipulated this district for a long damn time. Sounds like someone is well aware of your abilities in that department, and expects you to continue exercising that skill."

Guy exhaled, flushed, vacillating from anger to an inability to deny the accusation. "I have to put on a show, they said. Act like I'm in charge. Do my job as chair. Push enough others to vote properly to pass the proposal."

"What's the proposal?" Quinn asked.

"I do not know. They would not say."

"Seriously?" Jonah said. "Since when do you hold court and not know the docket, counselor? Surely you can speculate."

"I'm afraid to speculate," he said with ebbing energy. "The not telling me makes me wonder how off-the-wall it is. Why *not* tell me? I wonder if it's something we've never discussed before."

He talked in circles, and he went out of his way to say *they*, not *him* or *her*. "Are you keeping the meeting secret from the public?"

His brows about hit his hairline. "I'm not broadcasting it, if that's what you mean. Date and time will be discreetly posted on the website without fanfare, to keep things legal."

Just like Iona said. Iona . . . she knew before Guy did.

"We're wasting time," Jonah said, jaw tight, mouth flatlined. "Are you calling every board member to tell them how to vote?"

Guy didn't respond.

"I can't believe this." Jonah leaped to his feet. "We're wasting time, Quinn. Let's go."

Quinn stood, but didn't take her stare off the chairman. He'd turned in the money to authorities. He'd admitted he'd been bribed. "Guy, listen to me."

The man waited, legitimately listening, frozen like a trapped man sorely in need of options.

"Vote the right way," she said. "Not how they tell you to. Not like you think will be the least trouble. We cannot help you if you keep screwing up. What are you supposed to tell these other board members?"

"To vote like I vote. To vote like the board member who proposes the issue. To do what they are told."

"Then don't," she said. "Stop digging your hole deeper. Just show up Monday night and vote. We'll be there."

"But they'll know," he said.

"And we'll know," she countered. "I'm not sure what this proposal will be, but something tells me it'll be easy to tell the right vote from the wrong one or they wouldn't be pushing you so hard."

Guy blinked rapidly, processing.

"Think hard about it," she said, and nodded to Jonah to leave.

They made straight for the truck with no goodbye. Guy was confused, embattled with his decision.

Quinn texted Jule they were on the way again. "They've gotten to Guy plus one other," she said to Jonah.

He nodded. "My guess is Laney."

"Can't see these people trusting Guy, though. Did what you see in him in there give you confidence about Monday night?"

"Not in the least."

She called Ty. He picked right up. "How'd it go? What's your read on him?"

She gave him the abbreviated version. "He's being forced into voting for something he won't learn about until he gets to the meeting Monday night."

"That's it. I'm calling Aunt Laney whose not exactly being forthcoming," he said. "Why'd you call me?"

This is why she loved working with Ty. "Just to see if you could still read my mind, fella."

Another call came through. Iona. Quinn hit the automatic message stating she was on the phone and would call back. It was then she noticed texts from where Iona had tried to contact her while in Guy's. Iona had typed SOS, EMERGENCY, and 911 in six different messages, the last one in caps, stating CALL ME, QUINN. I'M SCARED.

She'd performed this flighty behavior before.

Quinn's ordinary reaction to Iona's overreactions would be to call her and calm her down. Just do this. Just do that.

But someone had gotten to Guy to make him confess to bribery. Someone had scared Laney into silence. Someone had run Jonah and her off the road. Who said someone wasn't making the rounds to the board members with individualized threats?

She called Iona.

"Thank, God," Iona exclaimed. "Are you paying attention to this? Threats! I'm afraid to answer my phone. Afraid to go outside. Afraid to—"

"What is the emergency, Iona?"

"Um, just, just . . . everything. What do I do if someone comes after me? Maybe I should resign, too. Talk to me, Quinn. You're the only person I can trust. Seriously, should I resign?" Her voice had inched up to a pinched squeal.

"No, just stay home, stay off the phone, stay off Facebook. Just consider this a hurricane, and you're riding it out."

Which reminded Quinn they hadn't had time to study Facebook in an hour or more. She needed to since social media was fast becoming a barometer for this whole damn board.

Jonah tapped her arm. "Quinn, please." He held up his phone, sounding nervous and serious at the same time. "Call Jule for me."

Quinn instinctively studied their texts to see where Jonah left off with Jule. He might hover over his mother, but his concern outranked that for Iona. "Gotta go, Iona." She hung up before the woman could argue.

"Call her," Jonah said again.

They texted routinely with Jule, the three of them, especially on matters of supper. There was the text from Jonah saying they'd be late. Then the text that they were about to leave. Then Quinn's saying they were on their way.

Jule always responded with a heart. There was no heart last time.

Quinn's own heart stuttered in her chest.

Any other night, she wouldn't have worried. But Jonah was in the thick of this school board mess, and someone out there was flexing their muscles to smack members in line.

Who says they wouldn't do so with everybody else involved, lessening their odds of anything going wrong?

She called Jule. Call went straight to voice mail.

Jule never turned her phone off. Especially if her two kids weren't home for the night.

Chapter 25

JONAH IGNORED THE speed limit, and he fishtailed, skirting the ditch taking the turn through Sterling Banks's entry gate. "I should've just kept to myself," he said.

"You helped an old woman," Quinn replied, trying to focus him while holding onto the door to not hurt the arm. "Jule thought you did the right thing. Just deal with what's in front of us, Jonah." Too many people ate themselves alive when bad things happened, which interfered with getting the job done.

Not that her pulse wasn't throbbing double-time up her neck.

The truck skid into Jule's drive. Jonah beat Quinn to the most used entrance, the kitchen door, and hesitated for a nano-instant finding it ajar. "Jule? Mom?"

They ran through the house, Quinn taking note to look in closets. Her doing so sent Jonah to the goat barn ahead of her, Jule's second home, and the place that had both their hearts in their throats from the past death of Bonnie Blue, the murdered nanny goat murdered by a hired man under the employ of real estate mogul Renault. A security system was put into place, supposedly to catch future people like that.

Jule wasn't there.

Jonah scurried through the place, meeting Quinn at the corral, his eyes searching hers knowing full well she would've shouted out if she found anything. The motion sensor spots sent their shadows across the dirt like an afternoon sun, accenting the pale fret on his face.

"Jesus, Quinn, what have I done?"

"Can't blame yourself for bad people," she said, dialing Ty.

"But what they did to Miss Abbott . . . I should have forecasted . . ."

Ty picked up. "Hey, I—"

"Change gears." Quinn's no-nonsense nature kicked in. "They've taken Jule."

"What?" Then he locked in his cop-sense. "How do you know?"

Panic-stricken, Jonah held up his phone to Quinn.

"Hold on, Ty." She read him the text. "You know what to do."

"Give me the number," he said.

She did. "Has to be a burner."

"Well, I can't not try."

"I know," she said. "Tell Uncle Larry and get here."

She hung up and tended to Jonah. "They have no need to hurt her," she said, afraid her words meant nothing. Another old woman threatened in the name of buying a damn piece of dirt for, of all things, a school for innocent children.

Counselling him kept her from losing her own shit, but having a plan would keep them sane. "Let's scour the house and barn again. We stay together, both our eyes on the same things. It's home to both of us, and it might be hard to see clues, but hunt for anything, regardless how minor, out of place, left behind, even broken. Start with the house."

They began with the kitchen where Jule spent so much of her time when she wasn't with the goats, or in the pecan building. She'd been expecting them for dinner.

Quinn checked the water for the pasta which was cold, waiting to be turned on, but the spaghetti sauce simmered on low, covered. Lifting the lid, she jammed a finger into the mixture, expecting to get burned but didn't. It hadn't heated through. Jule hadn't long turned on the heat, likely switched on after the text from Quinn stating they were on their way, seventeen minutes ago.

Quinn turned off the range top then scrolled through her contacts. It was late, and the person might be out, but once he saw her name, he'd answer. She was almost positive he would.

Until he didn't.

"Knox," she said into voicemail. "This is official. Call me ASAP. The school board corruption is now a kidnapping . . . a member of my family." She thought about going over his head, but she needed reliable guys on her side, and none of her red-head temper.

She and Jonah combed the house, analyzing everything from drapes being open to trinkets missing. They found Jule's phone in the bathroom, on the floor under the sink. When Jonah stooped to retrieve it, she gripped a fist-full of his shirt. "Don't touch it. Prints. She probably wasn't the one who threw it there." Instead, Quinn bolted to the kitchen where she recalled plastic gloves in a drawer, used during Jule's summer canning marathons. She returned, awkwardly forcing one glove half on her slinged arm, then the too-short extensions over the long fingers of her right hand. Then she picked up the phone, its power turned off.

Jonah recited the password, and the phone powered up, but no texts, emails or messages indicated anything untoward. Just the latest texts amongst Jule and Jonah and Quinn.

A heart-dropping feeling told her they had zero idea where Jule was. She would've left the phone on. She would've hidden it in her overalls, to be tracked.

Someone grabbed Jule slick, clean, and unexpected. Quinn guessed they slipped in the kitchen, probably left unlocked by Jule as a courtesy for Jonah and Quinn expected any moment. She'd just turned the sauce on to heat, waiting for them to arrive to cook the pasta. Then she took the opportunity for a bathroom visit. With the toilet flushed, water droplets scattered around the sink and the soap dispenser still damp from handwashing, the kidnappers waited for her outside, surprising her as she exited.

At least that was Quinn's best guess.

She eased Jonah out of the bath. "Don't touch a thing," she said. "Better yet, go outside. Be careful where you stand. Stay on the stoop." She kept thinking of the evidence they'd ruined already. Tire tracks. Footprints. Problem was, it was night.

"Quinn? I can help. I can—"

She held her good arm out, protecting any further violation. "We probably mucked up enough evidence as it is. Just do like I ask . . . please." She added the last to avoid hurting him. He barely held himself together, and alienating would only irritate. He wanted his mother back and wanted to be proactive doing so. Quinn fought to save enough evidence to increase the chances they could.

Silently, he did as told, while she mentally deciphered the crime. Where the hell was the sheriff's department?

She returned to the hallway. She and Jonah had not touched the door knob, just pushed the door with a foot. No rug on the floor to wrinkle or shift. Nothing on the wall had tilted from a bump. She visualized the shortest route from there to the most efficient exit, the kitchen, and she gingerly walked the path. They hadn't even knocked the coffee table directly in the line of egress, meaning they'd detoured around . . . or carried her over.

Then they navigated around the dinette table, already set for supper per the silverware and folded paper napkins. Through the kitchen, a used, sauce-covered ladle rested on a spoon holder. Unused utensils huddled in the deep red, cast-ironed container shaped like a rooster on the counter. Dishtowels hung neat except for the one near the stove. Gloves still on,

Quinn nudged the kitchen door open and eased out, each step studying for signs.

Not a damn thing out of place. *Son of bitch*, Jule would've left something to find. She was smart, aware who'd be hunting her. Fright crawled through Quinn's bones at this vacuum of evidence.

They carried Jule, no doubt, her unable to leave breadcrumbs. Just how incapacitated she was, however, was the scary part.

Sirens echoed in the distance, sound waves pushing their way. Quinn still wore the gloves.

Jonah stood terrified on the corner of the concrete, studying her face as hard as he'd hunted for his mother. "Quinn?"

"They entered here, I believe. She was in the bathroom, and they waited for her to come out." She wasn't sure how much more to tell him. Nothing was proven, and she had no gelled concept of why anything occurred. She did know Jule, though, and Quinn had a fairly crystalized notion of how things went down . . . maybe twenty minutes ago. But twenty minutes could be twenty miles in any direction, which could mean any of three counties.

Thank God Ty and two other cruisers distracted Jonah from picking more empty details out of her.

Quinn ran out and tried to wave them off the graveled drive, but too late. Now tire tracks ran over the place. She lowered her arm, yanked off the gloves, shoved them into her sling where she'd tucked the phone, and ran to meet Ty.

"They took her forcibly but somehow subdued her, I think," she said. "Phone was on the floor in the bath, turned off. Turned on, I found nothing out of the ordinary." She motioned into her sling for him to gently take the phone, talking fast but succinct about her theories. This was third shift. Only two other deputies waited, appreciating Ty ran investigations for the sheriff. Over their pay grade to think for themselves. The sheriff rolled up before Quinn finished, but her phone rang before he left the vehicle.

Knox.

She showed the caller ID to Ty.

"Jesus, Q." He recognized the name and spoke low, his lips mashed in a rebuking stare, but Quinn gave him enough acknowledgement to let him see just how much she didn't care and walked far enough from her uncle to avoid him hearing.

"I need you, Knox," she said, backing up to a pecan tree on the edge of the grove, facing the darkness that seemed to have no end. Far enough not to be heard from those in the driveway.

"Talk to me," he said, no longer the man humoring her about her legs or her two-bit PI business.

The years of separation shrank between them. Her hate for the FBI evaporated. They'd been well-trained for the personal to vanish at first sign of a distress call, and when dealing with one of their own, well, the shift was instantaneous. She'd been one whom the field agents wished the bureau had kept.

She filled him in.

"The school board business is still awful tenuous to this," he said.

"Don't do this to me, Knox. This is the third casualty in a week over a damn school being built, with a bribe involved and questionable parties from outside the county."

"Your uncle—"

"Allowed my daddy to get murdered in his own house then couldn't solve the case. He's well proven his incompetence when it comes to anything other than domestic disturbances and speeding tickets. This is the woman who raised me, Knox." Her voice intensified. "This is the woman who miraculously was only injured when my daddy was killed. She's stood by me. She's the mother of the man I'll probably marry."

"Quinn."

It took her a second to realize the voice wasn't Knox's. She spun around.

Uncle Larry's furrowed forehead showed he'd heard. He held out his hand. "Give me the phone."

She twisted, putting the phone on her other side, away from his reach. "Hell, no."

"Quinn?" Knox called.

The sheriff stood fast, pushing his hand out. "Let me talk to whoever you're asking to come in here."

But Quinn stood fast, using the phone to motion to the house, then to his uniforms. "Go do your job, Uncle Larry." *Or try to*, she wanted to say. "This is about Jule this time, and we have no room for error. Jule raised me. She and Jonah have sacrificed for Sterling Banks as if it was their own."

Her voice shook in holding up the real words she wanted to spout. *I cannot afford for you to screw things up this time.*

No tears. She was too angry for tears, but he was about to nix the bureau coming into Craven County. In spite of Jules being the one missing, regardless that her uncle's past transgressions had almost cost

Quinn her life and *had* cost them Graham's. Larry Sterling was digging in in the name of turf.

"Quinn," Knox shouted from the phone. "Is that the sheriff?"

She spoke through her teeth. "Yes."

"Pass him the phone."

She pressed the phone closer to her ear. "Knox, you don't realize—"

"Pass him the phone, Quinn. You're too close, honey. You're too close to the situation."

She peered to her allies for support. The ones she wholly trusted. Jonah itched to come to her, but Ty held his sleeve, understanding the play going down.

Quinn's jaws ached from the battle. "If you fuck this up, Uncle Larry, I will never forgive you. I will never accept you in my house, and I will forbid you to set foot on this farm." She quivered, not asking if he understood nor if she was clear enough. She thrust out the phone. He accepted the challenge.

For Jule. Only for the sake of Jule.

The sheriff left it off speaker and walked further into the trees.

Quinn returned to the others, shivering. She finished explaining events to Ty, what she presumed, and what she couldn't figure out, but in the telling kept staring into the trees after her uncle.

"We need to search the entire farm," Ty said.

Quinn doubted Jule was on the property, but where else were they supposed to search? They had no clues leading elsewhere. So Ty gave his orders, his men taking the manor and the river.

"It's dark," Jonah said. "How are we supposed to see her in the dark?"

"We do the best we can, dude," Ty said, a grip going to his friend's shoulder. "Sheriff Sterling will notify highway patrol, Colleton County, Charleston County, everyone. She's easy to spot with those overalls and long braid. Her age. We'll find her, man."

"Her bandanas," Quinn added.

Jonah had more questions. They hung on him, waiting to be said. Exactly how would they find her? Where else would they look? What were her odds of being found unhurt, much less alive?

But he was also smart enough to see there were no answers. Not yet.

Quinn came around him to reach over with her strong arm. At first he stiffened, but she pulled him tighter, and his resistance turned into a smothering hug. The pain in her hurt shoulder shot into her fingers and up her neck.

"I cannot lose her," he said. "She's all I've got."

"We're not losing her," she whispered into his head pressed hard against her collar. "And she's not all you have." She rubbed circles on his back. "I'm here." He squeezed harder. "I'm always here," she said.

He jerked, the sudden movement shooting a reminder of her injury, and she peered at the ground to avoid him seeing. She sucked in and got in front of the pain.

"We gotta search," he said.

"You stick close to home," she said, craving to cocoon him and box him up from this. "In kidnapping cases, someone needs to be home."

"Son of a bitch," he said. "We know why this happened."

Yes, they did. They might not be able to connect the board or their puppet masters to Jule, but the invisible strings were there.

Quinn scooted to her uncle. She needed him to finish with the FBI so she could retrieve her phone and join the deputy searching the manor. From there she'd lead him along the acreage toward the highway.

Ty already left to search alongside the river, but nothing was as dark as the Edisto River ecosystem. If this were another situation . . . not Jule and not Jonah . . . Quinn would've said don't bother with the river. A kidnapper normally left the victim's area, taking them to his own comfort zone, but this was different. What comfort zone? Who's comfort zone? This was a message to Jonah to do what they wanted him to do, and he didn't need a ransom note or letter of instruction. The question was whether he'd get her back even if he did as they wanted.

Her uncle hung up, strode over, and handed her her phone. "The bureau is on its way."

She was stunned. "Um, thanks." But instinct kept her from singing his praises. "Gotta go search."

"She's not here," he said.

"We have to make sure. You do the bulletins and we do what we can. This is different, Uncle. Jule is a statement, not someone they want to exchange for money. They're manipulating Jonah."

These people went too public with this. No way this could go well long term. How stupid were they?

Or were they? Like the board using Iona, maybe someone higher took advantage of idiots, remaining in the shadows. Maybe the power behind this was nowhere in plain sight, giving the visible people a lot of rein, with promises of repercussions downstream for screw ups. These were sacrifices for the greater good, or at least that felt the theme.

She dared to wonder if this was personal, toward her, toward those she loved.

"So sure of this direction, are you?" Larry said.

"Solid." She had to sound that way to him.

"Well, your FBI people are coming to help. Are we good?" he asked.

Startled, she took the win. "Yes." Then added again, "Thank you."

But in spite of Uncle Larry's concession, her mind dwelled on the type of surroundings Jule would spend the night in and whether she felt safe enough to close her eyes. If only she'd had a chance to send a phone message, but that phone text might've gotten her killed, too.

The night would be long. Somewhere in the middle of it, Quinn would take a moment to catch her breath. Maybe then she'd call Iona, because somehow calling a school board member in the midst of hunting Jule right now would only make her vomit. These people made her sick.

Chapter 26

THEY CALLED FOR the search dogs about ten p.m. to scour Sterling Banks, coming up empty, leaving them nowhere else to look. With no ransom note or phone call or some sort of direction, they could only wait. In the meantime, a Senior Alert was distributed and police departments notified across the state. *Be on the lookout* felt like such an empty gesture but what else could be done?

The morning sun peered through the pecan canopies indicative of a clear day. *Thank God.* Quinn wasn't sure Jonah could've handled dreary drizzle atop of worrying about his mother.

No call for money. No call, period. Jonah paced most the night, inside then out, frantic at the lack of progress, Bogie on his heel until Quinn scolded him to get out of the way. His fret ultimately exhausted him, and Quinn told him to rest while she took Knox and a few others to her place up the driveway. She left Bogie with him for consolation and to have something to take care of. A SWAT team remained on standby. Quinn played go between from there to Jule's place, where Ty and an agent kept Jonah company.

Jonah had received only the one text. *You know what to do.* While Knox wasn't a hundred percent sold yet, Quinn was concrete sure that this was about waiting for Monday   night's board meeting. Nothing for Jonah to do but attend the meeting and follow whatever direction he felt in his gut was the right one to follow once this, whatever this was, went down.

The general consensus of everyone but Knox was this was some sort of attempt to devise a major development move on Craven County. He held onto the alternative that someone simply hated the Sterlings for being rich landowners, the haves versus the have nots, or some fool thinking he could win the lottery via a kidnapping, but he remained surprised there'd been no ransom.

In Quinn's opinion, a lot of seeds had been planted leading up to this. She worried she stood on the precipice of a different Craven County. The people who wanted change stood on the outside, hungry to take for themselves, and those on the inside weren't powerful, savvy, or financially solid enough to stop the coup.

Even Sterling Banks couldn't stop the shift of an entire county.

She was tired, and her thoughts too often took off on skids in one direction, then another, before rebounding to worry about Jule. She even worried about calling in the FBI for what little it had accomplished, and concerned if word got out, their presence could do more damage than good. Always that chance when it came to hostages. She'd received the training.

Sore and spent to her bones without any sleep, Quinn could barely move out of the rocker on her porch. The breeze played tag in and out of the trees, some finding a way to her, the soothing brush across her weighting her eyelids. Her shoulder was stove up bad, the pain relentless. The wreck apparently jerked muscles from her neck into her hips, and Tylenol didn't touch it. She'd finally swallowed one of the prescription pills about three in the morning when her adrenaline had ebbed and Knox had wanted one more time to pepper her with questions.

Knox brought her a coffee and slid up another chair, waking her from a twilight sleep. She appreciated the gesture and hadn't the strength to tell him he'd used the wrong milk. Then the memory of Jule hooking her on goat's milk pushed fresh apprehension to the surface when Quinn thought she couldn't worry more.

"You ought to get some real sleep," he said. "How's the shoulder?"

"Protesting," she said, voice thick as if she'd already slept. She'd tried laying the sling on the arm of the chair but the angle was wrong so she let it hang. No telling what she smelled like. She needed a shower but handling the arm for that would be a trick. She'd call Jule for that sort of help. Guess she could call Jonah. She was too exhausted to care.

"What time is it?" She hoped at least Jonah slept.

"A little after six," Knox said.

She reached into her sling and pulled out her phone. Iona might be up by now. After the string of emergency acronyms Iona put in her texts last night, Quinn hoped she wouldn't mind.

"I'm putting this on speaker," she said, balancing the device, dialing with her thumb. "This is my client I told you about."

Knox put a notepad on the arm of his chair, the one he'd carried around all night, jotting things. "Might as well start with her. I'll be reaching out to each of the board members before this day's through."

Quinn stopped the call. He told her hours ago, when she'd briefed him on Miss Abbott, Miss Birdie, and her conversations with assorted board members, that he might want to interrogate each of these people.

She'd listened, said nothing, but now she questioned that move, or at least the timing. "You sure you want to let yourself be known to these people? We have no direct connection between them and the kidnapping."

He leaned back in his chair, judging. She usually ran like gangbusters seeking clues and dogging suspicions. Felt odd to switch roles with Knox. Felt even odder to be thinking more like her uncle about the FBI's tactics.

"Jule, the fires, the board, the gossip, hints, and talk in county council about development. . . it's all likely connected," she said. "But if board members are being coerced, they're too untrustworthy not to inform Chance or Mauney or whoever is yanking their chain. We aren't sure which board member is on the inside, on the outside, involved, or ignorant. And if everything hinges on tomorrow's meeting, we could get Jule killed."

"Okay," he finally agreed after some thought. "But don't mention Jule to Iona." He waved for her to proceed, promising no interference, but he stayed put to listen. Quinn dialed again and put the call on speaker.

"Where the heck have you been, Quinn?" Iona's speech crackled, as if she'd awoken too early, full of annoyance.

"Settle down. I've been in a wreck, remember? What happened with you?"

A big gasp, then Iona whispered. "Sorry. Was it them? Did they get to you, too?"

Maybe they had. The BOLO for the Ram pickup remained active with no reported sightings. The driver surely tucked that truck out of sight somewhere safe, pending body work, but that discussion wasn't Iona's to have. "Sorry I didn't call right away," Quinn said. "What's so dire?"

"First, I was skipping the meeting tomorrow night, but I have to go now. Fripp came home yesterday with a list of demands. Stay home on Sunday. Don't go to church. Keep our daughter out of school on Monday. Sounded like you until he ordered me to show up and vote accordingly Monday night. What's happening, Quinn? What's accordingly mean?"

Quinn cut her eyes at Knox. "I was about to ask you the same question. What *does* accordingly mean?"

"No idea. He got irate when I asked him. Oh my gosh, then Laney called and told me the same exact thing."

Quinn stopped rocking and sat forward, ensuring Knox heard, him now familiar with the names. "What did Laney say?"

"That something was going down Monday. Told me to vote like she does, and that the result was *defining for us*, for the community. Her words. She wouldn't say what that meant, and trust me, I asked."

Quinn saw why Laney didn't elaborate. Iona wouldn't keep her mouth shut. Here she was being told to protect her daughter and stay out of the public's eye, and she picks up the phone and calls Quinn. Laney knew what she was doing. "Who has Fripp been talking to?"

"He didn't say. I didn't want to know."

God, the woman could be dense. Quinn understood Fripp needing to protect his daughter, but he wouldn't be so enrapt in the board unless he had something to gain . . . or something serious to lose. "What about Miss Abbott's funeral on Monday?"

"Oh shit, you're right." Silence from Iona. "Not sure how, but we maybe caused that, didn't we, Quinn?"

Pretty sure that's a solid yes. Quinn couldn't tell if those were tears or not in Iona's morning voice. "I believe someone got to Fripp, Iona. Go over what he said again."

Iona blew out long. *"There's a lot riding on Monday night*, he said, and *A lot could go well or bad things could happen. Don't fuck it up."*

Well, that was clear as mud.

"When I asked him for more, he chewed me out. Made me so mad I started to kick him to the curb, but if things get dangerous, he's better than nothing for protection around here, don't you think? I'm armed, but not the best shot."

Quinn couldn't begin to imagine that woman wielding a weapon and not doing more damage than good. "Put Fripp on the phone, please."

"Oh, Quinn, if he found out I'd hired you . . ."

"I'm serious. Put him on." Knox nodded in agreement.

"He's not here."

Of course he wasn't. So much for protecting his family. "Who have you spoken with besides Fripp?"

"Just Fripp and Laney, both telling me to be quiet and invisible until the meeting. So I am." She hesitated. "I'm afraid to go, Quinn."

Quinn looked to Knox with an imaginary I-told-you-so. "Expect added protection there. Just go, okay? Bring your daughter with you. Park her off to the side, out of the audience but so you can see her. So everyone can see her. She's safer in public than alone."

Iona didn't respond at first. "I'll think about it."

Quinn didn't want to browbeat the woman into putting herself or her family at risk. Jule missing was enough. "Take care and stay safe."

"Quinn?" Iona said, like a nervous child afraid to let go. "Are you and Jonah okay? Y'all are sort of involved now. Has anyone called you?"

Quinn gave Knox an even harder I-told-you-so stare. "Just take care of you and your daughter, hon. I'll see you Monday."

She hung up but shook the phone a few times toward Knox at the reality of things. "They went to Fripp instead of Iona. They understand the dynamics of that board well enough to tell Laney to make Iona tow the line, and threaten Fripp as backup insurance. Iona's too flighty to approach direct."

"Or Guy or Laney just educated these people. Give me Fripp's number. I'm taking one of your deputies and running this one down. I need some names."

She retrieved the number for him. "He's a blowhard," she said, recalling her confrontation with Fripp outside Jackson Hole a few days ago. "But he might fight you. And if you talk to him, and leave him out there, he'll blab your conversation to the world."

Knox gave a light chuckle tinged with darker, more serious intent. "He won't do either, trust me." He left his chair, but then turned. "The APB on Jule will take on new life now that it's daylight. You showed me that Facebook page. I'm not so sure these kidnappers aren't hidden amongst those posters."

Quinn had to agree, but one or two out of seven thousand didn't sound promising. Lincoln20 came to mind. She hadn't decided which side of good he stood on yet. Dozens of others with loud mouths made appearances on that list, too. Silent ones, however, would be the more likely candidates, and those numbered in the thousands.

"Post that Jule is missing," he said. "It looks odd not to."

Made sense. She'd get on it. "Better Jonah do it," she said. With the condolence comments that would ensue, he'd have busy work to occupy his anxious mind.

"I'll have a guy working with him," Knox said.

She understood. No mention of the FBI. That alone could get Jule killed.

EAGER TO EMBRACE Facebook, Jonah took his coaching well. Be organic. Reveal that Jule had not been seen for twelve hours. Ask if anyone has seen her. Do not say how much law enforcement is involved. Or who.

Avoid appearing panicked.

"People will ask questions." His handsome face had lost some tone, a grayness dull in the skin under his eyes.

She hugged him tight, sad he wasn't resting. He gripped a coffee mug across the kitchen table from Ty and an agent. Everyone watched their phones. She couldn't help but want to hug him again and hold on.

"We're studying the dynamics of the group," Ty said. "Our agent buddy's helping, but you and Jonah are probably our best gauge in reading these people."

Jonah needed to stay busy. They may have nothing to do outside of this until tomorrow night. She didn't tell him about Fripp, either, which might give him someone to pursue.

With Knox gone, she remained and found her own chair at the table, Ty giving up his so she could sit next to Jonah. The three men rested elbows on placemats and entered the online group with Quinn resting her phone on her sling. Silence entombed them, short of the different degrees of clicks and beeps on their devices.

While the others read reactions to Jonah's posts and replies, Quinn did a search for each board member for their posts. No one had since the resignation announcements yesterday. Short and sweet, each of them, then nothing. Miss Birdie announced how much better she was and how she'd be home tomorrow. Remarks ranged from blaming the board, protecting the board, and blessing Miss Birdie. Prayers were promised from a hundred different people, many the same souls wanting to fire, picket, arrest, and God-knows-what to others.

But the post that caught Quinn's attention, the one that had collected almost as many comments as Miss Birdie's condolence post, was that from Lincoln20 blaring to the public that the board planned to hold an emergency board meeting on Monday night, and they'd tried to keep it secret. A last minute affair, he said. He ranted how they were notorious for this sort of *clandestine comportment*. Those words. The phrasing told Quinn this person was educated but not young. She leaned toward him being a generation older than herself. She still assumed him male.

The post spiked, the readers white-hot. How dare members slide in a hush-hush meeting, thinking people went about their Sunday business, too absorbed in family to take note. Again, the board behaved in its atrocious ways. But phones were read on the way to church if not in church, and what they read was discussed afterwards in the parking lot.

Ty spoke first. "The sheriff hasn't told us anything about a meeting."

She tried to give a shrug and paid for it with another shot of pain. "He will, I'm sure. With all of this . . ." she did a circle look around the table at the four of them. "There will be more than a couple badges at the meeting."

Ty stared longer at her than necessary, then seemed to decide not to ask his question. Not in front of Jonah, she guessed.

But Jonah caught the exchange. "What?"

"Just post about Jule and answer the feedback," she said.

"Quit placating me."

She eyed Ty who gave a barely appreciable nod.

"The first priority is Jule's safety," she said.

Jonah stiffened, waiting for her to finish whatever she seemed to be painting as a prologue.

"Nobody is interviewing the board before Monday," she said.

His frown etched as deep as she'd ever seen. "What? They ought to be the starting point. You saw those three on Miss Abbott's place, trespassing and inspecting their handiwork before the old lady was cold. What the hell is the FBI here for if not to flex muscle and get answers?"

"One would think that, yes." She'd played this in her head as well, repeatedly. "But the priority is your mother. For some reason this meeting is important to whomever is behind this. You were there when Guy admitted he'd been bribed. You were there when Laney avoided our questions about the pressure on her. Iona's in hiding. We haven't even spoken to the other four. A meeting is on, and we believe they can't not show up without fear of someone acting on assorted threats."

"To include Jule?" His question cracked on the end.

She dropped her phone on the table and reached over, rubbing across his upper back. "You got your own text, Jonah. It means you have to be there, too. If nobody follows through, if anyone screws up, we may never see your mother." She swallowed her own lump at the desperation in his eyes. "We don't expect to hear anything until tomorrow night. We can't tell anyone about the FBI, your directive, any of this. We just have to play it out. I know it's hard."

"But we don't even know we're doing the right thing."

Quinn had thought that so many times she'd lost count. "Just post about Jule, okay?" She tired of saying that.

The posts from Jonah robbed some of Lincoln20's energy and redirected Miss Birdie. Like Miss Abbott and Miss Birdie, the Craven community respected Jule Proveaux. Folks offered to hunt for her and make calls; others asked how they could help.

With Jonah's attention on responses, Quinn sagged in her chair. Ty winked approval over at her. She smiled, welcoming the sympathy Jonah hadn't the strength to give her.

Chapter 27

SUNDAY DRAGGED into the evening without a word from a soul. Knox and a deputy found Fripp, after a three-hour search of his assorted stomping grounds, taking him to the old sheriff's office Quinn liked to use.

Fripp admitted listening to Chase's enticement of future work, so that conduit was established, though an independent person like Chase asking a local contractor like Fripp to do what he could for the greater good, wasn't exactly breaking the law. Iona doing what Fripp wanted was just her not using the brains God gave her. At worst, she could be considered more of a culprit than her husband since her vote directed work to herself.

Supposedly, Chase had bragged about representing money with the clout to do as *they* pleased. Was that using a general, catch-all pronoun, or was there a consortium involved.

"Jesus," Jonah kept saying. "Who goes to this much trouble for Craven County?"

Knox gave Fripp the option of remaining quiet, staying home, and hiding up to the Monday meeting, or remaining in FBI custody to insure the same. He headed home, making Quinn feel sorry for Iona.

Quinn and Jonah bowed out of church. Iona stayed away as well, but not from the grapevine, i.e., the Facebook group. Laney showed up for service. Guy didn't go to church anyway, and someone mentioned they'd seen Piper take communion. The entire day, social media chewed on the meaning of the board meeting, broadcast sightings of its members with pictures, commended Miss Birdie on her recovery, and prayed for Jonah in finding Jule.

What everyone on Sterling Banks hadn't expected was folks and their respectable manners wanting to come by to speak to Jonah, bring casseroles, and sit in his momma's stead to offer peace. After six impromptu drop-ins when agents had to disappear in bedrooms, Jonah posted his thanks to the group, begging folks to keep their distance for the time being. He had to focus on Jule. Those who didn't get the message were deterred by Ty at the door, the bureau agent keeping out of sight.

When Quinn could, she pried Jonah out of the house to walk Bogie.

Sometimes they said nothing. Other times they spoke of their childhood experiences in the trees, on the river, up in Windsor, the treehouse. Escapism. But each time they returned to the house and reality, Jonah's shoulders drooped, and he plopped on the den sofa, Facebook open, the dog beside him. Not even the television came on.

Lenore had brought them homemade breakfast biscuits in the morning, sandwiches at lunch, and a pot of chili as well as one of potato soup for dinner, determined to feed the whole lot of them. She asked if she needed to stay, and Ty convinced her not to. The diner needed her more than they did sitting around watching each other. She hugged Jonah three times before she reluctantly left.

Everyone half ate dinner, and by seven, Quinn had had enough of the whole damn mess. She went outside, disappeared into the trees, and called Iona.

"Are you okay?" she asked, antsy about nothing to do.

"Did they have to restrict Fripp to home?" her client whined.

"Thought he was your protection."

Iona said nothing to that.

"Run through the board members for me," Quinn said. "Surely y'all took a head count as to who would be at the meeting tomorrow night after that resignation talk. Start with Laney." Always give them something easy to answer to make them cooperative.

"She's coming and told me to come, remember?"

"Right, good. Piper?"

"She's coming. Laney said so."

Quinn kept delivering direct questions to invite direct answers.

"Harmon Valentine."

"Don't know."

"Curtis Fuller?"

A scoff on the phone. "He always comes. Mr. Red-White-and-Blue never misses a meeting . . . never misses a vote."

But these weren't normal times, and Curtis ran rogue. Quinn bet he never received a phone call.

"And Ella Mae," Quinn concluded.

"Whatever Guy does—"

"Ella Mae does. Can you call them for me? Tell them you're under the weather, and are trying to judge attendance?"

"They'll think I'm lying. Have you found Jule?"

"No. We need your help, Iona. Can you make the calls? It's important."

Feeling needed, Iona agreed. Wasn't thirty minutes before she called with her reply. "Couldn't get Guy or Curtis, but the rest said they'd be there. Ella Mae was iffy, but I believe her answer was closer to yes than no. Does that help?"

"It does, thanks. See you tomorrow."

"At the funeral?"

Once again, Quinn forgot about the funeral, and guilt spilled over her. Even worse, Jule had handled the arrangements, and Jonah or Quinn might have to pinch hit for her. "I'll leave that up to you."

How horrible for the memory of Miss Abbott to be marred by this.

She headed to Jule's place, stopping to check on the goats like she would want. Jonah had tended them throughout the day, but Quinn peered in once more. They dozed already, mommas and babies with a billy to one side of the corral and another on the other. All good. On the way back to the house, however, she dragged, rethinking what she'd thought about umpteen times already.

This board might be elected officials, the politics lending itself to shadiness, but they were still bright, each in his or her own way when it came to their profession and skill. They weren't career criminals. Some of them bullied to get their way, and most of them had misspent funds in one way or another during their tenure, but nothing that reeked of incarceration. She didn't see them risking jail time by killing, maiming, or kidnapping anyone. Even Guy, as opportunistic as he was, didn't have the balls to cause injury.

She felt sorry for them, frankly, and she prayed she wasn't being naïve about that.

They were being driven by someone smarter, hungrier, and much more powerful in money and influence. She staked her pecans on it. Charleston land cost too much these days and Colleton was too far from the major cities. Someone had set sights on the easy, cheap land in between.

Her daddy had forecasted this sort of movement as inevitable, and had warned that land grabs would be Quinn's and future Sterling Banks heirs' biggest challenge in facing the future. Taxes were high enough and to turn everything around Sterling Banks into commercial or residential would only raise taxes more.

Quinn decided she wasn't ready to go inside yet and perched on the fence railing, dismay clinging to her. The motion sensor triggered the lights. Deputy Harrison moved aside a curtain and peered out, as he should. Ty had gone home to catch up on sleep with Harrison taking his place. She waved and the curtain fluttered back into place.

She left the fence, for no reason other than she'd been there a while.

As she entered the kitchen, the bird clock on the wall sounded with an oriole call. Eight at night. Not a damn thing left to do this day but pray again that Jule watched the same moon they did, safe.

Quinn wasn't staying in the manor again. Tonight she'd stay with Jonah and Bogie. Here. And Harrison could tell everybody in the county if he wanted to.

THE CHURCH SERVICE was set for two p.m., the graveside for four. Presley Funeral Home had done a fine job listening to Jule's directions for Miss Abbott's memorial, and with her missing, they went the extra mile as if in honor of her as well. The music, the dress, the casket, even the way her hair was done seemed to represent Miss Abbott to the letter.

Jonah drove Quinn to the church in her pickup, his truck still in the shop from the wreck and her arm still tender. "I can't," he said, not reaching for the door. His voice was thick. "She planned all this."

"Most people don't know we had the accident. Hold onto me, like I'm an invalid or something," she said and reached across him with her good arm, wriggling fingers for him to take her hand. "Look at me."

He did.

"The board meeting is tonight. It comes together then. We will get Jule back." She squeezed for emphasis. "But right now we honor Miss Abbott, and in these arrangements we respect your mother. Let's do this, okay?"

He left the truck, came around, and helped her out. They hadn't left the parking lot before someone asked about Jule. Quinn interceded, put the attention on her, and evaded the inquisition. Rinse and repeat, she did the same with ten other attempts.

People loved Jonah, and they loved his mother. They loved the concept of Jonah and Quinn, and she made it look like they united even more over these tragedies. Wasn't long before Jonah had memorized the short phrases that Quinn used, and they cut through the crowd.

Jonah was as close to family as Miss Abbott had and had been properly placed up front. The Abbott niece had already sent her regrets though leaving her address, phone number, and questions about when the will would be read.

They sat through the service teary-eyed, phones at the ready. Jonah did a little jolt when his vibrated. Discreetly he eased it out. She felt him stiffen.

He tilted it for Quinn to see. *Be there tonight.*

With everyone in the church facing the backs of their heads, Quinn tried desperately not to turn around and scan the crowd. Instead, she took the phone, saved a screenshot of the text, and forwarded it to Knox . . . who invisibly sat tucked in the loft section, scanning the crowd.

Quinn ticked off in her head the familiar identities who came in. Iona showed along with the rest of the board. The superintendent of the school. A fair share of teachers. Numerous white, blue, and gray-haired ladies. Uncle Larry. Lenore, who sat with Ty in uniform, no doubt on duty. But in being politely early in their arrival, she and Jonah had missed too many who'd cut their clocks short in straggling in. The church held three hundred people, and it was packed to the rafters.

Quinn twitched in her pew, dying to stand and snap the sanctuary, but chances were Knox already had someone doing that from a more clandestine position. She hoped to God he did anyway.

The organist, tears glistening in the sun reflecting through the left front stained glass window, played a soft version of *Lord of All Hopefulness* as everyone stood and the pall bearers took away Miss Abbott. Jonah's own eyes moist. He worried this was a rehearsal for his mother, because if Quinn's heart ached at the thought, his had to, too.

She didn't take pictures, but she scoured the crowd as the casket made its way slowly up the aisle. No Chase. No Mauney. Nobody she could claim was a stand-out anomaly.

The wait between the service and the graveside was the worst, with too much time built in for folks to reach the cemetery. The memorial park as ancient as the church, headstones covered a wide slope down to a dark border of woods, live oaks, and cedars planted by families years ago. Finally, the funeral director clipped a lavaliere to the minister so he could be heard, and the short, final appreciation sermon began.

The sermon lasted half the time it took for them to break free of the curious and escape the parking lot. Slowly, Jonah and Quinn made their way out, but once they reached the highway leading to Sterling Banks, Jonah suddenly pulled over to the side of the road.

The engine idling, he laid his head on the steering wheel. She thought him exhausted until she saw his shoulders shake from a good cry.

Her left arm kept her from doing much other than twist awkwardly and lay her right on his. "Jonah. It's okay," she said.

"Don't say it's okay, Quinn. Don't say it's okay until it is. Give me a moment."

She let him sob. Not loud, not ugly, just painful tears needing a release.

A car pulled alongside. Knox. Wiping her own face, she sniffled, not caring if he could see everything, and waved him on. *All was good* being her message. Instead, he eased his vehicle in front of their truck and waited.

"What time is it?" Jonah asked, head still into the steering wheel. He raised up and, cheeks blotchy, turned to her.

"A couple minutes after five," she said.

"The board meeting is at seven."

She could tell he'd turned a corner. "Yes, sir, it is. So, what are we doing?"

He coughed once and resorted himself in his seat. "We seem dressed for a special occasion. Why change? Let's go by Lenore's and grab a bowl of okra and a tea then head to the high school. This has to be about Jule now."

As if she were done crying. This gracious side of Jonah touched her heart almost to the point of breaking. He could do this. What had he said? *Don't tell him it's okay until it is?* No, she wouldn't say it now, but she damn sure hoped to do so before this night was through. One way or another, however this turned out, Quinn would make sure Jonah's life was damn sure okay.

Chapter 28

KNOX APPEARED IN Jackson Hole diner just as Quinn and Jonah slid into the booth, confirming he was Jonah's guard for the night. "Just okra and tea," Quinn said. Lenore would already know where they had to be. The food arrived fast, and though surprised at the fried okra, Knox was Southern enough to partake. The three opened up the Facebook group.

"It's exploded," Jonah said. He hadn't asked for an update. By now he recognized the fact he'd be the first to know if they had a lead.

"The fire is fueled," Quinn said. Death, injury, and the grab of three old ladies, the three connected to the school in one fashion or another, had shed a spotlight on the unfairness and greed of recent board events. No mincing of words or dancing around suspicions. The eight thousand Facebook participants type-screamed, ridiculed, and semi-threatened every side of this equation. The board, teachers, some parents, and anyone in construction on one side . . . Jonah, the Miss Abbott lovers, and people with land to sell on the other. The haves and the have-nots, too. The young versus the old and the age-old conflict of who should pay the taxes.

There were no clear sides. This was a free-for-all, and despite Miss Birdie's best efforts, the rancor grew, making for an opportune display of on-screen mob-violence.

"I've never seen anything like this," Quinn said, tired of staring at her phone but finding it hard not to, her soul bruised at watching her beloved county behaving so vehemently. She turned her screen toward Knox. "This is not our community."

Knox nodded. "This board and whoever they are in bed with have underestimated this sleepy village."

Jonah continued to scroll. "Jesus, read what Thomas said from the hardware store. And Rebecca from the flower shop. These people aren't even afraid of what it might do for their businesses and jobs."

"Mob rule," Quinn said, but to Knox specifically, said, "This thing is getting scary, by anyone's standards."

"We gotta get this right," Jonah replied, closing his phone, absent-mindedly picking at the okra. He didn't have to add that Jule's life depended on tonight. That went unsaid.

Quinn leaned against him, a quick moment of her head on his shoulder. "Nobody here would dream of doing otherwise. Finish your tea, and let's go. It might be hard to find a chair."

Jonah smiled a sad, dark smile but it carried purpose. He was ready to do this.

Quinn would be there no matter which way this ordeal fell tonight. Parties had accidentally killed Miss Abbott. Who's to say they couldn't do the same with Jule?

Lenore waived them on, minus a ticket, and blew Quinn a kiss as they went out the door. Quinn bet a thousand dollars that Ty told Lenore not to go.

THEY ARRIVED AT the school at six thirty, to the closest spot six rows from the entrance. Knox parked an additional row over. Every sheriff's cruiser lined the first row. A Charleston television van shined like a new penny from amongst the front line of cars, having arrived early to capture whatever went down.

Protestors walked the sidewalk, placards held high, and a uniform kept them from straying into the walkway leading to the entrance. *Approve the school* on one side. *Don't raise taxes* on the other. *Save Craven County from the greedy* waved high and proud beside a few pretty and tastefully designed signs saying *Remember poor Miss Abbott.* A couple of protesters pumped their signs up and down to the beat of music from someone's phone. *We need more like Miss Birdie.*

Quinn sent up a silent thank-you that none of these hot-heads mentioned Jonah, or Jule.

The district had used every one of their black SUVs to bring the board members, escorted, as if they were senators chauffeured to a vote on waging war on a foreign country. They'd entered through the cafeteria door. A metal detector had been set up at the main entrance where the public funneled through.

Knox wasn't waving his badge, but his protection conduct fooled nobody. Quinn did her best to do the same, keeping her protected arm between them.

"Do the right thing," someone shouted. Both Quinn and Knox jerked to see who might've hollered the too familiar phrase. Too many people made the shouter too difficult to spot.

They weathered the metal detector, Knox being granted a discreet pass thanks to one of his agents hanging close to the sheriff's deputies working the people coming through. Entering the auditorium, Quinn could hardly hear herself think. The public jockeyed for best seats, but nobody denied Jonah and Quinn their preference to be up front and center.

"Thanks for what you've been doing," said one gentleman, shaking hands hard with Jonah.

"No word on Jule?" asked a woman, while another tagged on, "We're praying for you."

Quinn placed Jonah between her and Knox.

The time was ten till seven.

Some admin type from the school took the mic. "Everyone attending the meeting please take your seats. We will not be adding extra chairs, so once chairs are filled, we'll shut the doors and control entry."

People scurried like mice for places before the poor woman could lay down the mic. Then she scurried out of site behind the curtain as if saving her own skin.

Chairs scrubbed, talk turned to whispers, then the double doors shut like a tomb. A deputy posted himself at the door, but someone soon knocked. The deputy opened them wide enough for people to see Miss Birdie in her wheelchair, a friend pushing. The uniform peered back into the room, his look querying for someone to tell him whether or not to let one more person in. Especially this person. Especially since she had her own seat.

Guy gave his nod of approval, and though bandaged Miss Birdie had taken the time to dress in her best business attire. Her cohort wheeled her in and moved up toward the front as if by being handicapped, she needed to be closer to hear. A muttered ripple sounded, mostly positive from what Quinn could tell.

But she couldn't hear everyone from her own seat up front, and people with ulterior motives didn't necessarily broadcast themselves.

Wasn't this turning into a major event.

While turned, Quinn scanned the rest of the big room, catching sight of the suits. Literally. This time, Chase and Mauney really donned suits, as did a handful of folks who chose not to change out of their funeral clothes. Over there was Sy Bowers, a contractor, next to Fripp Bakeman, and the Bakeman daughter beside her father, brought to the meeting as Quinn had suggested. She guessed her father, even Fripp, was as safe a body guard as the child could have.

She didn't recognize another two or three. Never seen them before, and they sat differently than the people she could easily label as Craven residents. Sat like visitors. Backups to Chase and Mauney? Allies or insurance? But then they could be contractors who heard about this hubbub in Craven County, and attended to see if they spotted potential work if this school really happened.

For a second, one guy reminded her of Chevy Castellano, which was ludicrous. Chevy was dead. He'd bled out in her living room, atop her braided rug, a bodyguard to real estate mogul Ronald Renault and his daughter. Chevy had paid the ultimate price for being a double agent between the two.

She didn't want that memory in her head right now. Instead, she focused on the folks she did know. So many souls waited with baited breath to see how the group of seven would impact their futures professionally, personally, and financially. Would their daughter have access to the new school, or would their son be able to remain at the old school he was accustomed to. Teachers wondering if they'd have to transfer, or if they'd be allowed to. So many lives in seven pairs of hands . . . plus whatever other sets of hands worked behind the scenes, which by now, a lot more citizens suspected.

Quinn's uncle occupied the same seat as before. He'd called her once yesterday, briefly, but his force's presence in seeking Jule spoke for him otherwise. She assumed he called Jonah. He better have.

Tonight, she wasn't sure where he stood: on the side of the board or the side of keeping this event safe. Maybe both. Or maybe because he couldn't *not* be seen there after what had unraveled of late in his county, the unraveling reflecting on him. Politics. Always the politics.

The board filed out and took the same seats as every meeting. Guy sorted papers, laptop, and phone before him, mentally preparing. Iona looked about to throw up. Ella Mae waited wide-eyed and scared. The others, however, functioned business as usual. Guy lifted his gavel and dropped it once. "This meeting comes to order." The room quieted. Deputies crossed arms across their chests, backs against the walls.

Glares radiated from the audience while gazes from the stage darted anywhere but into the crowd. Mixed aromas of cologne and body heat already took hold with doors closed. For fifteen minutes, the board conducted routine business of okaying the last minutes, remembering Miss Abbott, finally reminding those in attendance that this was a civil function . . . and if anyone turned uncivil, they would be escorted out.

People hadn't wanted to hear a warning, and grumblings sprinted up and down the rows until the gavel reminded them of the rules. Quinn would be surprised if Guy got reelected next time, assuming he didn't resign tonight, regardless his tenure . . . regardless how many long-legged, dancing girls he put in his outdated commercials.

He announced that several board members would tender resignations, but before these certain members did, who'd remained unnamed thus far, the board needed to vote on other matters at hand. Otherwise, they might be minus a quorum and business would be bottlenecked until a special election could be held a couple months downstream.

"Get rid of them now," yelled a man from the rear. A whistle and a few claps tailed his remark.

"We don't like their votes anyway," yelled another.

The gavel pounded.

"Not fair letting them vote and run," hollered a woman, pursued by more claps and harumphs of agreement.

The gavel pummeled louder. Uniforms stepped off the wall to the edge of the audience.

"They act like friggin' Gustapo," Jonah whispered.

"It's crowd control," Knox murmured. "Pay it no attention. Your phone on?"

Jonah raised it to show him.

"All right." Guy started off loudly, as much to take charge as to be heard. "We have two items on the agenda tonight. Will the board member who requested this meeting, please address the board?"

Quinn's attention immediately went to Laney. She'd told Iona to follow her lead. However, Ty's aunt remained undisturbed and unmoved. Instead, still decked out in her black suit and stark silver scarf, pearl earrings, her hair recently trimmed into its short bob and tinted to hide gray, Piper Pierce moved her mic closer and took the floor.

"Mr. Chairman and the board . . . public attendees and guests . . . we've wasted so much time, months really, in moving forward with a new elementary school."

Low level grumbles traveled the room, but in the interest of hearing Piper, remained controlled.

"There were errors and unforeseen tragedy. Arguments and conflicts. While there's nothing wrong with healthy debate, we have to realize the underlying purpose." Piper swept her hands wide. "This meeting, these discussions, and yes, the picketing, protesting, and Facebook posturing, are for one reason and one reason only. To serve the needs of our children. I think we can agree with that."

People weren't ready to fall in line with her. Instead they waited on the edge of their seats for some sort of other shoe to fall.

"We need to proceed with the school we've already invested in, on the ground we've already purchased." Each word was practiced, and she enunciated succinctly reading from a page.

"We must be efficient. We must move forward." She waited for applause. She got minimal, hesitating a bit to give people more time to do so. Quinn thought she saw the first flash of nerves.

How exactly was Piper playing this? They could not move forward. The first tract was too small, and the second tract not available. Quinn knew that. Jonah knew that. While everyone knew the facts of that, a good many still thought *that* could be ignored and the right amount of land just happen. *For the children.* People eagerly hushed, waiting for Piper to address *that.*

She motioned like a queen stiffly beckoning with her right hand. "Mr. Armstrong, please stand."

Peering at Quinn, Jonah looked concerned. Mr. Armstrong was an attorney, currently the one held on retainer for the board. There was nothing spontaneous about this night whatsoever.

"Tonight," Piper began again. "I move that we purchase the remainder of Miss Abbott's acreage at the same cost per acre that we purchased the original land. A total of forty additional acres. For those unfamiliar, the current thirty acres we bought from Miss Abbott proved unable to pass standard for parking, ingress, and egress, and rather than just buy the extra ten acres that would grant us to meet that standard, we propose to purchase the remaining land."

"What the hell?" Jonah mumbled.

"Hear it out," Quinn whispered, while Knox's stern expression showed he listened for the catch.

Short of a spotlight, the entire room stared at a flushed Jonah.

This was what one of his three mysterious texts had meant. *Sign the papers.*

Threatened by the room's disturbance, Piper let Guy gavel for silence. "And included in that motion, I ask we name the school Abbott Elementary School in honor of Miss Amy Abbott's ultimate sacrifice."

Part of the room gave applause. Part didn't.

Jonah's phone lit up with another text. *You know what to do.*

Not without proof of life, he typed without waiting for Knox or Quinn to approve.

Do it, came the answer.

Proof. Of. Life. he replied. *No picture. I want to talk to her.*

Knox put his hand over the phone. "Stop. We need to—"

"I don't give a damn what you think you need," Jonah hissed. "Nor what you want, feel or think, Agent Knox."

Quinn understood Knox, but she felt more like Jonah. This moment was important for the power behind the scenes, and if Jonah didn't behave as they wanted, right now, the plan could go awry. Whatever that plan was. No doubt delegated eyes were in the room, watching in live time.

But she, like Knox, also feared what would happen to Jule.

Damn gutsy move by Jonah.

Piper's attention rested on them. People nearby twisted in their seats as Jonah rose, excusing himself as he passed in front of these people in his row, then walked as if to exit the room. Quinn leaped up in chase.

"Mr. Proveaux?" Piper's indignance rang loud and clear over the loudspeaker system.

Startled, Jonah looked over his shoulder, even more startled at the entire sea of attention on him.

"We're trying to conduct a meeting here," Piper said.

"Jonah," whispered the closest uniform. "Man, take it outside."

"Do not leave the room, please," Piper said, befuddling the uniform.

"Go right ahead," Jonah said to Piper, then, "Out of my way," to the deputy.

Quinn followed him to the far back corner.

His phone lit up. Quinn worked her own phone to record. "Update on Jule," she yelled up to Piper.

Which shut up everyone. Piper had been bested and she continued to pontificate on the advantages of her proposal, but few listened. Her face reddened. She started repeating herself.

Quinn and Jonah turned away from the crowd. Quinn didn't get the chance to read caller ID before Jonah picked up on the call, and she held her own phone close. "Mom?" Jonah leaned in for Quinn to hear. "Are you okay?"

"Yes, son, they're treating me like the queen," she said, then the phone went dead.

Knox came up. "You get more texts?"

"We got a call," Quinn said, letting him listen to the recording.

He reared back. "Is that her?"

"Yes, it was her," Jonah said low.

"I second that motion!" came loud from the front.

"More discussion," yelled an attendee.

Guy launched into his gavel mode, raising the noise level. Like an incoming tide, the crowd showed its impatience.

Knox pushed them out the double door into the hall, hitting a wall of quiet. "Did anyone else speak?"

"No."

Jonah had his proof of life, but instead of giving him hope, it seemed to have stymied him more. "I'm taking the board's offer, Quinn. Whatever it is, I'm giving them the land. Jule isn't worth this."

Quinn rested an assuring hand on his chest. "You do whatever you need to do. It's only dirt. It's only money. There is no other Jule." Then to Knox, "They're watching us in there. They know what we're doing almost before we do."

Knox couldn't take Jonah's phone to check the number. Jonah needed it handy, in case there was another call, another text. "Then I suggest we get in there."

The confused deputy poked his head out. "They asked if you're coming back in before they take a vote."

"See?" Quinn said, trying to slow this thought process down. The kidnappers hadn't hurt Jule. They wanted Jonah's presence in the meeting. None of the resigning board members had left, even with their threats of resignation. "They need us on the chess board," she said. "We are a serious part of this game. What if we change the strategy?"

Knox and Jonah appeared skeptical, Jonah just eager to go back inside.

"No time for this," Knox said, before turning to follow Jonah through the doors.

"Wait," Quinn said. "Give me a sec." She stared at the dirty lines in the old linoleum floor, trying to let an idea take shape.

Jule wasn't a jokester and was known for no real sense of humor. She spoke literally, to the point, without room for misinterpretation. *Treating me like the queen*, she'd said. Not *a* queen . . . *the* queen.

She snatched Knox's sleeve before he got through the door. "Jule's at Windsor." Then to Jonah. "She's at the treehouse."

"But we searched there," Knox said.

"Saturday," she said. "But not in the last two days."

Knox wasn't on board. Jonah was afraid to alter the course.

"Just send someone there, Knox. Jule said she was being *treated like the queen. The* queen! Jule doesn't talk like that. She's giving us direction."

But Jonah stood conflicted, short-circuited outside the double door the deputy held open for his return. He struggled choosing his mother's hint or this blustering bunch of fools' demands.

"Jonah, if you're not there for the vote, they might move her." Or worse. "They can call to move her quicker than Knox can get there, but he has people in place. There is no risk, guys!"

The men took parting glances at each other.

"I'll stay with Jonah," she said.

Just like that, Jonah snapped a wave for Knox to take off, then entered the auditorium. Knox exited, giving orders on his radio. "Call the team and launch the drone," was the last thing Quinn heard before rushing in to be at Jonah's side. Then she texted Ty. Bless him, he'd volunteered to stay at the house . . . just in case.

Chapter 29

"WE ASSUME ALL is well?" Guy Cook asked into his mic, comment bouncing off the high walls, directed at Quinn and Jonah as they returned, minus Knox.

"We have hope," Jonah said.

Undertones of support traveled the auditorium. Those within reach touched them, touched their chairs. Then another double-tap of the gavel returned the room to order.

"Now." Guy's deep, saucy chairman voice returned to life. "We have a motion by Piper Pierce to purchase forty acres owned by the Abbott estate, Jonah Proveaux, executor, currently adjoining the tract already purchased and previously owned by Amy Abbott, at the same price per acre as was paid for the first tract, to enable us to build an elementary school that is also proposed to be called Abbott Elementary School." He sighed after reading the long script. "Does that about say it?"

The board nodded concurrence. Observers spoke low amongst themselves. "Yes, Mr. Chairman," said Piper.

Jonah seemed resigned to end this. He would sell the land for a nickel right now. He could only think of Jule.

Guy peered to his left, then his right, down the long tables. "Since this is such a critical vote, I'll call each board member's name. Please answer yay or nay. Let's begin with the member who proposed the motion. Mrs. Piper?"

"Yay." Clipped and firm.

Guy made an elaborate sweep of recording the choice. "Very good. Mr. Harmon Valentine seconded the motion. Your vote, sir?"

"Yay."

Again with the flourish. Guy was addressing his compatriots first, putting pressure on the others. Quinn could sense the acquiescence entwining itself in and out of the rows of onlookers. This was how the Corps did things. It was how they'd always held control. Why should this time be any different. Even if some of them did resign, they would go out on a high, leaving the mess to clean up in the laps of whoever was elected next.

This was how the invisible powers-that-be got their way, and unless bribery, kidnapping, corruption, and assorted other law-breaking activities could be proven, they would acquire their land, which would lead to other deals, other construction, and goodness knows what else that would forever change the personality of Craven County and put millions in the pockets of parties who didn't give a damn about the altered quality of life.

"Mr. Curtis Fuller?"

"A serious nay, Mr. Cook. That's N-A-Y. Do you need me to repeat that?"

Bless him, Quinn thought.

Guy cut him his I'm-the-chair look. "No, your nay is duly noted, sir."

Jonah wasn't even watching the vote. He remained glued to the phone laying in open palms in his lap, waiting for a response.

"Mrs. Laney Jackson Underwood. Your vote, please?"

Quinn softly leaned into Jonah, reminding him she was there. With Laney's vote would likewise go Iona's, and the deal would be done. Four was a win for the proposal.

Laney didn't immediately respond. She peered down the black-covered tables toward Iona, who waited for the unsaid directive for how she was to respond. Of course with Guy would come Ella Mae.

Jonah didn't have to sign the deed. This proposal was to make him the offer, and he could still rightfully refuse. But he wouldn't. He watched his phone, and Quinn wondered if he even heard what was going on.

Laney stood.

Members never stood to vote. They never stood to even make a proposal. Everyone hushed, side-glancing at each other. Piper had already given her speech about the pros of moving ahead. What more could Laney add?

Laney smoothed her skirt and adjusted her suit jacket, raising her lowered chin to something much more regal. Was that a fleeting look at Quinn?

"Mr. Chairman," she commenced. "Laney *Jackson* Underwood votes nay in the name of Craven County and all it holds dear."

Iona jumped up. "And Iona Bakeman votes nay, too."

Then Ella Mae vaulted to her feet, and at first forgetting she needed her mic, she snatched it from its table stand. "And Ella Mae Dewberry votes nay, your honor." Her high pitched voice carried the day as most of the two hundred people roared in excited ovation, overpowering any of the opposition as the four votes killed the proposal.

Piper sat stunned, her false eyelashes touching her bangs. Harmon froze like being still made him invisible.

People slapped each other, congratulating. They congratulated Quinn, tried to praise Jonah, but he was too intent on his phone. Quinn sat back down, the cacophony igniting around them. "Nothing?" she asked.

He shook his head. In the midst of that rejoicing melee, the two of them held their breaths, intensely aware that each second was critical. Each second ticked with the power of stealing the number of breaths Jule had left to live once the kidnappers heard the board's decision.

The plan had fallen short and Jonah had not signed the paperwork. This deal, and no telling how many others, vanished into the air.

Jule's life could've just been traded for the millions of dollars lost in contracts.

Somewhere in the middle of the chaos, Quinn thought to stand and hunt for the suits

But no way she'd leave Jonah.

Out of the corner of her eye, she glimpsed Chase navigating through the bodies alone. Guess Mauney had already made his way out. She thought to text her uncle, but he didn't know them, and they'd be gone before she could describe them to him. She'd leave them for Knox.

"Quinn!" Jonah snatched her from behind as his phone vibrated. "Look!"

"Victim secure," said the message. "Medical assessment pending."

But the second one from Ty said it best. "Jule's safe, y'all. Thank the Lord."

Jonah wrapped Quinn in a hug, half laughing and half crying, her doing the same. Then he reared, smiling so huge, and kissed her hard on the mouth. Wolf calls and laughter crescendoed around them, but to Quinn, all she heard was Jonah's moans of relief against her lips.

When they parted, he gave her another quick peck. "Pardon me for a minute." He shoved two chairs aside and excused himself around people, them patting him on the back and saying things in his ear he wasn't hearing. Finally, he reached the tables and took a mic.

"May I say a few words, please? Everyone?" Then he repeated, "Please, may I say something here?"

Shushes went from person to person, everyone policing the noise level until Jonah could be heard.

"Jule is home!" he yelled.

Yells and whoops circumnavigated the auditorium, and he beamed at the communal response, the overhead spots meant for the board reflecting off the tears on his cheeks. "But I want to say this. Please, let me speak."

It took a while, but they honored his wish, him laughing at their restraint when they only wanted to cheer. Everyone always listened to Jonah.

"I propose the board sell me back Miss Abbott's original land, at which time I'll donate twenty thousand dollars to their search for another piece of land."

Huge applause.

"Order, order," came a female voice. Unaccustomed to hearing this person, people hunted for the source. "I propose the board accept this offer." Iona climbed up on a chair, mic in her hand. "Do I hear a second?"

"I second it. I second it," yelled Ella Mae, hopping on stage.

"Then I vote yay," Iona said on her heels.

"Me, too!" yelled Ella Mae.

"For the record, I vote yay," said Laney into her mic.

"Damn right it's a yay," boomed Curtis.

Then came Guy, of all people, and after that it didn't matter though the video would record the official count.

Someone rolled Miss Birdie down the side aisle, the retired teacher waving her bandaged hand, wanting her say as well.

But a burst of light lit up the picture windows, right before the sound wave hit the assembly.

The boom sent folks to the floor. Screams filled the air. Those in the open ducked behind folding chairs, husbands covering wives, others diving under the board's tables. Uniforms, however, bolted to the exits. Along with Quinn.

A sedan in the front row of the parking lot was in flames, fire celebrating as it reached to the sky. Alarms went off in vehicles across the parking lot, the last bits of glass and shrapnel still tinkling from their fall to the asphalt and cement.

Attendees ran frantic hunting loved ones, officers grabbing extinguishers from their vehicles and the school. Sheriff Sterling caught up with Quinn. "Good God Almighty," he said.

Quinn's mouth remained open, just as it had fallen agape when she identified the gray sedan being the car afire. In spite of the twisted metal, flames, and flumes of smoke, she recognized that car. And amidst the odors of rubber, metal, and gasoline, she caught the whiff of flesh.

Jonah caught up to her.

"Chase and Mauney," she said. "Or one of them anyway. That was the car at Laney's on Saturday."

A young deputy seemed unaware what to do. The sheriff strode over, giving him the orders he so desperately needed, then took charge. A crime scene line was set up, distancing onlookers. A nurse appeared from the crowd and offered her services, but thanks to everyone being inside the building, there were no other injuries.

Quinn stepped to the side, closer to the building to stay out of the way, watching, still stunned at this course of events. A surreal bubble enveloped her as she tried to click blocks together while inventorying attendees, hunting for someone out of place. The kidnapping . . . a car bombing. This was a whole other level of wrongdoing.

This wasn't the board's doing. They hadn't sought partners. The partners sought them. They'd acquired unofficial partners who'd reined them in using well researched weaknesses and foibles. These partners had tapped into human shortcomings and imperfections to run over them, twisting their morality to the point they didn't have the gumption to stand up to them.

Guy had tried to rectify his compass by returning his bribe money. After what Quinn now saw as a lot of soul-searching, Laney showed them up by going against the grain, taking down the plan in domino fashion. Bless Iona and Ella Mae for finally standing up for what was right. Bless Laney for showing them the way.

The suits left the meeting once they saw the writing on the wall. Their strategy crushed, with everyone inside celebrating, commiserating, listening to Jonah announce what he hoped the board would do, they gave in to the reality that the tide had turned on a dime.

Quinn wasn't trained in bombs, hadn't been in the FBI long enough to talk it much, but in scoping the area from her vantage from the crowd, she noted a couple things. Things like the blood and flesh on the brick wall of Craven High School. Some on the windows of the second floor. She could taste the melted car components and smell the burning human being.

Most of these people did, too. They just didn't know it yet.

She wouldn't be surprised if the FBI didn't call in ATF on this one. This wasn't just small town politics squabbling anymore.

The powers-that-be couldn't be happy, but worse than that, Quinn saw they seriously hated leaving loose ends. Nope, this case was no longer the sheriff's, and it wasn't just a little case of buying thirty or forty acres. There were other ways to build a school and get a permit approved for a subdivision, and from what Quinn surmised, money wasn't the soul issue.

Something else was.

Jonah came up and slid his arm around her. People were still full of questions, and they trailed him, as if he'd taken control of everything. They sought a hero, and he filled the bill.

"Go tend to them," she said, after the umpteenth person wanted Jonah's take on the situation, or queried about Jule. "People are concerned. Do your thing."

"You don't mind?" he asked.

She shook her head. "Go make people feel better. It's part of your magic."

He kissed her quickly and let himself get pulled into the people.

Being left alone let her reflect on these more serious complexities she wasn't ready to let loose of. This wasn't exactly déjà vu, but it damn sure dug up memories of how someone else handled his business, and his memory had been haunting her off and on throughout this case. God Almighty, Quinn prayed she was wrong, but on the other hand, she prayed she was right. She hated to think there were two such players like Ronald Renault loose in the world. The real estate kingpin wasn't used to not getting his way, and if Quinn's senses were correct, Sterling Banks had just bested him again tonight.

Chapter 30

MID-JUNE WARMED up fast, but the late-morning shade on the patio kept morning temps in the upper seventies, at least until noon. Comfortable if you're Southern. Quinn had dressed for the occasion and waited for her road-trip partner to pick her up and head into Charleston for the day. He was late.

Not Jonah. He'd barely let Jule out of his sight since her return, plus this trip wasn't his to make. His mother came home uninjured from Windsor, but he wasn't discounting any residual emotion. Nor would he risk someone unexpectedly trying again, though he'd been assured by Quinn the chances were nil.

Quinn wanted to double down on that assurance, and this trip was insurance to that end.

Knox had been stymied and somewhat embarrassed about where they'd found Jule since they'd thoroughly canvassed the property via dogs, drone, and agents two days before, especially with agents on the property the whole time. But with Jule reasonably tended and conveniently returned to the farm via Windsor, Quinn suspected that no harm was ever intended.

The kidnapping was a statement in a language only Quinn and Larry Sterling would understand.

Just like Miss Abbott was supposed to be only scared into selling, and Miss Birdie was supposed to trip on the wire and not make it as far as the truck fire, Jule was probably insurance for events to play out as desired. The manipulation was to scare simple, rural folks that they better build a school and put it on the Abbott land. The total end game. At least the supposed end game to the hired players on the ground. Things just sort of . . . got out of hand. Too many layers of too many amateurs involved made for one mistake too many and had cost them the game.

She had a keen theory of what happened, and she'd asked to assist the FBI's investigation in proving this wasn't the board's manipulations. Call it protecting her county's people, not that she expected Knox to sanction the request, but the urge in her said she had to try.

He'd surprised her and suggested she reapply to the bureau instead. He would work hard to bring her back in. The age cutoff was 37 so she still met the requirement. He'd love to have her in Charleston, though both had a strong inclination that headquarters would ship her to Los Angeles or Chicago as payback for having left to begin with. The bureau could play hardball.

Besides, her old problem would reemerge anyway. Sooner or later some issue with Sterling Banks would lasso her in and hand-over-fist ease her return until she was again amidst those hundreds of acres of pecans. Nobody served two masters. At least not with one being the FBI and the other a three-hundred-year-old legacy, each too Type A to tolerate the other.

Out of courtesy, Knox had kept her up to speed though. By the Wednesday after Monday's historic meeting, the FBI identified Chase as the body in the gray sedan, the same guy Quinn and Jonah had crossed paths with at Laney's. Mauney wasn't located yet, but Knox expected to have him located by the end of the day. Said he wasn't hardcore, never was suspected of bloodletting, with only a history of bullying. Seems he was an actual scout that specialized in connecting developers and school projects. Not quite the badass he presented himself to be.

Quinn didn't quite believe he would be rolled up by days' end. Especially given the way the cabal had disposed of his buddy. Loose ends had to be tied up tight.

The bureau would tease loose threads of their own in assorted covert and overt manners, seeking who told who what to do. Contrarily again, she doubted they'd find those responsible for the two arsons, mainly because they were too far down the food chain. Setting fires didn't take much gray matter. Ordering them took the higher IQ, especially if done right with sufficient buffer in between.

Just like someone higher up put Chase and Mauney in charge of strong-arming the board.

Quinn doubted the same person menaced Miss Abbott, Miss Birdie, and Jule. Different people with different tasks with no one aware of who the others were or what they were doing. A hired hand from a day-labor line likely set a house on fire. An illegal was paid enough to set a truck ablaze and string a trip wire on an old lady's front stoop. Jule never saw her captor, her head covered. She happened to know the lay of the land so well that the smell of the pecan trees and the sound of the Edisto River they returned her to had clued her in. Her captor probably bolted as soon as Jule's proof of life was given, being out of the county before Jule was found.

The developers interviewed, those with pending permits for homes and commercial development down the highway, would only say they were hoping to build near a new school they heard about, appalled at being accused of anything but offering a good price to Craven citizens. Contractors like Fripp already identified the developer who promised them good work by the end of the year if the board approved the project. Nobody admitted to or could prove that Iona's ownership was even known about, much less capitalized on, to include the board.

Meanwhile, Quinn guessed the puppet master went about other puppet shows, tweaking the tension and setting stages from one community to another.

Craven County wasn't out of the woods, and they couldn't stop the slow erosion of its old timey character, but they could interfere with this backdoor crap in hope the county could create a controlled development plan that local folks preferred. Infrastructure requirements, impact fees, and mitigating aesthetics could be designed to prevent outsiders from making messes and ruining the lives of rural property owners. A method was needed to direct the madness, so to speak, and not let it run wild and loose for someone else to dominate, control, abuse, and leave behind destructed. They considered this a wakeup call.

Jonah hadn't owned an acre of land until Miss Abbott bequeathed him his forty acres, now seventy since the board wasted no time drawing up the deed. He'd made them an offer they couldn't refuse. His story of Miss Abbott had taken on a life of its own, too. His attempted rescue of her brought tears to women's eyes, and he'd supposedly schemed the takedown of the board's wanton behavior. His remark to Laney about him running for school board took deeper root than expected, and several of the county's business owners had suggested he take his charisma more seriously to include something more like county council. Maybe the state legislature.

"Quinn?"

"Out back," she hollered.

Uncle Larry had dressed down for this appointment, forgoing the uniform and its regalia used the last time they made this move. "I'm driving."

"Cruiser?"

"Makes the drive easier, plus no point in you taxing that shoulder," he said, waiting for her to catch up to escort her to the driveway.

He tried to help her into the car.

"I got it," she said.

"I know you do," he replied, helping anyway before getting in to head to Charleston.

After Monday's board meeting, after Larry Sterling had herded the school explosion aftermath, he'd gladly passed the reins to Knox and his people, offering his services as backup, of course. If the FBI thought they were big and bad and all that in their abilities, he'd let them have it. Or so that's how he painted it with bluster and show.

That was more the uncle she once imagined as a child, which gelled an idea. An idea that originated Monday night.

Tuesday morning, Quinn called her uncle for an amazingly rare conversation—a plea for his assistance, and his take on her theory. Ty was off duty. Jonah couldn't take his eyes off his mother. The timing was perfect since she didn't want them involved.

Quinn hadn't organized anything one-on-one with Larry since their last Charleston trip, and while they usually butted heads, this subject matter outranked anything of a personal nature between them . . . just like last time. Over this they could bond. She asked he meet her at Jackson Hole diner for breakfast where she'd laid out a theory she couldn't prove . . . but felt needed addressing nonetheless.

Over coffee Uncle Larry'd listened. Over Lenore's ham biscuits, he'd meditated on her notion. Over the final cup of coffee, he offered to accompany her to Charleston. *A Sterling thing,* he'd said. *The sooner the better,* he added. So, not forty-eight hours after the board meeting, they ventured to the Holy City in a united front, with no proof . . . but with plenty of gut talking to them both.

There might not be much Sterling blood left, but in this instance, it was concentrated, potent, and determined to remind a certain party it was not to be overtaken.

They pulled up to the Broad Street office of Ronald Renault and parked right out front, a patrol car exempt from feeding a meter, so that those inside had time to note their arrival. Only two months prior, this city's papers spoke of two rich spoiled women going at each other, with Renault's devious, blind daughter the loser. Quinn had fatally shot her in a scramble over a gun after the blind bitch shot Quinn in the arm, attempting to put her down . . . the same arm currently in a sling. At this rate, that arm would never be right.

The dead girl's work-for-hire man had tried to kill Quinn and go after Jule, killing the goat. The tragedy served as an attempt to take Sterling Banks, the daughter aching to prove to daddy her worth by snaring the only piece of land the man had never been able to acquire.

For this meeting, Quinn purposely donned a sharp-as-shit green, fitted pants suit from an upscale Savannah dress shop, her red hair swept into a loose Dutch braid. Her three-inch heels echoed across the marble and old-wood lobby, a posh stereotypical balance of old money and Charleston history, and she had to admit Larry Sterling made a handsome presence of his own in suit and tie.

Not her normal choice of attire, nor his, but they were meeting a man who judged quickly and acted accordingly, his seconds worth hundreds of dollars, and without saying so, he made you believe it. She wanted all of his attention she could get. There was a reason actors held dress rehearsals, the clothes calling upon their best performance.

The assistant greeted them first in her King Street jewelry and pointy shoes, ushering them into an empty office, soon returning with coffee service and tiny biscotti wafers, the fresh baked kind, not the airplane-in-a-wrapper variety. Quinn and her uncle sat in the same place as last time, on either end of a navy leather sofa, and after serving them, the assistant left, her back zipper flaunting curves from neck to knees.

Round two. Quinn didn't want a round three. She didn't want to perpetually look over her shoulder, or worry about Jonah or Jule watching over theirs.

Jonah would have a fit knowing she was here. For a change, she trusted her uncle to keep a secret. He didn't want to be here anymore than she did, but Quinn had come too close to jailtime the last go around, and she admitted his dedication to the family name had helped her out of a tight spot. Normal wasn't a word that fit any part of the Sterling/Renault affiliation, which meant both tended to color outside the lines, legal or otherwise. The twelve-foot high paneled double doors opened without noise, and Ronald Renault walked in noiseless shoes to assume his place before them in his high-back, wing-back chair. Quinn was sure their host saw few individuals unless equipped with ample money and plans to make him richer, so this prologue to a meeting that did neither was no doubt staged to make a statement. He still considered them beneath him.

Quinn smiled and waited until the man stilled before addressing him. She wasn't about to stand. "No recordings," she said. "Just like before."

He responded, "Agreed."

Yet both expected the other to do otherwise. Quinn's recorder was in her purse, Renault's hidden in his office.

Men like him lived in bugged offices, recordings seamlessly toggled on and off, but that was okay. He wouldn't want any of this to hit a third party's ears anyway.

Renault had mastered a reptilian grin quite some time ago. "To what do I owe this pleasure?"

Pleasure. She doubted that. Who'd want to socialize with their daughter's killer?

And why would she want to share coffee in china, dressed in a complete pretense, with a man whose burning goal was to absorb Sterling Banks into his empire?

This is what money did. Jousted with words and innuendo.

"Strike two," she said, cutting through the bullshit. She set down her cup and saucer.

Renault gave not the slightest recoil and no sort of denial. Quinn didn't even have to explain what she meant. "I'm curious," he said, his head almost imperceptive in its tilt. "What happens at strike three?"

"So there will be another attempt?" Larry Sterling said.

Leave it to her uncle to get straighter to the point. "We admit your disguise carried its weight . . . for a while," she said, "but your signature became apparent. At least to me. Exploding body parts across a high school building sort of gave it away. Nobody wants land as ruthlessly as Ronald Renault."

Renault oozed facade. "Yes, I heard about that. Sounds rather desperate that destruction for acreage in the middle of nowhere, but you can never tell how far people are willing to go to get a foothold into the future."

"Or make a statement about the past," she said.

"Or make a point, period," Larry added. "Of course, money might factor in there somewhere." He tired of holding a coffee cup, and laid both hands on his knees. "Will there be another time, Ronald?"

Quinn tried not to chuckle at her uncle's red-neck, straight-talk use of the man's first name without his permission.

Renault recrossed his legs, arms rested parallel and precise on either arm of the chair like an oil portrait in Buckingham Palace. "Someone will always attempt to develop undeveloped land with potential, Ms. Sterling. You won't be around forever. Neither will I. Neither one of us has an heir, so that puts a ticking clock on matters, doesn't it?"

She hadn't wanted to discuss Catherine's death. Quinn didn't relish taking that life. Catherine's dying expression as she faded into a lush gray carpet soaked with her blood recurred often to Quinn during the most unexpected moments.

She wasn't surprised he pissed on her about not having offspring. The entire Lowcountry real estate community watched with baited breath to see who'd inherit Sterling Banks with Quinn being single . . . the last heir of the oldest family in the oldest county in the state of South Carolina.

She didn't put it past the man seated across from her to hasten her demise, either, so he could again attempt to manipulate who acquired the deed. His daughter had almost succeeded.

"Let's make something clear, Mr. Renault. This, you and me, is about Sterling Banks, and it is not for sale," she said. "I'm putting more acreage into a conservation easement to restrict development, and I'll deed it to charity before letting it reach your hands."

"Some of us have no say as to when we leave this life, and some of us can pay enough to entice the most altruistic among us."

She fought to put a lid on any heat reaching her freckled cheeks, wondering if this was a threat.

"As for charity, I have a healthy foundation that would be more than interested," he said.

"Not interested in a self-serving cover for your wealth."

Palms still on the arms of his chair, he lifted his weight forward and crossed his ankles. "Miss Sterling, what is your point? My time is money."

"I've made my point, but if you're missing it, let me simplify the message. Stay away from Sterling Banks. Stay away from my people."

"And stay away from her," Larry added.

"Need I worry about any sort of . . . threat against my person? Does land mean that much to you to come all this way to put me on notice?" he said.

"They'll be no threat for your recording." Larry rocked forward to stand. "Niece, we're done here."

Quinn could've said *Message delivered* or *Stay away*, or something about getting even or watching over her shoulder for him, but she didn't. A man like Renault dealt in nuance, and anything more would only come back to bite her. Indeed, they'd said enough.

She stood, Quinn and Larry Sterling looking down on the rich broker from Broad Street. Then arm in her uncle's, they left before the assistant on the outside could do her clandestine trick of opening a door before someone got to it.

By the time she reached the cruiser, little shakes traversed Quinn from head to toe. From anger, definitely not from fear, and maybe from the reality that this man's life's goal might be to do the Sterlings in.

She feared this was not over.

Traffic typical for a Charleston weekday afternoon, Larry had to flash a blue light to inch into it. Quinn let him focus on his drive for five or so miles until they'd reached West Ashley, still with forty-five minutes ahead of them.

"That went well," he said.

"The hell it did," she replied. "You smelled Renault early on, uncle. Had you spoken to him about any of this before today? Made any backdoor promises or assurances to stay out of his way?" He'd had a nasty relationship with Renault before Graham died, had even promised to help him buy Sterling Banks at one point. Quinn liked to think Larry had changed after his brother was murdered, his niece almost taken out. He'd seen what Renault was capable of.

But Larry Sterling wasn't exactly a strong man of substance. He'd come around since the daughter's death and Quinn's endangered freedom. She liked to consider him answering the call of his bloodline. He might not be the hero type, but when it came to her she'd hope he'd come to the rescue. She wouldn't place too high a wager on the bet, though.

"No," he said, "I haven't seen Renault since you and I visited him two months ago."

"Yet you limited Ty to just investigating in Craven County, specifically stopping him from straying into Charleston. You suspected Renault," she said. "Why didn't you tell me?"

Larry watched the road hard, like he couldn't afford to take his attention off it. "I didn't want to poke the bear, Quinn."

"I see," she said, disappointed. "This was just about a stupid school and a few houses, so you were letting him get away with a land grab in your own county."

"At least it wasn't about Sterling Banks," he said, jaw taut. "I promised you I'd not jeopardize the farm anymore."

Yet he'd risk the rest of the county. That hurt. His callousness, laziness, ignorance, any or all of it, hurt. "In the long run it would have."

"You're dramatizing this."

"You know better," was the only comeback she had.

Jesus, this man. He carried so many of the same genes as Graham Sterling, yet none of the traits, style, or decency. He fell so damn short, so many times. Did he not see himself in the mirror? She could only pray he loved her enough to protect the legacy. He swore he did, and maybe a small part of him still cared he belonged to the family, but God sure played cruel games sometimes, whittling such a strong family down to just the two of them.

"I think I might be marrying Jonah," she said, out of the blue.

Larry side-eyed her. "Has the boy even asked, or is this just her highness selecting which of her suitors makes her happy today?"

Damn him.

No, Jonah hadn't asked. Well, he had, but some time ago, and he'd sort of taken it back. Lately he'd made the proper moves, and clearly he was invested in Craven County. Even more in Sterling Banks. Undoubtedly in her.

"Maybe I'll ask him," she said.

Her uncle's head cocked askance, challenging her sincerity.

Now she hated her uncle for making her second guess Jonah's intentions.

"God knows you've pounded into my head that I needed to marry, and you've been rather mean about it, too. Our family tree is losing its leaves pretty fast."

"Queen bee," he reiterated.

She gave a half smirk. "He already calls me princess."

Larry didn't accept the humor. "Don't play with people, Quinn. You've been privileged. You've been blessed. No doubt you've also been loyal to Sterling Banks, which counts in your plus column."

Says the man who toyed with a mistress who ultimately ratted to his wife, costing him his third of Sterling Banks.

"Marrying you comes with responsibility," he continued, a lecture ensuing. "Think about your father. His father. All those planted in the south quarter." Meaning the family cemetery.

"Maybe I don't need a husband, then," she said. "I just need an heir. That's easy enough."

He stared her down this time, his voice rebuking. "Quinn."

"Don't chide me, uncle. You lost the right some time ago."

She'd had enough, and she rode the rest of the way in silence, not sure exactly what her uncle meant.

She'd been an obnoxious brat growing up, and a handful as an adult. She didn't tell Larry that Jonah's term *princess* wasn't often complimentary.

She thought she'd outgrown some of those old habits. She'd tried. Guess she could try harder.

Chapter 31

AFTER A WEEK, Quinn was out of her sling but back in physical therapy. She'd heard nothing from Renault, but she'd briefed Jonah and Ty. Not a one of them wouldn't be watching over their shoulder for any underground, covert, disguised, or side-armed attempt to come at Sterling Banks, but she still envisioned Renault as a lot darker enemy than they did. Money made people irresponsible. Big money created toxic demons.

Miss Birdie's Facebook page hadn't missed a beat in discussion of what happened to who, as well as suspicions on how it came to pass. She regained her health, her newspaper column, and her control of the group, and she'd behind the scenes asked Lincoln20 to retire in an effort to calm the masses, and she announced his departure to the group.

Lincoln20 disappeared, and Curtis Fuller joined the group, singing the praises of the forthright, civic-minded strengths of Laney, Ella Mae, and Iona. The Corps had taken on different identities, but Curtis also asked that the board's nickname be put away and forgotten. Fresh slate and all that.

Lincoln20 had been mothballed in Curtis's closet much like Ty's cape for Miss Birdie's class. But nothing could stop the gossip-mongering, the very nature of what made Facebook what it was.

I heard FBI was involved.

I heard it was state guys, not the feds.

For a school board? Doubt either one got involved. Sheriff Sterling wouldn't allow it.

I'm confused who's still on the board. Who got arrested?

Someone did. Probably Piper Pierce and her uppity self.

LOL. Nobody got arrested. Just saw her in town this morning.

On went the conversation, posts having lessened into entertainment more than mob. Of course nobody was actually *in* jail, but Piper Pierce and Harmon Valentine had been charged, arrested, and released on bond until their cases appeared before a grand jury. They might be walking the streets, but they faced a serious future with potential of bars on the windows, thanks to Guy Cook plea bargaining for his own skin.

Weeks ago, Harmon had felt too cozy with the chairman and too eager to share, and he had inquired if Guy had been offered money for his vote.

The chairman played attorney to the end, ratting on Harmon, and while he lost his license, he only got probation. Guy quickly hired a partner, as if he'd planned to do so all along. Television commercials changed overnight from *Don't cry, call Guy*, to *Don't sob, call Bob*, the music the same. Some cats always landed on their feet.

Quinn had hoped that horrible jingle was as dead as Chase. Speaking of which, Mauney hadn't been found, and his family pled with the public for assistance as to his whereabouts. Knox told her. Quinn did an *I told you so*. She didn't share Mauney's situation with Jonah.

Three weeks later, the board called another emergency meeting to order at the same high school, scrubbed clean of the last meeting's aftermath. Three empty chairs and three resignations were presented before Laney Underwood, the lone remaining officer. The auditorium filled, the community cried hard for a special election, but not before Laney was unanimously chosen as the chair to see them through the transition.

Jonah and Quinn sat in the audience, this time toward the wall, neither caring to take the mic. Ty appeared as the solo uniform, half as the veneer of security, and half as support for his aunt.

No Sheriff Sterling this time. Quinn like to think he listened to her in not coming. He seemed to be listening a little more these days.

Iona asked to speak. Laney graciously gave her the floor, and Quinn held her breath wondering if Iona was about to do the right thing. One never knew.

"As much as I love serving on this board . . ."

To which Quinn rolled her eyes. Iona had hated the board almost from the start . . . except for her shining moment voting down the Abbott property.

". . . I must tender my resignation. As you are aware, my husband received repair contracts from this district, to which I voted for. I could justify my actions by saying the vote would have carried in his favor anyway, but that's not the point. I want to do what's right. I was inexperienced and not ready for public service. Thanks for the support, though. I guess there are now four open seats for the special election."

The assembly gasped, people agreeing and disagreeing, the tone rising. Quinn heard folks around her talk about repercussions and others saying Iona's ground-breaking vote three weeks ago more than made up for anything in the past.

Iona decided not to divorce Fripp. After he was interviewed several times by the FBI, he convinced her he'd strayed from common sense, and he'd erred abusing her position on the board. The GPS tracker was his doing, claiming he was only following his wife.

Truth was he'd come too close to being labeled a con and ethically inept, both by authorities and the community. Quinn wasn't sold on the remorse act. He simply realized that with Quinn offering to stand by Iona in court and the daughter choosing her mother, divorcing Iona wasn't wise. Iona, on the other hand, admitted she hated giving up her childhood sweetheart.

If she were Laney, Quinn would ask for a forensic audit and start this board off on a clean ledger by breathing fresh life into everyone's reputation.

Laney let the crowd have its say a few moments and studied Iona with a slight smile. Finally the gavel came down. "Thank you for your service, Ms. Bakeman. Your offer is accepted, and we'll miss you." The vote carried.

Savvy on Iona's part. Leave on a high note with people remembering you in a positive light.

The agenda's public participation time came easily, with one man throwing his hat in the ring for the election now scheduled two months downstream. More would be forthcoming with the power team dismantled and four chairs beckoning for honest leadership and transparency.

People kept glancing at Jonah.

Quinn was surprised when Jonah didn't make the least effort to leave his seat. Announcing his own candidacy was why she assumed he'd wanted to attend. They'd cut short limbing a row of trees in the east quadrant to shower, eat, and make the meeting. "Thought you told Laney you were interested."

"Not here, not now," he said. "Still thinking."

Laney's voice sounded firm, calling upon the next person in line. "Miss Birdie Palmeter. I believe it's your turn to speak."

Miss Birdie had healed nicely in the last few weeks, and she walked herself to the front, grasping the mic from its stand to give her more liberty in movement. "Ladies and gentlemen, I stand here pleased as punch at how our community has come together." She gave a dramatic pause. *"How poor are they that have not patience! What wound did ever heal but by degrees?"*

Of course she had a Shakespeare quote. Which play, Quinn could not say.

"Othello, Miss Sterling," the teacher said, a warm smile pointed Quinn's way. Then to the audience, "We might have scars, and we might still be licking our wounds, but we are healing." She held her arms wide, herself the example. Her bandages were down to band-aids.

The room clapped wildly for a few seconds.

Miss Birdie sure loved a stage. "We might have been deceived, but we became wiser."

"Amen and yes, ma'am!" hollered a woman against the east wall. Guy would've chastised her, possibly even removed her from the room for such an outburst, but Laney only smiled at the enthusiasm.

Birdie continued. "And we might not have the money of some of these zealous parties wanting to swoop in and consume us, but we have land, people. I am one of those landowners, too, and I'd like to offer them enough acreage for the school at a reduced price. It might not be exactly where you wanted it, but—"

Her words drowned out to the standing ovation, Quinn and Jonah rising with them. People here and there wiped tear-streaked cheeks, beaming. This was community. The too familiar gavel sounded, though not as ominous, not raised nearly so high to make its point. The crowd quieted, excited to hear more.

"My, my," Birdie said, chuckling. "Y'all can make quite the spectacle of yourselves." More tittering traversed the room. "As I was saying before you dear friends and neighbors made such a to-do, my land is closer to town and not on the main county highway like the other one, but if my memory serves me right, the need is still there." She turned to Laney. "You know where to find me. Thank you."

Hands clapped in honor of Miss Birdie as she returned the distance to her seat. Quinn did the same, leaning into Jonah. "She needs to run for one of those seats. Did you two get together on this land thing?"

People were peering again at the two of them, or rather more so at Jonah. He turned to talk in her ear. "No, but I'm not surprised. Good begets good, Quinn, and these people are hungry for this sort of camaraderie."

She nodded for him to turn so she could talk in his ear. The room's applause likened something from the President's State of the Union. "Then do it."

"Do what?" he said, turning to speak in her ear.

"Run for one of those seats," she yelled back.

"I didn't sign up to speak tonight. The rules say you have to sign up at the door."

But then something caught Jonah's eye. She followed his gaze seeking what he saw only to realize it wasn't something to see . . . it was something to hear. A small rumbling cheer had started to swell, each repeat louder. Of course it had caught his ear before hers.

Jo-nah. Jo-nah. Jo-nah.

A seed of pride sprouted in Quinn's chest, and she nudged the lovely man beside her. "They want you to go up there. Time to decide, Tree Man." She clapped, falling in line with those around her, even in the chanting.

He wanted this. He'd learned that a school board mattered in a county. It held the potential to stop change, initiate it, or mold it. To not stand up and run for office meant accepting whatever happened to this county through others.

Jo-nah. Jo-nah. Jo-nah.

Everyone clapped and whistled when he leaned over, kissed Quinn on the cheek, and strode forward.

Though a tad timid, he soon worked his way past his reddened cheeks, and mic in hand, thanked people, speaking of how much the community meant to him. How even though he didn't have children, and yet someday hoped to . . . making half the room grin at Quinn . . . he would love having a hand in creating an environment that developed children into people eager to learn, willing to give back, and aiming to succeed. He couldn't have planned that statement any better with a day's preparation.

Quinn scanned the assembly, recognizing people, touched at how much Jonah was openly admired . . . then her eyes caught Ty. The man practically cried for his friend. Then his gaze caught Quinn's, and across that sea of heads, they smiled at each other, the warmth reaching her in what appeared a sense of acceptance.

He winked. She winked back.

Movement at the double-door exit distracted her, and she wondered who would be leaving at such a passionate height of revel. Wait, could it be . . . Quickly, she scrolled her contacts list and dialed the number. He answered outside.

"What are you doing here?" she asked.

"Still checking boxes. Touching base with people. I heard about this meeting and just wanted to make sure all was well," Knox said.

"Aren't you sweet?"

"FBI agents don't say things like that," he said.

She laughed. "Then I guess I'm not FBI agent material," she replied, putting the nail in the coffin that she wasn't coming. "Keep in touch, dude." She wished she could see him.

"I'd be at your door tonight if I didn't suspect you were about to be taken off the market," he threw in when she thought he'd about hung up.

The comment caught her off balance. Knox's jokes were one thing. This was Knox being real. "I miss you," she said. "I miss the bureau."

"Our loss, sweetheart. Our loss. Take care of yourself." Then he really was gone.

What felt like ages took only minutes before Jonah returned flushed, adrenaline pumped, and pleased with his knee-jerk decision to jump on board this train. "Want to go out and celebrate?" she asked.

"No." He reached down and took her hand. "I need to get to Jule."

Of course he did. Quinn loved that about him.

The second the meeting adjourned, they made for her truck and reached it promptly only to spend twenty minutes addressing handshakes from people swearing their allegiance and asking how they could help with the campaign.

Jonah smiled the whole way to Sterling Banks.

They parked at her manor. He would walk the rest of the way to Jule's. Quinn would invite him in, but he'd distanced himself from overnight trysts since Jule's incident. She could ask, though. She wanted to ask. But she'd determined he needed to make that first advance, sort of like her uncle said about a marriage proposal. She felt herself standing on the precipice of change, a lot of change, but regardless where that next step took her, she had about decided it had to be initiated by Jonah. She wouldn't be so standoffish this time.

"Good night," he said, leaning in to kiss her. The kiss lingered.

They separated and he quickly returned for another. God, she wanted to make the first move. That was her nature. *Behave*, she reminded herself.

They parted, and this time he grinned and turned to leave toward home. She would watch him till she couldn't see him, taking in the whole of him. Maybe she did love him.

Bogie scratched on the door, sensing his owner home. "Poor baby," she muttered. "Bet you're about to bust in there. Hold on. I'll let you out."

"Hey, Quinn!" Jonah yelled from the darkness.

"What?" she shouted, hesitating to let Bogie out until Jonah was home. Otherwise, the dog would take off after him.

"Would you ever marry someone like me?" he hollered from the distance.

The shock about knocked her down. "Why, are you asking?" she yelled back.

She caught him in the edges of the house's spotlight. He raised his arms out to the side. "No. Just testing the waters."

Opening her mouth to retort, she found herself empty of words.

Which sent Jonah off toward Jule's place, his laughter bouncing off the wide canopy of pecan trees.

The End

Acknowledgements

Thanks first and foremost to hubby. Gary asks almost daily, "You need to write?" or "Do you have a chapter you want to read to me?" When I accepted the writing profession, he accepted his assumed role as taskmaster, or as he named himself, my uncompensated, executive, personal assistant.

Thanks to the community of Chapin, South Carolina who have unofficially dubbed me "Chapin's Author." Somehow, during COVID, when all of us were confined to smaller circles, my Chapin circle grew tremendously stronger. That especially includes Jerry Caldwell and his staff at The Coffee Shelf who tout my books front and center to the slew of coffee aficionados they serve.

Thanks to Karen Carter and The Edisto Bookstore. During COVID, she lost her staff but exploded in sales. Bless her, she's been tested this year, but risen from the viral ashes successful. She is my mainstay on Edisto, and a staunch supporter I could not do without.

Thanks to SC's Talking Book Services for grooming me these last five years on how to be an audiobook narrator. Through them I've come to appreciate the audiobook in terms of serving the needs of those who cannot read a traditional book, which in turn encouraged me to branch out into audiobooks of my own.

Thanks to my core groups of readers who are so incredibly sweet to me. Some tell me that they feel they know me, and that we are friends. Of course we are friends. As intimately as we've shared stories over the years, how can we not be?

Finally, thanks to my publisher, editor, and partner in all things caregiving. Debra Dixon has shown me that a publisher indeed can have a heart . . . a big one.